Of Earth and Flame

THE ITHENMYR CHRONICLES
BOOK ONE

ELAYNA R. GALLEA

First paperback edition July 2022

Cover by Getcovers

Map designed on Inkarnate

Paperback ISBN: 978-1-7781920-2-9

Ebook ISBN: 978-1-7781920-3-6

Hardcover ISBN: 978-1-7781920-8-1

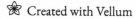 Created with Vellum

For women.
Because somehow, in the 21st century, we can drink pumpkin spice lattes, but misogyny still exists.

Map of Ithenmyr

FOR A LARGER VERSION, PLEASE GO TO:
HTTPS://WWW.ELAYNARGALLEA.COM/MAPS

Pronunciation Guide

Hello dear readers,

Ithenmyr is a fantasy world filled with mythical creatures and interesting names.

I have included this pronunciation guide in case you find it useful. (But please feel free to ignore me and pronounce the words as you see fit.)

After all, the beauty of reading is that books are never the same from one person to the next.

Aileana: Ay-lee-ah-na

Kydona: Key-doh-na

Ithiar: Ih-thee-ar

Thyr: th-ur (Like sir, but with th)

Ithenmyr: Ih-thin-meer

Xander: Zan-der

Paeral: Pay-ral

Daegal: Day-gal

Myhhena: my-hen-na

Orvyn: Or-vin

Irriel: ih-ree-el
Uhna: ohh-nah
Niona: Nigh-oh-na
Saena: Say-nah
Elyx: Eee-licks
Elyxander: Eee-licks-zan-der
Rathian: Ray-thee-an
Hironna: He-ro-nah

Contents

Author's note   xi

1. Dreams Were for the Weak   1
2. A Mutually Beneficial Arrangement   14
3. I was Wrong   25
4. Nonna Doesn't Bite   36
5. A Gift and a Departure   46
6. A Gilded Cage   58
7. Seen and Not Heard   69
8. Rumors Abound   80
9. Heretics Among Us   91
10. I Hate You   104
11. Change of Plans   117
12. I Should Have Known   132
13. Protectress of the Woods   142
14. The Picture of Hilarity   153
15. The Feeling was Mutual   164
16. A Multitude of Explanations   173
17. Once Upon a Time   181
18. Run   193
19. The First Battle   205
20. Eternal Blessings   215
21. A Long Journey   229
22. A Truce and a Tale   242
23. The Sound of Death   251
24. Wedding Bells and Darkness   261
25. The Pines   273
26. Research and Whispers   284
27. A Brief (and Incomplete) History of Dragons   291
28. You are Mine   293

29. The Red Shadow   308
30. Not So Naïve Anymore   317
31. I Would Rather Die   331
32. Stand Your Ground   342
33. Death Smells Like Smoke   350
34. I'm So Sorry   360
35. Stay With Me   370
36. What are We Going to Do?   379

The next part of Aileana and Xander's story is out now!   385
Acknowledgments   387
About the Author   389
Also by Elayna R. Gallea   391

Author's note

Welcome to Ithenmyr.

Of Earth and Flame takes place in a medieval setting that contains violence in several different forms.

This book contains references to violence, including violence against women and children. It also contains language, death, assault, sexism and severe misogyny.

There are flashbacks to Aileana's childhood where she suffered punishments at the hands of the king.

Dreams Were for the Weak

I tightened my grip on the rope, my hands growing clammy as flashes of lightning streaked across the early morning sky. The tower itself shook as rolls of thunder roared with their displeasure. It was as though Kydona herself was angry with me.

Breathing in deeply, I tilted my head towards the gray sky as large raindrops plastered long strands of hair the color of burning sunsets against my face. The sun was tucked away behind the heavy clouds, its watchful gaze nowhere to be seen as the storm ravaged the land.

A brisk wind swirled around me, causing my already tenuous position to become even more life-threatening. Water streaked down my face, blurring my vision as I tried to look around. Everything was a fuzzy mess. Grunting, I wiped my eyes on my shoulder before continuing my descent down the slippery stone exterior of my prison.

A groaning sound came from above, and my eyes darted up the slick gray walls. My mouth tightened in a straight line as my heart pounded more quickly in my chest. I could hear each beat as I descended slowly.

Thump

Thump

Thump

My heart's rhythm spurred me on as I lowered myself down the side of the tower. Inch by inch, I worked my way towards the ground.

"Come on," I muttered, adjusting my grip on the thick, wet cord. It was slippery in my hands, my fingers unused to what I was asking them to do.

The makeshift bag on my back bumped against me as I shimmied down the wall. There would definitely be bruises on the small of my back tomorrow. If I made it to tomorrow.

My words were little more than pleas, drowned out by the raging storm. "Don't fail me now."

The rough, brown rope ran from my hands up the gray stones and through the open window far above me. On the other side, it was tied to the large four-poster bed that occupied most of the small space.

Hopefully, the bed frame would hold my weight. I just needed it to last long enough for me to get to the ground. It wasn't as though there was really anything else I could have used as an anchor. Other than the bed, the only furniture in the circular space was a small wardrobe, a desk, and a chair. That was all.

The entirety of my twenty-three years of existence boiled down to everything in that room.

"Breathe," I ordered myself as I continued my descent. "Don't look down."

As though mocking me for my foolish commands, my treacherous eyes disobeyed me almost instantly. Bile rose in my throat as I took in the distance between the bushes below and my current position dangling against the side of the tower. It hadn't seemed so high when I was looking out the window, but now it was as though every inch was a mile.

Suddenly, I was regretting the life choices—the few I had been allowed to make, seeing as how being locked in a tower had meant that said choices were few and far between—I had made that brought me to this moment.

A knot formed in my stomach, and my muscles fluttered as my body protested my current course of action. My head pounded as the reality of my current predicament slammed into me like a tidal wave. It crashed against my defenses as I dangled from the rope. My eyes stung, and my vision blurred once more.

"Don't. Don't you dare cry," I commanded myself through gritted teeth. Taking a deep breath, I forced myself to move down another inch. "Keep going. Think about what will happen to you if you don't make it."

Visions of red magic and trails of blood flashed before my eyes, and I shimmied down a bit more.

"You can't let them have you," I told myself for the hundredth time. "You *have* to make it down. If you don't..."

You'll never escape.

The words reverberated through my mind. I couldn't let that happen. I wouldn't. If he got his hands on me...

That thought alone was enough to spur me down the wall.

When I was five years old, I watched a wedding procession. They hadn't invited me, of course. But I had watched from my window in the tower. I remembered staring so intently that my nose had gotten stuck to the pane of the glass. I had dragged my chair over so I wouldn't miss a single thing.

The bride had been so beautiful, with her translucent pale pink wings fluttering in the quiet breeze as her white silk gown flowed all around her. Her groom had been resplendent in black, his dark horns reaching high into the sky as he had led her away from the temple. The path had been lined with well-wishers who had cheered as the couple had taken their first walk together after the ceremony. High King Edgar had even attended the wedding.

Not grasping the severity of my situation, five-year-old me had spent months daydreaming about my future wedding. At the tender age of five, I'd been blissfully unaware of the exact circumstances of my captivity in the tower. I hadn't known what was coming. If I had, perhaps I would have allocated a little less time to daydreaming and a little more time to trying to escape.

Five-year-old me had imagined that perhaps I would have woken up and eaten a delicious breakfast before having been pampered by my many servants. There might have been a long, hot bath, complete with scented soaps and bubbles. Maybe I would've eaten cake for breakfast. There definitely would have been copious amounts of sweet tea.

I had dreamed of the freedom that my wedding would bring me. Of the escape from the circular walls that were my constant companions. Even at that age, I had known exactly how many bricks made up the walls of my prison.

Having counted the black and gray stones so many times, I could recite the numbers in my sleep. I knew every inch of the glimmering surface of the black rocks that seemed haphazardly strewn throughout my room. The way they burned when I touched them.

Even at the age of five, I knew I was different. Living in a tower was not normal. But at least I'd had dreams to keep me company. I had imagined that the one who would marry me would be kind and loving. I'd dreamed countless times about my betrothed and his undying love for me.

I used to have dreams.

But not anymore.

Life had already taught me its most important lesson: dreams were for the weak and powerless. Daring to dream meant watching your hopes shatter into a million tiny pieces on the floor. Dreams only led to one thing: death.

Case in point: my current predicament. Never in my wildest dreams would I have imagined that as the sun rose on the day that was supposed to lead me into matrimonial bliss, I would have been dangling out of a window high above the ground. Nor had I imagined that instead of the traditional wedding dress, I would have been wearing thick black tights and a tunic that stuck to my every curve as I repelled down the tower that had been my home for my entire life.

I would have scoffed if someone had told me I'd trade my wedding jewels for rope, a traveling cloak, two sets of clothes, and throwing knives. The entire idea would have been preposterous.

And yet, here I was. Having done all of these things. Thank the gods for a few faithful servants who had been willing to help me. I hated they took pity on me—being known as the king's pet was bad enough without adding pity to the mix—but I couldn't deny that their aid was instrumental in my escape.

Suffice it to say, my wedding was *not* going the way that five-year-old me had planned.

My fingers stung, signaling that I needed to continue my perilous descent. Taking a deep breath, I begged my stomach to remain calm as my eyes dipped towards the ground. It was maybe thirty feet below now, but the smooth stone of my tower would not make for an easy descent. Glancing up, I stared at the open window.

Biting my lip, I forced myself to decide. If I went up, I would have been as good as sentencing myself to a very long, very miserable life. Down led to almost certain death.

"Aileana?" a feminine voice cried out from inside the tower. All the blood drained from my face, and my heart pounded in my chest. I could hear the doorknob rattling inside. Before leaving, I had taken the chair and wedged it up against the knob, but I knew it wouldn't hold them for long.

Shit.

The servant continued, "Aileana, this isn't the time for one of your games. Open up!"

Pressing myself against the tower, I looked down. Counting to ten, I made up my mind. Certain death was the better option. At least then, I had a chance, no matter how small, to be free. To live.

If I went up, I would never taste freedom.

I slipped down the rope, but it wasn't fast enough. Every second felt like an hour as I inched downwards. Soon, the pounding on the door from the room above intensified, and I knew I had to move faster.

Inhaling deeply, I let my grip on the rope loosen. Instead of sliding down at a manageable speed, I flew down the rope. My hands felt like they were on fire, and I knew without looking that they would be red and burned by the time I made it to the bottom. They'd heal, of course, but I would be in a world of pain until that happened.

But better pain than marriage to *him*.

Gritting my teeth, I pushed past the agony in my hands. The ground grew closer by the second, and before I knew it, branches were cracking under my feet as I landed in a crouch.

The breath blew out of me in a *whoosh* as I yanked on the rope as hard as I could. For a long, painful moment, nothing happened. The rope dangled in my hands, tense and unmoving.

No.

I knew I only had seconds before they noticed me. Not willing to give up, I drew in a sharp breath and tugged as hard as I could. Yanking on the rope with all my might, I jumped up and used every ounce of my weight against it.

A moment passed as the cord grew taunt before a loud snapping sound came from above.

Biting my lip, I swallowed the cheer that was rising in my throat. My heart raced as I flattened myself against the tower. Seconds later, a carved piece of wood the length of my chest rushed through the air before landing with a *thud* near me.

I took a step closer, noting the way my knots had held. The rope was still firmly tied around the middle of what had been a bedpost. A smirk rose within me at the sight, but I quickly tamped it down. This was not the time for laughter or frivolousness. I was far from freedom.

But this... being outside. Breathing fresh air. Not being contained within the tower. This was a huge accomplishment and one that I wasn't soon to forget. Even if they caught me now, I was experiencing something that I'd been denied my entire life. I'd tasted freedom, and it was far better than anything I'd ever had before.

Gathering the rope and the wood that had aided in my escape, I tossed them into the bush. Breathing in deeply, I gave myself three seconds to look around.

Three seconds to take in the dark forest that stood before me, the stone wall at my back, and the sudden rush of freedom that was flooding through my bones. Three seconds to pat myself down and feel the reassuring hilt of my daggers.

I'd traded everything for those blades, and they carried with them a sense of security that I desperately needed. Three seconds to look up and see the dark wings of the soldiers patrolling the walls of the keep.

My prison looked... unremarkable from the outside. Like I imagined any other stone tower attached to a keep would look. How was it possible that something that had contained my entire life was so... small?

Then the shouting began.

"Where is she?"

"Someone find her."

"Tell the king."

That was all I needed to hear. I shook myself free of my thoughts. There was no way I would let the king get his hands on me today. I had already risked everything by befriending one of the servants.

It had taken me nine months to convince Lithani to help me escape. In the end, she'd only been able to do so much. She had brought me the clothes I now wore and the daggers strapped to my thighs. Hopefully, the jewels I'd given her would be enough to see her to safety.

Straightening my tunic and pulling on my hood, I wrapped my cloak around myself before taking one final glance at my childhood prison.

"Good riddance," I muttered before darting into the welcoming embrace of the King's Forest.

TWIGS CRACKED, and leaves crunched beneath my feet as long, thin branches whipped at my cheeks. My face stung from the force of a dozen small lacerations, and my lungs burned from the effort of exercise. Within ten minutes of running through the forest, my body was aching like never before.

Tiny bugs flew around me, nipping at my skin and leaving painful reminders of their presence on my face and arms. I swatted at them, never stopping the constant movement of my legs.

And still, I pushed forward.

For years, I had stared at the trees longingly from my window, but now that I was in their midst, I realized the forest was much larger than I could have ever imagined.

Being outside was... exhilarating. The vibrant colors of the trees were unlike anything I'd ever seen before. The fresh air was intoxicating. No one had ever told me that. Granted, no one had really spoken to me unless commanded by the king, but still.

Even breathing *felt* better. It was different. I hadn't realized how stale the air had been in my tower until now. At that moment, it struck me. One second, one minute, one hour of freedom from my tower would not be enough. It would never have been enough.

Freedom, I was finding out, was like a drug. Once you tasted it, it opened your eyes to all the things you had been denied. It was addicting, this thing called freedom.

Leaving, it seemed, would teach me far more than I had ever thought possible. The entire world was waiting for me to discover its hidden treasures, and I was an eager pupil.

I ran, and I ran, and I ran.

Every second felt like an eternity as my feet pounded through the muddy terrain. Glancing at the still dark and stormy sky, I hoped the storm would cover my escape. The King's Forest surrounded my tower on all sides. At least they would have no inclination about which direction I was headed.

My feet squelched through the mud as my every breath sounded far too loud to my nervous ears. My lungs burned, and still, I ran. The further I went into the forest, the thicker the surrounding growth became. Trees of varying shapes and sizes loomed over me, their leaves a lesson in shades of green.

Seeing them, being surrounded by *wilderness* for the first time in my life, I regretted my lack of education surrounding all things flora. I did not know what they were called, only that they were providing me with my escape.

My heart was hammering in my chest, my muscles aching as I pushed my body harder than I ever had before. The exercises I had done with my guard Matthias in the tiny attic above my room had done nothing to prepare me for this mad dash through the woods.

Birds chirped from their positions in the trees, their songs providing much-needed encouragement as I continued my trek through the woods.

I ran until I came across a small stream rushing along the forest floor. The moment I laid eyes on the crystal clear water, I dropped to my knees. Ignoring how small rocks cut into my legs, I cupped my hands and greedily dipped them into the water.

Bringing my hands to my mouth, the cool liquid ran down my throat, providing a momentary reprieve to the aching of my muscles. Even the water smelled and tasted different when it wasn't brought to me in a jug. It tasted like the morning air, fresh and cool, as it dripped down my throat.

Wiping my hand across the back of my mouth, I panted and drew deep breaths as I leaned back against a nearby tree. Closing my eyes, I allowed myself a moment to relax. The bark was rough against my back as I focused on slowing my breathing.

The wind blew around me, sending locks of my hair flying into my face before a voice echoed through my mind.

Greetings, daughter of Uhna. We have been waiting for you.

A scream crawled up my throat as my eyes flew open. Drawing one of my daggers in one swift movement, my heart pounded in my chest as I bolted to my feet.

"Who is there?" I called out.

No response. My heartbeat sounded like a drum.

"Show yourself," I hissed.

The wind rustled, but there came no reply. Wide-eyed, I took in the dark trees and bushes that surrounded me. Thunder still roared above, but I couldn't see anyone. I turned in a circle, my dagger outstretched, as my gaze swept through the forest. The rain continued to fall, the steady pitter-patter of raindrops sounding like drums as they beat against the leaves.

"You've been in that tower for too long. Now you're hearing things." Scolding myself, I kept a firm grip on the hilt of my dagger as I looked around one more time. I was alone. After a few achingly long minutes, my heart rate settled.

The forest was empty. They hadn't yet found me. I was still free. Exhaling a ragged breath, I pushed back my hood and ran my hand through my damp hair. I couldn't stay here any longer. My reprieve from running had cost me and I knew the king's guards wouldn't give up so easily. I had to keep going.

Cursing, I rubbed the palms of my hands over my eyes before pulling my hood back onto my head. Letting a calm wash over me, I began picking my way through the forest once more.

I didn't pray to the goddess Kydona for safety or protection as I started running again.

She had abandoned me long ago. Matthias, my guard—and only parental figure—had taught me to pray every night when I was little. For protection, he had said. It was because of the gods and goddesses that we were still here. He had insisted that we pray to them every night.

Matthias prayed to Ithiar, the God of War. And me? I was supposed to pray to Kydona, the Mother Goddess. For protection. But I had put a stop to that tomfoolery when I was thirteen.

Why would I pray to a deity who obviously cared so little for my well-being? She hadn't stopped the king from taking everything from me. She hadn't released me from my captivity. Obviously, I was invisible to her. And so Kydona was invisible to me, too.

I knew Matthias had disapproved of my lack of reverence, but he had never said anything. And now he was dead, so he couldn't. Matthias had been the one constant in my life.

From the day I had turned five, he had shown up daily to take me to the attic for my 'walks'. Away from the prying eyes of my other guards, we had trained and sparred until we had both been breathless and sweaty.

At least, that's what we had done until he had up and died on me a year ago. The Plague had swept through Ithenmyr, taking more than a third of the servants and guards with it. Ever since the day they had burned Matthias' body on the pyre, I hadn't seen outside the circular walls of my room once.

Until today.

And so, I didn't pray. I ran. When the voices became nothing more than whispers on the wind, my shoulders relaxed enough for me to slip my dagger into the sheath on my forearm.

The rising sun illuminated the surrounding forest, and I kept picking my way through the trees. Dawn gave way to morning, and soon my footsteps slowed as a gnawing hunger rose within me. At the same time, I noticed just how wet my cloak and clothing had become. Everything was completely soaked, and my run through the forest hadn't helped matters at all.

Spotting a small cave carved into a large hill up ahead, a small smile crept onto my lips. Perhaps Kydona hadn't forgotten about me after all.

I ENTERED THE CAVE, sitting on a rather uncomfortable stone that marked the entrance before opening my makeshift bag. Pushing aside the leather wrapping that was thankfully somewhat waterproof, I pulled out a loaf of brown bread and a piece of hard cheese. The bread was stale, but after a few moments in my mouth, it grew soft enough to chew.

Soft enough was all that I needed. I would rather have eaten dozens of loaves of hard bread and cheese than have spent another moment in that accursed tower. Bland, stale bread was nothing compared to the life I had already faced.

It was nothing compared to the prospects of the marriage I was running from.

Having filled the gnawing pain in my stomach, I took a moment to look around the cavern that was providing me shelter. It was small and didn't appear to go much further than a few feet back. A few leaves dusted the rocky ground, but other than that, it was completely empty. Shrugging, I dug through my pack.

A groan escaped my lips. "Of course."

My only other pair of clothes were completely soaked. Cursing, I shoved them back into my pack. I couldn't stay here long enough for them to dry. I needed to get further from the tower.

Stewing about my bad luck, I threw my bag on my back and stood. I made it out of the cavern and back under the leafy canopy before the hairs on the back of my neck prickled.

A deep, gravelly voice came from behind me, sending shivers down my spine. "You must be the reason there are soldiers everywhere."

A Mutually Beneficial Arrangement

At the sound of the voice, my mind emptied of all rational thought. Only one thing remained.

Drawing in a deep breath, I centered my thoughts.

I will not go back.

In the space of one breath, my fingers wrapped around the hilt of the throwing knife sheathed against my right thigh. Ignoring the rope burns on my palms, I focused on the *zing* the metal made as it met the air.

In the time it took me to inhale, I was already pivoting on the balls of my feet. My mouth was pinched in a straight line as I drew back my arm, the familiar weight of the blade welcome in my hand.

As I exhaled, my eyes narrowed. I took in the extremely large, burly male standing less than ten feet away from me. He was the largest being I had ever seen in my entire life. Mind you, I had been... sheltered. But even so, I could recognize someone big when I saw them.

And he was *big*.

I had to tilt my head up to look at him. My hood slipped back, and I

14

kept my gaze firmly on him as I reached up with my free hand and tugged it forward.

Based on my limited experience with the servants and guards, I knew I was tall, but my height had nothing on the being standing in front of me. He was imposing in a way that I hadn't known was possible.

For a moment, neither of us moved as our gazes swept over each other. My eyes traveled down his face, starting at his rounded ears and moving down from there.

His long, silver-white hair was being held back by a leather band that accentuated the strong boning in his face. Silver stubble dusted the bottom half of his face, adding an air of aloofness to him. He had a strong, chiseled jaw with a nose that was slightly bent out of shape, like it had been broken and reset one too many times. He was the palest being I had ever seen, but with my lack of life experience, that didn't mean much.

His strong jaw was clenched, and his bright, golden eyes narrowed as he gripped a large wooden bow in his hands. He was muscular. Strong. And he looked like he could kill with a singular glance.

The wooden bow in his hands almost seemed like a joke, except it currently held an arrow that was nocked and trained on me. My would-be assailant opened his mouth to speak, but I didn't wait to hear what he had to say. Large or not, I was fast, and I knew my aim with the dagger was true. Taking aim, I released the knife before I grabbed my bag and began to run once more.

I was already flying through the forest when a cry of pure outrage filled the air. A guttural roar came from my assailant as a grim smile crept onto my face. I vaulted over fallen logs, rushing past another babbling brook before ducking into a thick grove of trees.

I kept my eyes on the sun, constantly running away from the castle.

Always away.

My heart pounded in my chest as the scents of the forest filled me.

The fresh air invigorated me, giving me the strength to continue to move despite the many hours I had already been running.

Behind me, loud crashing sounds made me run even harder.

Pushing myself harder than before, I raced through the forest in an effort to increase the distance between the two of us. I knew my dagger had hit him. Hopefully, it had caused enough injury to slow him down. If it hadn't, and he decided to bring me back to the tower...

I wasn't going to let that happen. I couldn't—I wouldn't—go back.

Venomous curses came from behind me as I continued to run. My every breath was ragged as I pushed my body harder than I ever had before.

Seconds became minutes, and still, he pursued me. Our matching footsteps echoed through the forest as we ran. Soon, my lungs were burning. Every breath felt like a million flames erupting within me. I knew I needed to take a break, or my body would force me to do so.

Ducking behind a tree, I fought to catch my breath as I withdrew the dagger sheathed on my forearm. My eyes darted around wildly, trying to find the best route forward when a large hand landed on my shoulder.

No.

I screamed, raising my second blade in the air as I turned toward my attacker.

His eyes widened at the sight of the blade in my hand. Colorful curses escaped his lips as his nostrils flared. He snarled, "You have *got* to be kidding me. How many knives can one female carry?"

It took me a moment to understand what he was saying. His voice was deep and had a strange accent to it. His words were more clipped than I was used to hearing. While I was processing his words, one of his hands wrapped around my wrist. The moment he touched me, it was as though sparks erupted underneath my skin. I gasped, trying to yank my hand back.

"Let me go!" I raised my foot, intending to stomp on his, but he shifted his body away from me.

He laughed. Laughed! That sent a wave of rage through my body.

"I don't think so, little lady." He eyed my dagger.

"Little?" I sputtered. Anger like I'd never felt before roiled through my body. "I'm not little. You're just a giant!"

"Giant or not, I don't plan on getting stabbed again."

I huffed. "Maybe you shouldn't sneak up on people if you don't like being stabbed."

"Maybe you should just practice kindness and not jump to conclusions!" he retorted. His nostrils flared as he loomed above me. "Did you consider that perhaps I just wanted to talk to you?"

"I wasn't aware talking required a bow and arrow," I snapped, looking pointedly at the weapon currently hooked on his back. I couldn't help but notice the way his muscles bulged as he held onto me.

"Maybe I had a reason," he said. "Do you make a habit of stabbing every male you encounter in the woods?"

I dragged my eyes up to his, forcing myself not to notice the way his golden eyes seemed to look right through me into my soul.

"I don't know," I said through clenched teeth as I tried to wrench myself free from his grasp. With every yank, he tightened his grip. I huffed. "You're the first person I've met out here. Why don't you let go of my hand and find out if there's a repeat performance?"

He raised a brow, his gaze darting between me and the knife in my hand. "I'd rather not." Lips twitching, he gestured to his right shoulder. "This is enough damage for one day, thank you very much."

I smirked at the sight of the fresh blood trickling down his navy blue tunic. A hole the size of my index finger marred the otherwise untouched piece of clothing.

"Too bad my aim was off," I grumbled.

Choked laughter escaped him as he continued to grip my wrist. His fingers were so tight, that I knew I would have bruises there tomorrow. If I was still alive tomorrow. At this rate, I wasn't sure if that would be the case.

But one thing was certain. I wouldn't go down without a fight. If he thought he could use me, he would be in for a rude awakening. No one would touch me without my permission.

That's why I was in this mess in the first place.

Gritting my teeth, I twisted away from my assailant before raising my knee and aiming it for the sensitive spot all males have. He jerked back, and my knee connected with his thigh instead.

Damn.

He cursed, still holding onto me. "This is unbelievable." He threw his free hand in the air before running it through his hair. I tried to kick him, to no avail.

"Would you stop that?" he snapped.

"Let me go!" I insisted.

He shook his head, muttering to himself. "Go to Thyr, they said. It would be easy, they said. A two-day trip. Get what you need and get out. It's not like I've been waiting for a very long time for this. No one was even supposed to know I was here."

My brows furrowed as I tried to make sense of what he was saying. I asked, "Who are 'they'?"

He ignored me, continuing to rant as though he wasn't holding me captive in the middle of the woods. "Here I am, making my way through the King's Forest when an entire contingent of Winged Soldiers flood the area. Then, as if that isn't enough, I get attacked by some female who apparently doesn't know how to do anything except stab people."

"Hey!" I shouted, trying to yank my hand out of his.

He tightened his grip as he stared at me.

"What?" he snapped.

"You're the one who attacked me." My eyes widened as I glared at him. "I was perfectly happy before *you* approached *me*."

"I just wanted to talk to you," he growled. "You're the one who stabbed me before I could utter a single word."

Then, before I could stop him, he reached up and wrenched back the hood of my cloak. I flinched, pulling away, but it was too late. A flash of recognition went through him, before his mouth set in a thin line.

Blinking, he stared at me for a second too long before dragging his gaze back to mine. His mouth opened and closed, as though he was lost for words.

I did not have the time or the patience for this.

"What?" I snapped, my nostrils flaring.

"You're..." his voice trailed off, his grip on my hand tightening to the point of pain.

"A female?" I filled in for him. "Beautiful? Dangerous?"

"An elf. A female elf." Still holding onto my wrist, he continued to stare at me. His eyes swept over me, starting at my head and slowly running down my body.

His gaze was heated, and it caused my insides to twist in a way that I had never felt before. It wasn't altogether uncomfortable, but I didn't like it. I needed to be in control, and right now, he was making me feel... out of sorts. That was the last thing I needed right now.

"Let go of me," I snapped.

My attacker returned his gaze to mine, his eyes sharper than before. He tilted his head, a knowing gleam in his eyes. "It's you they're looking for, isn't it?"

My heart pounded in my chest, and a roaring filled my ears. My entire body felt too tight as I struggled to breathe. I couldn't go back. I wouldn't go back. Not now. Death would be better.

A strange sensation washed through me moments before the ground began to shake all around us. I clamped my mouth shut as tremors threatened to overtake me. Forcing the feeling of helpless terror deep down within me, I shook my head. I wouldn't give him the satisfaction of knowing he frightened me.

"What in the seven circles of hell?" my captor sputtered, staring at the shaking ground.

He turned his wide eyes towards me. He loosened his grip on my wrist, and I yanked my hand back with a triumphant cry. The moment he released me, the trembling stopped.

He blinked, his eyes narrowing as he studied me. Suspicion leaked into his voice as he snarled, "*What* are you?"

"We're not talking about me right now," I huffed, shaking my head as I took a step back, then two.

There was no way I was going to tell him that even if I wanted to answer his question, I couldn't. Family history hadn't ever been on my tutors' approved lessons. Knowledge of myself and my past was just one of the many things I'd been denied. I had no idea what kind of elf I was, although I supposed I was probably a Light Elf. They were the most common breed, after all. Even I knew that.

I stumbled over a fallen log, but managed to remain upright as I said, "I don't go around talking about myself with strangers I met in the forest ten minutes ago."

He shook his head, prowling towards me. Instinctively, I raised the dagger, moving back.

"Stop," I ordered through clenched teeth. "If you value your life, you'll stop moving. I won't miss a second time."

To his credit, he did. Raising both hands, he paused. A vein pulsed in his neck as he said, "Look. I don't want to hurt you."

I snorted. "You attacked me!"

He shook his head. "A misunderstanding."

"I don't think that pointing a nocked arrow at me is a 'misunderstanding'," I snapped.

"You stabbed me!" he yelled.

"I—"

A guttural growl rose in him. It was almost animalistic as he bared his teeth. "Lady," he snarled, "let me speak!"

A heavy moment went by as both of our chests heaved.

My nostrils flared, and I glared at him. "What?"

"I think we can help each other."

"Is that so?" I asked cooly.

He furled his fist at his side. "I'd tell you if you'd stop threatening me long enough to listen."

Scoffing, I brandished my dagger in his direction. He took another step back, and I smirked. "How can you help me? I was doing just fine before you showed up."

"You were running for your life through the forest. I trailed you for half an hour before you even realized I was there. I don't think that qualifies as 'fine' at all."

Forcing myself not to let my surprise show, I glared at him. I had no idea he had been following me. That was... problematic. If I wasn't aware of him, who else might I run into in the forest?

Trying to regain the upper hand, I gestured at his bloody tunic. "And yet, I'm not the one with a stab wound, am I?"

He winced, raising a hand and rubbing it on his wounded shoulder. "That's true. I'll give you that. You have good aim. It was... unexpected."

I crossed my arms, careful not to stab myself with my blade as I turned away from him. "Then it's settled. I bid you good day, sir."

I got all of five steps through the woods before his hand landed on my upper arm. I whirled around, holding my dagger aloft once more. He seemed to have learned his lesson and had already jumped back.

"Listen," he said through clenched teeth. "Could you *please* stop trying to stab me? I have an offer for you."

"An offer? What makes you think you have anything I need?"

He motioned at me with his hand. "Let's just say that *hypothetically*, you are the elf that the Winged Soldiers are combing the forest for right now."

I glared at him, raising my brows. "Hypothetically?"

He nodded. "Yes. *If* that were the case, where do you think you would be going? It's not like there are hundreds of elvish females in Ithenmyr with your rather distinctive coloring or your height."

"Well, I was..." My voice trailed off as I realized he was right. My plan, as carefully thought out as it possibly could be, had consisted of exactly three things: Bribe the servants with my jewels. Escape the tower. Run away.

I didn't really have many plans after that. It was hard to make plans when you had lived your entire life in one building.

Dammit, Matthias. Why didn't you prepare me for any of this instead of just teaching me to wield a blade?

A pang ran through me as I thought of the guard I had lost, and I winced. Running a hand through my long hair, I turned around and leaned my palms against a nearby tree.

I was aware of his eyes on me, but for some reason, I knew in my core he would not hurt me. If he wanted to, he already admitted he could have done it while I was unaware of his presence in the forest.

A moment passed before I turned back around. Biting my cheek, I sighed. "Look. Not that it's any of your business, but I was going to head north until I hit the Indigo Ocean."

He raised a brow. "How were you planning to deal with the Accompaniment Law?"

"The what?" I snapped.

He looked at me like I was stupid. "You must know what that is."

"Humor me," I ground out through clenched teeth.

"The Accompaniment Law. The one that states that all female citizens of Ithenmyr, regardless of species, cannot travel without their father, brother or husband."

"The Accompaniment Law," I repeated, my voice monotone. My heart was racing, and it took everything I had not to react. I didn't want to give him anything over me.

He raised a brow. "Yes, the one put in place two hundred and fifty years ago after the Females' Rebellion." His eyes crawled over my body, a strange gleam entering them before his lips tilted up in a wry smile. "The only females exempt are those of... questionable morals. Which you don't appear to be, despite your knife-wielding tendencies and your very unfeminine attire. Did you forget about that?"

I had not forgotten. It was impossible to forget something that you didn't know.

But there was no way I was going to tell that to *him*. I dragged my eyes up to his, tilting my head back so I could look him in the eyes.

"Hypothetically," I took a step towards him, keeping the dagger between us, "what would you suggest we do?"

His eyes flashed, and the tiniest smile lit up his face. The way his expression made my insides twist was... odd. But that was a matter for a different time.

"I propose a mutually beneficial arrangement," he said, smugness lacing his tone.

"Oh?" I raised a brow. "And what would that be?"

"Well," he drew out the word like it was an entire sentence. "We've established that you are a female."

"Yes." I tapped my foot on the ground, ready to get this conversation over with. "I most certainly am."

"And *I* am a male," he said, drawing his hand over himself like he was showcasing his very large body.

"I gathered as much," I said dryly. "Tell me, why would you help me?"

He coughed, avoiding my gaze as he rubbed his foot on the ground. "There are certain people looking for me. But they don't exactly know what I look like and they won't expect me to be traveling with anyone, let alone a female. I'll help you get to where you need to go, and in turn, you'll help draw their gaze off of me."

Biting my lip, I tapped my fingers against my thigh. I hated to admit it, but this plan made some sense. I had no way of knowing where to go after the forest. For Kydona's sake, I didn't even know about the laws of the very country I had lived in my entire life.

It was becoming painfully clear to me I needed someone's help. Otherwise, I would likely be back in my tower by nightfall, never to leave again. I sucked in a deep breath. It appeared I was out of options.

"Okay," I said, sheathing my dagger before extending my hand toward him.

He clasped my hand in his and I jumped, not expecting the surge of heat that seemed to constantly run under his skin. He raised a silver brow. "Do we have a deal?"

I nodded briskly. "Yes. I'll help take eyes off you in Thyr, and in exchange, you'll get me out of Ithenmyr."

"It's a deal."

We shook on it.

I was Wrong

It turned out that without a dagger pointed at him, my new companion was not very talkative. That was fine with me, considering that my plans for this day had gone in a completely different direction from what I had originally intended.

We hiked in complete silence for the next four hours. The only time we stopped was to relieve ourselves, which only happened once I ensured he was going to give me complete privacy.

We had walked so far, and the burning in my muscles had given way to numbness hours ago. I hadn't known it was possible to be so tired, so sore, so worn out that my body no longer felt like it belonged to me.

The good thing about the exhaustion was that the constant tingling in my hands was no longer the most prevalent source of pain in my body. As we walked, I focused all my energy on remaining upright, determined not to falter in front of this warrior I didn't know. Weakness was dangerous. I knew that. And being weak, in Ithenmyr, was deadly.

When the trees finally thinned, a ripple of excitement ran through me. My mysterious companion stopped a few feet in front of me, shifting from one foot to the other, his fingers tapping on his thigh as I came up to stand beside him.

He cleared his throat, breaking his silence. "The city awaits. We should be within the walls of Thyr by the time the sun sets, my lady."

He extended his arm towards me, bowing extravagantly in my direction.

"Don't call me that," I muttered as I pushed past him to look at the winding road that climbed over rolling hills and valleys. On one side of the road was a long river, and on the other was yet another forest. If I squinted, I could see the very beginnings of what looked like an enormous wall far off in the distance, but I couldn't be sure. "I'm not your lady."

He raised a brow and huffed, crossing his arms. "Well, what should I call you?"

Pinching my lips together, I smoothed out an invisible wrinkle on my cloak. There was no way in the seven circles of hell I was going to tell him my real name. That he knew I was an elf was trouble enough. If he knew what the king would do to get his hands on me again...

I wouldn't let that happen.

"You can call me Ana," I told him after a moment.

"Ana." He rolled my name around on his tongue, tasting it as though it were a fine wine. It must have pleased him, for he bowed again. "Thank you for allowing me to escort you, Lady Ana."

Huffing at his mocking display of kindness, I narrowed my eyes. "And what shall I call you? Lord Snuck-Up-On-Me-In-The-Woods somehow just doesn't quite roll off the tongue."

He chuckled. The sound was low and deep and made my stomach twinge in a not-at-all unpleasant manner. "You can call me that if you want, Ana, or you can simply refer to me as Xander. Either is fine."

"Xander," I murmured, testing his name on my tongue as his eyes twinkled in amusement.

His lips twitched as he said, "Since you didn't know about the Accompaniment Law, Ana, am I to assume that you've never been to Thyr?"

For a moment, I considered lying to him but then decided that the easiest path forward would be the truth.

"Yes." I sighed, running my hands down my cloak for what felt like the hundredth time. "I've never been there before."

I've never been anywhere, I added silently.

Xander nodded, his brows furrowed as he studied me. "Does what you've seen so far meet your expectations?"

Blinking, I returned my eyes to the scene before us. My gaze swept over the countryside. I stared at the winding road and the dots that I assumed were people heading into the city. From here, Thyr looked larger than life, but I knew from my very limited education that it was only the third-largest city in Ithenmyr. I took in the plethora of tall stone buildings dotting the horizon.

How could anything be bigger than this?

Not for the first time since escaping my tower, I regretted that I barely knew the country I called my home. I had lived in a cage for so long, and only now was I realizing that there was an entire world that was waiting to be explored.

People to meet. Things to see. Places to go.

I was beginning to realize that I'd had experiences stolen from me because of my secluded upbringing. That by keeping me locked in a tower, the king had done more than take away my freedom. He'd stolen my ability to choose. To learn. To grow. What good was life if one didn't have these things?

Suddenly, I couldn't wait to get to Thyr and see what the city looked like from up close. I couldn't wait to experience life.

The afternoon sun was warm as it bathed the hills in its rays. The storm clouds from earlier had cleared, leaving shimmering pools of water on the road. It was stunningly picturesque. I had no idea something so beautiful existed less than a day's walk from my tower.

What else had been hidden from me?

My fingers twitched at my sides, and I wished for a piece of charcoal to memorialize the sight. Instead, I settled for locking the memory away in my mind.

Later, I promised myself. *I'll sketch it later.*

If there was a later.

There *had* to be a later. Freedom tasted far too good. Now that I was out of the king's clutches, I already knew. I would never go back. I would run as far away from here as possible and experience *everything*.

"To be honest, so far, it's more than I thought it would be," I whispered. The words came out of my mouth unbidden, and immediately, I slammed my mouth shut. That was far more information than I had ever wanted to give to this male who had forced me into coming with him.

Xander glanced at me, a brow raised, but he didn't say anything. Instead, he reached behind him. His mouth twitched as he said, "Before we continue our trek, I thought you might like this back?"

My eyes narrowed, but then my lips tilted up. The sun glimmered on the silver blade of my dagger as Xander withdrew it from the waistband of his trousers. He had obviously wiped it clean, and he was extending the hilt of the weapon to me.

I reached for it, but before I could touch the hilt, he snatched it back. "Just try not to stab me with it again, Ana. Please."

Grabbing my knife, I tried not to sigh in relief at the familiar weight of my blade. I slipped it back into its sheath before shrugging. "Try not to sneak on me, Xander, and I'll see what I can do."

A chuckle burst out of him, and I could tell I had surprised him. He extended his arm towards me in clear invitation. "I'll do my very best, Ana."

"Thank you." I reached over and grasped his elbow. Over the years, I'd spent countless hours watching couples walking outside my tower, and I understood what he wanted us to do.

He cleared his throat. "Are you ready?"

The question rang through me as I considered Xander's words. There was no way he could know how much going into Thyr meant to me.

I could feel his eyes on me as I mulled over his words before I let a small smile creep onto my lips.

"More than you'll ever know, Xander." Tugging on his arm, I walked towards the river separating us from the city. "Let's go."

AFTER CROSSING over the large stone bridge separating us from the road into Thyr, it took us another hour on foot to join the thin stream of traffic heading into the city. With every step, I felt a thrill growing within me. This was the life that I had been denied. How dare the king keep me from everything?

Anger, red and hot and fueled by the sight of the stone walls surrounding the city in the distance, roiled through my veins. He had kept this all from me. Beauty. People. Freedom.

Not anymore.

Even though we could see the walls surrounding Thyr, the city was not close. It turned out that walking over rolling hills was far more time-consuming than I had ever imagined. I was lost in my thoughts as we walked, the murmurs of conversation filling my ears as we continued towards the city.

I wondered what we would do if the sun dipped below the horizon and we were still outside of the walls. My education regarding the animals who lived in Ithenmyr, along with nearly everything else, had been non-existent.

When I had made my plan to escape, I had thought my weapons would be enough. I'd thought that if I got away from the wretched fate the king had planned for me, I would somehow figure everything else out. I had believed the skills Matthias had taught me would be enough to help me survive.

Well, it was already clear to me I was wrong. I was woefully under-prepared for this journey. It hadn't even been a full day since my escape, and there was no doubt in my mind that I had misjudged the entire situation. Not only was Ithenmyr far larger than I had been led to believe, but there were dangers I hadn't even anticipated.

The road wasn't too busy, although there were a few wooden carts being pulled by donkeys and horses as travelers hurried down the dirt road. A somber mood seemed to settle on everyone as we approached Thyr.

Most of the other travelers were walking by without even looking at us, although every so often, we seemed to attract their attention. At first, I thought Xander's size drew their gazes over to us, but soon, I realized that was not the case.

When the stone walls of the city were still far off in the distance, a plump older female met my eyes before spitting on the ground and crossing her heart.

"Hear me now, Ghemra," she prayed as she hurried past us, clutching onto the arm of her companion. "Be with us and protect us from this heathen."

Once she was out of earshot, I pulled on Xander's sleeve. He glanced down at me, raising a brow in silent question.

"Xander," I hissed, "why did she pray to the Goddess of Virtues when she looked at me?"

He jolted, his eyes widening as they swept over my body. "Dammit," he cursed. "This isn't going to work."

"What?" I asked, but in response, he simply pulled on my sleeve and dragged me off the road. No one stopped as we hurried past them, allowing us to get off the path without issue.

Xander ran a hand over his face, his features contorting as he stared at me.

"I can't believe I didn't think about this," he muttered. "This will put us back a day, at least."

"What is going to put us back?" I tugged on his sleeve, but he continued to ignore me.

Tapping a finger on his chin, his eyes narrowed as he mumbled to himself. "Think, Xander. You need a solution. She can't go into the city like that. You'll attract too much attention. But what about—" Suddenly, he stopped, and his eyes lit up. "That's it."

"What is *it*?" I huffed, my fingers subconsciously picking at the hilt of my dagger. When I realized what I was doing, I let go of it, crossing my arms in front of my chest instead. My eyes narrowed. "If you don't want me to stab you again, you will fill me in on what is going on."

He stopped pacing, mirroring my position as he glared down at me. "Really? We're back to threats?"

"It seems to be the only thing that makes you act," I replied, not trying to temper the snark in my tone. There was just something about Xander that set my teeth on edge. Every single emotion within my body flared as he scowled down at me. It was as though my entire body was on fire as I snapped, "Are you going to tell me what is going on?"

"Patience really isn't your strong suit, is it, Ana?"

I tilted my head, baring my teeth at him. "I don't know. Most people don't try my patience like you do, *Xander*."

"Fine. You want to know what I'm thinking?"

"Yes," I ground out through clenched teeth. "That's exactly what I said. Do you have problems hearing? Maybe it would help if I yelled it a little louder so everyone could hear?"

He shook his head, his nostrils flaring. "No," he hissed, lowering his voice. "We don't want to attract attention. It's dangerous to stand out from the others. And you and I both know we are trying to stay *safe*."

"Then explain to me what is going on!" I whisper-yelled.

"Come with me." He grabbed my hand, huffing as he adjusted the bow slung over his shoulder before dragging me into the forest. "We can't go into the city with you looking like this." He moved his hand in front of me.

I sputtered, my eyes widening. Blood rushed to my face as I clenched my fists and fought the urge to stomp my foot on the leafy ground. "You just gestured to all of me!"

He nodded, his eyes firm. "We won't get within ten feet of the walls. You look like... well, I won't say the word because it isn't appropriate for your maiden ears."

Gasping, I lurched away from him. "I'm not a maiden, you pig-headed fool," I seethed. Blood rushed to my face, and I knew my ears were likely turning red beneath my hood.

Raising a brow, he tilted his head. "You're not? I could have sworn you gave off a maidenly aura."

"I-I... ugh!" I threw up my hands and stormed away from him. This infuriating, vexing, horrible male. Not only could he tell I was lying, but he just wouldn't stop pushing my buttons. Of all the people I had to run into. Pivoting on my heel, I shook my finger at him, my eyes narrowing. "I dislike you immensely."

Something that sounded like a snort came from Xander's direction, but when I glared at him from over my shoulder, an impassive look was on his face.

"I'm not so fond of you either, Sunshine," he muttered.

I inhaled sharply, my eyes widening as I pulled my dagger out from its sheath. The metal zinged in the air as I asked through clenched teeth, "*What* did you call me?"

He stood his ground, widening his stance. He somehow looked even more imposing than he had before. Larger. More dangerous. I could have sworn heat was coming off his body as he snarled, "You heard me. Sunshine. Because of your *sparkling* personality."

"How dare you?" I gasped. "You don't speak to me for hours, and now you have the gall to call *me* names? I'm shocked that more people aren't lining up to stab you with how you talk."

He snorted. "Thank you for proving my point. In all my years, I've never met someone as inclined to violence as you seem to be. Now, will you make us stand out here until the moon rises, or can we get going?"

I crossed my arms, careful not to stab myself with my dagger. "I'm not going anywhere with you until you explain what's happening."

One second, Xander was standing at least ten feet away from me. The next, he was right next to me, grabbing my elbow with his too-hot hands.

"How did you—" I started, but he ignored me, pulling me through the woods. His grip was tight, and I tried to pry his fingers off me, to no avail.

"Listen, Ana," he growled under his breath as he ducked beneath a branch. "That lady won't be the last one to look at us like that. We can't go into the city until we find some better clothes. Like it or not, you don't look 'right'. And that means you'll keep drawing attention, which is the exact thing we don't want."

My lips tilted down as I considered his words. "Okay," I said slowly as

I sheathed my blade. "But where exactly are we going? We're in the middle of the woods. I don't see where you think we will find some 'better clothes.'"

"Leave that to me," he said, shifting his grip to my elbow before leading me deeper into the forest.

We continued to stumble through the trees. The woods grew darker with every passing minute as the sun made its last farewells to the winter day. All around us, animals called out as the day slipped away. The evening air grew colder and seeped through my still-damp clothing, causing my already terrible mood to go from bad to worse.

Infuriatingly, the cold didn't seem to affect Xander at all. He rushed along, seemingly unaware of the drop in temperature.

I hurried behind him, ducking around trees and over branches while trying to stop my teeth from chattering. Despite my best efforts to see where we were going, it didn't appear we were following any sort of path.

"So, what is your plan?" I panted, stepping around a fallen branch. It seemed as though we had been hiking into the woods blindly for what felt like hours, but I knew it was probably thirty minutes.

"We'll have to delay our visit to the city until tomorrow. We will have to visit her."

Xander didn't sound out of breath at all as he led us through a grove of trees. This brought me enormous amounts of frustration. After everything I had put my body through today, it was protesting violently. My lungs were burning, my muscles aching as I put one foot in front of the other.

Blowing out a long breath as a wolf howled somewhere in the distance, I stumbled alongside the much larger male. "Who is she?"

There was no response.

No matter how much I pushed and prodded, Xander refused to

answer any of my questions. It seemed as though he lost himself to thought, for every single question I asked got the same answer: a grunt.

Eventually, I gave up all hopes of discovering who this mysterious *her* was. I trudged along in silence, listening to the sounds of the forest as we trekked. When an hour or so had passed, Xander finally stopped.

My mouth fell open as I took in our surroundings.

This was his solution?

Nonna Doesn't Bite

❧

"Let me get this straight. Your master plan is to bring me to a ramshackle cabin in the middle of the woods?" I hissed at Xander, digging my feet into the ground as he dragged me towards the decrepit cabin.

He was so large that my feet were barely making grooves in the dirt as he pulled me along against my will.

"Do you have a better plan, Ana?" he asked, his voice sharp. Any trace of kindness that might have been in his voice earlier was long gone. "One that will allow us to spend the night somewhere safe and give us the opportunity to dry off before going into the city tomorrow?"

"Well, I don—"

He shook his head, his grip tightening around my arm as he continued to rant. "A plan that perhaps involves finding appropriate clothing in the woods? One that might also, as an additional benefit, not get us killed? Despite your seemingly natural inclination towards violence, *I* would prefer to make it through the night alive."

I pinched my mouth shut. I didn't have a plan, but I still didn't like the look of this... this... shack. And that's what this was.

A shack in the middle of the dark, deserted woods. This cabin looked like the kind of place only someone with nefarious intentions would go. Which was precisely what I was beginning to suspect of Xander.

Not only was he rude, disrespectful, and arrogant, but it also seemed that he might have been planning to murder me. Of all the things I'd planned for today, being murdered was not one of them. I could just imagine what the servants would say as they hurried along the halls of the king's castle.

She escaped, only to be killed and taken apart limb by limb in the woods by a crazed lunatic. Fitting. She got what she deserved.

A shudder ran down my spine.

"Come on, Ana," he hissed.

I shook my head. "No."

Wooden shutters hung on the walls where broken glass covered what had been, at one point, a window. A lopsided chimney stack reached above the cottage, and even from here, I could see that bits of stone and mortar were missing from it. To say it looked unsafe would have been an understatement of vast proportions.

Green vines crawled up the walls of the log cabin, and a garden that looked like it had seen better days took up most of the clearing. Even in the dimming light of the evening, I could see that this was *not* somewhere I wanted to spend any amount of time.

Blowing out a deep breath, I grabbed onto a large tree limb and held on with all my might.

He scowled, the sound sending shivers down my spine. "What are you doing, Ana?"

I shook my head, kicking him as he tried to come closer. My voice was high-pitched as I said, "I'm not going in there with you. How do I know you won't just murder me?"

Xander's nostrils flared as he threw up his hands. He snarled, "If I were going to murder you, Ana, I would have already done it ten times by now."

I narrowed my eyes. "Says the one walking around with a stab wound."

He shrugged. "I let you stab me."

"It didn't look like that from where I was standing," I snorted, releasing my grip on the branch and crossing my arms as I widened my stance. "If you want me to go in there, you'll have to carry me. I won't go willingly."

Xander clenched his jaw and pinched the bridge of his nose. "Kydona, save me," he muttered under his breath before taking a step toward me.

We stared at each other, anger radiating off both of us as everything else seemed to fade away. The air was charged with something that felt thick and heavy, and my heart pounded in my chest. I fingered the hilt of my dagger, a snarl rising in my throat as I prepared to defend myself.

Just then, the wooden door of the murder cottage creaked open.

"What is going on here?" a withered voice spoke, shattering the weighted silence that had been stretching across the clearing.

I shook my head, stepping back from Xander, before peeking around him. Standing at the door of the cottage was the shortest female I had ever seen. She had long white hair that was twisted into a bun on the top of her head. A lantern dangled from her fingertips, casting eerie shadows on her face as she bustled forward.

"Xander?" she asked. "Is that you?"

Then, the strangest thing happened. A smile broke out on my would-be murderer's face as he turned around and spread his arms. The sight was so shocking that I let out an audible gasp.

"Hello, Nonna," he said. He bent, wrapping the old female up in his arms.

She was so much smaller than him. His body engulfed hers as he lifted her off the ground. I noticed he was careful not to jostle the lantern, something I was very grateful for. An accidental forest fire was not on my to-do list for today.

From my position on the ground, I couldn't help but notice that she wore threadbare stockings under her long dress. Blood rushed to my cheeks, and I looked away.

"Put me down, Xander," she complained before hitting the male on the arm with a wooden spoon I hadn't noticed before. "Introduce me to your lady friend and tell me why you're here. Don't tell me you just came to visit your old Nonna, because I won't believe you for a moment."

Xander did as she asked, quickly explaining that we were looking for a change of clothing and shelter for the night. When he was done, the old female turned around. She placed her hands on her hips, pinching her lips together as she studied me. I shifted on my feet as the one called Nonna hummed.

"Ah. I see the problem. You did the right thing, Xander. A female dressed in leggings and a tunic would draw far too much attention."

I sputtered, my eyes still wide. "This was all I had access to," I huffed.

It was true. The servant I had traded my jewels to had only been able to get me the tunics and leggings. Anything else would have drawn too much suspicion.

"When I was dressing this morning, I had far bigger problems than trying to impress males."

Despite the bite in my words, Nonna simply nodded as she studied me in the dimming light. "What is your name, child?"

I just stared at her. I wasn't used to talking to people, and there was something about this female that was... different.

"Did you hear me, girl?" She stepped forward, lifting a hand as though to pull back my hood.

Instinctively, I shuffled back. "Yes, ma'am." I raised my hands. "I heard you."

She smirked, patting her hands with the wooden spoon. "Good, good. Why don't you tell Nonna your name?"

"Ana, ma'am," I replied quickly.

She smiled, revealing a toothless mouth. It took everything within me not to shudder. "That's a good girl."

Just then, a shiver racked through my body. I tried to stop my teeth from chattering, but it was too late. The old female noticed, springing into action.

"Oh my goodness," Nonna muttered to herself. Her long dress swept in the air as she turned around. "I've been a terrible hostess. Come on inside, children. I'll get you both warmed up in no time."

I raised a brow, crossing my arms and glaring at Xander. "As I mentioned to your grandson, I'm not going in there."

He huffed, grabbing my elbow and drawing me near to him. I tried not to jump at the way the heat of his hand rushed through my skin. "Listen, Sunshine. I will make you a promise."

A promise. One of the few things I had been taught was that making promises and vows was never something to take lightly. They held weight in Ithenmyr. There was magic behind promises. They could hold weight and be binding.

No one in their right mind made promises to someone they had just met. That he would suggest making one for me...

I raised my brow. "I'm listening."

"I promise you will not die inside this cottage," he said gruffly. "You have my word. Nonna doesn't bite."

Something about his words made me stop. No one had ever sworn a promise to me before. Xander's tone was so sincere that it almost sounded like he was pleading with me to go along with him.

This day had been so long, and suddenly, all I wanted to do was sit down. Chances were fairly decent there would be some sort of furniture in the cottage. At least, I hoped that would be the case.

"Fine." I ground out through clenched teeth. "I'll come. But if I die in this murder cottage, I promise you, I will come back from the seven circles of hell and haunt you."

"It's a deal," Xander chuckled, tugging on my elbow. "Come on."

I sighed, praying to anyone who would listen to keep me safe.

THE INSIDE of the cottage was nothing like I expected. On the outside, the building had appeared as though it was at risk of collapsing on itself at any moment.

But once Xander pulled me across the threshold, I found myself unable to move. All the manners that had been drilled into me evaporated as I slowly turned on my feet. My jaw fell open, and I had trouble comprehending what I saw.

"Ana," Xander whispered in my ear, his warm breath tickling my neck, "come on." He tugged on my elbow, breaking my reverie.

"I... How is this possible?"

He blinked, those damn golden eyes large as he looked around. "Do you mean the shack?"

"Xander." Nonna's voice was chiding as it lilted out from behind a closed door. "You know better than to misuse your words. This isn't a shack. It's my home."

I gestured towards the door, stomping my foot on the wood. "*That* is what I mean. This dinky little cottage shouldn't have a second room, let alone look as... as... as palatial as it does!"

And it did look palatial. The cottage's interior was filled with cream-colored walls, beautiful furniture, and artistic renderings of streams and mountains hanging on the walls.

There was even a mural of a giant green dragon flying over a high mountain range painted over the fireplace. The artist had painted a female riding on the back of the dragon, her long red hair flying behind her like a river. It was.... incredible, completely unlike anything I had ever seen before.

Xander opened his mouth, then closed it as he stepped back. "Nonna is... special," he said after a moment.

I crossed my arms. "Explain."

He stared at me, blinking several times. He had a maddening look of incomprehension on his face. "Excuse me?"

"You heard me." I waved a hand in the air. "Explain what you mean. How is *this* possible?"

"Well... she..." Xander cleared his throat, his feet shifting on the floor as he avoided my gaze.

"I'm a witch," Nonna said as a door slammed shut behind her.

I blinked once, then twice, trying to understand what I just heard. My mind was racing. I knew the word, but I thought witches were nothing more than tales. "I'm sorry, a what?"

Nonna appeared at my elbow, looking up at me. "A witch."

"A witch," I repeated.

The old female—the witch?—stared at me for a moment, her brows furrowed, before turning to Xander and putting her hands on her hips.

"Xander." Her voice was chiding. "Am I understanding correctly that you finally brought someone home to meet your precious Nonna, and you didn't even tell her who I am?"

So many questions ran through me all at once.

Who was she to Xander? If she was a witch, did that mean other mythical creatures were also real? Ones that I thought were long dead and gone from Ithenmyr? Mermaids, dragons, faeries, vampires—did they still exist, too? Moreover, was this Xander's home? Why had he acted like going into Thyr would be a day trip and nothing more? How come she thought Xander and I were together?

All the questions fought for dominance in my mind, but finally, I settled on the most important one.

"Xander and I aren't a couple." I crossed my arms in front of my chest, a scowl on my lips. "He and I are the furthest thing from that. We aren't even friends. We were supposed to go into Thyr, but apparently, I wasn't dressed properly, so... here we are. A non-friendly, non-couple, in the middle of the woods."

I finished my tirade, suddenly exhausted. My feet seemed to be unable to continue to hold me, and I slumped against the back of the nearest chair. My vision blurred, and I blinked, rubbing my hands in front of my eyes. That sent shooting pains down my hands, and I pulled them away from my eyes, staring at the red flesh that greeted me. I'd forgotten about that.

Nonna took one look at my hands and tsked. "Xander. Why didn't you tell me she was in such a bad state?" She lurched forward, grabbing one of my hands in hers. I tried not to flinch when her thumbs ran down the rope burn that still marred my skin.

"I didn—" he started.

"I'm fine," I muttered, interrupting him as I tried to pull my hand away, but Nonna wouldn't listen.

"Nonsense, young one," she scolded. "You will let me take care of this right now."

I frowned, "I'm not—"

Nonna shook her head, speaking in a tone that made it clear she was used to getting her way. "Xander, don't just stand there. Make yourself useful. First, you need to wash." She pointed at his ripped tunic, wrinkling her nose. "Get changed. I won't have you smelling like you rolled around in a pigsty."

"But Nonna, I jus—"

She shook her head, shoving Xander. "No buts. I didn't raise you to question your elders. Now, you will wash. Then, you will make us some dinner. I won't have you lazing around my home."

I smirked as Xander jumped to attention. He hurried off to do Nonna's bidding, leaving his bow resting against a wall before disappearing from sight. Once he was gone, the witch turned back to me. She took my hands in hers, turning them this way and that. I watched as she nibbled on her lip before sighing.

"Hold still, Ana. This will be over before you know it," Nonna said.

The witch took my hands in both of hers, and I tried to ignore the way her papery skin felt against my hand.

A warm, tingly sensation spread through my hand as Nonna murmured under her breath. As she worked, a soft blue glow began to emit from the witch. It was as though a thousand tiny stars were embedded beneath her skin. I stared at her, enthralled.

"There you go." She smiled, releasing her grip on my hands.

Snapping out of my trance, I turned my hands over. I couldn't stop the gasp that escaped from me. My hands were immaculate. There wasn't a single trace of the burns. In fact, my entire body felt better than I had in days.

"Thank you, Nonna," I said sincerely.

The witch's lips tilted up, the lines around her eyes crinkling. When she smiled, she looked at least a decade or two younger than I had initially thought. She patted my cheek. "Not a problem, my dear. It's been too long since someone has needed me to heal them. It was my pleasure."

All of a sudden, my stomach twisted. My gaze darted around wildly as I searched my pockets. "I can't... I don't have any money to pay you for the healing."

Nonna stared at me for a long moment before bursting into laughter. She bent over, clutching her middle as hysterics overcame her. I watched with furrowed brows until she straightened once more.

"Oh, my dear," the witch chuckled, wiping a finger under her eyes. "Meeting you was payment enough. I never thought the day would come when I would meet the female whose aura was tangled with my Xander's."

Raising a brow, I tilted my head. "Thank you?" My voice betrayed my confusion as I continued, "I'm not sure what you mean about auras, though, Xander and I—"

Just then, a loud crash came from the other room, followed by a steady stream of curses.

Nonna winked, stepping away from me as she turned toward the source of the sounds. "Don't worry, my dear. You'll see in time." Pulling the door open, she turned. "Now that your hands are healed, I'll leave you to get change. You'll find everything you need in the loft."

Without waiting for a reply, Nonna disappeared from sight. Once the door snicked into place, quiet murmurs of conversation came from the kitchen. The promise of clean clothes beckoned me forward, and after one last glance at my now-healed hands, I climbed the ladder.

A Gift and a Departure

~

Moments after I ascended the ladder and entered the loft, I decided I had *definitely* underestimated Nonna's powers.

This so-called loft was more like a suite, with a full-sized bed and an attached bathing chamber. Nonna must have been an extremely powerful witch. The moment my feet came in contact with the wooden floorboards, a fire sprang to life in the fireplace. Above it, a kettle holding water began to boil almost immediately, providing me with warm water for my ablutions.

As soon as I checked every inch of the space and ensured I was alone, I removed my cloak. Shaking my hair free, I muttered as I pulled off my damp clothes.

"How is it fair that no one questions if a male wears leggings, but a female wears the clothing of a male, and all of a sudden, she's too 'inappropriate' for the city? I'd like to meet the person who decided this was okay."

Continuing to grumble to myself, I folded my clothes in a neat pile. I wasn't an animal, after all.

My skin bristled as a cool breeze blew in from an open window, and I quickly pulled on a long, black silk robe as I walked over to the nearby wardrobe. Yanking the doors open, my eyes widened at the sight.

I had never seen so many dresses in one place. A dozen gowns, ranging from the palest yellows to the deepest blues, hung from a row of pegs. For a minute, I just stared at them. The colors were so different from the crimson red gowns I'd been forced to wear my entire life. I'd be happy if I never saw that red again.

After a few minutes of deliberation, I decided on a simple but beautiful dark green gown. Silver trim ran around the hem and the bottom of the long bell sleeves. The laces of the stays themselves appeared to be made of the same silver material, and the entire dress shimmered in the firelight.

Running my fingers down the dress as I laid it on the bed, I marveled at the softness of the gown. I had never been given clothing so fine to wear before in my life. The king had allotted me two dresses per year, and that had been it. This was an unexpected luxury.

Having picked my clothing, I shed the housecoat and walked around in nothing but the skin Kydona had given me at birth.

I used the warm water to wash the grime of this never-ending day off me before brushing my hair and leaving it in soft red waves that rippled down my chest and back. Glancing in the mirror, I saw the tips of my long ears poking out from among the waves. Shaking my head, I tried to tuck them away, to no avail.

I supposed it was useless, anyway. Xander already knew I was an elf and would probably tell the witch. There was no point in hiding.

Once I no longer carried layers of dirt on my skin, I rummaged through a nearby trunk and found a set of clean lingerie. Sliding on a linen shift and underwear, I pulled on three petticoats before stepping into the gown itself. It conformed to my frame as though it had been made for me.

Perhaps Nonna was a witch and a seamstress.

Looking down at myself, I couldn't help but run a hand over the stays and down the fabric. Hidden pockets had been sewn into the gown, and I took pleasure in finding a home for both of my knives.

Satisfied that I had adequately hidden my weapons, I took a deep breath and descended the ladder. The main room was empty, but by the murmur of conversation, I knew Nonna and Xander were nearby.

Holding my breath, I tip-toed across the room. I had overheard dozens of conversations in this manner when my guards and servants were too liberal with their voices outside my door.

"... Be careful," Nonna whispered. "Are you certain?"

"I have to go into the city," Xander said. "I need to get to The Opal Spoon tomorrow, and with her at my side, it'll be easier."

Nonna hummed as her voice lowered. She whispered something I couldn't hear before raising her voice once more. "I know you heard me tell her your auras are intertwined, Xander."

I stilled, pressing my ear against the door. There was that word again. Auras. I had no idea what it meant, but the witch kept bringing it up.

Xander laughed. He *laughed*. It wasn't just a chuckle but a full-on belly laugh. The kind people made when someone told them a hilarious joke.

Bristling, I pursed my lips. Obviously, Xander knew what auras were, and he found the entire situation humorous. I huffed, crossing my arms. Everything he did aggravated me.

"Nonna," he chided, the laughter still present in his voice. "That... female is not my mate. She *stabbed* me. And she's an elf. You know that it's rare that..."

His voice dropped lower, but I wasn't paying attention anymore.

Mate.

The word clanged around in my mind. It shook something loose within me. Mate. I'd heard the word whispered behind closed doors when no one thought I was listening. Mates were *rare*. But then again, until a few minutes ago, I thought witches were nothing more than mentions that appeared in history books, so what did I know?

But even if mates were rare, I already knew.

There was *no way* Xander was my mate. Mates were supposed to be your person—the one who cared for you when no one else would. Mates were supposed to love you until you Faded. When people decided to accept a mating bond, it was for life. Accepting a mating bond wasn't a decision to be made lightly.

Once bonded, mates would never be with anyone else. When one of them Faded, the other would be so overcome with grief that they would quickly follow.

To lose one's bonded mate was to lose one's other half.

Two of the servants in my tower had been mates. After Matthias, Paeral and Adan had been the two kindest people I had ever met. Their love for each other had been a shining example of what I had been missing in my life. They made being mates look easy. They were always helping each other and finishing each other's sentences. As I thought of them, a pang went through me. I hoped they wouldn't be punished for my escape.

"Elf or not," Nonna whispered, jolting me out of my thoughts, "your auras are intertwined. Have you ever known me to be wrong, boy?"

"No, but Nonna, I can't be with anyone. You know that. I won't risk it. Not after what happened to..." Xander's voice lowered, and I clenched my fists.

Whatever was between me and Xander was *not* easy. It was not simple. Putting aside the fact that we had just met, I couldn't ignore that he was the most infuriating person I had ever met.

Dammit.

"Xander," the witch chided. "Remember who you are."

"Nonna," he hissed, as something loud slammed onto the table, "you mustn't speak of such things. When I was at the university..."

Xander's voice lowered, and I couldn't hear him.

Who is he? He went to university? Where?

I only knew of two universities in Ithenmyr. When I tried to picture the big, burly male bent over a desk with a quill in his hand, the entire idea seemed utterly preposterous.

"My child," Nonna sounded like she was moving around in the kitchen as she spoke, "You can't choose who your essence..."

Her voice lowered, and moments later, I decided I'd had enough. Not wanting to be discovered eavesdropping, I coughed as I pushed open the door.

"I hope I'm not interrupting anything," I exclaimed loudly.

My brows rose as I took in the two of them. They were both sitting at a tiny wooden table with a porcelain teapot between them. My stomach grumbled at the sight of an overflowing plate of biscuits resting among tiny tea cups painted with flowers.

"Of course not, dear. Your presence is never an interruption." Nonna pushed back her chair and stood. She had changed her apron and pulled another wooden spoon out of a large pocket. I raised a brow as she walked to the fire, reaching in to stir something in a large pot balancing over the flames as she continued to speak. "Isn't that right, Xander?"

At the sound of his name, Xander's gaze flicked up from his teacup. The moment his eyes met mine, it felt like my heart stopped in my chest. Everything seemed to slow as his eyes widened.

A beat passed before his jaw fell open. Xander's golden gaze swept over me, starting at my hair and crawling all the way to my feet before coming back to meet my eyes. The fire in his eyes startled me, and I stepped back.

"You look..." He coughed, his cheeks reddening. "Better."

Nonna looked up from the fire. "Better?" Waving her wooden spoon in the air, she admonished. "That is no way to speak to a lady, Xander. Especially not one as stunning as the one before you."

"No, it's fine," I said as I slid into the seat Nonna had vacated. I spread my skirts, settling them around me. "I'm not a lady."

Nonna raised a brow, turning from the fireplace with her hands on her hips. "Nonsense, my dear." She gestured to all of me with a smile, and suddenly, I knew where Xander had learned the gesture. "You cannot look like that and not call yourself a lady."

A retort rose to the tip of my tongue, but before I could say it, Nonna shoved a plate in front of me. I hadn't even seen her prepare it, but biscuits with slices of meat and cheese were sitting next to a bowl of the best-looking stew I'd ever seen.

"Thank you," I said as gratitude welled within me. My stomach grumbled at the amazing aroma coming from the steaming bowl.

The witch nodded. Her voice was full of authority as she said, "You are far too thin. You will eat, and then you must sleep. I won't allow you to go into Thyr without being well-rested."

"Yes, ma'am," I said as I brought the first spoonful of stew to my mouth. It somehow tasted even better than it looked. The moment the first spoonful hit my tongue, my eyes widened. Flavors of deep, warming spices hit my palate, and I devoured the entire bowl within a few minutes.

I hadn't realized how hungry I was, but once the food entered my body, I could do nothing more than eat.

Nonna's stew and biscuits filled every crevice within me, and before I knew it, I was back in the loft. Crawling under the covers of the enormous bed, I reveled in the softness of the mattress. I'd never slept on anything so nice before in my life.

Sliding my daggers beneath my pillow, I lay on my back and closed my eyes. The crackling fire downstairs filled my ears, and soon, sleep was beckoning my name.

Releasing my grip on reality, I slipped into the welcoming darkness.

"Ana, you need to wake up."

A deep masculine voice reached me, pulling me out of my dreamless slumber. Blinking, I rubbed my hands over my eyes and took in the male standing over me.

Xander was nothing more than shadows, his large frame blending into the inky blackness of the night. I could have sworn his eyes flashed green in the darkness before they returned to their regular golden color.

"What time is it?" I mumbled.

"Time to get up," he snapped.

I yawned, snuggling into the warm bed. "Could you be more specific? I'm still so tired."

"It's almost dawn," he said moments before something heavy landed on me. "Get dressed. We need to leave."

"What's the rush?"

He huffed, irritation lacing his voice. Even though I couldn't see him, I knew he was making a face at me. "My contact will only remain in Thyr until tonight. We need to see them before it's too late. They have something for me, remember?"

His words made sense. But his tone made me feel... unsettled. He kept doing this. There was just something about him that made me feel off-kilter. Even his closeness to me right now made me feel unstable.

And I *despised* feeling unstable.

Frowning, I got a distinct impression that he was studying me. Which was completely unfair because I could barely see anything in the dark.

"Do you mind?" Snapping, I pulled up the blanket and crossed my arms over my chest. "Unless you're in the mood to be stabbed again, I would appreciate a few minutes alone."

My words seemed to startle him because he jolted upright and hit his head on a rafter. He cursed, muttering as he straightened. "You're so full of threats."

"Leave, please," I said through clenched teeth.

"Hold on a minute, Ana," Xander said before the distinct sound of shuffling filled my ears. I reached under my pillow, grabbing my blade, just as a flame flicked to life on a candle I hadn't seen before. He placed the taper on the table, backing away.

"You couldn't have done that earlier?" I snapped.

He ignored me, climbing down the ladder. His voice carried to me as he descended. "I'll make some tea and say goodbye to Nonna. Come and meet me when you're presentable."

IT TOOK me twenty minutes to get ready.

During every one of those minutes, I cursed Xander while taking care of my needs. I brushed my teeth and hair before pulling on my lingerie and the same dress I had worn last night. I huffed as I sheathed my weapons on my body, thinking of ways to get back at Xander for his horrible attitude.

Once I went downstairs, I glared at him as I drank Nonna's tea. It was warm, delicious, and invigorating. In other words, it was perfect. Of course, it was. I couldn't hold Nonna's association with Xander against her, but I wondered why she put up with him. She seemed so delightful.

To my utter dismay, Xander seemed to be entirely at ease despite the early morning hour. My eyes narrowed as I took in his all-too-chipper attitude. He chattered with Nonna about inconsequential things, talking about people I didn't know while he devoured a massive breakfast.

It was all terribly irritating. *He* was terribly annoying. No one had a right to be so chipper before dawn. Especially not someone as inherently bothersome as Xander. It seemed like every single thing he did was geared towards irking me.

Finally, it was time to leave.

I stepped outside, the fresh, crisp morning air finishing the job the tea had started. I blinked as my lungs filled with air that tasted like freedom. This was something I would never get used to.

In the early morning, the clearing around the cottage seemed less menacing than it had the evening before. A breeze blew by, and I shuddered.

Nonna tsked, rushing inside the cottage. "Wait a moment, young ones."

I watched her go, the door slamming shut behind her.

"It still looks like a murder cottage to me," I mumbled.

Xander shot me a glare, his voice rising as he put his hands on his hips. Anger emanated from him in waves. "Seriously?" He made a face. "We're going to do this *again*?"

"*Seriously*," I mimicked his tone of voice, "it does." I gestured to the cottage. "It was a simple comment. There's no reason to bite my head off."

He grumbled something rude under his breath that I chose not to hear.

"Why are you so quick to anger?" I knew I was pushing his buttons, but something about him made it too easy. I couldn't stop myself.

He raised a brow. "*I'm* quick to anger?"

I nodded. "That's what I said. Do you need to have your hearing checked?"

"As I recall, you're the one who attacked me yesterday."

Groaning, I ran a hand through my hair. "That's not fair. We have already concluded that *you* were following *me*, and you were aiming a nocked arrow at me! My blade just got to you first."

"Fine," he hissed. "I acknowledge that perhaps sneaking up on you hadn't been the best idea."

"You do?"

"I do. If I had known you were so ornery, I probably would have just left you in the woods."

"Ornery? I'll show you ornery!"

He turned, taking a step away from me, then two. A long moment passed where we just… stared at each other. The air was heavy as he sighed, running his hand through his hair. "Let's call a truce. For the next few minutes. Please. For the love of the gods, we have enough to worry about without adding any injuries to the mix."

I narrowed my eyes. "I'll tell you what. You focus on your behavior, and I'll do the same."

"Fine." He huffed. Crossing his arms, he stared at the cottage door, waiting for Nonna to return.

A tense minute passed before the witch reappeared. She held a pair of navy blue cloaks with large hoods.

"These will keep you both warm at night," she said, seemingly oblivious to our previous interaction. "Now, Xander, don't make me wait years before you come back to see your Nonna."

"Yes, ma'am," Xander replied gruffly. He uncrossed his arms, shifting on his feet.

I smirked. The witch's head barely reached the middle of Xander's chest, but it was clear he was scared of her. She reached over, handing me the cloak.

"Here you go, dear," she said.

Chuckling as I thanked Nonna, I clasped the cloak around my neck.

The witch smiled, patting Xander's cheek before stepping back slightly. "Tell me your plan one more time."

Xander sighed, crossing his arms. His muscles rippled as he huffed, leaning against a tree. "Nonna—"

"Please, Xander. Put your Nonna's mind at ease."

He sighed. "Fine. We are meeting Jo at The Opal Spoon tonight, and we will be out of the city by sunrise tomorrow."

"From there?"

Xander shook his head. "We'll know more tonight."

"You'll remember what I told you both?" Nonna asked, her gaze darting between us.

I stepped forward and clasped Nonna's papery hands in mine. "Of course. We will be careful."

Nonna smiled, pulling her hands out of my grip to reach into her apron.

"Good girl," she said. Her wrinkled fingers came out of her pocket, holding a golden chain between her fingers. "I want you to have this."

My eyes widened as I looked at the gilded necklace. It was delicate, and a small charm hung off the chain. It looked like a locket, although I couldn't see where it opened.

"Oh, no, I couldn't." I shook my head, backing up into a tree. The rough bark pressed into me, but I didn't move.

Nonna came forward, grabbing my hand and pressing the jewelry into my palm. She wrapped my fingers around it, beckoning me to lower my head.

"I insist," she whispered, squeezing my hand tightly. "You will need this for the time to come. Swear on Kydona, you will never take it off."

Something about Nonna's tone made my ears perk up. It felt as though every word was laced with a double meaning, but I did not know what it was.

"Swear it," the old female repeated. Her eyes were glowing blue, and cold sweat appeared on my forehead.

"I-I swear on the goddess herself, I will keep it on," I vowed. A tingle ran through me, and I could have sworn I felt a hum from the tree behind me. But it must have just been in my head.

"Put it on now," she insisted, releasing my hand.

I nodded warily. Lifting my hair, I clasped the necklace around my neck before pulling on my hood. "I promise, Nonna, I won't take it off."

My words seemed to mollify the witch. She stepped back, and the blue glow receded from her eyes. "Good girl," she repeated. Nodding to both of us, the witch smiled. "You should both be going now."

Xander stepped forward, drawing the old female into a hug. He picked her up off the ground, squeezing her tightly. "Thank you, Nonna."

Placing his grandmother on the forest floor, Xander turned to me. All traces of kindness vanished from his eyes as he scowled in my direction. Of course. I'd come to expect nothing less from him. His voice was gruff as he asked, "Ready, Sunshine?"

Pushing off from the tree, I narrowed my eyes at him. "As ready as I'll ever be."

He chuckled as he swung his pack over his shoulder. Nonna had been kind enough to give us enough food and coins to last us a few days, with strict instructions to buy more supplies in Thyr.

Xander started down the path, calling to me over his shoulder. "Let's go, then."

Huffing, I followed him. Even though I was going to the city with this less-than-pleasant company, I was excited.

Today, I would finally see Thyr.

A Gilded Cage

The trek through the woods back to the main road was different in the sunlight. The cloaks Nonna had given us were warm, and even with the added swooshing of my petticoats and dress, it was much easier to pick my way through the forest now than it had been the previous evening. For that, I was grateful.

I kept my eyes on Xander's back as he led us through the woods. The irritable male maintained a healthy distance between us as he picked through the forest. He hadn't said much since we had left Nonna's cottage behind, which was fine with me.

It gave me time to think everything over.

After having lived my entire life in solitude, the last twenty-four hours had been overwhelming, to say the least. Nothing about the past day had gone as planned. Yesterday morning, I had been escaping what would have been, at best, a loveless union and at worst, a marriage to a psychopath.

My intended's father had already proven himself to be a ruthless murderer who cared little for morals, and I knew his son followed in his bloody footsteps. That was why I had left.

There had been no way I would let myself be shackled in marriage if I could help it. Even as sheltered as I had been, I had seen the institution of marriage for what it was: a gilded cage.

The moment I swung out of my tower window, I vowed I would never let anyone trap me again. Not now that the glorious taste of freedom had made itself known to me.

"Good riddance," I muttered as I hurried to catch up to Xander.

The forest cover was becoming less dense, and I could see snippets of the road through the trees. Every time a branch brushed up against my cloak, I felt a stirring within me, but I didn't have time to unpack what it meant.

Xander stopped ahead of me. His face pinched in an impatient scowl as he watched me push back a heavy branch. I could hear the quiet murmur of conversation rising above the chirping of birds as people traveled toward the city.

"Come on, Ana," he said gruffly, motioning for me to hurry. He waited until I was beside him before he said, "We don't have all day."

I narrowed my eyes at him, a retort on the tip of my tongue, but I lost all ability to speak when he bent down and laced our hands together.

A spark ran through me at his touch, and I pulled my fingers back as though he had burned me. I snapped, "What in Kydona's name do you think you're doing?"

He raised a brow, grabbing my hand once more. The same spark rushed through me, and when I glanced at him, I knew he felt it too. His brows were furrowed as he stared at our joined hands. Our eyes met, and for a moment, it was as though I couldn't remember my own name.

A beat went by before my senses came flooding back.

This wasn't just any person holding my hand. This was *Xander,* and he irritated me like no one else. Xander wasn't nice. He wasn't affable. He didn't make me feel good. On the contrary, he made me feel angry. Spiteful.

He ignited a fire in me that no one else ever had before. He wasn't amicable, and he wasn't my friend. Far from it, in fact. We were very much not friends.

I needed to remember that.

Yanking my hand away from his, I reached into one of my hidden pockets and shifted away from him.

"Don't touch me," I spat.

He crossed his arms as he loomed over me. His tone was laced with superiority as he asked, "Did you forget the terms of our agreement already, Ana?"

I shook my head. "Of course not. I said I would help keep eyes off you in Thyr, and in exchange, you will get me to the Indigo Ocean. I'm not stupid, you know."

Xander just raised a brow, his face clearly telling me precisely what he thought of me.

Huffing, I narrowed my eyes and continued, "Do I need to remind you of my ability to defend myself? I don't need you to look after me."

He leaned, closing the distance between us as he lowered his voice. "I know that, Sunshine."

"Do you?" I snapped. "It seems like you might need a reminder."

The air between us thickened as his nostrils flared. He smelled like smoke and the deep woods, and my insides twisted at his proximity. I hated that. But more than that, I hated him for how he made me feel.

"Good gods," he snarled. "I've never met a female as resourceful with a blade as you are. You'd think we'd get along, yet you infuriate me at every turn."

"What kind of backhanded compliment was that?" I snapped. Blood rushed to my cheeks as I whisper-yelled, "I can't stand you!"

He snarled. "Believe me, this would be a lot easier if you were stupid. Maybe we wouldn't be stuck together. But unfortunately for both of us, we will have to put up with each other."

"That still doesn't explain why you touched me."

He heaved a heavy breath, running a hand down his face as he groaned. "Unbelievable. Am I seriously going to have to spell this out for you?"

I narrowed my eyes. "Spell what out?"

"Kydona, have mercy on me. Of all the females, I had to get stuck with this one." He continued to swear colorfully under his breath, mentioning something about fire as he turned around. He slammed his closed fist into a nearby tree twice, then three times.

The wood splintered, and spots of red blood appeared on his pale knuckles.

I stepped forward, extending my hand towards him before I remembered I was supposed to be mad at Xander. Whoever he was... he was not to be trifled with. This outburst of anger only served to remind me of that.

Xander huffed, wrapping his bleeding knuckles in his cloak as he turned back to me.

"Listen, Ana," he snapped. His tone was dripping with barely contained violence and anger. "I am not old enough to be your father. Nor could we pass as siblings. We look nothing alike, and I'm much bigger than you."

I nodded, pursing my lips as I tried to follow his train of thought. Avoiding his gaze, I studiously ignored the small trail of blood running down his right hand. It dripped onto the leafy floor, the blood bright red against the green leaves.

After a moment, I said, "I agree. Neither of those options is plausible."

The infuriating male in front of me stared at me until I raised my gaze to his. He lifted a brow. "Since I am accompanying you, but I cannot be your father or your brother that leaves..." He smirked, his voice trailing off as he waited for me to fill in the blank.

When I finally realized what he was saying, I raised my chin and met his eyes.

Curling my fists at my side, I stepped closer to him. When we were standing a mere foot from each other, I breathed, "You knew about this all along, didn't you?"

He tilted his head. "Honestly, Sunshine, I thought it was obvious."

"Not. To. Me." I ground out through clenched teeth. "If I thought for a second that you and I would have to... to..."

"Pretend to put up with each other?" he supplied unhelpfully.

"Pretend to be married," I hissed.

His mouth twitched in amusement, but he remained silent.

Huffing, I crossed my arms. "If I had known, I wouldn't have agreed to your deal."

"Is pretending to be my wife so reprehensible to you?"

Reprehensible? What kind of person uses words like that in real life?

I pursed my lips, but before I could say anything, Xander stepped even closer to me. "Am I really so terrible?" he asked. His eyes flashed, and for a moment, his icy exterior cracked. I could have sworn a flash of pain appeared in his eyes as his mouth tightened in a firm line. Just as quickly as it had appeared, it was gone.

My stomach twisted as I stared at him. "You're not... terrible to look at." I conceded, waving at his body. "The goddess obviously blessed you physically."

A noise that sounded like a cross between a choke and a cough came from him. "Not terrible to look at. I think you might have just complimented me, Sunshine."

I huffed, crossing my arms as I leaned against a tree. "Don't get used to it."

"Oh, believe me, I won't." Xander moved toward me, and I sucked in a breath. His eyes flashed as he glared at me. "If there's one thing I know, it's that the two of us are not suited. I could have told you that the moment you stabbed me."

"On that, we can agree," I said, blowing out a long breath. "And my problem... it's not you."

"Then what is it?"

Behind us, the sounds of conversation were growing louder as more and more people flooded the road.

"It's just..." I threw my hands in the air. "Never mind. I don't know how to explain it."

"Try," he ground out. His chest heaved, and we were so close... my heart was racing in my chest.

I sighed. "It's not really..."

"Give me a reason, Ana," he growled. He raised his hands, boxing me against the tree. I felt the rough bark against my back as he stared at me. He was so close thatI could reach up and touch his face if I wanted to. Thinking became far more difficult than I'd ever thought it could be.

"I..." my voice trailed off.

"Tell me," he breathed, a note of pleading in his voice. "Make me understand."

My breath caught as my mind raced. How exactly did one explain an aversion to the entire institution of marriage? Xander had no way of knowing what I had just escaped from, and I wasn't keen on telling him.

Gnawing on my lip, I considered the situation. His gaze was locked on the movement, and I sucked in a deep breath. "You won't... make me do anything, right? This is just pretend?"

"Of course." Xander nodded, his voice gruff. "I would never force you to do anything." His face grew somber as his eyes took on a far-away look. He grimaced, pushing away from me.

I sucked in a deep breath as space grew between us. "Do you promise?" I whispered.

"You have my word," he replied forcefully. "I'm not that kind of male."

"Okay." Stepping towards him, I placed my hand on his arm. He looked down at where I was touching him, and I realized that this was the first time I had initiated contact between us. I whispered, "I trust you."

When the words came out of my mouth, I realized they were true. For some reason, I trusted Xander. There had been plenty of opportunities for him to turn me into the king's soldiers yesterday, but he didn't.

I ran my hand down his arm before lacing my fingers through his. Ignoring the spark that came as I touched his warm hand, I glanced up at him to find him staring at our intertwined fingers.

"Let's go, husband," I said jokingly.

The moment the last word left my lips, a strange warmth filled me. I didn't have time to think about what it meant because Xander was already pulling us through the forest.

WITHIN MINUTES, we were standing at the edge of the dirt road. Picking off various twigs and leaves that had attached themselves to my cloak and gown, I stared at the commotion.

The quiet bustle of the road from yesterday was nowhere to be seen. Instead, we were confronted with a steady stream of traffic. People were yelling in the Common Tongue, but there were also several other languages I had never heard before.

I sighed. Yet another thing I needed to learn. Storing the thought in the back of my mind, I watched as dozens of carts pulled by horses and donkeys went by us. People hurried alongside their animals, their eyes trained on the city walls looming ahead. The walls of Thyr broke up the horizon, the city at odds with the beauty of the woods surrounding it. If I squinted, I could make out the shapes of soldiers marching along the top of the wall.

Those who didn't have carts carried enormous packs on their backs, and young children darted between skirts and ran up the road. Many travelers wore cloaks that kept their faces obscured from view. But even so, I knew not everyone was human, like Xander.

A traveler walked past us with glowing orange eyes and long black hair held in braids that ran down his back. His dark arms were thick with muscle as he held a young child on his hip. He had another in a sling on his back.

Turning his head, his lips peeled back in a snarl as he stared at us. I shivered at the sight of his canines. He glared at me for a moment before turning and speaking in a rapid stream to one of the children on his hip. His words were fluid, but I didn't understand anything he was saying.

"A werewolf from Vlarone," Xander whispered in my ear.

I watched the werewolf with wide eyes. From my limited studies, I had known that they existed—they were a part of the triad of species that lived in Ithenmyr: humans, elves, and werewolves—but I had never seen one before.

"Don't most werewolves work in the province of Osafeld?" I asked Xander.

He nodded. "Yes. He probably has a whole litter of pups. They're a long way from home. I wonder what brings them up north."

I watched, entranced, as a tall, dark-skinned female came up behind the werewolf, her swollen stomach reaching far ahead of her. Even in this state of advanced pregnancy, she was stunning. She wore a richly colored cloth tied around her head that matched the colorful dress that barely covered her bump. The werewolf wrapped an arm around her—his wife, I presumed—drawing her in tight against his chest as they continued.

As soon as there was a break in the flow of traffic, Xander pulled me onto the road, and we joined the crowds of people heading into town.

"Why is it so busy?" I whispered after a few minutes. Xander still hadn't let go of my hand, and I hadn't forced the issue. The rough skin and callouses that spoke of someone who worked with his hands daily were a warming, grounding presence among so many new people. It was providing me... comfort.

I refused to think about why that was.

"It's market day," he said in a low voice. "I hadn't realized. This is going to make getting through the city more complicated."

"What—"

Before I could say anything else, a shout came from behind us.

"Make way! Move out of the way for Lord Greenriver."

Xander paled, his grip tightening on my hand as he drew me against himself and to the side of the road.

With his free hand, he tugged on my hood, ensuring my face was covered, before repeating the action on his head. My heartbeat was loud in my ears as all the chatter on the road died down almost instantaneously.

I went to turn my head when Xander's voice reached my ears. "Don't turn around," he whispered, his hand on my lower back as he held me close. The heat emanating from his body seemed to wrap around me like a warm cloak as he murmured, "Just keep looking straight ahead."

Something in Xander's voice was different from before, and I nodded. My hands turned clammy as I stood still, wondering what was happening.

It didn't take long for me to find out.

I watched, wide-eyed, as an elf walked past. My chest seized as I stared at him. There he was, baring the ears I had so carefully tucked under my

but never had I ever imagined that something like this could even happen.

I swallowed, my gaze following those poor people as I tried to understand. To think of what to do. We had to help them.

"This isn't right," I whispered. I went to pull my hand out of Xander's grasp when, suddenly, the slaves began to yell. They were marching through a large mud puddle when a female in the middle of the group stumbled and fell to the ground. Her long, stringy brown hair dragged in the mud as she cried out, trying to return to her feet.

The others didn't stop. Before I could question why, a loud crack sounded as a whip unfurled in the air, shattering the final remnants of the peaceful morning.

My back clenched in agony, and for a moment, my vision blurred. Echoes of pain rippled through me as unwanted memories threatened to come flooding in.

I sucked in a deep breath. *Focus,* I commanded myself. *Pay attention. You got out. He can't hurt you anymore.*

She screamed, and I shoved all thoughts of the past away. My heart fractured as a second crack; then a third echoed all around us. My lungs grew tight as her wails became louder and louder.

No one moved.

Even Xander stood still, his mouth in a grim line as he watched the nightmare taking place before us.

The fluttering of wings filled the air, and soon, I realized maybe marriage wasn't the worst thing that could happen to me in Ithenmyr.

Seen and Not Heard

ᕙᕤ

ooking up, I watched as Lord Greenriver's wings flapped in the air as he hovered above the fallen human. I trembled as bright red tendrils of magic erupted from his hands. The deadly ribbons snaked out of him, writhing in the air before enveloping her from head to toe.

The slave's mouth opened in a silent scream as her shackled hands went to her throat. She clawed at her neck, her fingernails making tracks in her skin, as tears ran down her dirt-stained face.

Lord Greenriver was a Death Elf.

My breath caught in my throat, and my heart raced in my chest as I shrunk back into myself. The human's eyes bulged, and the Death Elf chuckled. The sound was sinister, malicious, and *familiar*. It was far too similar to a sound that haunted my nightmares.

His wings flapped as she fought valiantly against his magic. She struggled, her hands scrabbling at her throat as she fought to breathe. Even from here, I could see her face paling beneath the layers of dirt that coated her features.

"Why isn't anyone helping her?" I whispered in horror. She was less than two hundred feet from us, and there were many others lining the roads between us and the slaves. And yet, no one was moving. Urgency filled my voice as I said, "We have to help her."

Xander's arm tightened around my waist, and even though I struggled, I couldn't break free.

"Don't," he hissed in my ear. The word was filled with warning. Something about his tone sent shivers down my spine. He moved his other hand, reaching to grip my fingers with his. His skin was pale, but even so, I could see his white knuckles as he held firm onto me. "Ana, you can't stop this. Don't draw attention to yourself. To us."

I heard him, but there was no way I would stand by and watch... whatever was happening here.

Not all Death Elves were evil. I knew that. Evil wasn't something that we were inherently born with. It was something that we became over time. Circumstances created evil beings. No one was born good or bad. They just were.

But the Death Elves that I knew... They were as far from good as they could get.

I wouldn't stand by and watch this happen. I couldn't. Not when my own back was riddled with similar scars.

My mouth was pinched in a firm line as I yanked against Xander's grip again, but he tightened his grip. I snarled, "Let me go."

"No," he hissed.

And then it was too late.

Her struggles ceased. She dropped to the ground, her lifeless body twitching once, then twice, before it stopped moving altogether.

The Death Elf twisted his hands, and the deadly red ribbons of magic raced back into his skin, disappearing from sight.

The lord gestured to someone nearby, and I watched, wide-eyed, as the soldier with the whip hurried to unlock the shackles around her feet. He grabbed her body like she was a sack of grain, throwing her over his shoulder before tossing her into the back of a nearby cart.

Lord Greenriver nodded, flicking his fingers. "For your troubles," he said in a nasally voice.

My stomach churned as something gold arched through the air. I watched, my fists clenched as the soldier pocketed the coin. The lord turned his back, continuing towards the city with a spring in his step. As though he hadn't just committed a heinous crime in broad daylight. As though he hadn't just murdered that helpless female.

Then people began to walk once more. The slaves continued on their path toward the city, and the chatter picked up as though nothing had even happened. I couldn't get the limp body out of my mind. The way life had slowly disappeared from her eyes.

"Oh my gods," I whispered.

Wrenching my hand out of Xander's grasp, I rushed towards the bushes on the side of the road.

Footsteps pounded behind me as someone jeered, "Get your wife under control."

Xander snapped at them, but I paid them no attention as I dropped to my knees in the damp grass. My stomach was at war with the rest of me. I was barely aware of a warm hand pulling back my hood and holding my hair before I lost the contents of my stomach.

When I was well and truly empty, I crawled away from the bushes. Resting my back against a nearby tree, I took deep, shuddering breaths and pulled my hood back over my bright red hair. Xander crouched before me, producing a flask out of his pack. Behind him, I could feel the weight of people's stares as they walked by, but I didn't care.

"Here, Ana," he whispered, holding the flask up to my lips as he brushed strands of hair away from my face. His voice was softer than I had ever heard before. It was almost caring. *Almost.* "Wash your mouth out with this."

Accepting his offering, I took a tiny sip of the liquid. It burned, and I swished it around before spitting it into the bushes.

"What is that?" I rasped.

"Golden Fire," he said, taking a swig of the flask before handing it back to me. "Take another sip and keep it down this time. It'll help."

Reaching out, I grabbed the flask with trembling fingers. I took a swig of the liquid, and sure enough, the Golden Fire burned on the way down. Within moments, I felt some of the tension leave my body.

"He killed her," I whispered, dragging my eyes up to Xander's. "The slave. She fell, and then he killed her."

He nodded, his golden gaze somber as he placed his hand on mine. I stared at the spot where our bodies were touching. The slave would never be touched again. Never speak again. Never have the chance to do anything again.

Lord Greenriver had stolen her future.

Xander's voice was low as he said, "He did."

"I've never..." I shook my head, rubbing my fingers on my thighs. "I've never seen something like that happen before." Raising my trembling hand, I stared at my shaking fingers. "No one fought for her. No one even cared. He murdered her in front of hundreds of witnesses, and no one did anything to stop him."

Would anyone have cared if that had been me lying in the dirt?

I took a shuddering breath before a pair of warm hands landed on my cheeks. Blinking, I watched wordlessly as Xander pressed my forehead against his. A second went by as we just... breathed in the same air.

A luxury that human no longer had. Thanks to Lord Greenriver.

"It just isn't fair," I whispered.

Xander's voice was soft as he said, "I'm sorry you had to see that."

We remained like that for a long moment, barely touching as my mind settled. I nibbled on my lip, asking softly, "Do things like this happen often in Thyr?"

"More than they should," was Xander's only reply.

I pinched my lips together. "That's... horrible."

"It is." Blowing out a long breath, Xander gently wrapped my fingers in his right hand before pulling us both to our feet.

"We'll talk more about it once we leave the city," he murmured as he drew me against himself. Xander was so warm, and after what we had just seen, I needed that. He studied me, his eyes soft. "Do you think you can walk?"

I took a moment, swallowing as I assessed myself. My heart rate slowed, and my chest wasn't as tight as before. "Yes," I murmured. "I can."

"Good."

He squeezed my hand before we rejoined the crowd marching towards the gates. We walked in silence, each lost in our thoughts.

It wasn't until I could make out the faces of the soldiers guarding the entrance to Thyr that I realized something. When Xander had held my face in his hands, his knuckles hadn't carried a trace of the earlier beating.

"WHAT IS YOUR BUSINESS IN THYR?"

The guard crossed his arms, his voice low as he leaned against the stone wall. He wasn't even looking at me, addressing his questions to Xander.

I didn't mind. We had spent the past hour trudging along in the long line that had formed near the city gates. As we waited, I watched as the same thing had happened over and over again.

The soldiers only spoke to the males. It was as though the many females accompanying them didn't even exist.

For my part, I was happy to remain unnoticed. My stomach was still in knots from witnessing the murder, and my hands were clammy as I ran them down my cloak.

"We are looking for a place to spend a night or two before continuing north," Xander replied gruffly. He wrapped an arm around me, drawing me against his chest.

The soldier eyed me, his gaze traveling up and down my body. A lecherous sneer appeared on his face as he stared too long at my breasts. As he stared at me, I desired nothing more than to acquaint him with the blade sheathed against my thigh.

You are trying to go unnoticed. Stabbing a guard is not a good idea, even though he deserves it. Someone needs to teach this pig a lesson.

"This is your wife?" the lecherous guard asked, pulling me out of my thoughts. He directed the question to Xander, never removing his eyes from my body.

Despite the heavy cloak, it felt like he was stripping me naked. My fingers flexed at my side, reaching towards my pocket as I fought to remain silent. Xander must have sensed my desire to teach the guard some manners because he grabbed my fingers and wrapped them up in his much larger hand. He squeezed tightly, drawing my gaze to his.

His golden eyes were burning into me, the warning within them clear: stand down.

Xander pasted a smile on his face before shifting his attention back to the soldier. "That's correct," Xander replied smoothly. He dipped his head ever so slightly, his voice going even lower. "We're newlyweds."

The guard grunted. "Do you have your travel papers?"

My chest seized as I stared at the guard blankly. Papers? I had no papers. Nothing of the sort.

Visions of whips cracking and red ribbons of magic flashed before my eyes. I could already feel the oh-so-familiar burst of pain as the knotted leather ripped across my back for the first time. The first was always the worst. When the whip tore across newly healed skin and broke through scars of older beatings.

How many lashes would they give me before turning me back over to the king?

A moan rose in my throat, and I swallowed.

What was I going to do? Here I was, moments away from being taken down by something as simple as a lack of papers.

Black spots filled my vision as my heart pounded in my chest. I was seconds away from fainting when Xander reached into his pocket and withdrew a wrinkled sheet. I couldn't read the words from where I stood, but it appeared to be some form of identification.

"Here you go, sir." Xander handed the guard the sheet of paper. Staring at it, I wondered exactly where Xander had gotten it.

Did he just walk around with fake marriage identifications? Did he get them from Nonna? Was this whole thing a setup? I resisted the urge to look behind my shoulder to see if the Winged Soldiers were there, waiting to catch me unaware.

Before I could continue down my spiral of fear, Xander squeezed my hand. He leaned in close to the guard and winked, lowering his voice as though he was imparting a vital secret.

"My wife and I are traveling to Breley for business. We had hoped to take a detour through Thyr. Extend our trip for a couple of days away from the eyes of her parents." He winked at the guard. "We are seeking some time alone—if you know what I mean."

The soldier laughed crudely, slapping Xander on the back.

"Do I ever," the guard chortled. "All right then..." He scanned the paperwork. "Mr. and Mrs. Whitefall, go right ahead. Might I recommend you take your pretty wife to the Winter Market, Mr. Whitefall? She looks like she may enjoy some of the baubles being sold today."

The soldier blatantly ogled me once more, his lecherous gaze remaining on my breasts as he handed Xander back the papers.

A snarl rose in my throat at his continued disrespect, but before it could come out, Xander was already tugging on my elbow and dragging me through the city gates.

The moment we stepped through the city gates, it felt like we had entered another world. My eyes widened at all the sights.

Tall buildings towered on either side of us as puddles of questionable origin filled the gutters lining the cobblestone streets. People hurried down the road—so many people. I hadn't even known this many people could exist in one place. They moved with purpose towards their destinations.

I looked up, taking in the lines stretched between the buildings overhead. Garments swayed in the wind, blocking the view of the clear sky.

"Look out!"

A shout came from behind us, and Xander pulled me aside just as a horse and rider barreled past us.

"Hey!" I yelled. "You idiot! Watch where you're goi—"

Xander drew me against him, pulling us both into a nearby alley before pushing me against a wall. He bent down to whisper in my ear, his breath warming my skin.

"Get a hold of yourself, Sunshine," he growled with his hands on my shoulders. "I know anger is your first response to every single thing that happens, but you can't go around yelling at everyone you meet."

"That horse almost ran us over," I hissed, standing on my tip-toes so I could meet Xander's gaze. "Not to mention the soldier who was practically undressing me with his eyes. It was disgusting."

Xander shifted back, crossing his arms as he stared at me. "Who are you, Ana? Have you never met anyone before in your entire life? If you think that the guard's behavior was bad, you are in for a rude awakening. I've met people ten times as bad as him. Most people in this country wouldn't blink an eye before putting a female like yourself in her place."

"Is that a threat?" Widening my stance, I clenched my jaw. Pressing my back against the grimy brick wall, I ignored the people walking by and kept my eyes locked on the male towering over me.

He shook his head, his nostrils flaring as he huffed. "Good gods. This *female*. No, Sunshine." He took a step towards me, glowering. "I wasn't threatening you. I'm *telling* you that people here won't hesitate to deal with someone like you."

"What does that even mean?" I snapped.

"It means that there's only so much that I, as your husband—"

"Fake husband," I interjected, my voice hard. "Fake. I would rather die than be married for real."

He growled, running his hands over his face. "There's only so much I, as your *fake husband,* can do for you if you step out of line."

"Is that so?"

"It is," he ground out through clenched teeth. "It would behoove you to behave."

Xander stepped forward, putting a hand over my head as he leaned in close. I stared at him, the air becoming charged between us. Our chests heaved, the foot between us seeming at once both a mile and no space at all.

I seethed, "Perhaps if people want me to behave better, they would act deserving of such conduct."

Xander tilted his head. My gaze was locked on his lips as they opened slightly. I tracked the movement with my eyes as he sucked in a deep breath, whispering, "Listen to me, Mrs. Whitefall."

I bristled at the sound of our fake last name but didn't move. I couldn't. It was as though he had me in a trance.

Xander seemed to take my silence as leave to continue. His voice dropped even lower as he closed the distance between us. He put his finger on my chin, the touch gentle and at odds with the rough tone of his voice. "The sooner we get out of this city, the sooner I can fulfill my end of the bargain and get you to the Indigo Ocean. That's what you want, right?"

I swallowed, my eyes wide. My chest was growing tight as my insides twisted. Xander's closeness made me feel things I had never felt before, and I hated it.

If he knew how he made me feel, he would taunt me with my emotions. Use them as yet another weapon against me. I was sure of that.

"Yes," I whispered, my gaze locked onto his. He seemed to be staring into my soul, his eyes filled with storms as they studied me. I repeated firmly, "Yes, I want to leave."

"Then you'd better ditch the attitude and become the obedient wife people will expect you to be. I don't know where you came from, but females in Ithenmyr are expected to be seen and not heard. Can you manage that?"

"You're insufferable, and I can't stand you," I hissed. He didn't even flinch, my insults washing over him like they were nothing. "But even so, yes. I'll... behave." I winced as the word came out of my mouth, and Xander's mouth twitched.

"Will you?"

"I'll even try not to stab anyone so we can get your meeting over with and get out of here." I crossed my arms, forcing my gaze away from his. "The sooner we can split up, the better."

"Thank you," he said. Xander pushed himself off the wall and tilted his head towards the busy street. "I would much appreciate going a day without adding another scar to my collection."

"I'm sure you would," I muttered.

Xander's lips twitched. "Jo won't wait forever. We should get going."

He took a step away from me, offering me his arm. The moment he moved, a long breath whooshed out of my lungs as the tension between us dissipated.

It was only then that I realized just how loud the city was. A cacophony of predominantly masculine voices filled the air, along with the braying of various animals.

I pushed away from the brick wall and slid my hand through my fake husband's arm. I avoided touching him, ensuring my hands remained firmly on his sleeve. Gesturing to the street, I painted what I hoped was a placid smile on my face before batting my lashes in Xander's direction.

If he wanted a good fake wife, I would be the most docile, non-violent wife in existence. I'd show him how well-behaved I could be. My voice was sickly sweet as I said, "Well, Mr. Whitefall. We should get going, don't you think? I really should hate to keep Jo waiting."

Xander looked at me, his eyes narrowing. If he was wondering where this suddenly pliant female came from, he didn't say anything. Instead, he simply grunted before leading us both down the street.

I walked silently beside him, one thought running through my mind.

The sooner we get this over with, the better. I cannot wait to get this insufferable male out of my life.

Rumors Abound

～⁂～

I hated playing the meek female.

Maybe it was the fact that I had spent the past twenty-three years of my life in a tower, or maybe it was the presence of the male strolling beside me, but nothing felt natural about what he was asking me to do.

From the moment that Xander and I had left the alley, I had done nothing but hold on to his elbow and smile demurely as we walked down the streets of Thyr.

Every second felt like an eternity. Every footstep was like we were walking a mile. With each breath and moment I wore a fake smile on my face, a little piece of myself slipped away.

How did the people of Ithenmyr do this every day?

As much as I loathed to admit it, Xander was right. Even though the city was loud—and it was louder than anything else I had ever heard in my life—once I began to listen to the cacophony around us, I realized that all the noise had one thing in common.

Other than the children yelling as they ran through the streets, I couldn't hear any female voices. It was as though they didn't exist. Not only were they not speaking, but they were also standing right next to the males accompanying them. If their husband took a step, they quickly followed. If he stopped, they did as well.

Unlike me, their gazes were pointed at their feet. They didn't look at anything or anyone. Even though they weren't trapped in a tower, it became abundantly clear that they, too, were caught in cages of their own.

How was this fair?

I might have been playing the part of a demure female, but I would not waste my first opportunity to look around.

And so we walked. And I stared. I drank in the city: the loudness, the bustle of activity, the *people*.

The city was beautiful and strange and far more incredible than I'd ever thought it would be.

Keeping me close to his side, Xander whispered in my ear as we hurried through the city.

"We entered through the Western Gate," he said as he pulled me around a suspicious puddle on the ground. Wrinkling my nose at the aroma, I lifted the hem of my gown as I skirted the mess. He continued, "The Opal Spoon is on the eastern edge of town, so we will have to go through the market square."

Being the dutiful, silent wife he had asked me to be, I didn't say anything. Xander shot me a look that said he wasn't buying my act, but he didn't say anything as he led me through the throngs of people crowding the narrow streets.

We passed storefront after storefront, proudly displaying their various wares. I ogled them as we hurried by. There was so much.

The world was so much bigger than I'd ever thought possible.

One store boasted a dozen barrels overflowing with fresh fruit, while the next was filled with bolts of fabric of every imaginable color. I could even smell fresh-baked bread coming from a bakery up ahead. The aroma overpowered the stench of unwashed bodies that seemed commonplace in the city, something for which I was very grateful.

As we approached the bakery, my stomach let out a most unladylike grumble. Blood rushed to my cheeks as I tried to ignore the sound. Moments later, Xander pulled us off the street and into the bakery. A bell rang as we entered the small but homey shop. We were the only customers.

"Hold on!" a low voice shouted from the back. "Magdelina, go see to the customers."

"Right away, Alfonzo."

Footsteps came from the back of the bakery as I looked around. Small wooden shelves were laden with dozens of freshly baked goods. My nose filled with the intoxicating scent of warm yeast, and my hunger grew.

A plump baker—Magdelina, I presumed—came out of the back wearing a floury apron. Her brown hair was tied in a bun, and her eyes lit up as she saw us.

"Welcome," Magdelina said as she dipped her head. "What can I get for you?"

A kind smile flitted across her face as she surveyed us.

Xander stepped forward, reaching into his pocket before pulling out a gold coin. "My wife and I will have two of your delicious loaves, please."

Magdelina's eyes widened at the sight of the coin. I didn't know how much it was worth, but it was obvious by her reaction that Xander was overpaying for the bread.

"O-of course, sir." Magdelina curtsied low to the ground, her apron fanning out before her. "Can I get you and your wife anything else?"

Xander rested his arms on the floury counter, leaning in close to her like they were sharing a secret. His golden eyes twinkled as he smiled at her. He looked... charming. Likable. Charismatic, even. The transformation was disconcerting, to say the least. He looked like a completely different person.

He asked, "What's your name, ma'am?"

"M-mistress DuBois, sir."

"My wife and I were wondering, Mistress DuBois, has anything strange happened lately?"

Magdelina's eyes widened as she looked between Xander and me. "I-I, what do you mean, sir?"

Sliding his hand into his pocket, Xander produced another coin. He tapped it with his finger before placing it on the counter.

"Anything odd? Something that someone as beautiful and pleasant as you would have noticed. We're simply seeking information," he said, winking at her. "But we're willing to pay for it."

Her eyes bulged at the sight of the second coin, and she stammered for a moment before she slid them into the large pocket of her apron. They clinked together as they disappeared. Mistress DuBois gestured for us to lean in.

"I don't know anything for sure," she started, laying her hands on the counter. "I've just heard rumors."

Xander nodded. "Anything you know is helpful, Mistress."

"There was a contingent of Winged Soldiers in town yesterday," she whispered. "Rumor has it they were searching for someone who escaped from the other side of the Niphil River."

My chest seized as the blood drained from my face. I couldn't move as suddenly the walls of the small bakery felt like they were closing in on me. The Winged Soldiers were here...

Was *he* here?

Gods. If that was the case...

I could hear the whip slashing through the air. Feel the way it burned like a thousand fires across my back. Smell the sandalwood mixing with the coppery tang of blood.

My mouth opened as I struggled to breathe. Everything was becoming too much. If he was here...

I shook my head.

I wouldn't go back. Death would be better. Not now that I'd gotten a taste of freedom. One day wasn't enough to make up for a lifetime of imprisonment.

Beside me, Xander ignored my panic and chuckled as though nothing was wrong. "Really? I wonder who High King Edgar has them searching for?"

"My husband heard..." Her voice trailed off, her head tilting as she checked to make sure we were alone before lowering her voice even further. I had to strain to hear what she said. "Prince Remington was supposed to be married yesterday, but the ceremony never took place."

"No!" Xander gasped, slapping a hand on the counter. He shook his head sorrowfully. "Such a shame. And to think we could have had a new princess."

She sighed, shaking her head. "Yes, isn't it so sad? "

Xander nodded solemnly. "Terribly so."

Magdelina, clearly caught up in the zeal of having someone to gossip with, continued in a whisper. "In fact, I heard people say the bride-to-be *jilted* the Prince. He was waiting there, dressed in the colors of the House of Irriel—you know, no other colors would do."

Xander nodded sagely. "Of course not."

"And she never showed up! Can you imagine? Who wouldn't want to be married to him? Heir to Ithenmyr *and* the second most powerful Death Elf on the entire continent? I can't imagine what female wouldn't want that kind of life."

Snorting, I covered the sound with a cough. Both Xander and the baker stared at me. I turned away, coughing into my elbow.

"Forgive my wife," Xander whispered, patting me on the back as I adjusted my hood. "She has a touch of illness. You were saying about the soldiers who were here yesterday?"

"Yes, there were three doz—"

Just then, the bell above the door rang. Magdelina jumped, her cheeks reddening as her mouth slammed shut. She roughly shoved two loaves of bread into brown paper before handing them to Xander.

"Here you go, sir," Magdelina said. Her voice was much higher-pitched than it had been moments before. "Have a great day."

Xander nodded, grabbing the bread, before placing his hand on the small of my back. Even through all my clothes, I felt the heat from Xander's skin like a brand as he led me to the door. "Thank you, Mistress DuBois."

Once outside, he handed me one of the loaves before steering me down the street. Somehow, it had gotten even busier while we were in the bakery.

I had so many questions and things to say, but one look at Xander's hooded face told me to keep my thoughts to myself. His eyes were wide with warning as he steered us through the growing crowds. I was getting used to the sounds of the city and found that they weren't bothering me as much as before.

We ate our loaves in silence as Xander navigated us through the busy streets. He only removed his hand from the small of my back when we entered a massive square.

I felt the lack of heat the moment he pulled his hand away. Part of me —a very small part that I refused to acknowledge—mourned the loss of his touch.

"Welcome to the Winter Market, Sunshine," Xander whispered, offering me his arm as a rare smile flashed on his face.

I took the proffered limb as I slowly turned in a semi-circle. My mouth fell open as I took in my surroundings.

"Xander, this is…"

He grinned. "It's quite large, isn't it?"

"Mhmm."

I couldn't quite find the words to describe the market.

Large didn't quite cover it. The Winter Market was massive. It was unlike anything I had ever seen. I was thoroughly impressed by the number of people packed into the square. Dozens of tables filled the open area. Baskets were scattered about, with every kind of ware imaginable on display.

We walked over to a table, and I stared at the baskets and jars filled with dozens of spices. Together, they smelled hearty and delicious. Despite the bread I'd just eaten, my stomach grumbled.

Xander chuckled, leading me away from the table. "Hungry, Ana?"

"A bit," I muttered.

A corner of his lips tilted up. He seemed more… relaxed now that we were in the city. There was a twinkle in his eye as he said, "Well, that won't do. We can't have someone as lovely as you be hungry. We'll make sure to feed you when we get to The Opal Spoon."

My mind caught on to the word lovely. Did he think *I* was lovely? No one had ever said such a thing to me before.

I was thinking this over when a woody scent filled the air. My nose twitched as my mind suddenly went blank. The market disappeared as I was thrown back into a memory I had no desire to relive.

Tears rushed down my cheeks, my back in utter agony, as I stared at the stone floor beneath me. The muscles in my arms ached as the leather cord binding my wrists to the bedpost tightened.

A chuckle came from the other side of the room, and I tensed.

Tap

Tap

Tap

"Look at me!" a voice roared.

Lifting my head off the cool stone, I sniffled despite myself. The punishment was still too fresh to ignore. "Yes, my king?"

High King Edgar snarled, coming to kneel before me. His tunic—crimson, like the blood dripping down my back—filled my vision, and I instinctively winced at the spot of blood on his black shoes.

His favorite instrument of torture dangled from his hands as he grabbed my chin and forced me to look at him. The scent of sandalwood drifted off him, filling my nose and burning away the iron scent of blood.

My blood.

It was always my blood.

"Why do you think you are being punished?"

I bit my lip. I knew there was no correct answer. There was no reason. There never was. I dared to reply, "I don't know, my liege."

"Wrong answer," he barked.

He pushed himself to his feet, taking the scent of sandalwood with him.

It was a momentary reprieve.

A peaceful second passed. Then two.

He chuckled darkly as a cracking sound filled the air.

And I screamed.

"Sandalwood," I whispered as I turned around despite Xander's tight grip on my hand. People were milling about all over the place, but I didn't see the familiar head of brown hair. I couldn't see his curling horns or blue eyes that seemed to brighten at the sight of blood.

Where was he?

My heart pounded in my chest as my wide eyes flew about the market square. *There.*

A few tables down was a male with dozens of tiny glass vials. Oils. It was just a vendor selling oils.

Relief flooded through me as my knees weakened. "He's not here," I murmured.

"Who?" Xander's voice was gruff as he drew me towards him. His mouth was pinched as he studied me. "Who isn't here? What's wrong?"

I shrugged, trying to force the thoughts of the king out of my mind. My back twitched, and I knew bloody nightmares would be my companions tonight. "I thought I... saw someone I knew, but I was wrong."

Xander tilted his head, his eyes shrewd as they studied me, but he didn't pry. I was grateful for that.

We continued walking through the Winter Market, and I fell silent. Over and over again, I watched as the same scene played out.

A couple, or sometimes a father and daughter, would walk over to a table. A female would point to something, and the male accompanying her would pay for it. She would never, under any circumstances, speak.

The only feminine voices in the square were those of children running around their mothers' skirts. Even their voices were subdued, as fathers, brothers, and husbands reprimanded the children whenever possible.

I pulled my cloak tight around myself, feeling more uncomfortable than ever. I had thought that leaving the tower would mean freedom, but this... I was beginning to question what freedom really meant. What good was escaping my captors only to land in another cage?

More than that, would I ever escape this one? I had no idea what I would find if I made it to the coast of the Indigo Ocean.

What if freedom didn't really exist? What if it was all a lie concocted by our minds? A desire to believe that something—anything—would be better than our current lives.

Were we all just lying to ourselves?

Panic began to take hold of my heart when a shout came from behind me.

"Excuse me!"

I jolted backward as a young brown-haired boy dressed in little more than rags ran into my legs. I stumbled back a step as the child pulled on my skirts. He couldn't have been more than five or six. His hands were covered in dirt, and I could barely make out the brown of his eyes through the grime coating his skin.

His voice was high-pitched as he asked, "Do you has some money, ma'am?"

"Oh," I started. "No, but—"

Xander reached down, prying the child's hands off my skirts. He growled, "Get lost, urchin."

The boy's blue eyes widened, meeting mine for a moment. "S-s-sorry, sir. Ma'am." he stuttered, stumbling away from us.

My jaw was agape as the boy ran up a set of white marble steps that led into a massive temple. The building was made of pink stone and filled with dozens of intricate stained glass windows. A tall steeple housing an enormous bell hung within the steeple.

In front of the temple, a massive statue of Kydona stood watch over the square. The artist had chiseled the goddess out of white marble, her long, flowing hair covering her supple body from sight.

The boy ran around the temple and disappeared.

When he was gone, Xander turned to me and put his hands on my shoulders. His brows were furrowed as he checked me over. "Are you okay, Ana?"

I nodded, picking at a loose thread on my cloak. "Why didn't you help him? I know you have money."

Xander continued to propel us both forward. A moment passed in silence as we walked past a booth before he sighed. "If we helped every orphan running through the streets, we'd never get out of Thyr."

"That doesn't seem right," I whispered.

Xander made a non-committal sound, and we walked silently for a few minutes.

We were approaching the temple when Xander abruptly skidded to a stop. For someone of his size, he moved so fast. "You have got to be kidding me."

He turned towards me. His face was paler than I had ever seen, and he grabbed my arm.

"I need you to listen carefully, Ana," he hissed, drawing me against him. He wrapped an arm around my waist before he moved us with purpose towards the edge of the temple steps and the streets that lay beyond. "We need to get out of here."

"Xander, stop," I insisted, pulling on his cloak as he yanked me behind him. "What is so urgent?"

"Ana—"

The warning died on his lips as I turned and looked over my shoulder at the Winter Market.

My legs wobbled, and my eyes widened as everything else in the square seemed to fade from view. Knots filled my stomach as I stared at the scene before us.

Heretics Among Us

❧

Less than a hundred feet from us at the base of the temple steps, six Winged Soldiers stood in a semicircle.

Black feathered wings protruded from the soldiers' backs. Their tunics and trousers were the color of a starless night sky. It was a stark contrast to the bright cloaks and tunics all around us. Their very presence seemed to suck the sunlight out of the square.

The chatter died down, and a somber mood replaced the cheer that had filled the market only minutes before.

A tall, lanky elf knelt between the soldiers at the foot of the stairs. I could see him clearly from where Xander and I were standing to the side.

He was naked from the waist up, and he shook uncontrollably. His long ears pointed towards the sky as dark brown locks curled down his back. As I watched, the prisoner lifted his pale hands before him as though he were praying.

Unlike the Death Elf we had seen earlier in the day, this elf looked like he had been beaten until he was moments from The Fade. He was clearly

Mature, but I had no way of knowing how old he was. He could have been three decades or three centuries old.

Heavy black chains held his hands together, and it was clear he couldn't move them more than six inches apart. My chest tightened at the sight of the rivulets of blood that ran down his bare chest.

The wind carried whispers to my ears.

"... prohiberis on his wrists..."

"Never seen him before..."

"... stops the use of magic..."

"Who is he?"

Many of the same questions were bubbling up on my tongue. I had never seen an elf so close to Fading before. Blood covered every available inch of flesh on the injured male.

"Don't move, Ana." Xander's grip tightened around my wrist as he pulled me closer to him. He lowered his head to mine, forcing my gaze to his. Xander drew his lip through his teeth as he looked around the square. His eyes were assessing as he stared at the Winged Soldiers. "We need to be very careful."

I had no words. All I could do was stare as one of the Winged Soldiers pushed the elf forward onto all fours. The prisoner grunted, taking the weight of the impact on his elbows. Another soldier grabbed the chains and dragged the prisoner along, pulling him up the stairs. An ominous silence descended on the square as everyone watched the soldiers.

No one moved. No one spoke. No one did *anything*.

Again. For the second time in one day, I watched as people stood, unmoving, as cruelty unfolded in their midst. Their expressions were a mixture of fear, apprehension, and hatred.

Anger stirred within me like a red-hot flame.

What kind of hold does the king have on these people that they would disregard the lives of their fellow beings? Why don't they fight back?

The Winged Soldier continued to drag the elf up the marble stairs of the temple until he was standing before the statue of Kydona. I gasped as the soldier shoved the elf onto his knees once more.

Silence, thick, heavy, and entirely foreboding, coated every inch of the market. Even the children stopped their incessant shrieking as they hid behind the skirts of their silent mothers.

From within the temple, three figures dressed in flowing white robes appeared.

"Burning hells," Xander cursed. "That's just what we need."

His jaw was in a tight line, and the arm wrapped around my waist was growing tighter by the moment.

"What's wrong?"

"Those priests are dangerous," he whispered without moving. "More so than the Winged Soldiers. We need to get out of here."

I nodded, my gaze never straying from the scene unfolding before us.

Two of the mysterious priests were unmoving, while the third stepped forward and conferred with one of the soldiers. Their heads remained together for a minute before the priest nodded. He lifted his hands, the sleeves of his robe slipping back to reveal pasty, white skin covered in swaths of black, winding tattoos.

The priest walked halfway down the steps before stopping.

"My children." The deep register of the priest's voice echoed through the square. "Today, Kydona smiles down on us. His Supreme Majesty High King Edgar's soldiers have uncovered an Earth Elf living among us. This male has been masquerading as a Light Elf in our very city, living under our noses."

A collective gasp echoed through the market. My heart was pounding as the reality of what was happening set in.

The priest's voice thundered through the square once more. "If the marking on his back wasn't proof enough, the Winged Soldiers found a shrine to Thelrena in his home."

Thelrena.

Thelrena.

Thelrena.

The name echoed through my mind as I gasped. The square faded away as a long-forgotten memory forced its way to the surface of my mind.

Flashing, searing, burning pain erupted on my back over and over again. Salt filled my mouth as the cracking of a whip filled the air. Time and time again, it slammed onto my exposed back as I cried out. The scent of copper and sandalwood filled the air, mingling with the salt of my tears.

"Help me, Thelrena," I whimpered the only prayers I knew as I drew my legs up to my chest and tried to escape my tormentor.

"Don't ever say that name again," a voice growled behind me.

"Please," I whimpered.

"There is no room for Thelrena here," they continued as I sobbed into the mattress. "You are my pet. You will forget you ever knew of her. She is a false goddess. If she weren't, she'd be saving you by now. No one will come for you. Not today. Not ever."

I shoved my fist in my mouth, and the goddess' name echoed in my mind, but I wouldn't say it. I couldn't.

Thelrena.

I was pulled back to the present by a loud clap. The priest paused as whispers rose all over the square.

"The elf worships the false goddess."

"... Heretics among us..."

"Earth Elves..."

"... I thought they all died two decades ago."

The whispers were like voices calling to me in a dream as I swayed on my feet. My skin felt too tight as I struggled to draw air into my lungs. It took me a moment to realize that the priest had continued speaking.

"... Kydona, in her eternal wisdom, has allowed our illustrious High King to bring the heretical Earth Elves under control."

Another priest stepped forward, climbing down the steps as he spoke. "Remember, children of Thyr, the horrors the Earth Elves inflicted upon our lands. It is only because of our glorious king that our forests became free of these wicked creatures twenty years ago. Their shrines to their false goddess were destroyed alongside the temples where they sacrificed their young in her name."

The second priest fell silent, dipping his head.

Jeers rose from the crowd as emotion swelled all around us. People's faces contorted as they sneered at the trembling elf on the steps. Shouts erupted from the crowd as I pressed myself against Xander. I wanted nothing more than to be out of this square.

Gods forbid if their attention turned to me... I swallowed, pulling my hood down even more. At that moment, I wished I was somewhere else. Anywhere else.

"Death to all the Earth Elves!"

"Kydona is the true goddess!"

"Praise Kydona!"

The priest allowed the yelling to continue for a moment before speaking again. The Winged Soldiers watched him carefully, their eyes trained on his every movement.

"Earth Elves were a scourge on this continent. Their false beliefs made them a danger to Ithenmyr." Nodding to the soldiers, the priest gestured for the prisoner to be brought to him. "This elf is not worthy of Fading away with time. Thank Kydona; she delivered him into our hands. We must expunge the scourge the heretics bring to Ithenmyr!"

A cheer went through the crowd, and my stomach twisted in knots. A whimper escaped me as the priest's words settled on me.

Xander's other hand reached up and wrapped around mine. His breath warmed my neck as he lowered his head.

"Ana," he whispered, "I need you to listen to me very carefully. In a moment, we are going to leave the square. On my command, I need you to follow me and not look back. Can you do that?"

I stared beyond him to the Earth Elf, who was being dragged down the steps like he was an animal. My mouth felt dry as I rasped, "I can."

Xander squeezed tightly. I focused my attention on the heat coming from his hand and not on the sword one of the Winged Soldiers had just drawn.

"Good," Xander said, shifting his stance. "Look at me."

The atmosphere in the market was changing. The air itself seemed to be churning as dark emotions bubbled to the surface. I was certain that horror was painted on my face as the Winged Soldier raised his weapon in the air because, all of a sudden, Xander drew my head against his chest. Sucking in a deep breath, I squeezed my eyes shut. For once, I didn't fight him.

Burrowing against him, I wished I was anywhere else. The sword whistled as it swung through the air. The Earth Elf let out a strangled cry, and then I shuddered as deafening silence reigned once more. I clenched Xander's cloak as he rubbed his hand on my back.

A minute passed in complete silence. A long, eternal, never-ending minute.

And then the priest cleared his throat. "The heretic's blood has been spilled as an offering to Kydona. You are safe from the threat of the Earth Elves. Go about your days and remember: the true goddess always looks after her people."

"Thank Kydona," the crowd intoned as one.

A beat went by before the sounds of life began filling the market again.

Exhaling, I shook my head against Xander's cloak. I dared a peek, watching from the corner of my eye as the Winged Soldiers descended the temple steps.

Crimson streams colored the steps where the Earth Elf had been standing, and shudders threatened to overtake me as Xander pulled on my arm. I whimpered as his warmth disappeared before he touched my chin.

"Look away, Ana," he whispered.

I nodded, forcing my gaze to his. Despite the hood covering Xander's face, I could see his eyes. They were heavy and lined with pity. Something flickered brightly within them that made me catch my breath.

I tilted my head, but he blinked, and just as quickly as it had appeared, the emotion was gone. Xander pulled my hand, leading us out of the market.

I didn't fight him.

It wasn't until the cobblestone streets had long since given way to packed dirt roads that I understood the emotion I had seen lurking in Xander's eyes.

Rage.

Pure, unadulterated rage.

WITH EVERY STEP we took towards The Opal Spoon, my feet dragged like I was walking through thick mud. Exhaustion plagued me. I was grateful that the tavern was within the city walls.

The walk passed in a blur of tall stone buildings and dirty streets. As the minutes passed, the riches of the market square gave way to poverty.

Xander didn't speak. For that, I was grateful. Everything felt heavy. Far heavier than I had known possible.

If yesterday had been a day of freedom, today was a day of death.

The entire day was stained in red. Red magic. Red blood. I picked up a stray lock of my hair, scowling at it. Red hair. So much red.

I *despised* it.

My mood only worsened when Xander finally pulled us to a stop in what I assumed must have been one of the poorest parts of Thyr.

Where the market had been filled with life, the streets now carried a sense of unease. Dirt roads had replaced the square's cobblestones, and the air was permeated with the stench of unwashed bodies, urine, and alcohol.

I wrinkled my nose, lifting my skirts and stepping around a mysterious puddle. Not for the first time that day, I wished that I could have been wearing my leggings and tunic. It would have been much easier to move around in less restrictive clothing.

Xander tilted his head, pushing open a creaky wooden door tucked into an alley.

"Come along, Ana." He sighed. "The sooner we get what I came for, the sooner we can leave."

I scowled as I read the painted letters on the wooden sign above our heads. *The Opal Spoon.* Each letter was the same color as the crimson blood that had marked the temple's steps. The same color as the House of Irriel. The same color as the fate I was running from.

I decided then and there that red was my least favorite color.

Xander didn't seem to notice all the red. He was too focused on scanning the dim interior of the tavern. I followed him closely, pressing against his back as my eyes adjusted to the darkness.

The surprisingly large space was packed. After a long day of barely hearing any females speaking, it was jarring to hear high-pitched laughter intermingling with a chorus of much deeper chuckles. For a moment, I wondered about the Accompaniment Law, but I soon realized why I was hearing females alongside males.

Despite the late afternoon hour, The Opal Spoon was filled with people who were in the middle of partaking in what Matthias would have called *improper activities*.

As the king's pet, I'd never participated in such things. I wasn't allowed. I couldn't even imagine the punishment I would have received for thinking of doing such a thing. Even so, I'd heard enough from the servants and guards to understand what Matthias meant. And now, I was watching as the preludes of such activities took place right in front of me.

Jugs of ale were being served around the tavern as scantily clad courtesans sat on laps. The females wore little more than scraps of fabric covering their breasts and bottoms. I had seen more flesh in the past minute than my entire life. The courtesans laughed and pushed their chests forward, grinding their bodies in a very suggestive way.

Blood rushed to my face, and I pulled my cloak tighter around myself. I shifted uncomfortably as I watched one courtesan whose breasts practically fell out of her bodice nibble on a male's ear before leaning forward. She whispered something inaudible as she placed her hand on his lap and rubbed suggestively. The male grinned, tossing his cards on the table and saying something in a low voice to his companions, who laughed as he followed her up the rickety stairs.

I must have made some sound, because Xander looked over his shoulder at me. He raised a brow. "You alright there, Sunshine?"

"I'm fine," I snapped.

That was a lie.

Every time I blinked, I saw the crimson stains on the temple steps. I wondered how long that scene would haunt my nightmares. A long time, I thought. It wouldn't be easy. I wasn't even sure I *could* banish the memories of the Earth Elf's execution.

But this... this I could do. Talking. Exchanging barbs with Xander. Each word that came out of his mouth pulled me a little bit further from the memories of the Winter Market.

A smirk danced on his infuriating lips as he looked me over. "Are you sure? You're looking a little pale."

Huffing, I crossed my arms. All the emotions from earlier today were bubbling inside me, but I kept shoving them down. Dealing with those emotions would not be easy, and it was not something I wanted to do right now.

This, though, I could do. Arguing with Xander felt as easy as breathing. And right now, that's exactly what I needed.

"I am absolutely fine," I retorted, raising a brow. "Let's get this over with."

"Get what over with?" a high-pitched voice asked.

I turned, eyeing the buxom female standing behind the bar. Human. She was definitely human. The dark brown counter stretched the length of the tavern, and there were several unoccupied stools in front of it that looked like they had seen better days.

"It's been a long time, Xan," the barmaid said, turning to my companion. Her brow rose as she glanced at the door. "I was expecting you yesterday. But Daegal said you were running behind. You're lucky you got here in time. I'm leaving tonight."

"I ran into something... unexpected," Xander grunted. "Will your brother take over the day-to-day affairs after you leave, Jo?"

This was Jo? With that name, I'd assumed—wrongly, clearly—that we were meeting a male.

Jo nodded. "He will. I don't expect to be back until the Winter Solstice or later."

Xander nodded. "Must be nice to have a partner in business."

My brows hit my forehead. I hadn't even known females could own establishments. And this Jo was a... partner here?

Interesting.

I had so many questions, but Jo turned her assessing gaze to me before I could ask them. "Daegal didn't mention you were bringing company, Xander. Who is *she*?"

Jo looked at me shrewdly, and I stepped back, sliding my hand into my pocket. The hilt of my dagger was a comfort against Jo's gaze as I sorted through her words. Who was this Daegal? Was he the brother?

Xander stepped forward, pulling out a stool before gesturing for me to sit on it. I did, but not before sending him a withering glance.

In response, he placed a large hand on my shoulder. Infuriatingly, the possessive action felt... right, somehow. Xander drew me against his chest before clearing his throat. "This *company*, Jo, is Ana. My wife."

Fake wife, I added silently.

The barmaid paled, her eyes darting between me and Xander. "*You,* the male who refuses to see anyone twice, got married?"

Xander nodded, his voice grave. "I did."

"To her?" Jo gestured to me, the question clear in her voice.

"Yes, to me," I snapped. I felt oddly insulted that Jo thought Xander's marriage to me was strange. Our marriage was fake, but her disbelief irked me. I added, "You're not exactly what I was expecting, either."

Jo raised a brow, pausing mid-wipe of the bar to put her hands on her hips. The cloth dangled from her hands as she tilted her head. "You were expecting someone else?"

"I-I..." I blinked as the admission slipped out, "I thought you were going to be a male."

Xander chortled, and Jo looked amused as blood rushed to my cheeks.

I hurriedly continued, wishing the ground would open and swallow me whole. "I suppose I shouldn't have made any assumptions."

"Don't worry about it," Jo said, leaning forward. I averted my eyes as her breasts appeared moments away from spilling onto the countertop. Several males and a few females eyed her appreciatively.

Still holding my gaze, Jo grabbed a cup and wiped it with a new cloth as she said, "You aren't the first one to make that assumption. Most people find it easier to deal with a male, so I don't mind helping them to that conclusion. Usually, by the time they realize they were wrong, they're too invested to back out of our dealings. My brother is more of a... silent partner in the business."

"I see," I lied. There was still so much to the world that I had to learn.

Xander claimed a stool beside me as he braced his arms on the counter.

"I need to talk to you," he said to the barmaid.

Jo nodded, her brown eyes shrewd. "I figured you would. *It's* upstairs." She placed the cup she had been cleaning on the counter and waved her rag in the air. "Daegal, come here."

I turned, my face paling as a dark-skinned elf with pointy ears and black curls began walking towards us. My stomach tightened as the elf approached.

A dozen thoughts ran through my mind at once. Was this a set-up? Was this another Death Elf? Were they going to sell me out to the Winged Soldiers?

I was sure the king would pay handsomely for my return.

My gaze darted all around the tavern, marking an escape route. A dozen or so patrons blocked my path to the front door, but there appeared to be a route out the back.

Just as I was about to bolt, a warm hand landed on my arm. I tensed as the warmth of Xander's touch leaked through every layer.

"Easy, Sunshine," Xander rasped. His breath warmed my cheek as he said, "Daegal is a Fortune Elf. He's not going to hurt you."

"That's right." The Fortune Elf slid behind the bar, nodding in my direction. His eyes glistened in the candlelight as he picked up a glass. "I don't believe in hurting females."

I narrowed my gaze, still deciding whether to leave, when Daegal looked at me again. He raised a brow, placing a hand on the countertop between us.

"I wouldn't do it if I were you." He shook his head back and forth. "A patrol of Winged Soldiers would find you within the hour, and they're out for blood."

My brows furrowed as I stared at the elf. "I-What?"

Xander chuckled, pushing his stool back. "Take it easy on the fortune-telling, Daegal. Ana here isn't used to your ways yet." He turned to me. "Daegal can See what will happen in the future. You would be wise to listen to him."

The Fortune Elf nodded before turning to Jo. "You'll be needed upstairs in seventeen minutes," he said cryptically.

I raised a brow. That was... odd.

But apparently, no one else seemed rattled because Jo just put her rag down, wiping her hands on her apron. "That should be more than enough time. Come on, Xan. It's upstairs."

It. What was this thing that Xander was getting?

My curiosity peaked, but this didn't seem to be the right time for questions. Placing his hand on my arm, Xander cleared his throat.

"Stay here, Ana," he ordered. "I'll be right back. Don't talk to anyone except for Daegal."

I narrowed my eyes. "You're so bossy," I muttered, but he didn't respond as he turned to follow Jo.

Sighing, I turned my attention to the Fortune Elf, who was currently staring at me with wide, unblinking blue eyes.

"You wouldn't happen to have anything to drink, would you?"

I Hate You

Daegal smirked, reaching under the counter before pulling out a cloudy, green bottle. I eyed it warily as he poured a small serving of an amber liquid into a shot glass.

"I think you'll want some of this," he said as he slid the shot glass over to me.

Narrowing my eyes, I inspected the liquid warily before shrugging and tossing it down my throat. The moment it landed on my tongue, I jumped. I had been expecting a burn like the Dragon Fire, but it tasted sweet, with just a hint of fire as it went down.

Smacking my lips together, I leaned back on the stool. "Thank you," I said. "What is this?"

"The merchant who sold it to me called it Eaflower. It comes from Eleyta."

Gaping at him, I blinked rapidly. Did he say Eleyta? I must have misheard him. "I'm sorry, I thought you said Eleyta?"

"I did," he replied.

"The Northern Kingdom beyond the mountains?"

He nodded. "The one and only."

I tilted my head, studying the Fortune Elf. "I thought the Koln Mountains between Ithenmyr and Eleyta were impossible to cross."

A grim chuckle escaped the Fortune Elf. "Impossible just means you don't know the right people." He nodded at my empty glass. "I'm glad you liked it."

"I did. But you said I would need it?"

He nodded. "Yes, I—"

Before Daegal could continue, the pupils of his eyes disappeared entirely as a silver gleam took over his features. The elf's hands stopped mid-air, his face going slack for an entire minute, then two, before life seemed to return to him. "Shit. Stay here."

Without waiting for a response, the Fortune Elf hurried into the back.

"Yeah," I muttered to myself, pulling my hood even further over my head as I turned the empty shot glass over in my hands. "Because that wasn't weird."

Sighing, I slammed the shot glass down and narrowed my eyes. What were the chances that Winged Soldiers would be waiting for me if I left out the back? I didn't know Daegal and had never heard of a Fortune Elf before.

But the way his eyes had gone glassy, and then he had disappeared... It had struck a chord within me.

"Dammit," I muttered. I was going to stay. Even the thought of being captured by the king's guards sent shivers down my back.

Resigning myself to staying put for the time being, I set the shot glass down on the bar top. Angling myself to see the tavern's entrance better, I took a deep breath.

If there was one thing living in the tower had taught me, it was that the ability to listen and learn was a gift from the goddess herself. One that I wouldn't let go to waste.

Exhaling deeply, I let the sounds of the tavern wash over me. High-pitched giggles reached my ears, followed by a much deeper masculine voice.

"... come upstairs, Polly."

Her reply made me blush. The worldly response and barely veiled innuendo reminded me that despite what I had said to Xander, I was, in fact, a maiden.

Scowling, I shifted my attention away from the amorous couple. Pretending to straighten my skirts, I tilted my head and eyed a pair of older customers seated by the front door. They were leaning close together, their voices low as they whispered.

"Did you see the Winged Soldiers patrolling the city, Bard?" the young one asked.

His older friend coughed, gesturing to a cane leaning against the table. "My leg doesn't work as well as it used to, Godwin, but I'm not blind. Of course, I saw them."

Godwin nodded. "When I was younger, my great-grandmum would tell me stories."

"Did she now?" Bard sounded like he was putting up with the younger male's conversation.

"Yes," he whispered, "she told me all about the Dragon Massacre. She said there were hundreds of soldiers throughout the kingdom during those days."

Bard's eyes bulged, and he grabbed his cane. In a swift movement, he whacked it against the side of Godwin's legs. I sucked in a deep breath at the sudden violence as Godwin bit back a yelp.

Bard hissed, "Bite your tongue, you fool. No one speaks of those days. Anyone who was alive then could tell you they were a nightmare."

"Were you... did you see it happen?" Godwin asked eagerly as he promptly disregarded the older male's advice for the sake of gossip.

I shook my head but leaned in to listen.

"Hush, you idiot," Bard whispered. "Of course not. It was over a century ago. But my grandfather was five at the time, and he told me..." Bard's voice lowered, and I struggled to hear what he was saying.

"Eavesdropping, Sunshine?"

I jolted, my hand flying to my chest, as I turned to stare at Xander. He was leaning over the bar top, his eyes twinkling as he studied me.

"No," I spat out.

He raised a brow, a knowing look on his face. "Liar."

Narrowing my eyes, I slammed my hand on the counter. "Don't call me names," I seethed.

A feminine chuckle came from behind me. I turned to see Jo barely containing her laughter as she said, "My goodness, Xander. It isn't often that I see someone who isn't falling all over you."

Crossing my arms, I glowered in the barmaid's direction. "People fall all over themselves for *him*?"

Xander placed a hand over his heart, his mouth tilting down. "Sunshine, you wound me. I'll have you know, I've had my fair share of females seeking my company over the years."

Jo nodded. "It's true. The last time he disappeared from Thyr in the middle of the night, three different hearts were broken beyond repair."

"Josephine," Xander hissed. "Stop spreading stories about me."

Jo... was short for Josephine?

She leaned in and smacked Xander on the arm playfully. I watched her, an odd spurt of anger bursting through me as her hand connected with Xander's arm. I'd never felt anything like it, and it was... discomforting, to say the least.

"Stop that," she replied. "No one calls me Josephine except my mother. Not even my brother. Don't you start now, Xan, or I'll be forced to tell Ana more stories about you."

Xander paled, but before he could reply, Daegal's head poked out of the back. "Two minutes, Jo."

Furrowing my brows, I watched as Jo walked up the stairs. Once she was gone, I turned to Xander. He was standing with his arms crossed, staring at the empty stairwell.

I cleared my throat. "Did you get the mysterious item you came for?"

He nodded distractedly, his gaze still firmly on the now-empty doorway. His fingers twitched at his sides as he stood, legs spread like he was preparing for a fight. "I did."

A twinge of something odd appeared in my stomach when I realized Xander was watching for *her*. Josephine.

This was a strange feeling and one I had never felt before. It left a bitter taste on my tongue and made me feel queasy. I wanted to walk up and grab Xander's attention for myself. I wanted him to pay attention to me.

It took a moment for me to realize what I was feeling. Jealousy.

Huffing, I rubbed my hand over my face.

Get a hold of yourself, Aileana. You have no business feeling jealous of Josephine. Xander can do whatever he wants. He doesn't belong to you. Just look at him. He doesn't even like you. And you don't *like him.*

I sighed because Inner-Aileana was right. I had no business feeling anything for Xander.

Whatever Jo and Xander had going on, it didn't involve me. Besides, Xander and I had only known each other for two days. He and Jo seemed to have a much longer history.

If there was one thing I knew for sure, it was that I didn't intend to know Xander long enough to have a history. I disliked him immensely. He rubbed me the wrong way and made me feel all sorts of complicated things. Things I had no time for.

The sooner the two of us could go our separate ways, the better.

Then, these pesky, horrid feelings would be in the past. And I could go on living like none of this had ever happened.

"Good," I said, nodding emphatically. I strove to sound calm, but my voice sounded off to my ears. This time, I repeated, "That's good. I'm glad you got what you came for."

Xander pulled his gaze from the stairs towards me, his mouth twitching. He leaned forward, cutting the distance between us in half.

I took a deep breath, my eyes finding his as all the tavern sounds faded. Xander tilted his head, his golden eyes sharp in the dim lighting. He smirked. "What's wrong, Ana?"

"Nothing's wrong," I huffed, pulling my gaze from his and staring at my hands. I would not get worked up over this male who clearly harbored immense feelings of dislike towards me. "I'm just ready to leave this city, that's all."

I'm ready to leave you and these confusing feelings behind.

The words echoed in my mind, but I didn't say them.

"Good," Xander said gruffly. "I'm sure you'll be happy to get rid of me." He muttered something under his breath that sounded suspiciously like, "that makes two of us," but before I could call him out on it, a series of loud shouts and scuffles erupted from the floor above us. It sounded like a herd of elephants had taken up residence upstairs.

Moments later, a crash reverberated through the floor. The chatter in the tavern stopped as Daegal's head popped out from the back. His cheeks were flushed as he gestured toward us.

"Change of plans," the Fortune Elf said hurriedly.

He pulled a heavy black cloak over his tunic, placing a large canvas bag on his back.

"What's going on, Daegal?" Xander asked.

The elf withdrew a long sword from under the counter and shoved it into a sheath at his hip. "We'll be leaving sooner than expected. Get ready."

"We?" I asked, but just then, several people came barreling down the stairs.

"I won't stand for this, Jeremiah," an elf with a long red beard said.

Jeremiah crossed his arms, getting in Red Beard's face. "Mariella made her choice, Lothar. And it wasn't you."

"You don't deserve her," Lothar sneered. "As if Mariella would pick a pig farmer's son over a wealthy merchant."

"She has picked, hasn't she, my dear?" Jeremiah glanced over, and I followed his gaze.

Then, I noticed a lithe, barefoot courtesan with hair the color of straw standing back on the stairs. She had a worn shawl wrapped around her shoulders, covering her night clothes. Her face was pale, and she was looking between the arguing pair with her mouth wide open.

Above her, Jo stood with her hands on her hips.

Jeremiah and Lothar glowered at each other, raising clenched fists as anger radiated off of them in waves. Jo pushed past Mariella, coming to stand between the two. Even though they loomed over her, Jo radiated authority.

"Gentlemen," Jo crowed in a soft, soothing voice. She looked between both of them, her gaze hard as she said, "Let's not fight over this."

"Go away, Jo," Lothar snarled. "This doesn't involve you."

Jo placed her hands on her hips, tilting her head. "Everything that happens at The Opal Spoon is my business, Lothar. Mine and Finn's."

Lothar raised a brow. "I don't see Finn here tonight."

Jo took a step forward. Her eyes were hard, and her fists furled at her sides as she said, "Just because my brother isn't here doesn't mean he won't find you if you hurt one of our girls. You know this. Besides, there are more than enough females in Thyr to go around. I'm sure you can find someone as beautiful as Mariella to warm your bed."

Sneering, Lothar stepped close to Jo as he glared down at her. "You're little better than a whore yourself, Jo. Running a brothel that fronts as a tavern. What would you do if the king's guards were to find out about your off-the-books operations?"

The moment the words left Lothar's mouth, it was as though the air had been sucked out of the tavern. All conversations ceased as a dozen pairs of eyes swung to the confrontation.

Out of the corner of my eye, I noticed Daegal standing near the door. He nodded subtly. I wouldn't have seen it if I hadn't been paying attention. My skin felt tight as tension permeated the atmosphere. Something was about to happen. I could feel it.

Jo's voice was icy, her jaw clenched as she tilted her head ever so slightly. "Did you just call me a whore and then threaten me, Lothar?"

He shifted on his feet, swallowing, but didn't back down. "I said what I said."

"Idiot," Xander muttered under his breath.

Faster than I could blink, many things seemed to happen at once. Jo dove forward and delivered a right hook to Lothar's face that Matthias would have been proud of.

Lothar gasped, tumbling backward as his arms flailed wildly. He fell onto a round table. The wood cracked under his weight as the dishes fell to the floor with a clatter. The moment the plates shattered on the floor, it was as though a spell had been lifted.

Suddenly, all the patrons were on their feet, their fists clenched as their faces contorted with rage. I lost sight of Jo as an older male darted out from his seat, shoving one of the scantily clad courtesans aside before slamming his fist into another patron's side.

I watched the fight unfold with wide eyes. Mugs and chairs were being used as makeshift weapons as patrons turned against each other. I had been trained to fight, but my training had been nothing like this.

Slipping my hand under my cloak, I reached into the hidden pocket of my dress. The quiet *zing* of my dagger whispered in my ear. I kept the weapon out of sight as I watched the anger take hold of everyone around me.

Keeping my grip firm on my dagger, I gathered my skirts.

A hand landed on my arm.

"Come on, Sunshine," Xander said quietly. I glanced down, noting a sword similar to the Fortune Elf's hanging off Xander's hip. "Daegal Saw this. We only have a few minutes before soldiers come to investigate the commotion."

He didn't need to say anything else. Tightening my grip on my dagger, I slid off the stool and followed Xander out the door.

A cool breeze slammed into us the moment we were out of the tavern. I bristled, letting go of my skirts to draw my cloak around me.

"We don't have any time to waste," Xander said gruffly, pulling me down the street behind him. "Jo and Daegal will meet us at the Traitor's Bridge."

Traitor's Bridge. The ominous name rattled within me.

"Where..."

My words cut off in a strangle as I caught sight of something that sent shivers down my spine.

Two tall soldiers with long, black, feathered wings were turning the corner. They were walking with purpose, their heads high and legs spread as they kept their fists at their sides. Swords hung from their hips, but I knew they didn't need them. Their bodies were weapons enough. Any moment from now, they would be right on top of us.

Winged Soldiers.

"Shit," Xander cursed, yanking up his hood and hiding his silver-white hair. Personally, I thought it did little to help him hide. His size was more of an issue. Even after two days together, I wasn't used to how... big Xander was. He muttered, "Dammit, Daegal, you had to be wrong today. Three minutes, my ass."

Xander grabbed me, his grip rough as he swung me around and pushed me up against a nearby alley wall. Bricks dug into my back, and I lifted a knee, intent on showing him my displeasure.

He smirked, anticipating my movements and pinning me against the alley with his hips. I struggled as he placed one arm against my hip and the other on the wall above my head. I tried to ignore the way warmth flooded through me as I shifted my hips, trying to escape his heated touch.

"I told you, don't touch me," I growled, but Xander simply pushed his forehead against mine as he angled our bodies away from the street. His chest was heaving, his breath warm as he loomed over me. If I'd thought he was big before, it was nothing on how he looked now. Up close, with his chest heaving and such little space between us, he was huge.

"If you want to remain free, Sunshine, I suggest you play along," he ground out through clenched teeth.

A snarky comment rose in my throat, but I shoved it down as the Winged Soldiers drew closer. I had some sense of self-preservation, after all.

"Fine," I hissed.

Xander's eyes sparked, and I could tell he thought he had won. But if he thought I would just stand there and do nothing, he was wrong.

Two of us could play this game. Whatever this game was, I knew I did not want to lose.

Narrowing my eyes, I sucked my bottom lip between my teeth for a moment before blowing out a long breath.

The Winged Soldiers drew nearer, their footsteps pounding on the cobblestones, as I raised my head. Xander's face was mere inches from mine, his jaw clenched as he stared at me. His eyes looked darker in the shadows, more of a dirt brown than the gold from before. They seemed to flicker as dark shadows passed through them.

"Xander," I whispered.

"Yes?" he ground out through clenched teeth. His pupils dilated as he stared at me.

"I cannot stand you," I murmured. My voice was husky as I leaned forward and cut the distance between us in half. His eyes widened as I drew nearer to him, but he didn't move. Pressing my hand against Xander's chest, I pushed myself onto my toes as I looked him in the eye. "I can honestly say I've never disliked anyone as much as I do you."

Not wanting to lose my courage, my eyes fluttered shut as I closed the space between us. I brushed my lips against his. Our first kiss—my first kiss ever—was light, tentative, and little more than a whisper on the wind.

It wasn't enough. The second I moved my lips off of his, I knew. I needed more. I wanted to taste him and make him feel the tumultuous storm within me.

Xander stared at me, his eyes unblinking, as I came back for more.

This second kiss was anything but fleeting. I moaned as I pressed my mouth against his, my eyes sliding shut again. He tasted *so* good. I hadn't known another being could taste this good.

I must have caught him by surprise because for a moment, Xander was nothing more than a statue against me. Then, a growl escaped him as he took over. He moved subtly, his hips pressing against mine as our kiss went from a light touch into something deeper, filled with urgency and passion.

As I kissed him, this male I despised, a feeling I had never felt before, began to spread through me like liquid fire.

He groaned, his hand tightening around my hip as he pushed me harder against the wall. I huffed out a surprised breath, my mouth opening slightly, and Xander's tongue darted in and brushed against mine. I gasped at the warmth that flooded from him into me as we became nothing more than lips and tongues and teeth.

In the back of my mind, I registered the sound of the Winged Soldiers as they walked past us. They chuckled, their voices low.

"Pair of lovers out for the night," one of them said.

The other whistled. "I wouldn't mind getting my hands on her."

"Damn straight, I would..."

The pressure of Xander's lips increased, and the soldier's voices faded. I had no room for anything except him.

He pulled away slightly, his voice deep and raspy. "Guess what, Sunshine?"

"What?" I breathed, too lost in the kiss to even open my eyes.

"I *really* don't like you, either." With that declaration, Xander pulled his hand from the wall. He slid it behind my hood and underneath my hair, cupping the back of my neck and tilting my head the way he wanted it. He drew me close to him, our bodies touching from chest to feet, as he pressed himself against me. I wasn't surprised to find that he was hiding hardened muscles underneath that cloak. Whoever he was, he clearly exercised.

A groan escaped him as he nipped at my lip. I squirmed beneath him as he said, "In fact, I think I might hate you for how you make me feel."

I pressed my hips against him as the feeling in my middle grew more intense. "How much do you hate me?"

Xander's eyes flashed, and his jaw hardened. He pressed his lips against my jawline. His kisses were forceful, brutal even, as he murmured, "I hate you more than anyone else I've ever met."

Then he reclaimed my lips, pushing me harder against the wall.

Seconds became minutes as we explored each other in a way I hadn't even known existed.

Everything I thought I had known about kissing—which was, admittedly, only what I had been able to glean from eavesdropping—had evaporated the moment Xander's lips touched mine. With every beat that passed, with every brush of his tongue, I felt myself melting against him.

Everything about him infuriated me. *Everything*.

From how he spoke to the hard line of his jaw when he got upset, Xander frustrated me to no end. No one else had ever made me feel this way. And yet, here we were doing something entirely unexpected. Something dangerous. Something that I knew was wrong. We shouldn't be doing this. He made it clear. He hated me.

The problem was—and it was a problem—it felt all too *right*.

I leaned against Xander, intent on running my fingers through his hair, when he grabbed my hand. He shoved my arm against the wall.

"No touching," he hissed.

"You're so bossy," I muttered, pushing against him. I could feel him smirk as he deepened our kiss. We were melting into each other when a voice came from behind us.

"I told you they'd be here, Jo."

Change of Plans

"Dammit." Xander pushed away from me, his eyes wide as he walked a few steps back. He shoved his hood off his head, running his hand through his hair. His muscles were tense as he paced like a caged animal, pinching the bridge of his nose.

A sharp stab of pain bolted through me at the sight of the regret that flashed across his face before I grabbed it and shoved it down. I couldn't get hurt over something that meant nothing.

And that's all that kiss was.

Nothing.

It was a distraction, nothing more.

Xander had made that perfectly clear. He hated me. I hated him. That was simple. And simple was all I had time for.

Pushing myself off the wall, I crossed my arms and glared at Daegal and Jo. They were standing a few feet away, both sporting matching expressions of mirth.

"Are we interrupting something?" Jo smirked as she glanced between

Xander and me. "Because if so, we can come back later..." She wiggled her eyebrows suggestively.

"You weren't interrupting anything at all," I replied quickly, ignoring the urge to raise a finger to my tingling lips. "We were just talking."

Xander growled under his breath, but Jo's knowing eyes caught mine as she smirked. "It didn't look like talking from here."

"Let it go, Josephine," Xander huffed. His voice was deeper than usual, his eyes dark and stormy as he crossed his arms. "What happened to meeting us at Traitor's Bridge?"

Daegal shook his head, and a vein popped in his jaw. "Change of plans. I have Seen many paths for today, but only one of them will result in all of us getting out of Thyr alive. We have to go *now*."

Xander nodded as though the Fortune Elf's words made complete sense to him. I, on the other hand, was utterly lost.

I shifted on my feet. "Excuse me? Can someone explain to me what exactly Daegal can do? What does it mean, he Saw many paths?" I gestured to Daegal. "How exactly does your magic work?"

"He's a Fortune Elf," Jo replied, as though that answered all my questions.

"I know that," I ground out through clenched teeth, "but—"

Before I could continue, Xander grabbed my arm. His touch, which had been so gentle only a few minutes ago, was now hard on my arm. Instantly, any remnants of warm and tender feelings dissipated into thin air.

Ah yes. This was *exactly* why Xander and I weren't suited.

"Not now, Ana," he hissed, dragging me behind him. "If we get out of this goddess-damned city, we can discuss it later."

"You're so damn bossy," I snarled.

"Better to be bossy than dead, Sunshine."

Having delivered that absolutely stunning pearl of wisdom, Xander stopped talking.

Daegal led us through the city as we ducked into alleys and under bridges. We moved quickly, avoiding the patrols of soldiers combing through the city.

Just like when the Earth Elf had died in the square, a somber atmosphere had settled over the city. It seemed like the king's guards were everywhere.

I couldn't wait to get out of Thyr.

THE SUN HAD SLIPPED below the horizon by the time we reached the city's outer wall. Covered in shadows, the stone structure seemed much more formidable than it had in the morning. The four of us stood, staring at the imposing wall.

I crossed my arms, looking one way, then the next. This part of the wall appeared deserted, but the entire structure reached far above our heads. I couldn't see any way for us to climb over it.

"What are we going to do?" I asked quietly.

My three companions were huddled together when Xander turned toward me. "We're going through the wall," my fake husband said matter-of-factly.

"Through the wall." I stared at him, putting my hands on my hips. "It has to be at least five feet thick!"

"More like ten," Xander replied, smirking as he dropped to his knees. He began crawling along the wall, running his hand down the bricks.

I blinked, dumbfounded.

What was it with these people and providing only half an answer?

Huffing, I marched over to Jo and Daegal. They were standing nearby, their hands on the hilts of their weapons as they stared into the falling darkness. Their backs were straight, and their bodies were tense. Everyone was on high alert.

"Is he serious?" I hissed. "Are we going *through* the wall?"

Jo nodded. "Yes," she said. "Xander doesn't really joke around much, in case you haven't noticed."

Oh, I'd noticed.

I smirked. "Yes," I drawled. "That is something I have definitely observed over our time together."

Jo raised a brow. "I'd love to know how the two of you got together. Xander is... interesting. I've known him for about five years, and I never thought he'd settle down. But he does seem happier now than ever before."

I coughed. She thought Xander was happy? In my opinion, he was aggravating. Infuriating. Maddening, even.

But *not* happy.

"Really?" I squeaked. "Happy?"

She smiled. "Yes."

Before she could reply, Daegal placed a hand on her arm. I watched as they stepped away and shared a conspiratorial whisper.

Feeling left out, I slid my hand into my pocket, feeling the reassuring metal of my daggers as I watched Xander crawl along the bottom of the wall. He was more shadow than corporeal form as the falling darkness enveloped him.

A minute passed in silence, then two, when a soft *thud* came from my right.

A beat passed before Xander's muffled voice came from right in front of me. "It's clear."

Glancing left and right, I tried to locate Xander's voice. All I could see were dark gray shadows.

Where is he?

"Come on, Ana," Daegal glanced in my direction before following the same path Xander had taken a few moments ago. "We don't have much time."

Nodding, I narrowed my eyes and tried not to turn my ankle in the darkness. Moments later, I saw where Xander had gone. Swallowing, I forced myself to shove my discomfort away as I stared at our route out of Thyr.

Xander hadn't lied.

A large stone had been cut out of the wall and rolled to the side, revealing a small hidden passageway that went through straight the town's defenses. Judging by the packed dirt, this was a tunnel that had been used by many people before.

"That's convenient," I muttered, eyeing the small hole. It looked barely large enough for me, let alone Xander.

"Very," Daegal agreed. He crouched, gesturing to the opening. "Ladies first."

Narrowing my eyes at the Fortune Elf, I drew my dagger before dropping to my hands and knees. Taking a deep breath, I tried to see beyond the tunnel. It couldn't have been over ten or maybe fifteen feet long, but that distance felt like a mile. Nothing more than dark, lumpy shadows greeted me.

"Come on, Ana," Irritation laced Xander's voice as it traveled from the other side of the wall. I narrowed my eyes, clenching my jaw as I thought about all the different places I'd like to stab him right now.

Unaware of where my thoughts had gone, Xander sighed. "We can't wait all night. You need to come through the tunnel. Daegal will go last and replace the stone."

Closing my eyes, I pushed aside my worry and fought to remain calm. *You can do this.*

Taking a deep breath, I entered the small tunnel. I couldn't see my dagger, but the familiar weight was reassuring in my hand as I shuffled forward. The stones felt like they were pressing down on my shoulders, and my chest was tight.

Breathe, I ordered myself. *You are strong. You can do this. Aileana, you* have *to do this.*

My hands dug into the compact dirt. It was cold and damp underneath my fingertips. Moments after I touched the ground, a soft green light came from my fingers, seeping into the soil. A sense of calm filled me as the dirt softened under my touch.

I blinked, but just as quickly as the green light had appeared, it was gone. I was left wondering if I was seeing things. When I was younger, I thought maybe my magic would appear. That it would be a clue as to who I was. What I was. But the years had dragged on, and I hadn't even been able to produce a drop of magic.

Eventually, I'd assumed that I'd been born Without. It made sense, in a way. Elves born without had no connection to the goddess, no magic of their own. It would be just my luck.

I'd never heard of anyone whose magic appeared in their twenty-third year.

Keeping my eyes on the end of the tunnel, I shoved the thoughts of strange green lights aside as I crawled toward the other side.

Every foot felt like a mile, and every second, a lifetime.

My heart was pounding in my chest, my lungs tight, until finally, I made it to the other side. The moment a cool gust of wind blew across my face in a gentle greeting, I blew out a long breath. Seconds later, I pulled myself onto the damp grass.

I panted, my head falling into my lap, as I drew myself against the wall. Closing my eyes, I focused on slowing my heart rate as I took long, deep breaths. After a minute, I heard shuffling coming from behind me. Peeking open my eyes, I made out the shapes of my three companions.

"Are you okay?" Jo asked, concern lacing her voice. She dropped to her knees. "You seem shaken."

Shaken was an understatement. At that moment, I didn't feel like myself.

Laughter bubbled up inside of me, and before I could stop it, a nervous giggle erupted from my lips. In the past forty-eight hours, I had escaped the tower that had been my prison for my entire life, met a witch, and gone into the city, and yet none of those had bothered me as much as crawling through that tunnel.

Coughing, I covered the sudden laughter as I dropped my head into my hands. I didn't even know what okay was.

Jo placed her hand on my arm. "Hey, Ana," she whispered. "If you need to talk... I'm here."

Narrowing my eyes, I nibbled on my bottom lip. I didn't know what to say. Not for the first time, I lamented my lack of social awareness. I was sure that conversational skills were right up at the top of the list of things that I should have learned.

Like many other things in my life, the king hadn't prioritized social skills. So here I was. To call me awkward would have been an understatement.

"I'm fine," I replied after a minute.

Jo pulled her hand away. "Okay," she said slowly, glancing at Daegal and Xander. They were engaged in a quiet conversation not far from us. "If you need to talk, I'm a good listener." She chuckled. "You have to be in my line of work."

"Thank you," I said sincerely. "I'll keep that in mind."

She smiled softly, pushing herself to her knees. Jo began brushing off her skirts, and I stood, doing the same.

When I was relatively clean, I marched over to Xander. Now that we were out of Thyr and he had his... whatever it was he had gotten from Jo, I needed some assurances. "I need to talk to you, husband."

Before Xander could answer, I grabbed his arm and dragged my fake husband away from his companions. Once we were far from the other two, he shook off my grip.

"What?" he snapped. He somehow managed to infuse a significant amount of irritation and anger into that one word.

My nostrils flared as blood rushed to my face. I stood on my tip-toes, holding my hand up between us as I waggled my finger in front of his face. "I wanted to make sure you don't forget your part of our agreement. We got through Thyr. Now, I need you to take me to the Indigo Ocean."

"I made you a deal, Ana, and I'll follow through," Xander ground out through clenched teeth. "I'm a male of my word."

"We'll see about that, won't we?" Stepping back, I crossed my arms and glared at Xander.

He looked like he was about to reply when, all of a sudden, shouts came from the other side of the wall.

Xander cursed as the sound of metal filled the air. "There's no time for chit-chat, Sunshine. We need to go."

FOR THE SECOND time in as many days, I found myself running through a forest away from the king's soldiers. This time, however, I was not alone.

Xander ran ahead and Daegal behind as Jo and I remained in the middle. For safety, they had insisted.

I hadn't fought them. There was no way I could find my way through the forest at night. With every passing moment, the woods transformed until the trees were shadows and stumbling blocks. I had no idea how Xander managed to pick his way through the trees so effortlessly.

My own movements were anything but effortless. The terrain was not flat, and it only took a few minutes before my muscles protested our course of action.

I knew from my limited studies that the forests around Thyr stretched over hills and mountains for miles. The leading economy in the province of Adatol was timber. Seeing the dense trees packed together, I wasn't surprised by that.

About an hour into our trek, Jo touched my arm. She asked, "How are you doing?"

"I'm tired," I replied honestly, exhaling a ragged breath. "This isn't exactly something I'm used to."

She raised a brow. "You're married to Xander, and you're not used to running through the woods?"

Oh no. I felt like I was a moment away from putting my foot in my mouth. I shrugged, trying to infuse nonchalance in my voice as I said, "Oh, you know." A dry laugh escaped me, and I hoped Jo couldn't tell how nervous I was when I said, "I meant not knowing where we were going. Usually, he tells me."

"Ah," she nodded. "We are most likely going north. I have never been good at navigating through forests, but your husband seems to have an uncanny knack for knowing exactly where he is at all times."

"Handy, that," I muttered under my breath. An insect buzzed in my ear, and I slapped it. The moment it was gone, two more appeared. Soon, dozens of the tiny insects were flying all around me.

Great.

I added bugs to the list of things I hadn't realized would be a problem when I escaped.

"It is," Jo replied, oblivious to the tone of my voice or the bugs swarming me. "He mentioned that you crossed the Niphil River yesterday."

"Mhmm," I muttered. I was distracted, trying to figure out how long it would take us to reach the Indigo Ocean.

My destination.

We walked silently for a few minutes, our feet crunching on the leaves as branches snapped beneath us.

"So..." Jo started again after we stepped over a fallen log. "How did you and Xander meet?"

I blinked. Was this how regular conversations went? Did one person ask a question, and the other tried to figure out if it was safe to answer?

Probably not. I was pretty certain I was missing some crucial part of this social exchange. The question seemed pretty innocuous, so I decided answering it couldn't hurt.

"We ran into each other," I said, deciding to keep the rest of the story to myself.

"Hmm," she said. A long moment passed before she sighed. "Do you care to elaborate?"

Shaking my head, I muttered, "There isn't much else I can say."

She turned, studying me. "Okay," she said after a moment. "Hopefully, you'll trust me with your story one day."

Trust.

My lips tilted up into a small smile. "I'd like that." Nibbling on my lip, I turned to Jo. "How did you meet Xander?"

"It's a long story." Jo laughed. "Let's just say that when Xander and Daegal showed up at my old house in Breley five years ago covered in blood, I was kind enough not to turn them away at the door. One thing led to another, and here we are."

Raising a brow, I lied and said, "I see." I didn't, really. Ducking beneath a low-hanging branch, I tugged as my skirt got caught on a bramble. "That's it? They just showed up, and you three were instant friends?"

She chuckled. "Well, I didn't say we don't have a history, but yes, the four of us have been friends ever since."

"Four? You, Xander, Daegal, and..." My voice trailed off.

"My brother Finn." Jo finished the sentence for me.

"Ah," I replied.

The mysterious brother who had remained in Thyr. Well, I supposed that solved a few of the mysteries.

After that, it seemed like neither of us felt like talking anymore. We fell into a comfortable silence, and eventually, Jo dropped back to hike beside Daegal. I took the time to think about what was to come.

I had no idea what lay beyond the shores of the Indigo Ocean. No plan. No thought about what I would do.

All I knew was that leaving Ithenmyr meant I would no longer be within the king's reach. And that meant more than anything. I would *not* let him put me back in that cage again. Not after I'd just discovered the truly wonderful taste of freedom.

As time passed, running became walking, giving way to trudging.

My energy was long gone as I moved through the dense woods alongside my companions. The late hour didn't seem to affect them, a point that was not lost on me. No one was speaking—a small mercy.

I concentrated on putting one foot in front of the other.

By the time the moon was high in the sky, my entire body felt like it was on fire. My lungs were burning, and my heart felt like it would burst out of my chest.

"Wait," I rasped, stumbling as I tripped over a root. My throat was dry, and my words scratched on their way out. By then, my eyes had adjusted to the darkness, and I could make out my companions' shadows as they all hiked silently beside me. The moment I spoke, they stopped.

I whispered, "I need a break."

"We can't jus—" Xander's words were clipped, but they cut off as I collapsed against a nearby tree.

My bottom landed on the ground with a very un-ladylike *thump*, and I cursed. "I need a minute," I ground out through clenched teeth.

Xander looked at Daegal. "Is it safe?"

The Fortune Elf's eyes went glassy, emitting the same strange silver light from before. I stared at him, panting as I tried to catch my breath.

When the silver receded, Daegal nodded. "We have time. Xander and Jo, why don't you go scout out up ahead? There should be a cavern within twenty minutes from here where we can spend the day. I'll stay and guard Ana."

"If anyone needs guarding, it'll be you, Daegal," Xander muttered, rubbing his shoulder as he glared at me. "Ana has multiple daggers and isn't afraid to use them."

"Don't you forget it," I replied haughtily. I winked at Jo, whispering loudly, "I think he's scared of me."

The bossy male snarled, and I giggled. I couldn't help it. Xander was so easy to rile. Making him angry was the highlight of what had become an exceedingly long day.

Jo laughed, muttering something about Xander deserving whatever he got. Every time she spoke, I liked her more and more. I couldn't wait to get to know her better. Maybe once we reached our destination, she could be my first friend.

I smiled at the thought. Jo seemed like someone I could get along with. Talk with. Share secrets with.

The barmaid continued to laugh at Xander as they disappeared into the forest, leaving me with Daegal.

I took a moment to look over the Fortune Elf. Where Xander was big, Daegal was lithe. Like me, he had long ears, but unlike my unruly mess of long red hair, he had black curls that stopped at the nape of his neck. Xander was rugged and wild, but Daegal seemed much more... contained.

The Fortune Elf raised a brow, dropping beside me as he pulled a canteen of water from his pack. He took a long sip before handing it to me. "Here."

The water was refreshing as it ran down my throat. Once my thirst was quenched, I turned to him. I finally had a chance to get some of my questions answered. "So you're a Fortune Elf."

He nodded, his voice low as he said. "I am."

"Can you tell me how you just seem to *know* things?"

Laughter erupted from Daegal. "You don't avoid questions at all, do you?"

I shook my head.

"Well, first of all, I don't *know* anything. But I See things that are likely to happen. Some of them are just potential paths people might walk. They're like water flowing in the river. Fluid. Changeable." He waved a hand in the air in demonstration. "Others are more certain. Etched in stone, so to speak. Those can't change, no matter what I do."

"Hmm." I sat back, resting my head against the tree as I tried to understand. "Can you See the future for everyone?"

"No." He shook his head. "It doesn't work that way. Magic demands a balance. If any one person had too much power... the consequences would be devastating."

"But you can See the future for some people?"

"Yes. The deeper my relationship with someone, the more I can See into their life."

"So for me..." My voice trailed off.

"I know your aura is tangled with Xander's."

I opened my mouth to protest, but Daegal held up a hand, chuckling. "You can't deny it. It's as plain as day. The two of you were meant to be.

But I never Saw you until the moment you walked into The Opal Spoon with him today."

"I see," I muttered. My brows furrowed as another question came to the forefront of my mind. "What do you See in the future for me?"

Daegal pushed himself to his feet. "Everyone always asks that question."

"Oh." I didn't like the thought that I was like everyone else.

"No, no, it's okay. I don't mind answering." He paused for a moment, his hand tapping against his side. "I don't See much other than a dark shadow pursuing you relentlessly."

My heart pounded, and I drew my cloak around myself as I whispered, "Is it the Red Shadow?"

A shudder ran through me at the thought. Repressed memories of searing pain and crimson blood filled my vision.

Gods. If he found me...

Daegal shook his head, his expression grim as he offered me his hand. "I can't tell. It's just... dark right now."

I frowned, placing my hand on his. "Is my future etched in stone? Will the shadow find me?"

"Many things can still change," the elf replied. "Your path is still fluid."

A breath of relief whooshed out of me. "Thank the goddess."

Daegal shifted on his feet, a beat passing before he sighed. "That's not the only thing that I have Seen." The Fortune Elf helped me to my feet but kept my fingers in his hand for a moment.

I tilted my head. "What else have you seen?"

A long moment passed as the wind carried whispers of Xander and Jo's voices. They were approaching quickly. Even in the darkness, I could see that Daegal was biting his lip. Indecision warred on his face as he fought a silent battle with himself.

"Tell me," I pleaded with him. "Things have been kept from me for my entire life. Please tell me what you saw."

"Fine," he said. "I've Seen what they called you. I know who you are to the king. Your... purpose."

My stomach fell to the pit of my body as I gasped and tried to pull my hand from Daegal's. "Please," I begged. "Please don't tell them."

The Fortune Elf looked at me quizzically. "Xander doesn't know? He's your husband."

I scoffed before I could stop myself. Deciding that avoiding *that* particular question was my best path, I forged ahead. "I can't go back." Hardening my voice, I continued, "I *won't* go back."

Daegal shook his head, his hand still squeezing mine. "I would never turn you in. Xander is one of my dearest friends. But there's one more thing you need to know."

My stomach twisted as I forced out the question, "What?"

"The path you are on now is dangerous. The shadow is determined to find you."

I Should Have Known

ᕯ

I've Seen who you are to the king.

The Fortune Elf's words continued to echo through my mind for the rest of the night.

Even after we found a place to camp and set up a watch, his words kept swirling through me. They were the last thing I heard as I fell into a restless sleep on the hard ground and the first thing that greeted me when I woke up a scant few hours later.

They became the backdrop to my footsteps as my companions and I continued to hike through the forests after having eaten a meager meal of stale bread and cheese. The wind rustled through the leaves, carrying the words to my ears as we hiked up hills and over mountains.

My heart pounded in my chest, and still, Daegal's words echoed in my mind.

The shadow is determined to find you.

I should have known I couldn't just disappear. I should have known that Remington and his evil father would chase me to the ends of the planet. There was no doubt in my mind that this shadow was the same person who had haunted me for my entire life even if Daegal couldn't confirm it.

Remington was a sadist, and his father...

There was a reason they called him the Crimson King.

Many years ago, when High King Edgar was still a young elf, he had bound the five provinces of Ithenmyr together not through diplomacy but through war. It was the bloodiest war Ithenmyr had ever seen.

I shuddered, drawing my cloak around myself.

After everything the two of them put me through, I should have known they wouldn't let their prized possession slip through their fingertips.

As we walked, the morning slipped into the afternoon. By the time the evening came around, memories I had successfully shoved away for years pushed their way through the flimsy barriers I had erected in my mind.

"LET me make one thing very clear, pet," High King Edgar of the House of Irriel said as he stood in the doorway of my room. His long brown hair hung down to his waist as red magic sparked from his fingertips. The horrid scent of sandalwood drifted off him, and it took everything within me not to wrinkle my nose.

"Your Majesty?" I asked quietly.

He snarled, "You belong to me. The only reason you aren't dead right now with the rest of your horrible people is because I need you."

"What did I do, my king?"

The words croaked out of my hoarse throat. I had been lying on my stomach for the past two days, unable to move after the last punishment I had received. Punishment for a crime I didn't commit.

As usual.

"You existed," he snapped at me before stalking away.

Not wanting to watch him, I buried my face in the pillow. Every movement sent shards of shooting pain through me. The door slammed behind the king, taking the scent of sandalwood with him. He didn't leave, though.

I could hear his horrid voice as he spoke to someone I couldn't see. "... I want an example made of her tutor. Tell Remington to take care of him."

Holding my breath, my eyes watered as I pictured Orvyn's kind face. The old human had been my tutor for the past eight years. My mind raced as I tried to remember what we had last been learning. Orvyn had been teaching me to do sums in my head and...

My stomach plummeted.

Three days ago, Orvyn had mentioned something about the War of the Four Kingdoms in passing. That was the last time I had ever seen him.

The guard outside my door cleared his throat. "Yes, Your Majesty."

"The next time someone decides that my future breeder should learn to do something other than reading poetry, looking pretty, and spreading her legs, I want them to remember the tutor's death. Remington is to make it last and make it hurt."

Future breeder.

That's all I was to him. A shudder of revulsion passed through me as I struggled to continue to listen.

"What shall we do about the girl?"

No.

Please, no.

Not another punishment. Not yet. It was too soon.

I whimpered into the pillow. If there were any good in the world, the king would walk away. I didn't think I could handle another punishment right now. Not when my back was still so raw.

"I don't want anyone talking to her," the king snapped. "She is not to

have any more outside influences. That tutor was the last straw. I won't have anyone corrupting her. She can read and write. That's good enough. No one except guards and servants will visit her without my permission."

My eyes burned as the king's footsteps retreated. I counted to a thousand in my head before I buried my face in my pillow. As soon as I was sure he had left, I screamed.

I screamed and screamed and screamed.

I screamed until my throat was raw. Until the pain in my back was overshadowed by the breaking of my heart. Until I had nothing left in me at all.

And still, no one came.

~

"Penny for your thoughts?"

Jo's voice pulled me out of the fog of my memories as her hand landed lightly on my arm. I jumped, drawing my dagger from its scabbard before I realized she meant me no harm.

"Sorry," I mumbled as I slid my weapon back into place. Ahead of me, I could see Daegal and Xander talking. "I'm a little jumpy."

She held up a heavy branch, ducking under it and waiting for me to follow. "I noticed," she said. "I've been trying to talk to you for five minutes, but I don't think you heard anything I said."

I shook my head, rubbing my hands over my face. "I was just... remembering."

Jo nodded, her voice dropping low. "Ah. The pull of memories can be funny, can't it?"

Something about her tone of voice told me she knew exactly what she was talking about.

I turned slightly, but Jo wasn't looking at me anymore. Her gaze was distant, her brows furrowed as she fiddled with her cloak.

"Yes," I agreed. "But I prefer to leave the past where it belongs. Somewhere where it can't bother me."

"Let me know if you ever want to talk about it."

"Thank you," I said after a moment.

We walked in silence for a while before Jo turned to me.

Even though she was shorter than me, she looked fierce with her arms crossed and a frown on her lips. "Look, Ana, I have to say something to you."

I shifted on my feet, unsure of where this conversation was going. "Okay..."

"I don't exactly know how you and Xander met other than what you told me yesterday..." Jo paused as though waiting for me to fill in the blanks, but I wasn't about to do that.

Somehow, "he stalked me in the woods, and I stabbed him" didn't seem like an appropriate answer, so I held my tongue.

After an awkward pause, Jo continued, "Xander is one of my oldest friends."

"You mentioned that." Something about her tone made me feel on edge. I felt my hackles rise as I looked at the barmaid.

"You seem like a nice girl, but I just need some assurances from you."

"Assurances," I repeated. This conversation was becoming odder by the moment, and suddenly, I wanted to be somewhere else. Anywhere else.

Jo nodded. "Yes. I need to make sure that you don't hurt Xander."

"Hurt him." My voice was monotone as I stopped moving and leaned against a tree. I'd already stabbed him, and he seemed to be fine hours after that, so I wasn't even sure Xander could *be* hurt. I asked, incredulous, "You think I can hurt Xander?"

"Yes," Jo replied. "I'm sure you know Xander has been through a lot."

Unbelievable. She wanted to make sure I didn't hurt my fake husband's feelings. To be honest, I wasn't sure he was even capable of feeling anything other than hatred, so this entire conversation seemed slightly laughable to me.

Hadn't we all been through a lot?

I hadn't realized I had spoken out loud until Jo nodded. "It's true, we have, but Xander has been through more than most. And I'm sure he's already explained to you what the map means and why this is so important to him, but I just wanted to—"

Putting up a hand, I pushed myself off the tree. "Wait, what map?"

She narrowed her eyes. "The piece of the map he got in Thyr. The one I've been holding onto for almost a year until he could get back into the city safely."

"Oh, that map." I nodded profusely as if I knew exactly what she was talking about. Internally, I grabbed onto the new information and stuffed it away to deal with later. "Sorry, I just forgot for a moment. I know about the map."

A nervous burst of laughter erupted out of my lips as I cursed myself for my lack of social awareness. Stepping backward, I awkwardly slammed my body against the tree.

At that exact moment, a gigantic bird flew out of the leafy canopy. It squawked, flapping large wings. Bright blue feathers showered over us as the bird took off. The nervous laughter kept coming out of me. Despite my best efforts, I felt unable to stop it.

Of course, that was the moment Xander turned around. He crossed his arms, raising a brow as he closed the distance between us. When he was just a few feet away from me, he spoke. "Something funny, Sunshine?"

I raised a brow, smirking at him. "Funny? No. But I need to talk with you about something, *darling*."

The last word stuck in my throat, but it was worth the effort of forcing it out when Xander's face contorted.

Jo laughed. "Yes, darling," she said, poking Xander in the arm before he swatted her away. "Go talk with your wife. Daegal and I will see what we can do about finding some horses."

My fake husband glowered at his friend before reaching into his cloak. He withdrew his hand, tossing her a small bag. The leather pouch jingled as it sailed through the air. Jo caught it easily, tucking it into her skirts.

"Thank you, Xan," Jo said before darting through the trees to catch up with Daegal.

"Don't spend it all in one place," he muttered.

Josephine threw up her hand in a rude gesture, laughing as she tugged on her hood and joined the Fortune Elf.

Once they were well and truly out of sight, Xander turned to me. "You wanted to talk, Sunshine?"

I scowled at him, crossing my arms. "Are you going to tell your friends the truth about us? About how we aren't really married?"

"Are you sure you'd like to do that?" he asked in a low voice as his golden eyes bore into mine.

I swallowed, taking a step back as he advanced toward me. He loomed over me, his height suddenly much more pronounced than before.

My heart pounded in my chest as the air between us became charged. I slid my hand into my pocket, but Xander was faster than me. His hand on my arm was like a brand.

"Let me go!" I insisted.

He shifted his grip on me, sliding his hand to my wrist and pulling me tight against him. Tsking, he tilted his head as he held onto me. "Come now, Ana," he hissed, "can't we have one conversation without you trying to stab me?"

Huffing, I tried to pull my wrist away from him. "Perhaps if you dislike being stabbed so much, you should be less aggravating."

Xander's eyes flashed as he leaned in, and he snarled, "*I'm* the aggravating one?"

"Yes, dear husband of mine, you are aggravating." I glared at him. "Also, in case you were wondering, you're irritating rude, and being around you brings me great displeasure. So pardon me if you inspire a desire for violence whenever we are together."

Xander pulled back but didn't remove his hand from my arm. "Unbelievable. You are a frustrating, vexing, horrible creature."

I gaped at him. "How dare you speak to me in such a fashion?"

"How dare I?" He laughed, and I got the horrible feeling that this conversation would not go my way. "How dare I? Let me tell you something, *Sunshine*. Why don't you stop trying to stab me, and we can talk about the *truth?*"

He hissed the last word, and my heart stopped.

Trying to regain my footing in what felt like a battle I was quickly losing, I nodded. "Yes. The truth. Tell me what you got from the city."

He shook his head, bringing his eyes within inches of mine. The air between us was charged, and I sucked in a deep breath as he stared at me. "No, Ana. I don't think I will. There's a more interesting truth than what I was getting in Thyr, isn't there?"

"What are you talking about?" I asked nervously. My voice squeaked, and I hated that. I tried to avoid his gaze, but he was right in front of me. All big and hot and angry. His nearness to me.... it was so much. Too much. My senses were overloading. My heart was pounding, my lungs tight. Even his hand on mine felt like it was searing my skin.

"There are so many truths to choose from," he said. "How about the truth about our pact to help each other? The way our auras are inexplicably intertwined?"

"I—"

He snarled, "Or perhaps you'd like me to tell my friends you are Remington's errant fiancée?"

How did he find out?

Suddenly, breathing became a chore. My mouth opened and closed repeatedly as my heart hammered in my chest. A roaring filled my ears, and my muscles trembled as Xander walked us backward, pushing me against a tree.

"Ah yes," he said, nodding as he boxed me in against the trunk. "I thought so."

"Did Daegal tell you?" I forced the question out through clenched teeth. My palms were sweating, and my entire body shook as I stared at the imposing male.

"Daegal? No." Xander's eyes narrowed before he shook his head. "I had my suspicions, but you just confirmed it for me, *Aileana*."

He wielded my name like a weapon. The moment it came out of his mouth, I forgot how to breathe. A choked, strangled sound came out of my throat.

"Why did you run?" he asked.

My heart froze, and my lungs constricted as I raised my wide eyes to his golden ones. "Xander," I pleaded with him. Tears filled my eyes, and I swallowed. "Don't."

"Don't what?" he snapped.

"Don't tell them. I won't go back," I whispered, my voice trembling. "You can't make me. I'd rather die than go back to him."

"Why not? You'd be a princess if you went back. Married to the High King's heir." Xander sneered as he tightened his grip on my hand. "Prince Remington. Lord of the entire province of Ocheka. Death Elf. Bearer of the Opal Scepter. And apparently, *your fiancé*."

"Being a princess is nothing if it means returning to my cage." My eyes flashed as Xander continued to press me against the tree.

"Tell me why you ran," he insisted.

"You want to know why I left?"

"Yes!" he bellowed. "Yes, dammit. Tell me!"

I glared at him. "I left because I won't *ever* let anyone tell me what to do ever again. Not him. Not you. No one!"

Xander just blinked at me as though my outburst surprised him.

"I told you. Now, you need to let me go." I pounded my free hand against his chest. His very large, very hard chest.

"Not yet. This conversation isn't over." A beat passed as he tilted his head, studying me. His voice was softer as he asked, "What did they do to you?"

"It's not your place to know!" I yelled.

I would *never* tell him all the things that were done to me. The things I suffered as the king's pet. The brutal whippings I'd suffered as punishments for crimes I didn't commit. Silence. Loneliness.

Those were my stories. My pain. They weren't his to pull out of me when he felt like it.

As I yelled at Xander, I felt something breaking apart within me. I gasped as a vibrant green light flooded through my skin.

Behind me, the tree *shifted*.

Welcome, Protectress of the Woods. We've been waiting for you.

Protectress of the Woods

⌇⌇⌇

A voice that was both young and old echoed through my head, and I screamed. I couldn't help it. The cry ripped through me, shattering the silence of the evening.

As my voice rang around us, something stirred in the woods. The ground beneath my feet trembled as dozens of green ribbons exploded from my fingers. Gaping, I was rendered speechless as a sense of vibrancy that I had never felt before filled me. The ribbons wove around me like slithering snakes before diving into the dirt.

For a moment, everything was deathly still.

The wind stopped howling; the birds stopped chirping; even the leaves stopped cracking. Time itself seemed to pause.

Xander lifted shaky eyes to mine as he opened his mouth. "Aileana, what are yo—"

"I don't know," I whispered. I stared at my fingers. A faint green glow still emitted from them. My voice shook, betraying the terror coursing through me. "I have no idea what is going on."

Then, one of the trees behind Xander moved. I watched with wide eyes as two large branches the size of my entire body reached out and wrapped themselves around Xander's waist.

"Stop this!" he yelled as the tree dragged him back into a tight embrace. Xander continued to shout, his cries furious as his limbs flailed wildly. "Aileana, help me!"

For a moment, I was frozen in place. This was... unexpected. How could this be me?

I had been born Without. I didn't have magic. This wasn't me. It couldn't be me.

Could it?

Cursing colorfully, Xander reached for his sword. Before he could do more than wrap his fingers around the hilt, the tree limbs pressed his arms against his side. Xander's hood fell off his head, and his silver-white hair streamed down his back like a flash of light as the tree bound him against it.

As I watched Xander struggle, a fierce desire to save him filled me. It was unlike anything I had ever felt before. I had no idea what was happening, but I knew one thing for certain. Xander needed my help.

"Stop!" I screamed as metal sang. Its song clashed with the stillness of the evening. I looked down, surprised to see my hands gripping my twin daggers. I'd drawn them without conscious thought. Running towards the tree, I shouted, "Let him go!"

This insolent male was attacking you, Protectress.

This time, the voice wasn't in my head. It was swirling all around me, carried by the wind.

I watched with wide eyes as hundreds of leaves, grass, and twigs lifted off the ground. They swirled in the air as a brisk wind blew my hood back from my face.

Long tendrils of red hair flew all around me, and I huffed. Wrenching my wayward hair away from my eyes, I blinked once, then twice, as I tried to comprehend what was standing before me.

A lithe female form made entirely of the forest stood mere feet from me. Her moss-green eyes were unblinking as she extended a leafy hand in my direction. She was naked, but what was a little nudity when your entire corporeal form was nothing more than leaves and twigs?

"Greetings, Protectress of the Woods," the leafy being said. Her voice sounded like the whisper of the wind late at night as it swirled around me.

"What in the seven circles of hell is that?" Xander hissed. His already pale complexion was as white as snow.

"You can see it too?" I asked over my shoulder, never taking my eyes off the green female.

Xander rasped, disbelief lacing his every word. "I can. I can't believe it, but I can see it."

"Who are you?" I called out to the leafy form as I tightened my grip on my daggers.

The creature opened her mouth, and the wind carried her words to my ears. "I am Myhhena. Your pain has awoken us."

I stared at her... at least I thought it was a 'her.' "What are you talking about?"

"You summoned us, Protectress."

Narrowing my eyes, I sheathed my daggers as I approached the leafy creature. Shaking my head, I reached out to touch her and then thought better of it. "I didn't mean to awaken you. I don't even know *how* I did it."

"And yet, you did." She swept into a sweeping curtsy, which was a feat considering she was made of leaves. "The hands of fate have determined that now is our time. You called me. Your sorrow echoed through the forest, awakening me and my sisters from our slumber."

"Okay." I sighed, pushing my hair behind my ears. I was tired, and this was a lot to deal with. "It's Myhhena, right?"

"You are correct," she replied in an ethereal voice. "I am one of the Twelve who reside within the forests of Ithenmyr. It is an honor to be summoned by you, Protectress."

Xander huffed. "Why are you calling her that?"

The winds began to swirl once more, and Myhhena's voice grew louder. "Silence! I will not be spoken to in such a disrespectful manner. Certainly not by *you*." The last word was dripping with undisguised disgust as Myhhena gave Xander what I could describe as a look of contempt mixed with utter hatred.

I opened my mouth, but before I could question the odd way Myhhena addressed Xander, she turned back to me. Her voice echoed through the forest as she said, "What would you have us do with this ill-mannered being? His kind has a history of being a menace in the woods."

His kind? Humans?

Based on the fires I knew were burning throughout Ithenmyr to keep people warm at night, I couldn't refute her claims. But the way she spoke about Xander irritated me.

Yes, he was rude and obnoxious and hard to deal with. But this... lady made of leaves had no way of knowing that.

Crossing my arms, I glared at her. "Don't talk about him like that."

Myhhena started, "But, Protectress—"

I held up a hand. "You said I summoned you?"

She curtsied once more, her leafy form rustling. "Yes, Protectress. My sisters and I exist to do your bidding."

"Then I demand you release my companion at once."

Myhhena hissed through her teeth. The leaves swirled around her as she advanced toward me. Her eyes glowed bright green as she protested, "But Protectress, it's not safe! He's a—"

"Enough!" I yelled. My voice rang with authority as I spoke, and I barely recognized myself. "Did you not say you exist to do my bidding?"

She nodded once, her lips in a tight line. "Yes, milady."

"Then you shall do as I ask at once."

Myhhena sighed, the sound long-suffering. "As you wish, Protectress."

The leaves around her hands blew as the tree holding Xander suddenly snapped its branches back. He tumbled to the ground, a curse slipping out of him as he fell face-first into a pile of mud.

"Dammit all," Xander muttered as he pushed himself to his feet, brushing off leaves and dirt from his tunic. "That was *not* pleasant."

The leafy female crossed her arms and scowled in Xander's direction. She had an imposing presence for a being whose corporeal form was made entirely of foliage. "You should thank the Protectress. If it were up to me, I would have left you to rot in the forest's embrace."

Xander's only response was to snarl at the female.

Myhhena's response was... harsh. Not that I didn't appreciate that someone else was *finally* seeing Xander for the vexing creature he was. It was just that insulting him felt like something that belonged to me.

A strange sense of protectiveness surged up within me as I stepped in between the two of them.

My voice rang through the forest. "That's enough. Myhhena, while I appreciate your... help, I think there's been some kind of mistake. I didn't summon you."

"Yes, you did," she insisted.

Huffing, I crossed my arms in front of my chest. "How?"

She stared at me, the leaves that made up her body shaking in the wind. "Do you not know who you are?"

Narrowing my eyes, I shook my head. "I am nobody."

Apparently, that was the wrong thing to say because all of a sudden,

Myhhena's leaves scattered. Just as quickly as she had appeared, she was gone.

In her place, a brisk wind blew through the forest. I stood still as the leaves swirled around me in a cyclone. I could hear Xander calling my name, but I could only see bright green.

Then Myhhena's voice echoed in my mind.

You are Aileana. Daughter of Uhna. Granddaughter of Niona. You are the last Protectress of the Woods.

"But what does that mean?" I pleaded with her as my heart pounded faster in my chest. Myhhena's words resonated with a part of myself that, until a few days ago, had laid dormant for my entire life. Even now, it was buried under years of pain and punishment. I whispered, "I have no idea what you're talking about."

One day, you will understand.

Frustration leaked into my voice as I stared at the swirling leaves. "Can you tell me anything at all? You claim to know who I am, but who are you?"

I am Myhhena. Spirit of the Woods. The eldest of the Twelve. Thelrena sent me to guide you. I am—

The spirit stopped talking abruptly. My heart pounded in my chest a few times before her voice returned. It was more harried than before, a sense of urgency tinging every word as she hissed in my mind.

Protectress, you must leave now. Run as fast as you can. The Red Shadow approaches. You must leave. Take your... companion and flee. I will come to you again. Now, run!

I blinked as the leaves fell to the ground in a blanket all around me, revealing Xander's looming form only a few feet away. His jaw was clenched in a firm line, his golden eyes flashing as he reached for me.

His warm hands grabbed onto me, jarring me out of my reverie. "Aileana," he barked my name. "What in Kydona's name is going on?"

147

Shaking my head, blood drained from my face as I stared at my trembling hands. "I-I don't know, but we need to go. The Red Shadow is coming."

And if he catches me, everything I've done to escape will be for naught.

To his credit, Xander took one look at my face and didn't question me. "Okay. Let's go."

Lacing our fingers together, Xander pulled me through the forest.

I let him, my mind too occupied with thoughts of the spirit we had just seen to do anything more than lift my feet. We stumbled over fallen logs and under branches, constantly pushing ourselves forward. Seconds ticked by into minutes, and still, we pressed on.

My lungs burned from the constant strain on my body, but we continued to run. When we came to a small stream, I dropped to my knees without a second thought and cupped my hands. The water streamed through my fingers, most landing on my chin and clothes, but I didn't have the energy to care.

Having quenched my thirst, I turned to Xander. He, too, was crouched by the stream, but he made drinking from his hands look easy. I hated that.

Clearing my throat, I wiped my hands awkwardly on my cloak. "How will Jo and Daegal know where we've gone?"

Xander shook his head. "They'll be fine. Daegal will See that we've left. We have a backup plan."

He fell silent. I stared at him, waiting expectantly. After a minute, I cleared my throat. "Do you care to fill me in on this mysterious plan?"

He jolted. "Oh. Yes. If we get split up, we are to find shelter and wait for the next two days."

"Two days," I repeated.

Alone. With Xander. That sounded like torture.

"Yes," he nodded, oblivious to my discomfort. "That should be enough for them to find us. I know of a safe place nearby where we can stay." He sounded so sure of himself that I just nodded.

Xander pushed himself to his feet, and I followed suit. My body was already aching, and I was not looking forward to running through the forest again.

Holding out his hand, Xander looked at me. "Are you ready to keep going?"

Since the only options seemed to be to run for my life or let the Red Shadow capture me, I knew I didn't have any choice. I swallowed, putting my hand back in his.

Forcing my voice to remain steady, I said, "As ready as I'll ever be."

We began to run once more.

Xander never let go of my hand.

WE RAN for three more hours. The forest was never-ending. Everything around us looked the same. Dark trees, shadows, and leaves surrounded us. Xander seemed to have an innate ability to see where we were going despite the late hour.

In the back of my mind, I wondered how far he had traveled in his life that he considered this length of travel time "nearby."

I had long since given up trying to remember where we were. Like before, Xander seemed to know exactly what direction we were going in. He led us with ease, his every stride filled with confidence. For once, I wasn't upset by his bossiness.

The night fell, the sun slipped below the horizon, and we continued forward.

Myhhena's words echoed in my mind, a backdrop to the symphony of our pounding feet and my hammering heart. Even the forest animals seemed to still as we hurried past.

Run.

Run.

Run.

By the time the moon was high in the sky, it was becoming more and more challenging to keep moving. My limbs were dragging, and my muscles were burning.

"Hold on, Aileana," Xander squeezed my hand. "The cavern is not far from here."

That's what he said three hours ago. I was so tired that I settled on making a huffing sound as I lifted my foot over a fallen log. Somewhere along the way, the forest had become even more wild and untamed. Trees were closer together, the bushes wilder, and vines hung from every available surface.

"We can spend the night in the cavern. It's secluded enough to keep us safe. Just keep moving."

"So bossy," I whispered, my voice hoarse.

He huffed a laugh. "What, no more threats about how much you'd love to stab me?"

I shook my head, keeping my gaze trained on the shadowy forest. "Too tired."

Xander slowed, his mouth pinched. "Are you okay?"

I mumbled a response. I didn't have the energy for anything else. Right now, all my strength was aimed at keeping me upright. I knew if I stopped, I wouldn't be able to get back up.

Tugging my hand, Xander brought us to a stop. He took one look at my face, and before I could decide whether I was going to take another step or simply collapse to the ground, a pair of muscular arms grabbed at me. Xander slipped one arm under my knees, the other around my back, before pressing me against his chest and walking again.

"You don't have to carry me," I protested weakly while nuzzling my face against his warmth. My heavy skirts and petticoats dangled from his grip, covering us in swaths of fabric as he picked his way through the woods. My body apparently didn't care that Xander hated me. He was a source of heat, and right now, I needed that. My voice was quiet as I said, "I can walk."

He huffed, tightening his grip. "And let you grab a knife and stab me because you're tired and angry? No, thank you, Sunshine. I'd rather keep you where I can see you."

Pressing my lips together, I rested my head against his chest. "I can still stab you from here," I whispered.

He chuckled, the sound rumbling through both of us. "I'm sure you can, but I would beg you to consider holding off on your violent tendencies until we reach the cavern. At least then, we might have a chance at finding some rest tonight."

Humming, I nodded. "Fine. Since you're being such a gentleman, I suppose I can keep my blades to myself for now."

"I thank you."

We fell into a companionable silence. I listened to Xander's heart beating in his chest, and he carried me effortlessly through the forest.

My eyes drifted shut as the heat emanating from this infuriating male warmed me through and through. I forgot to be upset by his closeness. It slipped my mind to be incensed by how he assumed I would hurt him.

Being close to Xander was causing my entire body to do things against my will.

I lost track of time as the night wore on, my hands clutching his tunic. Eventually, he stopped moving.

He groaned, the sound quiet before something hard brushed up against my back. Seconds later, a chill ran down my front as Xander stepped away. Instantly, I mourned the warmth.

"Rest," he whispered. Then, I felt his hands tucking my cloak tightly around me. It was surprisingly gentle. I opened my mouth, but no words came out. Xander continued, "When the sun rises, we will talk about... everything."

Everything.

Who I was. What that meant. The Red Shadow.

With that ominous declaration swirling around in my mind, I rested my head on the rocky ground.

"Goodnight, Xander," I murmured.

A long moment passed, and an owl hooted in the distance. I thought he hadn't heard me when a whisper came from nearby, "Night, Aileana."

At the sound of my rightful name on his lips, I shut my eyes.

Soon, I fell into a fitful sleep.

The Picture of Hilarity

"What have I told you about drawing, Aileana?"

My tutor's voice was reproachful as I glanced at him, the tiny piece of charcoal momentarily forgotten in my fingers. Black dust coated my pale skin, providing ample evidence of my crime.

I dropped the charcoal like it was on fire, hiding my black hands in my skirts. The gown's fabric was ratty and torn, the hem reaching no further than my ankles. I wondered if the king would find it within him to give me a new gown. This one was tight and made it hard to breathe.

Sighing, I closed my eyes and recited the reproof I knew was coming. "His Illustrious Majesty High King Edgar gives me charcoal to learn my letters so that I can be a good wife to Prince Remington when the time comes."

"And?"

"And it is my duty to be able to read and write. Charcoal is not to be used for frivolous activities like sketching."

Orvyn ran his hand down his face, grimacing. He shook his head. "You are correct, Aileana. Now, give it to me."

Frowning, I placed the charcoal in his waiting palm. I watched, eyes wide, as he slid it into his pocket.

"Do you... do you have to tell the king when he comes to see me?" My voice cracked on the last word as I instinctively cringed at the thought of seeing the king again.

I despised the way my voice sounded weak and wobbly. I was ten, for Kydona's sake. This was beneath me. I should have been able to control my emotions by now.

It had been three weeks and five days since the last time the King visited me in my tower. That meant he was due for a visit two days from now.

Only two days.

Orvyn winced, and I didn't need any words. He and I knew what would happen when the king learned I had disobeyed him. My tutor's eyes were lined with pity as he studied me. "You know I do."

My eyes filled with tears, but I shut my lips and nodded. There was no use crying over what was to come. After all, I couldn't do anything to change it.

I was the king's pet, and I belonged to him.

"AILEANA, WAKE UP."

Warm hands shook my shoulders as pain ripped through my muscles. Every part of my body was sore, including those I did not know existed.

Wincing, I rubbed my eyes. It was still dark, but the sun was beginning to peek through the trees just outside the cavern.

"What's going on?" I asked, my voice raspy.

Xander was sitting across from me, his legs outstretched before him. He was eyeing me; his head tilted to the side as though I was a puzzle he was trying to figure out. "You were crying out in your sleep."

I drew in a shaky breath as remnants of my dream returned. "It was a painful memory." I shrugged. He did not need to know that nightmares plagued me more often than not. I added as an afterthought, "Thank you for waking me."

"Of course." He nodded, a thoughtful look in his eyes. "Do you want to talk about it?"

"Not really." I wasn't ready to give my nightmares a voice. Not yet. Maybe not ever. His mouth twitched downwards, and I hurried to add. "It's not you. I just..." Coughing, I shuffled on my feet. "Is there somewhere I could take care of my needs? Alone?"

Understanding filled his eyes moments before the blood rushed to his cheeks. "Oh yes, of course. There is a clearing just beyond the grove of trees near the river. I'll take you."

We walked silently, and Xander was the perfect gentleman while I emptied my bladder. He kept his back to me, only turning once I said, "Thank you, I'm done."

Having relieved myself, I bent before a river running through the clearing. Reaching in, I began to wash my fingers in the running water when footsteps came from behind me.

Moments later, Xander came and knelt next to me. He ran the water through his fingers, splashing it on his face. "Are you feeling better?"

I nodded, relishing how the cool water felt as it ran through my fingers. "Yes, thank you."

"Good."

A shuffling sound came from behind me, and when I turned around, I saw Xander unclasping his cloak. I watched with narrowed eyes as he took it off with a flourish, spreading it on the grassy floor.

"Come on," he said, gesturing to the cloak. "Take a seat."

I glared at him, shaking my head. "I'm not sure I trust you."

"Of course, you don't. After all, I have violent tendencies." He paused, tapping his chin before turning his golden eyes to me. "Oh, wait. That's not me. *You're* the one who stabbed *me.*"

"You deserved it."

He huffed, running his hand through his hair. "Gods." Plopping down on the cloak, Xander kept my gaze. "Everything has to be a fight with you, doesn't it? This isn't a trap, Aileana. I just don't want to sit on the damp grass. Join me, or don't. It's up to you."

After that, he looked away. Sighing, I studied him. He looked so comfortable, and I was still so worn out from the day before...

"Fine," I said. "I'll try to be pleasant company, just for you."

He smiled, and something fluttered within me. Placing my shoes carefully beside the fabric, I unclasped my cloak before removing my daggers and putting them in a small pile beside me.

Xander glanced at them, smirking as I kept them within reach. He asked, "Do you think you'll be needing those?"

"You can never be too prepared," I replied sweetly as I spread out my stocking-clad feet. The early morning sun held traces of warmth despite the season, and the sky was clear. I hoped it would be a warm day.

A few moments passed in silence before Xander moved. Out of the corner of my eye, I watched as he pulled something red out of his pocket. His hands engulfed the spherical object, and I leaned in, curiosity overtaking my desire to keep some distance between us.

Xander turned, winking as he threw the mysterious object at me. "Catch."

It sailed through the air, and my hands jutted out. Gasping, I grabbed the ball right before it landed in the rushing water. It was heavy, and it smelled like a strong syrup. The crimson skin was hard, but it gave as I pressed my thumb into it.

"What is this?" I sniffed the mysterious fruit, and the syrupy smell became even more vital. I had never smelled anything like this, and it was enticing.

Xander reached into his pocket, withdrawing another sphere with a flourish. It looked comically small in his hand.

"They're rain berries," he said, biting into the fruit. He chewed and swallowed. "They bloom at night in this area. I foraged them last night while you were sleeping."

I turned my rain berry over in my hand as I watched him warily. The sickly sweet smell intensified as crimson liquid dribbled down his chin. Xander's tongue shot out, catching a tiny black seed threatening to escape. After devouring his rain berry in four bites, Xander gestured to me.

His golden eyes twinkled in the early morning light as he said, "Are you just going to watch me eat, Sunshine, or are you going to try it?"

Blood rushed to my face as I realized I had been staring at him. Fighting the urge to hide my face in my hands, I brought the fruit to my mouth.

Here goes nothing.

Watching Xander carefully, I opened my mouth and took a bite of the rain berry. Instantly, notes of sweetness exploded in my mouth. The pulp dripped down my throat, the sweet syrup carrying deep notes of warm spices as the flesh of the fruit nourished me.

"Oh, my goddess," I exclaimed after I devoured the entire berry. "I've never tasted anything so amazing."

Xander chuckled, reaching into the river with cupped hands. "I'm glad it made you happy."

Bringing some water to his lips, Xander quenched his thirst before splashing the water over his face. He repeated the motion three times, soaking his entire face and hair. I couldn't help but notice how the water droplets ran down his pale skin.

Xander's golden eyes gleamed in the morning sun as he shook his head like a dog, sending water flying. The water droplets sprayed me, and I shrieked as they landed on me. He smirked. "What's wrong, Sunshine? Don't you like the water?"

I hummed a response, but I wasn't really paying attention. He had given me an idea. My mouth tilted up, and I nibbled on my bottom lip. Before I could question whether or not this was a wise course of action, I leaned over. My hands landed on Xander's shoulders, and I pushed with all my might.

A loud shout escaped him as he tumbled headfirst into the water. Within moments, his entire body disappeared underwater. I held my breath, but he quickly bobbed back up.

"What. The. Hell?" he growled.

I giggled. *Giggled.* I couldn't help it. Xander's face contorted, his nostrils flaring as he stood in the river, water sluicing off him. His clothes were molded to his body, his tunic practically see-through as he caught my gaze.

And then the giggles dried up.

It was as though all the air was sucked out of my body as we stared at each other. I sucked in a deep breath and told myself to look away. But... I couldn't. Xander's gaze was completely and utterly captivating. Even if I had wanted to, at that moment, it felt like we were the only two people in the entire world.

"Aileana," he snarled. "Why did you do that?"

"What's wrong, Xander?" Tilting my head, I repeated his words from earlier. "Don't you like the water?"

He raised a brow, and I swallowed. A deep sound rumbled out of him as he took a step, then two towards me.

Gods.

I felt warmth rushing through me as I stared at Xander. My mouth dried as he walked out of the river. Coming out of the water, with his silver-white hair slicked back from his face, Xander looked especially... not terrible.

He smirked, his golden eyes blazing as he cocked his head. "Oh, it's like that, is it Sunshine?"

I considered that I might have misjudged the situation when Xander's lips tilted up into what I could only describe as a wolfish smile.

He clambered out of the water as a low growl escaped his lips. He stalked towards me. Shoving myself to my feet, I ran away from the river, squealing. Squealing!

Of all the new experiences I'd had over the past week, this was the oddest. I had never squealed before in my entire life, and here I was, having done so twice in the last ten minutes.

Who was this male that he made me do things like squeal?

I was no more than ten feet from the water's edge when warm, wet hands grabbed me from behind.

"Do you think you're funny, Aileana?"

A laugh escaped me as my feet were suddenly lifted off the ground.

"I think I am the picture of hilarity," I said with forced primness as I struggled against his grip. His hands were holding surprisingly firm for someone who had recently become well-acquainted with the water.

"Do you now?" he asked, a chuckle in his voice as he held me in place. "And here I was thinking, you didn't even know how to smile."

"I can smile, you big oaf," I replied, squirming.

He muttered something under his breath that sounded suspiciously like, "You could've fooled me." I wasn't entirely certain, because I was busy hitting him as he threw me over his shoulder like a sack of potatoes.

Slamming my clenched fists into his back, I ordered, "Put me down!"

He shook his head. "Now, who's being bossy?"

ELAYNA R. GALLEA

"Ugh. You're insufferable," I huffed, deciding to conserve my strength for a fight I could win. "You're getting me all wet!"

He chuckled darkly, and a bolt of worry shot through me. I was starting to believe I had *misjudged the situation when he growled, "Oh, Sunshine, you're going to be* wet in a moment."

I narrowed my eyes, but before I could reply, Xander's grip suddenly disappeared from around my waist.

"No!" I shouted, my eyes widening as the river grew nearer. I gasped, blood draining from my face, and I reached desperately for something to hold on to. Anything.

My fingers clutched at empty air until, finally, I felt wet fabric between my fingers.

Xander cursed as the water splashed all around us.

It was cold. So cold.

For a moment, my mind emptied as the frigid temperature of the water became my only thought. My teeth chattered as the frigid liquid seeped through my gown and petticoats, destroying their warmth in moments.

I shivered as my stockings met the sandy bottom of the river. It was gritty, and I struggled to find purchase. I took one step forward, then two, as my arms flailed.

Even though I was tall by female standards, I was much shorter than Xander. While he had been standing in the river without any problems, the water seemed much more profound now that I was in it.

The cold water lapped at my breasts. It felt like a thousand tiny needles were being pushed into my skin all at once. I drew my arms around myself as wet hair dripped down my face.

Behind me, I could hear Xander moving towards the water's edge. Soon, he was standing on the riverbank, his hands on his hips.

"Come on, Aileana," he huffed. Water dripped down his sodden tunic and trousers as he scowled at me. Fierceness and anger radiated off him in waves as he pointed at the grass. "Get. Out."

I glared at him as I picked my way through the water. "I'm moving as fast as I can," I snapped. "Be patient."

The bank was within reach when, all of a sudden, the sandy bottom was no longer there. One step, sand lay beneath my feet. The next, I wasn't standing at all. My legs buckled as my feet hit a smooth, wet stone. I gasped as suddenly I went flying back.

My eyes widened as the clear blue sky filled my vision. There wasn't a single cloud in the sky.

And then it was gone.

The river pulled me down so fast that I barely had the time to inhale before water filled my vision. I popped up and sucked in a deep breath, but it wasn't enough. I could feel the water's pull on my sodden clothing as it yanked me downstream.

My heart pounded in my chest, my lungs constricting, as the water seemed to yank me downstream. My arms waved in the air as I struggled for purchase.

In the back of my mind, I knew what this was.

A current. Swift, hidden, and deadly.

The water pulled me along so quickly that I barely had the time to blink, let alone cry out for help. Every single layer of my soaked garments felt like a massive weight trying to drag me to the bottom of the river. My head bobbed underwater, the murky liquid filling my vision.

I came up for air sputtering. "Help!" I screamed at the top of my lungs.

But Xander was already out of sight. Trees and rocks surrounded me as the water continued to drag me towards a watery grave.

Gasping, I tried to take in as much air as possible before the river pulled me back under. With each passing second, it was becoming more difficult. The water's deadly pull was getting stronger.

And stronger.

I was growing weaker and weaker.

Think, I ordered myself. *Think of something to do. Anything.*

But I couldn't think. Not now. I had no idea what to do. My ill-contrived prank would be, quite literally, the death of me.

"Xander!" I screamed as I came back up for air another time. "Help!"

Then I saw him. He ran along the riverbank, his eyes wide as the water sucked me under again.

When I came back up for air, he was closer.

But not close enough.

I cried out, "I can't swim!"

I saw the moment my words landed because Xander's already white face paled.

"Grab a branch!" he shouted as he dove back into the river.

He began swimming, his arms moving powerfully as he approached me. But the waters kept pulling, and my body was weakening.

Soon, it became a struggle to find the will to breathe when I came up for air. The length between breaths seemed to stretch as my lungs burned with the agony of a thousand fires.

Xander kept swimming, but it never seemed like enough.

There was a very real chance I would not make it out of this river in one piece. Hysterical laughter bubbled up inside of me at the thought.

Imagine that. I left the king's clutches, refusing to be his pet any longer, only to drown in a river.

Fitting.

It *would* be a fitting way to go. The girl who was locked in a tower her whole life was killed by something as innocuous as water.

I wonder if it will be a quick death?

A frisson of fear ran through me at the thought. The water sucked me underneath once more.

And I knew this was the end.

I couldn't survive much longer. Already, my body was drained. My limbs felt heavy. So heavy.

I could hear Xander yelling, but the water muffled his words. Exhaustion plagued me as my body became weaker by the moment.

From the conversations I'd overheard, I knew that most children in Ithenmyr received swimming lessons when they were young. Most people bathed in creeks, for Kydona's sake. But not me. Tepid bath water had been lugged up the many steps of my tower twice a week by the king's servants.

Swimming was one of the many things I never learned. Why would I need to swim when I only existed to be bred?

The irony of the entire situation was laughable. Or it would have been if my eyes weren't filling with black spots as my skirts finally succeeded in their mission to drag me to the silty bottom of the river. My lungs burned as every single muscle within my body protested the water weighing me down. I struggled against the pull of my garments to no avail.

This was it.

At least I will die free.

With that final thought, my eyes fluttered closed as I gave in to the cry of my lungs for air. My limbs were heavy, my body no longer belonging to me as I opened my mouth.

Cold water rushed into my lungs, a momentary relief to the burning desire for air. The river claimed me. Blackness drew me downwards.

And I was finally going to be at peace.

The Feeling was Mutual

"Wake up, dammit," a gruff voice said.

A pair of warm hands pushed on my chest as my entire body protested the rough treatment. The voice kept going, muttering to themselves as they continued the assault on my rib cage, "I won't lose my gods-damned mate to some fluke drowning accident. Not after everything else I've been through."

My lungs burned, and every single part of my body felt heavier than normal. I tried to open my eyes, but it was as though they were glued shut. My tongue felt thick and was stuck to the roof of my mouth.

Everything was dark and heavy and *not right*.

"Come on, Aileana. Wake up," they commanded. Panic was beginning to edge into their tone, but for the life of me, I couldn't figure out who the voice belonged to. "Yell at me. For the goddess' sake, I'd even be okay with you stabbing me right about now."

Another push against my chest, and this time, something shifted within me. I coughed as my lungs seized. A burst of pain was followed by sudden relief as water and goddess knew what else rushed out of me.

Turning my head, I gasped as precious air rushed back into my body. My lungs breathed in deeply as my heart began to beat once more.

A gruff exhale came from above me, and I realized I knew that voice. It was Xander. He groaned, "Thank Kydona, you're awake."

This time, my eyes obeyed my commands to open. I blinked rapidly at the onslaught of light. Xander's face was hovering above mine, his mouth pinched in a straight line as he stared at me.

"Hi," I said dumbly. I reached out a hand, touching damp grass and twigs. The water rushed nearby, and I instinctively tried to roll away from the river. My eyes searched Xander's as I tried to comprehend what had happened. I wasn't dead, nor was I sinking into a watery grave.

He had saved me. Why? I thought he hated me.

"Aileana..." Xander's voice trailed off as he seemed to lose his train of thought.

I stared at him, questions swirling in my mind.

Why did he do it? Save someone he hated? He could have been rid of me, and no one would have blamed him. No one other than Daegal and Jo even knew I existed.

But he did it. He saved me. And that meant something. Something I didn't want to deal with. Not right now. Maybe not ever.

So instead, being the very mature elf I clearly was, I coughed and looked up at Xander, who was crouched beside me. "I suppose I should thank you for saving my life after you tried to kill me."

Xander's face hardened before my eyes. His jaw tightened, and a look of anger flashed across his eyes. He snapped, "I wasn't trying to kill you. How was I supposed to know you couldn't swim?"

"I—"

He held up a hand, his jaw clenched as he glared at me. "Nope, not yet. You don't get to speak yet."

"You can't tell me what to do!" I yelled, struggling to push myself up on my elbows. Unfortunately, at that exact moment, my body decided to give out. I collapsed to the ground as Xander loomed above me. Even crouched on the ground, his size was impressive.

"Aileana," he hissed. "I'm *not* ready to talk about this. I'm soaked and shivering. We are unprotected in the woods, and everything we have is back in the clearing. Not only that, but I know that no matter how poorly I'm feeling, you are in a worse state. So here's what we're going to do."

I crossed my arms, glaring at him. Being serious while lying on the ground in a soaked dress was difficult, but I thought I pulled it off nicely as I said, "You're being bossy again."

"Too bad," he growled. "You brought this on yourself."

"How so?" I knew I was pushing Xander's buttons, but for some reason, I couldn't stop myself. This wasn't me. I was Aileana, the king's pet. I listened and did what I was told. Pushing back wasn't something I did. But with him... arguments just slipped out of me.

Xander huffed. His face was nearly as red as a rain berry as he clenched his fists at his side. Even on his knees, he looked ominous. "This morning, I woke up with every intention of being kind. I told myself, 'Xander, maybe you misjudged this female. Perhaps she has a reason for being so rude. Give her a chance.'"

"You—" I started, but Xander spoke right over me, "Nope. That was this morning. I was being kind, and you decided to repay my kindness by shoving me into the river. So, that plan is out the window. Now you're going to listen."

I stared at him, my eyes wide as my nostrils flared. His absolute *gall* shocked me. I exclaimed, "Gods! You are so bossy! I hate it when you act like this. Why won't you let me speak?"

I went to push myself to my feet, but by the time I was merely sitting, Xander had crossed his arms and glared at me.

"We're going to go back to the clearing, get our things, and head back to the cavern," he said. "Once we're there, you'll tell me *exactly* who you are. You will tell me about the memory that had you in tears this morning. You will answer my questions. No more half-truths, evasive answers, or lies. I want the *entire story*."

"Why would I do that?" I shook my head. "You can't force me to talk to you."

He shoved himself to his feet, huffing. "Goddess. I cannot *stand* this female."

"The feeling is mutual, you big oaf."

A sound of entirely male exasperation escaped Xander's lips as he ran his hands through his damp hair, pushing it back from his head. He turned back to me, glaring as he shook his finger. "If you don't tell me the truth, you're going to force me to re-evaluate the terms of our deal."

I gasped, pitching backward. "You wouldn't dare."

"Just try me, *Aileana*," he snarled, wielding my name like a sword. "We have a day before Daegal and Jo should be meeting us. That's plenty of time for you to be honest with me. If you are capable of such a thing."

"Or what?"

"I'm telling you, you do not want to push me right now."

Gathering my strength, I pushed myself to my feet. I wobbled for a moment before grabbing onto a nearby tree. The bark was rough in my hands, a welcome distraction from the anger flooding my body.

"Fine," I hissed. "But I'm only going to tell you because I want to, not because you're forcing me."

He glared at me, narrowing his eyes. "Keep lying to yourself if it makes you feel better. Now, let's go."

THE WALK back to the clearing was a lesson in tension.

Xander led the way as I stumbled along behind him, with my drenched skirts clenched in my fists. Neither of us spoke, and fire seemed to flash in his eyes every time he glanced back at me.

He was angry, that was clear.

Good. I was angry, too.

And exhausted.

And confused.

But at the moment, the anger I felt coursing through me was shoving all my other emotions to the wayside. How dare he *demand* I speak? Did he think he could force me to tell him my story?

Red spots filled my vision. I had already escaped from one cage. I wouldn't sit back and let him force me into another one. No one would ever bind me again. I wouldn't let them.

The insufferable male was muttering to himself as we walked. I could practically taste the anger coming off him in waves. His disdain for me was evident.

Well, the feeling was mutual. This morning's events had solidified one thing for me: Xander and I were *not* good together. Everything seemed to get out of hand whenever we were left alone.

With every step, I dove deeper into the pit of fury roiling through my veins. I didn't want to tell him anything. The problem was, I also knew that if he left me here, I would be lost entirely. I had no idea where we were.

The thought of being left alone in the woods while the Red Shadow was coming after me was enough to make me want to stab something. Unfortunately for me, my knives were back with my cloak.

I settled for stomping loudly as I huffed along behind Xander. If he was going to make me tell him everything, I would do it on my own time and only once I was ready.

A plan began to form in my mind, and I smirked.

I had overheard enough servants talk to know what made a male uncomfortable, even if it wasn't something I was especially familiar with. Never one to back out of a situation just because it was new, I knew exactly what I would do.

Xander would be *very* uncomfortable when I was done with him.

And that was precisely how I wanted him.

"GET YOUR STUFF, AILEANA," Xander ordered.

Without waiting for a response, he knelt. In one swift movement, he grabbed his cloak and threw it over his shoulders before stalking off through the woods.

I pointedly ignored the river, the waters deceptively calm as I picked up my cloak and daggers. A breath of relief slipped out of me as I slid the daggers into their rightful places.

Armed once more, I slipped on my shoes before glaring at Xander's retreating form. I wished with every fiber of my being that I could summon those green ribbons from earlier. Where was Myhhena when I needed her?

Alas, my simmering anger left me with nothing but bruised feet and a half-baked plan that would hopefully irritate my fake husband.

A large part of me wanted to sit down on a stump and refuse to move, but I knew what would happen. Xander would just come and pick me up.

He'd probably throw me over his shoulder like a sack of grain and carry me to the cavern like a prehistoric being. His grip would probably be hard. He'd growl. My body tingled, and my stomach twisted as I thought about his warm hands on me. Touching me. Gripping me...

Stop it, I ordered myself. *Focus. The last thing you want is for him to touch you again.*

The problem—and it was a problem—was that when Xander's too-warm hands were on my skin, my brain seemed to lose the ability to think rationally. And that was the last thing I needed right now.

Gathering my soaked skirts in my hands, I stomped after Xander. By the time the cavern was in sight, my hands were turning blue from the cold water seeping into my skin. That only ignited my anger further as I huffed my way inside the cavern.

Xander was crouched over a small fire about ten feet into the cavern, his back to me. "I hope you're ready to talk," he grumbled as he tended to the fire.

In response, I took off my cloak. It fell to the cavern floor in a heap as I lifted my hands to my wet stays and pulled one of the laces, then another. The layers around my waist loosened as I worked as quickly as possible. The sodden fabric stuck to my body, and I plucked it away from my skin as I shimmied out of it.

A few minutes later, a rustling of fabric hit the ground as a cool breeze rushed down my spine. I shivered but didn't stop to think as I stepped out of the fabric now pooling at my feet.

"I'm ready to talk," I said in a low voice as I picked up long locks of sunset-red hair and arranged them over my front.

After all, I was at least *attempting* to preserve what little modesty I had remaining.

"Good, then—" Xander pushed himself to his feet and turned around, his words dropping off as he stared at me.

His golden eyes flashed, and I could have sworn I saw a burst of green go across his eyes before they returned to their regular shade. He clenched his jaw, a vein ticking in his neck as he stared at me.

Xander drew closer to me until there was nothing but a few inches between my face and his own. I sucked in a deep breath as I held his gaze. Heat emanated from him in waves, and I had to fight to remain still.

"Aileana," he whispered hoarsely as he lowered his lips. They hovered just above mine, and I stared at him. His nostrils flared as his eyes darkened to a burnished gold. His breathing was ragged as he asked, "Why are your clothes on the ground?"

Holding his gaze, I blinked my eyelashes slowly. His fists were clenched at his sides as he waited for a response. I swallowed, taking my time. Eventually, I replied, "I took them off."

His jaw ticked even further. "I can see that. *Why* are you standing before me in nothing but a..." he coughed, his face reddening, "very white, very wet shift?"

I licked my lips, and I could have sworn he groaned.

"My clothes are still soaked from when you tried to kill me. If I keep them on, I risk getting sick." I continued to stare at him, raising a brow. "Do you have a problem with that? I'd rather not catch a cold, wouldn't you agree?"

Xander sighed, the sound somehow managing to be both long-suffering and entirely *male* at the same time. He ground his jaw, speaking through clenched teeth, "This is *not* what I meant, and you know it."

I gasped and threw my hand to my chest. My palm landed on Nonna's necklace, which I clutched as I stepped forward. We were so close that I could smell the rain berry on Xander's breath.

"Did I know it?" I whispered. Tilting my head, I fluttered my lashes. "I was just obeying your orders, *husband*. Isn't that what a good Ithenmyrian female does?"

The air seemed to crackle between us as we stared at each other for a very long moment. My heart raced as my skin felt too tight for my frame.

"You and I both know you aren't a *good* Ithenmyrian female," he murmured as he lifted a hand.

I watched in horrified fascination as he picked up a lock of damp red hair and rubbed it between his fingers. "No," he said, more to himself than anything else. "You are definitely not a good female."

"Maybe I am trying to become one," I said softly. I couldn't remove my eyes from his hands. The way he touched me was so at odds with the venom in his voice. It was as though he was at war with himself.

He tilted his head, still holding my hair, as he hissed, "Liar."

I sucked in a deep breath as my nostrils flared. "That's twice now you've called me a liar, Xander."

"If the shoe fits, wear it," he muttered. "I find it hard to believe that someone who carries multiple knives with her and doesn't hesitate to threaten stabbing someone is 'trying' to be good."

"Goddess, you are so horrible," I huffed as I moved back. A tug on my hair reminded me he was still holding onto me, and I stopped moving. "Why do you insist on saying things like that?"

"Why do you insist on being so aggravating?"

"Let go of my hair," I ordered.

Instantly, he dropped it like it was on fire. A look of shock passed over his face as though he suddenly remembered who I was. Who he was. What he was doing.

Xander stumbled backward, nearly falling over his tiny fire, before collapsing to the ground with a sigh. He dropped my gaze as he lowered his face into his hands and took a series of long breaths.

I stood there, unmoving, as I waited for him. The dripping of my wet hair on the stone floor was the only sound in the cavern for a very long moment.

Eventually, Xander looked back up.

His gaze was hard once more, his face steely as he gestured to a large rock across the fire. "Sit. I think it's time we talked."

A Multitude of Explanations

~~~

I remained standing.

If there was one thing I hated more than anything else, it was obeying orders. Especially *his* orders.

"Aileana," he ground out through clenched teeth. "Sit."

Who was Xander to command me around as though I belonged to him? I belonged to no one but myself. The king had kept me on a leash for twenty-three years, and I would be damned if I let someone else do the same thing to me.

"I'd rather stand," I replied.

Xander's silver-white brows rose as he studied me for a moment. His gaze was like a brand as it crawled over me, starting at my head and then dropping lower until it reached the hem of the shift resting above my knees. A steady dripping sound filled the cavern as small beads of water escaped the fabric and met the stone floor.

His voice rasped as he replied, "Fine. Suit yourself."

"I will," I replied. Silently, I congratulated myself on sounding prim and proper despite my inner turmoil.

"Good." Xander reached behind him and grabbed a flask. He lifted it to his lips, his eyes never leaving mine as he moved.

We were playing a dangerous game, one that I wasn't sure I knew the rules to. But it felt good to play. To tease. To watch him squirm.

And I really, really didn't want to lose.

He tilted back the flask, and I watched as his throat bobbed. I kept my eyes on him as he pulled it from his mouth, wiping a stray drop with the back of his hand. Holding his gaze, I bent, straightening my soaked dress and petticoats so they would have the chance to dry. The rustling of fabric was the only sound in the cavern as the air grew impossibly thick between us. I adjusted the material until it was perfectly flat against the stone floor.

When I straightened, Xander held out the brown flask. He asked, "Water?"

Suddenly, I realized a dryness in my throat. "Yes, please."

I kept my eyes on him as I stepped around the fire, extending my hand. My fingers were inches from the flask when Xander yanked it back at the last minute.

"Hey!" I scowled

Xander tsked. "Now, now, Sunshine. How about you start talking?"

I glared at him, crossing my arms in front of my chest. The movement was less dignified than I'd hoped, considering I was practically naked, but I watched as his eyes flew to my chest.

Xander's jaw clenched as I asked, "You're going to make me work for water? And you say I'm mean."

He tilted his head. "How else am I going to get information out of you? You're shut up more tightly than a bulb at the beginning of the spring."

I scoffed. I had reasons for being so secretive. And he did not inspire confidence with his exasperating ways and persistent questions. Sucking on my lip, I tapped my foot on the ground. "I'll make you a deal."

"A deal," he echoed.

I nodded. "Yes. You give me some water, and I will answer every question you ask."

He raised a brow. "I sense a 'but' coming."

A small smile danced on my lips. He wasn't wrong.

"*But...*" I drew out the word, "In return, you will answer a question of mine."

His eyes flashed before a smirk settled on his face. "So now we're bargaining?"

"Yes," I said firmly. "You want something from me, and I want something from you. Based on my experience, we have all the necessary pieces for a bargain. What do you say?"

A beat passed before he nodded tersely and held out the flask. "You drive a hard bargain, Sunshine, but I accept."

The water was refreshing as it dripped down my throat. Once I had drunk my fill, I handed it back to Xander. Our fingers brushed, and for a moment, a shock rushed through my arm. I yanked back my hand, rubbing my fingers over the spot where we'd touched.

"Thank you," I said.

He nodded, leaning back and seeming at ease in the rocky cavern. "So, Sunshine. You're an elf."

"Is that your question?" I crossed my arms. "If so, I will be forced to question the fortitude of your education."

Shaking his head, Xander chuckled. "My education was perfectly adequate, thank you very much. Not that you asked, but I happened to have spent a fair amount of time in university before I stumbled across you in the forest."

I raised a brow. Something about that answer niggled at me. Universities... there weren't many in Ithenmyr that I knew of.

Of course, they only accepted males. Why would females need higher education?

"Aileana," Xander said. "I asked you a question."

"Sorry," I replied automatically. "My mind drifted. What did you ask?"

He tilted his head as he said, "My question is this: have you reached Maturity yet?"

I wrung my hands together as I debated how to answer.

Every elf Matured at a different time, although most did so around their twenty-fifth year. Prior to Maturing, elves were just as susceptible to things like illness and injury as humans. Still, once they Matured, they would live for centuries or even millennia, until they Faded.

Eventually, I decided on the truth. After all, I couldn't see the harm in it. Xander already knew I was an elf. I shook my head. "No, I've yet to Mature. I saw my twenty-third autumn this year."

He kept my gaze, nodding slowly. "Interesting."

"How about you?" I asked, straightening my shift as I shuffled on my feet. "How old are you?"

"Old enough," he said, his voice gruff.

I narrowed my eyes. "Old enough?" I mimicked his response. "That's your answer? Old enough?"

"Yes," he said gruffly. "I said I'd respond, not that I would give you a specific numerical value."

I huffed. "Ugh. You are incredibly frustrating."

He shrugged. "Even so. Next question. Why are you running from your fiancé?"

"That's... That's..." My mouth opened and closed as I stood there in front of him. For the first time since I stepped out of my dress, I felt... exposed. My lungs tightened as I fought to breathe. My heart raced in my chest as a roaring filled my ears. I pressed my nails into my palms and forced myself to remember it was over.

I was out. I had saved myself. And I could do it again if I needed to.

I was strong.

"Aileana?" Xander asked. "Why are you running?"

A thousand different answers flitted through my mind.

I didn't ask to be married. My fiancé is a psychopath. I don't like him. His father is a murderer. No one asked me. I want to be more than a breeder. I want someone to love me. He's the king's favorite, and I'm his pet. I hate him more than I hate you. He haunts my nightmares. Life with him would be worse than death.

I didn't say any of that.

Instead, I lowered myself to the ground, finally sitting in front of the small fire. I extended my hands, allowing the warmth of the flames to seep into my skin. Staring into the yellow and orange flames, I breathed in deeply.

A minute passed in silence. Eventually, I raised my gaze and met Xander's.

"No one ever asked me if I wanted to marry him. The king just *assumed* his pet would do whatever he wanted. So he told me I would marry Remington."

I hated that my voice wobbled on the last word and that my eyes grew blurry as I stared into the flames.

Sandalwood, his favorite scent, poured off the crimson-clad king in droves as he loomed above me. He twisted his hands in the air, a stream of red magic flooding out of him. He held out his palms, the magic forming a sphere in his hands.

I flinched. I'd seen what balls of magic like that could do to a person. No one ever survived.

"It is time," High King Edgar said in a firm voice.

"My king?" I asked.

Please, no. It can't be. Not yet. I'm not ready.

He stalked over to me, his brow raised. This close, the sandalwood made me want to throw up. "One week from today, when the sun rises, you will marry Remington. Do you understand me, pet?"

I swallowed, staring at the black stones scattered through my tower. Inside my chest, my heart raced.

I had known this day would come, and yet now that it was here...

I wasn't ready.

"Yes," I whispered. My voice was weak, but the answer seemed to appease the king. "I'll do it."

"Good."

He stomped out of my room, and I didn't move.

One week.

Wiping my hands under my eyes, I blinked rapidly. I would not cry. Not after I'd gotten away. He had given me one week, and I'd taken it. During that time, I had gathered the courage required to break the leash binding me to the king.

I'd escaped, survived the King's Forest and made it through Thyr. Not only that, but I had magic. I wasn't born Without, as I'd thought initially. I'd summoned Myhhena. Power resided within me.

I'd already made up my mind. I would *not* let the king take me back.

For a long moment, the only sound in the cavern was our breathing. The fire crackled, filling my nose with the scent of ash and burnt wood, as I forced the thoughts of the Crimson King out of my mind.

Xander cleared his throat. "Why does the king call you his pet?"

My head snapped up. I hadn't meant to let that slip. Clenching my fists, I snarled, "It's my turn to ask a question."

Xander's face hardened at the tone of my voice, but I couldn't quell the anger rising within me. It was easier to be angry. Easier to yell and snap and be mean. Easier to avoid the question that meant revealing my pain. "What is so important about the map you got from Jo?"

A long sigh escaped Xander as he stared at me. He ran his hand through his silver-white hair and stared at something on the wall behind me. "Can I trust you?"

I narrowed my eyes. "Is that another question? You haven't answered mine yet."

"Please, Aileana," he whispered. There was something in his tone that made me look up. His eyes were soft, imploring, as he studied me. "Just answer this last one. Can I trust you?"

The air in the cavern felt weighty, and I realized this question was important. Somehow, I knew the way I answered this would change the course of my life forever.

Sucking in a deep breath, I met his gaze. "Yes," I whispered. "You can trust me, Xander."

His shoulders seemed to loosen at that admission, his entire body becoming more slack. "Thank you," he breathed. "You can trust me, too."

And I realized it was true. There had been so many opportunities for Xander to hurt me, to betray me, to rid himself of me, but he hadn't taken any of them.

Even after I had stabbed him, he had stayed.

A shiver ran through me, and I remembered I was still practically naked.

The movement must have caught Xander's eye because he added another log to the fire. He stood, grabbed his cloak off the ground, and walked over to me.

"Here," he said gruffly as he laid it across my shoulders, "this will help keep you warm."

The fabric warmed me within moments, and without even realizing what I was doing, I drew the cloak around myself. It smelled like Xander. Like smoke and ash and trees.

So much better than the sandalwood that haunted my past.

He cleared his throat. "I'm going to tell you a story."

I raised a brow. "Is it interesting?"

"Is that any question to ask someone who offered to tell you a tale?" he snapped.

"No one has ever told me a story before, so I don't know how to answer your question."

He stared at me. His brows furrowed as his voice softened. "What do you mean, no one has ever told you a story? What about your parents when you were young?"

I stared at the wall behind him, sighing as I twisted the cloak around in my hands. "I meant what I said. No one has ever taken the time to tell me a story. I..." My voice trailed off as I shut my eyes, burying my head in my hands as I admitted, "I never knew my parents."

I waited for a response, but there was none.

Eventually, I opened my eyes to find Xander studying me. Then he stood and bowed. "In that case, Aileana, would you allow me the honor of being your very first storyteller?"

A small smile crept on my face. "I would like that very much," I whispered.

Once Upon a Time

Xander shifted, leaning back against the rocky wall of the cave. He placed his hands behind his head, his muscles bunching as he shut his eyes. Resting there against the wall, he looked almost... peaceful.

He drew in a deep breath, his muscular chest expanding as he did so. I dragged my eyes away from him, studying our surroundings instead.

The cavern was roomy, and now that it was daylight, I could see outside. The sun shone through the trees, illuminating the deep greens and browns of the surrounding forest. Small animals darted back and forth on tree branches, and birds flitted over top of the forested canopy.

Far-off mountain peaks were hidden in mist. From here, it seemed like the forest was never-ending. The air itself was fresher here. Deeper. More invigorating.

I felt... safe.

That thought perturbed me. Xander had just tried to kill me. I had no right to feel safe around him. And yet, I did. I'd never felt as safe in my entire life.

Before I could delve deeper into these thoughts, Xander cleared his throat.

"Once upon a time," he began in a gravelly voice, drawing my attention back to him, "in a faraway land, there was a young boy who lived with his family."

"Does this boy have a name?" I interjected.

His golden eyes flew open, narrowing as he glared at me. "It's rude to interrupt a storyteller while they're talking, Sunshine."

I sighed. "I'm sorry, I just—"

"Seeing as this is your first story, I'll accept the interruption this once."

He nodded, closing his eyes once more. "We'll call the young boy Elyx. He had a much longer name, but no one ever addressed him by it. Elyx and his entire family lived in a village filled with people just like them. They were different from the other people in their country, but they had kept to themselves for centuries. They didn't bother the others, and the rest of the population steered clear of them. An arrangement, you might say. One that benefited everyone."

He smirked. "Actually, it was rather like ours. For many years, the people lived in peace. They spoke many languages and traveled throughout the Four Kingdoms, enjoying all that the continent had to offer."

Xander paused, and I stared at him. I was utterly entranced. As a storyteller, Xander was... remarkable. It was as though I could *feel* his words.

"One day, when Elyx was eight years old, he was looking after his younger sister." Xander's eyes opened, and he gave me a smug look. "I bet you want to know her name, too?"

"Yes, please," I whispered.

He smiled as though pleased he had anticipated my request.

"Saena," he murmured. As he said the name, his face grew soft. Warm. "Her name was Saena."

"Saena," I echoed the name, tasting the syllables. *Say-nah*. "That is a beautiful name. I bet she was a beautiful little girl."

"She was stunning," Xander agreed. "From the moment she was born, people knew she would be different. Special. Saena was three years younger than her brother and was the apple of his eye. Saena knew he loved her, and she had her older brother wrapped around her little finger."

Xander sighed. "She was the opposite of him in every way. Their father died when they were young, and Elyx took it upon himself to help raise Saena. Their mother used to say they were as different as night and day. Where Elyx was light, his sister was dark.

"Saena was full of energy, but her brother felt the weight of their tiny world on his shoulders. He tried to care for the three of them, but it was hard. The world wasn't kind to youth. Elyx and his family felt that harshness more than most."

"That's a lot of pressure for such a small child," I whispered.

My heart was breaking for the boy. I knew better than most the pain of having your childhood ripped away. The agony of having years stolen that could never be returned. Elyx hadn't grown up in a tower, but he hadn't had an easy life by the sounds of things.

I ached for children whose futures were stolen from them. Youth who were forced, like me, to grow up before their time. Those who lost their lives before they could Mature. Grow. Age. Before they could reach their full potential.

Children were our future. They deserved to be cherished. Loved. Protected.

They should not have been forced to know how heavy the weight of the world could be.

I had drawn closer to Xander and was sitting a few feet away from him. Reaching down, I picked up a small rock off the ground, rolling it between my fingers.

This story felt important. Crucial, even. And I didn't want to miss a single second of it.

Xander's face was grim, his jaw hard as he rubbed the back of his neck. "It was a lot. But Elyx was happy to take on the weight of the world for his sister."

There was a heaviness to his words that settled deep within me. Something terrible was coming. I knew it.

Trepidation filled my voice as I asked, "What happened to them?"

"One scorching day in the summer, Elyx decided to take Saena to the nearby river that ran through the forest. She had been begging him to go swimming from the moment she woke up, and he saw no harm in it. The river was an hour's walk from their home, but their mother seemed especially preoccupied that morning. The village elders had been in an uproar the past few days, and something had them on edge.

"Elyx could sense the tension in the air and wanted to give his mother a break. Saena was quite a handful, you see? She was five and had so much energy. She never stopped moving from the moment she rose with the dawn until the second her eyelids fluttered shut. She always had stories to tell, chattering about this and that. So that morning, Elyx kissed his mother on the cheek, told her, 'I love you,' and walked out into the woods with his sister."

"Elyx sounds like a wonderful brother," I said, rubbing my hands over my arms.

Xander's lips tilted up as he looked at me. "That's kind of you to say. I think he was."

"What happened next?"

"That hot summer day, Elyx and Saena played and swam in the river for hours. Morning gave way to the afternoon, and they remained hidden in the forest. It wasn't until their stomachs grumbled that the two siblings decided it was time to return to their tiny village. After all, Elyx was certain his mother would be missing them. But as they drew nearer to the village, he realized something was wrong."

"No," I gasped, drawing my arms around myself. "What happened?"

Xander removed his hands from behind his head, shifting to hold them in his lap instead. He began twisting them together, his voice deep and tinged with sadness as he continued.

"The forest was silent. The birds weren't chirping, the deer weren't moving, and even the insects had stopped chatting. As they drew closer to home, Elyx knew in his gut that something was wrong. There was a strange smell in the air that set alarm bells off in the boy's mind. His stomach twisted upon itself as each step became more difficult. When the edge of the woods came into view, Elyx grabbed Saena by the waist. He lifted her into a nearby tree and told her to climb to the top.

"Saena stared at him. 'Why can't I come with you?' He told her they were playing a game but that he had to go back to their home quickly. He'd come back for her, he assured her. Mollified, she scampered up the tree as Elyx grabbed his small pocketknife from his tunic.

"Armed with his tiny weapon, he left his sister in the woods and continued towards their home. He told himself that he was just being silly, that there probably wasn't anything wrong, but he couldn't shake the feeling that something had happened. And then..."

Xander's voice trailed off. A somber silence filled the cavern as our breathing was the only sound.

"What?" I breathed. I was a foot from Xander, and I grabbed his hand without thinking. Something within me knew I needed to touch him, to hold him, for what was coming. "What happened next?"

He sucked in a deep breath, lifting his silver-lined eyes to mine. A singular tear ran down his face. This male, who was almost larger than life, was crying.

And I knew.

This was the worst kind of story. The kind that spoke of ruin and death and destruction.

"Elyx's world fell apart," he said. "Thick, black smoke covered the entire village."

"No." The word was a whisper, a breath, a plea, as it left my lips.

"The destruction had been relatively recent. Flames, red and orange, were still licking the sides of the buildings. The stench was terrible, and there wasn't a single person in sight. Elyx cried out, running to the cottage he shared with his mother and sister, only to find that it was completely destroyed. Everything was gone.

"As he stared at the remnants of his home, a chill ran over Elyx. He screamed for his mother until his voice was hoarse, but there was no response. Over and over again, Elyx ran from one home to the next. Each one was a shell of what it had been. When he got to the seventh home, he heard something. A cry for help."

"Goddess," I breathed. I lifted my hands to my cheeks, surprised to find they came away damp.

"Inside was an older male, a village elder. Josef was his name. He was covered in burns that were so bad that Elyx couldn't believe Josef was still alive. As soon as Elyx approached him, the elder cracked open his eyes. 'Come here, son,' he said. Elyx complied.

"The old male extended an injured hand, grabbing Elyx's tunic. 'You must listen carefully,' Josef rasped. 'Inside the chest, you will find a piece of a map.' The boy jolted, but the old male continued. 'You must reunite the five sisters. Together, they will lead you to our people's salvation.' Before Elyx could say anything, Josef took a long, shuddering breath, and his eyes fluttered shut."

Xander stopped talking as he rubbed his temples with his free hand. For a long moment, he did nothing but stare at our intertwined fingers.

I asked, "What happened to Josef?"

"He died," Xander replied, his voice gruff. "Everyone died. Elyx and Saena were the only survivors from their village."

The only survivors. The words rattled around in my mind. There was so much death and pain and suffering.

For what?

I thought of the crimson red that marked the House of Irriel. The blood that now stained the steps in Thyr. The marks I bore on my own back.

This was wrong. It was all wrong. And I wanted to run away and leave Ithenmyr, pretending that none of this had ever happened.

A small voice inside me that had begun to speak in Thyr was growing louder. More persistent.

Running away won't solve anything.

A heavy silence settled upon us as Xander's words echoed through my mind. I warred with myself as his story settled within me. We sat, connected by our joined hands, until a chill passed over me.

Wiping tears from my eyes, I looked at him. I tried to force some levity into my voice as I said, "That was a terrible story. Are all stories so sad?"

Xander stilled, contemplating my question. Eventually, he shook his head.

"No," he murmured, rubbing his thumb on the back of my hand. "Not all stories. But all the ones I seem to know. Maybe one day, I'll tell you a story of a certain redhead I know who enjoys going for leisurely swims in the river and stabbing people she just met."

"Sounds familiar," I said, raising a brow. "How does that one end?"

A half-smile danced on his lips as he glanced down at our joined hands. I stared at our intertwined fingers as that familiar feeling twisted within me. I let go, bringing my hands into my lap and wrapping his cloak around me.

Xander chuckled, elbowing me in the side. "I don't know, to be honest. We'll have to wait and see."

I hummed before another question struck me. "Did Elyx find the map?"

There was a long pause, and Xander studied me. He leaned against the rocky wall, his eyes shrewd as they swept over me.

"Xander?"

He sucked his lip through his teeth, rubbing the back of his neck, before sitting up straight. Xander reached into the collar of his tunic and pulled out a piece of string tied around his neck, revealing a small tube attached to one end.

Holding my breath, I watched Xander carefully remove two pieces of worn brown leather from the tube and lay them before me. Each was about the size of my hand, worn with time and filled with long, black markings. They were written in a language I didn't understand, but it was clearly a map of... something.

My brows furrowed as I ran a finger down the markings etched on the leather. Chewing on my bottom lip, I turned to Xander.

His jaw was clenched, his eyes hooded as he ran a finger over the pieces of the map.

Eventually, I found my voice. "The story... you... you're Elyx?"

Xander nodded, his eyes distant. His voice was softer than before as he said, "When I was born, they named me Elyxander, but since that day..." He shook his head. "I go by Xander now."

"I'm sorry," I said. Grabbing his hand again, I waited until his eyes were locked onto mine. I hoped he could see the sincerity of my words. "Xander, I am so sorry. About your village, your mother, your friends... no one deserves to go through that."

After that, words seemed to escape us both. We remained there, our hands intertwined until the fire burned low.

I glanced outside and saw that the sun was high in the sky. Hours had passed since we'd first come in from the river.

Xander's thumb rubbed circles on my hand as he stared into the distance. I wasn't even sure he knew he was doing it. I wasn't sure why I was *letting* him do it.

All I knew was that things were more complicated now than ever before. I didn't hate him. I realized that now. Hate was strong. Too strong for what I felt about this male.

I wasn't sure that I liked him. I knew he provoked strong feelings within me. He seemed to go out of his way to push me. Xander definitely was not *kind* to me. But I didn't hate him.

And maybe he didn't hate me either? I wasn't certain. All I knew was he needed someone right now, and I was the only one there.

A long time had passed when another question struck me.

"Xander," I started hesitantly, "your sister... Is she here?"

It was like I had dumped a bucket of cold water on his head. He dropped my hand, pushing himself to his feet.

"She's gone," he replied gruffly.

His eyes hardened as he reached down and took the two pieces of the map. Xander carefully rolled them together before he slipped them back into the tube. I watched silently as he picked up my dress. I had forgotten all about it.

"Saena is *gone*," he repeated. The second time, it was as though he was telling himself, not me.

An air of deep sadness came over him. His shoulders were slumped, and his back stooped as he stood before me, holding out my dress.

"Oh, Xander." I took the dress in my hands. It was mostly dry, with just a hint of dampness remaining. "I am so, so, sorry."

189

And I was. Xander, who had been a stranger to me a week ago, was many things. But no one deserved to be left alone. Suddenly, so much about him made sense. No one could suffer as much loss as he did and not be affected.

I asked, "Is Nonna your real grandmother?"

"No. She found me wandering in the woods a few months after Saena..." His voice cracked, and he shook his head. "I was broken, and Nonna took me in." He rubbed his hands over his face, shoving his long hair back and tying it with a piece of leather.

When he was done, he looked at me. His face was hard; his hands clenched at his sides as he grabbed his dagger and sheathed it on his thigh. "I don't want to talk about this anymore. Get dressed. I'm going to go check the snares I set last night around the cavern while you were sleeping. I'll be back before nightfall. Keep your daggers by your side, just in case."

Just in case.

Those three words were a stark reminder of the danger we found ourselves in. The Red Shadow. The Winged Soldiers.

"Xander, I—"

He shook his head. "I can't do this right now, Aileana."

Before I could say another word, he stormed out of the cavern. I was left alone, reeling in the wake of the sudden shift in his moods. I got dressed and plaited my hair, all the while repeating Xander's story to myself.

This male was so much more than I'd originally thought. His story touched something within me. Changed me. And now, I knew I needed to make a new plan. One that didn't just involve me leaving Ithenmyr.

I was seeing Xander in a new light. Not only that, but I was beginning to realize that things weren't as simple as I had thought. Xander's entire village had been destroyed. His people had been wiped out. His sister was dead.

Evil reigned throughout Ithenmyr. This was bigger than me or the things I'd endured. Even the scars on my back seemed to pale compared to the pain and agony others suffered.

I had thought escaping Ithenmyr would bring me freedom.

But now I was doubting everything. What good was freedom if it came at such a steep price? If it left others to suffer in agony? If I got out, but others were living lives filled with despair and grief and hurt, was I really free?

Over the past few days, I had learned many things.

I had learned the taste of freedom. I had learned I was strong. But that wasn't all. I'd learned I wasn't born Without.

And perhaps, with the proper training and someone who understood who I was, *what* I was, I could change things. Do things. I could *be* the elf I was born to be. Whoever that was. Before the king had stolen my future, I'd had a family. Parents. Someone had to know who I was. What I was.

The minutes slipped into hours as I meditated, my thoughts keeping me company as the sun dipped lower in the sky. The evening was coming.

Eventually, my reverie was broken when a branch snapped outside the cavern.

"Xander," I whispered, pushing myself to my feet, "is that you?"

No reply, but I heard a small cascade of pebbles. I glanced around the cavern. Nothing seemed amiss, but my heart pounded in my chest.

Then the sound came again.

My breath caught in my throat as I slipped out a dagger, pressing my back against the rocky wall. I held my breath, moving carefully as I tip-toed to the entrance.

Matthias' many teachings echoed in my mind as visions of us sparring in the attic entered my head.

Be careful. Always be alert.

Always be on guard.

If someone comes close enough to touch you, you stab first and ask questions later.

Your life is valuable, Aileana. Never forget that.

And to that, I added my own mantra. The one that had given me the strength to escape before my wedding.

Even pets have teeth. No one can touch you without your permission.

I would not go back willingly. Not to that. To him. I was free, and I would remain that way.

I hissed, "Xander, if this is your idea of a joke, stop and show yourself."

Leaves crunched outside the cavern, but there was no response. I tightened my grip on the hilt of my dagger and let out a long breath. Remembering my teachings, I peeked around the corner of the cavern and saw... more trees.

And then I looked down.

A long breath escaped me as I sheathed my dagger before extending my hands. "Oh, hello, darling. What is a tiny thing like you doing all the way out here?"

Run

◠⌒◡

I bent, running my hands down the back of the small black cat that was rubbing up against my legs. Its fur was silky and soft beneath my fingers. The animal arched its back, a soft *purr* escaping it as I rubbed behind its ears.

I hummed. "Aren't you just the sweetest?"

In response, the cat licked my fingers. I laughed, continuing to pet the feline until another branch snapped.

"What are you doing, Sunshine?" Xander's gruff voice came from behind me.

I turned. He was holding a cleaned rabbit in his fist. The animal was comically small in Xander's large hands. Gesturing to the cat, I raised a brow. "What does it look like I'm doing?"

He glared at the animal, sneering at the small feline. "Get away from that thing."

I look at him, then the cat. "This? It's harmless! It just doesn't like you."

As if to prove my point, the cat hissed at Xander before rubbing itself against my legs again.

"Get away from that thing," he growled.

I scoffed, petting the feline behind its ear. "I can't say I blame him for his character assessment."

Xander shook his head, walking over and grabbing my arm. He dragged me away from the animal, who stood there, watching us.

"It's not *just* a cat," he insisted.

"Yes, it is," I said, putting my hands on my hips. "In my towe.... when I was growing up, I had a cat that visited me nearly daily. It would stay with me and keep me company when no one else did."

In fact, that cat looked just like this one. All black, except mine had a white moon under its neck.

"Aileana," Xander started again, "this is a—"

Just then, hoofbeats came from behind us. Xander turned away from me, dropping the rabbit on the ground and grabbing his sword in a practiced movement. He widened his stance. "Arm yourself," he hissed. "We will continue this discussion later."

I bristled at the order but after a moment, did as I was told. Daggers in hand, I watched and waited as the sound of hoofbeats got louder.

The cavern was surrounded by trees, and from the corner of my eye, I saw my feline friend scampering up a nearby tree. I made a mental note to ask Xander what all the trees were called. With every passing moment, my heart pounded faster in my chest.

Waiting was excruciating. Every second felt like an hour. As we stood still, the wind blew through the trees, whispering in my ear.

The spirits of old are waiting for you, Protectress of the Woods. Call upon us if necessary.

The wind's voice was everything and nothing. A whisper and a yell. It sent shivers down my spine, but a pair of horses appeared before I could reply. I relaxed as Jo and Daegal came into view.

"Hello there, you two," the Fortune Elf called out. He rode up to us, his face drawn. "I'm glad to have found you both in one piece." Daegal dismounted, coming to stand before us. "When we came back, and you were both gone, we had a bit of a scare."

"We ran into some... trouble," Xander said, glancing over at me. He sheathed his sword, reaching over to shake Daegal's hand. "I figured you'd know where to find us. We weren't expecting you two until tomorrow. I'm glad you're here."

Xander reached over and grabbed the reins of Jo's horse, tying the creature to a nearby tree. The barmaid dismounted, a haggard look coating her features. Her long brown hair was flying all over the place, her face worn as she glanced between us.

"You two seem to be getting along better than when we left," she noted. A wry smirk graced her tired features. "I'm glad you worked out your little lovers' quarrel."

A low growl escaped Xander, but I shrugged. "We did. We seem to have come to an understanding of sorts."

Beside me, Xander's mouth opened in surprise. Then his face softened as a rare smile graced his lips. "Yes," he murmured. "I suppose we did."

In front of us, a silver gleam overtook the Fortune Elf's features as his lips tilted into a frown. I watched him carefully. I had to find out more about Fortune magic. Death Elves could shape their magic into different objects—deadly ones—but I had no idea how Fortune Elf magic worked.

A minute passed before the silver cleared from his eyes.

"I Saw what happened in the woods. The spirits are upset," Daegal said abruptly.

The way in which he spoke and Saw things... that would take some getting used to. But I could already see how magic like his could help keep us safe.

"Upset," I echoed. "That's one way to put it." Personally, I could think of other words to describe Myhhena's attitude. Curt. Strange. Bizarre.

I studied the Fortune Elf. Perhaps he could See something that would help me understand what was happening to me. Or, at the very least, help keep me safe. "Can you See anything in my future? The spirit we met gave us a warning, but she was unclear about what was coming."

The Fortune Elf shook his head, taking a step towards me. "The path ahead is filled with shadows. Everything is cloudy, hard to see."

I sighed. "There's nothing? Still?"

Daegal extended a hand, touching my shoulder. "Trouble follows you, doesn't it?"

Xander snorted. "Aileana *is* trouble."

"Hush," Daegal commanded. He took a deep breath, clenching his fists at his side. "This is not the time for humor. Darkness is stirring behind your wife, Xander, leaving death in its wake."

I shivered. This was *not* what I was hoping to hear.

Beside me, Xander moved closer to me, brushing his shoulder against mine. "It's going to be okay," he whispered.

"No, Xander," I replied, shaking my head as I stared at Daegal. "I really don't think it is."

The silver gleam took over the Fortune Elf's eyes once more, his voice deepening as he spoke, "Listen carefully. The shadow is still coming for you. The way ahead is as black as the night and filled with evil."

One of the horses whinnied at Daegal's words, a foreboding air settling over us all.

Xander tilted his head, placing his hand on my shoulder and squeezing. "Is there any chance you could be less ambiguous, Daegal? Give us something more than sinister words? Something concrete would be very helpful."

Jo shook off her skirts, dust flying as she huffed. "Daegal's been like this ever since we split up. Ominous seems to be the theme of the day."

Xander straightened, shooting her a look. "Is it worse than normal?"

She nodded, lowering her voice as though she was imparting a secret. "Daegal has taken cryptic to an entirely new place in the past few days. I think—"

Whatever the barmaid was going to say was cut off as something whizzed through the air behind me.

Time itself seemed to slow as Xander yelled, "No! Get down!"

His warm hands landed on my back, shoving me hard. Gasping, I tumbled towards the ground. I slammed into the dirt, my cheek stinging as something ripped into my skin.

At the same moment, a strangled cry came from above me. My heart seized.

I knew cries that sounded like that. They had come from my mouth far too often in the past, mingled with the scent of sandalwood and iron.

The only thing that caused people to make sounds like that was pain. Horrible, terrible, excruciating pain. The cry ripped through the silence of the evening, and instinctively, I clenched my fists.

Take a deep breath. It didn't hit you. You're not hurt. He's *not here.*

A pulse of relief rushed through me, but a wave of guilt and worry quickly followed it. Someone was hurt. Who?

Blinking, I pushed myself onto my elbows and looked around. I saw trees and grass and...

"No," I whispered. "Oh, no."

I looked up, meeting Jo's wide eyes as her hands trembled at her sides. Her face was pale, her lips opening and closing as her breath came in ragged bursts.

"What?" she whispered.

I took a deep, shuddering breath, pushing myself to my knees.

My gaze lowered from Jo's face, my hands shaking as I stared at the feathered shaft of wood protruding between her breasts. Deep crimson blood was pouring out of the wound, staining her gown.

Standing next to Jo, Xander and Daegal stared at the arrow with equal looks of horror and shock. They seemed frozen in time as I stared at the wound.

Jo raised a trembling hand, touching the arrow. The moment her finger connected with the shaft of wood, she gasped.

Her legs shook as she moaned, falling to the ground.

"Ana," she mumbled. "I don't think I'm going to have the chance to get to know you better."

"Don't say that," I whispered. Crawling over to Jo, I grabbed her hands in one of mine. "Daegal. Xander," I snapped. "Help us."

My voice cracked on the last word, and Xander seemed to come back to life. He and the Fortune Elf each drew their weapons, their faces grim. Metal zinged in the air as they widened their stances.

I returned my gaze to Jo. The last two deaths I'd witnessed had been nothing like this. I'd thought those were bad, but this...

This was horrifying. Jo wasn't nameless. She wasn't just someone I had seen in the streets. We'd been on the way to becoming friends.

And now she was bleeding out in front of me.

What could I do?

My breath was coming in bursts as I tried to think of something. I couldn't just sit here as she bled out in front of me. I did not know how to treat an arrow wound, but the way the blood was pouring out from her chest... she wouldn't survive. Not with an injury like this. Not here, in the middle of the woods, far from any healers.

Eventually, I settled on pressing my free hand against the wound. Jo's blood was wet against my skin. It was frighteningly reminiscent of the way my own blood had coated the tower floor too many times to count.

No. Stay in the present.

I shoved down the shudder that threatened to rip through me as I whispered, "It's going to be okay, Jo."

Behind me, a branch snapped in the woods. Xander's head jerked, and he withdrew a dagger from its sheath. He spared a look down, snapping, "Ana, stay here."

He drew back his arm before sending the dagger hurtling through the woods. I watched in awe as he ran after it, a warrior's cry escaping his lips. Moments later, a loud snapping of bone came from the direction in which he had run.

And then a heavy silence fell around us.

A choking sound came from the barmaid as she shook her head. I returned my gaze to her. "Be still, Jo," I said in what I hoped was a soothing tone. "We'll get you to safety."

"Don't lie to me." She coughed. Her skin was growing paler and paler as seemingly endless amounts of blood seeped out of her chest. A rattle escaped from her lungs as her entire body shook.

"Jo—"

A trickle of crimson blood came from her mouth as she turned wide eyes to me. A branch cracked somewhere in the woods, and time seemed to return to normal.

"Run," Jo ordered, her voice rasping. Her chest rattled as she drew in a deep breath. And then there was... nothing.

Her lifeless eyes stared up at me.

A strangled cry rose in my throat as I stared at her unmoving chest. From afar, death was terrible. But up close and personal... It was so much worse.

Death was a horrid mistress who stole what wasn't hers.

I couldn't move. My mind told me it wasn't safe to remain where I was crouched, but my body... It was refusing to react. Jo, who could have been my first female friend, had been alive one minute ago.

One minute.

That was all that it took for her to die.

A single minute.

I had no idea time could be so cruel. Yesterday, she had been alive. Now, her lifeblood seeped into the ground before me.

For what felt like an eternity, I stared into her unseeing eyes.

Then, Xander's hands reached for me. I ignored the black, ink-like spatter on his skin as he grabbed my arm.

"That was just a scout," Xander said, his voice low. "But where there is one, there will be more."

He drew me to my feet, forcing my eyes to meet his. Black blood marred Xander's pale face, which was contorted into that of a fierce warrior. I glanced at Daegal, but the Fortune Elf stared blankly at Jo's body.

"Listen to me carefully," Xander said gruffly as he widened his stance. Black covered the blade of his sword, the color at odds with the brilliant greens and browns all around us. "When I tell you to run, Aileana, you will get as far from here as possible."

"What?" I protested. "No, I'm not going to do that."

Reaching out an arm, Xander shoved me behind him. I stumbled as my back met a large rock. "You heard me," he hissed. "You will run. It isn't safe for you here."

Staring at his back, I shook my head. "I'm not going to run like a coward. I have my daggers. Jo just..." The words dried up in my throat, but they echoed through the evening, unspoken.

Jo just died because of me.

There was no doubt in my mind. I was a beacon of trouble. This was my fault.

As though the wind could read my mind, a cool breeze brushed against me in a strange caress.

Xander snarled as he stared into the woods. Beyond us, I squinted. Dark shadows were shifting through the trees. I could have sworn they hadn't been there moments before. "Aileana, daggers aren't going to help you here. I count at least twelve soldiers in the trees. The scout I killed was the least of our problems. They're all armed to the teeth."

How can he see so well in the dark?

"If you think I'm going to leave you to fight without me, you don't know me at all." I widened my stance, pushing past Xander to stand between him and Daegal. I glanced at the Fortune Elf. He kept looking between Jo's lifeless body and the forest, his hands shaking as they held onto the hilt of his sword.

"I didn't See it coming," he whispered. "I should have Seen it."

A wave of pity mingled with grief rushed through me.

"I'm sorry, Daegal," I said. "I didn't know Jo well, but I'm sorry."

My words seemed to have a calming effect on the Fortune Elf because he took a deep, shuddering breath. "Thank you, Ana. I know you mean that."

Daegal looked past me to Xander. They seemed to communicate something silently before the Fortune Elf said, "Jo would have fought with us. Allow your wife to do the same if she wishes."

Wife.

I had forgotten that we hadn't cleared up that particular misconception, but obviously, this wasn't the right time for that.

And honestly, I wasn't sure that I wanted to. Not now. Not after Xander's story.

There were a lot of things we had left unsaid. Things we needed to talk about. Lying there, holding Jo's hand as she had died, I had decided. I had no idea how Xander would react to my decision, but I knew I needed to tell him.

Soon.

But not right now.

As if to confirm that this wasn't the right time for talking, a branch cracked in the forest beyond. I flung my head towards the source of the sound, my eyes widening as a dozen soldiers walked out of the forest as one.

My legs quaked, and my heart pounded as I stared at the soldiers who had come for us. For me.

I hadn't been fast enough.

A snarl rumbled through Xander as we stared at the soldiers in front of us. There was no question in my mind about who they were. Violence and pain radiated through the air.

"Winged Soldiers," I whispered. My eyes ran over the guards that I'd hoped never to see again in my life.

They were the personification of brutality.

Enormous, black wings hung from each of their backs. Stretched to their fullest, I knew they would be at least as long as a male. Feathers the color of the deepest night filled out their wings, absorbing the light from all around us.

Each soldier wore a black helmet obscuring most features, but I knew what we would find underneath. Elongated ears with three rings on each side. Lips pierced with a hoop in the middle. A shorn head showcasing the red sword tattooed on the back of their heads.

I imagined parents would tell their younglings stories of these soldiers to keep them in line. Winged Soldiers were birthed with the sole purpose of serving High King Edgar. Their blood ran as black as the soul of the one who controlled them.

Black covered them from head to toe, except for one thing. The crimson sigil of the House of Irriel rested on their chests. Even without that, I would have known who they worked for.

They belonged to the king.

They were here for me.

I gulped as the Winged Soldiers began advancing toward us. None of them seemed concerned about the three of us; honestly, I couldn't blame them.

There were only three of us against a dozen of them. Not only that, but I was a female. Even with my training, I was sure I was no match for the king's elite forces.

My knees shook, and my fingers grew clammy around the hilts of my daggers. At the same time, I hardened my resolve. I *would not* go back. Death would be better than returning to the king's clutches.

I was no longer the king's pet, and I refused to let him put me back on a leash. Even so, his soldiers were terrifying.

As I stared at the soldiers, imagining what they would do to me, I felt myself falling into a pit of despair. My stomach twisted, and a cold sweat appeared on the back of my neck. A whimper escaped me as I stared at our attackers.

Then, Xander's fingers brushed the back of my hand.

"Stay strong, Sunshine," he whispered so low that only I could hear it. His words ran through me, and I took a deep breath, allowing his touch to ground me.

One of the soldiers stepped forward. By the two small horns on his helmet and the flying bat surrounded by three stars, I knew him to be their leader.

"We mean you no harm," the commander said.

I scoffed. That was a bald-faced lie, even for a Winged Soldier.

The commander continued, gesturing towards me. "Give us the girl, and we will let you go peacefully."

Xander raised a brow, shoving me behind him once again. I didn't fight him this time as my back landed against the rocks. "Bullshit. You've already killed our companion."

"A warning." The commander shrugged.

Daegal spat, "A murder."

The Winged Soldier sighed, drawing his sword as his wings snapped behind him. "Fine," he said. "This could have been easy. You two would have been granted quick deaths. But now, you will find yourselves in so many pieces, your loved ones will never be able to put you back together again."

Xander sneered as he widened his stance. He tilted his head to one side and replied, "I'd like to see you try."

The Winged Soldier whistled in three short bursts.

As one, the company of soldiers behind him drew their weapons. They glimmered in the lowering sun, the numerous blades at odds with the beauty of the forest.

For a moment, everything was still.

The soldiers seemed to be waiting for a command. I stared at them, spreading my skirts and widening my stance. Xander and Daegal stood on either side of me.

The wind stopped howling. The birds stopped chirping.

Then all hell broke loose.

The First Battle

$\sim\!\!\sim\!\!\sim$

I inhaled, and everyone was standing still.

When I exhaled, the stillness shattered into a million pieces. All of a sudden, chaos reigned. Xander glanced at me once, a warning in his eyes, before he darted forward.

He raised his sword and shouted, "We will never surrender."

The commander laughed as one of the Winged Soldiers met Xander's blade with their own. The sound of metal against metal rang through the forest as fights erupted around me.

Beside me, Daegal lunged forward. He yelled, ducking under an outstretched sword before thrusting his blade into the guard's stomach. There was a horrible squelching sound as Daegal withdrew his sword, and black blood gushed out of the Winged Soldier. The dying guard cried like an injured animal before falling to the ground.

As his body tumbled to the ground, another guard ran toward me. I tightened my grip on my blades, sucking in a deep breath, before rushing toward him.

I was much smaller than the Winged Soldier, and as he raised an arm, I ducked underneath his outstretched wings. Despite the weight of my garments, I was able to move swiftly.

Lifting my dagger, I recalled Matthias' instructions.

No matter who you are fighting, child, if you aim for the back of their neck, you will deliver instant death.

And so I did. Twisting my hand in a fluid movement, I thrust my blade into the back of the soldier's neck.

He yelled, collapsing to the ground as black blood spurted from his neck.

I didn't wait to think about what I had just done. Later, I would recall the way he had crumpled like a piece of paper at my feet. I would never forget the way his wings fluttered one last time as he lay dying on the forest floor.

The midnight blood that had covered my hands would haunt me for the rest of my life. Later, I would remember every last moment of this male's death. The death that I had caused.

Later. If there was a later.

Right now, I needed to focus on fighting for my freedom. I would not go back. I refused to go back.

THE SOUNDS and scents of battle were soon all I knew.

Death was waiting in the wings, and I knew more bodies would join Jo's. I only hoped they wouldn't be ours.

Turning on the balls of my feet, I watched as Daegal and Xander each fought their own battles.

The Winged Soldiers were well-trained, but it quickly became clear that Daegal and Xander were equally skilled. They were both fighting multiple guards simultaneously, engaged in a deadly waltz with death.

My heart lurched in my chest when one soldier approached the two males.

"Xander!" I screamed his name as the soldier yelled, swinging his sword.

He question turned to look at me, his golden eyes glinting as he moved faster than I had thought possible for humans. He darted around the charging soldier and, in one fluid movement, raised his sword and sliced clean through the male's wings.

That was when I learned exactly what would happen to a Winged Soldier if their wings were removed from their bodies. It was horrifying.

The soldier screamed when Xander's blade went through the black feathers. The sound was not unlike that of a mourning mother.

One time, a funerary procession had taken place right under my tower. I had watched as a human dressed in all-black stumbled behind a tiny casket. She had screamed to the heavens, begging the gods to change their minds and spare her child. Her mourning wails had been so loud they had haunted me for weeks.

This soldier's cries for mercy sounded like that. I shivered as blood the color of the night spurted from the Winged Soldier's back, coating everything around him.

The maimed soldier stumbled towards me, his weapon raised as his features contorted. Despite his injuries, he was a formidable size. I gasped, adjusting my grip on my daggers as I ran forward.

He swung his sword, the blow landing short as I plunged my blade into his heart. The injured soldier's screams stopped abruptly as he tumbled in a mess of black blood.

There was no time to celebrate, though. In that soldier's place came another.

Despite being outnumbered, the three of us fought as hard as we could.

I ducked, lunged, blocked, and attacked until my muscles screamed from the exertion. Everything else disappeared as fighting for my freedom became the song that fueled my movements.

Exhaustion plagued me, and still, I fought.

MOMENTS WERE SLIPPING into each other. I lost track of time as the battle raged on. All that mattered was staying alive.

A sword swiped along my cheek, the stinging informing me the weapon had hit its mark. I shrieked, slicing my dagger down the arm of my attacker.

"Bitch," the Winged Soldier yelled. "I'm going to kill you."

I seethed, but the commander yelled from behind me before I could respond, "Don't hurt the king's pet. The prince wants her alive."

I screamed, taking my anger out on the nearest soldier. "I am *not* the king's pet!"

Despite my rage, the commander's order meant that his guards were watching themselves around me. Their caution gave me the upper hand.

Using every advantage I could find, I sliced through one of our attacker's arms. I spun on my heel, narrowly avoiding the spurt of black blood as I raised my second dagger and sent it hurtling through the air toward another guard.

Behind me, Xander snorted. "Nice shot," he said, panting as he fought two Winged Soldiers.

The clash of metal filled the air as the battle raged around us.

"Thanks," I replied as I grabbed a sword from a fallen soldier. Spinning around, I threw the blade as I moved. It twisted in the air before catching another guard by his wings. The sword *twanged* as it pinned the soldier against a nearby tree. He screamed, the sound ear-piercingly loud.

I turned, my face paling as I saw Daegal fighting a trio of soldiers less than twenty feet from me. He was doing his best, but even I could tell he was slowing down. My heart lurched in my chest as the soldiers fighting him forced him into a defensive position, his back against a tree.

The tallest of the trio drew their sword, angling it toward Daegal's face.

"What a pretty elf," the Winged Soldier crooned. "If only we weren't enemies. I'd quite enjoy spending an evening alone with you."

The commander scoffed, his voice coming from behind me. "Keep it in your pants, Dray. You can take his pretty head back as a trophy."

Apparently, the commander didn't believe in fighting his own battles. *Coward.*

Dray chuckled, the sound mirthless and tinged with barely contained violence. "Good idea, Commander. I'll definitely do that."

I spun around, shoving my opponent aside as I ran toward Daegal.

"Stop trying to kill my friends!" I shouted as I jumped. Sailing through the air, I shoved my dagger into the back of Dray's neck.

A sense of satisfaction bubbled through me as the soldier collapsed in a heap. I would have no guilt over his death.

My elation was short-lived, however, as Daegal's eyes widened. He jolted forward, yelling, "Duck!"

I did, but within seconds, I realized the command wasn't for me.

A scream came from behind me. The second I heard it, something shattered within me. I paled, my heart stopping in my chest as I pivoted.

"No," I whispered. "It can't be."

I blinked, hoping the scene would change.

But it didn't.

Xander was on his knees as bright red blood dripped down his tunic. A sword was lodged in his left shoulder, pinning him to a tree. He was panting, still fighting with his right arm, as a trio of Winged Soldiers circled him. They taunted him, jeering, as one of them lurched forward and grabbed the hilt of the sword.

The Winged Soldier pulled on the weapon, and a shriek came from Xander that I *felt* in the depths of my soul.

A terrible squelching sound filled the air as Xander's entire body seemed to waver in front of me. Sweat glistened on his face as he lifted his head. His golden eyes seemed to burn as his gaze caught mine. "I'm so sorry," he whispered.

Something within me cracked at the sight of Xander on his knees. His silver-white hair was covered in black blood, and his tunic was torn where the sword had penetrated it.

I stared at Xander, the infuriating male whose presence had been haunting me since I'd escaped the king's clutches, and a barrier I hadn't known existed within me shattered. This could not happen. I would not let it. Not like this.

At that moment, I knew. Nonna had been right. There was something between us. Something that was frail and intangible, but if we gave it room to grow...

It could become something beautiful.

And these males, these soldiers who worked for the Crimson King, were trying to kill Xander.

They were going to do it.

Unless I did something.

Reaching within myself, I begged anyone who would listen to help me. Turning my eyes to the heavens, I screamed. I screamed and screamed and screamed. The wind itself seemed to echo my cry as it swirled around us, picking up leaves and twigs from the forest floor.

"Don't touch him," I said in a voice that was not mine. It was deep and ancient. My words echoed through the air as dark green ribbons tinged with silver erupted from my outstretched palms. They swirled through the air before diving into the ground.

The Winged Soldiers stared at me, stepping back as I raised my hands in the air. A look crossed the faces of the remaining soldiers. It was fear.

They were afraid.

Of *me*.

Good. They should be.

Their fear emboldened me, and for the first time in my life, *magic* rushed through my veins like water pouring over a broken dam. It thrummed in my blood, singing to me like the call of the wind.

Protectress of the Woods.

"Hear me now," I said in that strange voice. "I am not the king's pet any longer. I will never return. And you will leave my companions unharmed."

The cowardly commander scoffed. "Nice light show, but I don't think a few green ribbons will stop us from fulfilling the king's orders."

I tilted my head. "Perhaps not. But how about this?"

Reaching deep into myself, I grabbed onto something I had no idea how to control. The magic—*my magic*—felt as slippery as silk. I tried to grab onto the ribbons, to command them, but precious seconds ticked by, and nothing happened.

One of the Winged Soldiers laughed while another raised his sword. "Let's finish this and take the bitch back to the castle where she belongs. Maybe the prince can beat some sense into her."

That was it. I was not some pet to be dragged around and used for pleasure.

Anger surged through me, and with it came the ability to grab the threads of magic. I drew in a deep breath as the ground shifted beneath us.

"I will never return to the king. I would rather die," I proclaimed as a flash of bright green light erupted from within me.

It was radiant, vibrant, and utterly blinding.

And it was *mine*.

SECONDS THAT FELT like hours passed as the vibrant green light flooded the forest. A jolt of power unlike anything I'd ever felt rushed through me, and I inhaled sharply.

As I closed my fists, the light faded.

And my mouth fell open.

The forest was empty. The Winged Soldiers were gone. In their place was life. *New* life. Nine new trees had sprouted in the forest. Their skin had been replaced with gnarled bark, hair with leaves, and clothes with branches.

They were dead, and we were alone.

"We won," I murmured as I stared at the clearing. "I can't believe it. We won."

Daegal turned to me, his sword falling on the ground as he tilted his head. "You're an Earth Elf," he breathed. "Kydona have mercy on us. I thought the king had destroyed the entire House of Corellon."

Xander lifted his golden eyes to mine. "Is that true? Are you an Earth Elf?"

I shook my head, stumbling back a step. "I-I don't know..."

No one had ever spoken of my heritage. Who I was. What I was. All I'd ever been told was that I was a *special* elf. That I was kept alive so I could marry Remington. *Breed.*

But this...

Could this be the answer to all my questions?

The wind swirled around me, whispering in my ear.

Protectress of the Woods. We are here to serve you.

"Protectress of the Woods," I echoed the wind's whispers.

Xander's mouth tilted up slightly as he studied me. "Aileana of the House of Corellon. Last female of her kind. Earth Elf. Protectress of the Woods. You have to admit, it has a nice ring to it."

Reaching his good hand behind him, Xander pushed himself to his feet. He took one trembling step before he pitched forward with a cry.

I rushed towards him, my hands grabbing his shoulders as he tumbled to the ground. Blood gushed from the wound on his shoulder, and he groaned.

"I'm fine, Aileana," he muttered. "Don't worry about it."

I raised a brow, pointing to the pool of blood gathering on his tunic. "This doesn't look like 'fine' to me."

He continued to protest, but I put my hand on his good shoulder. "Listen to me, you big-headed fool. You're hurt, and I'm going to help you. Now lay still, and let me do it."

"Fine," he sighed. "But let it be known that I am cooperating under protest."

I scoffed. "Noted."

Xander lay down on the ground, and I knelt beside him, hiking up my skirts. I turned my head to Daegal, speaking quickly. "We'll have to leave. I am certain there will be more soldiers where those ones came from."

The Fortune Elf nodded, his expression grim as he turned. "I will get the horses ready."

Xander turned his gaze to me, wincing as he jostled his shoulder. "You give orders well."

I smirked, lifting my overdress and taking hold of the petticoat closest to my body. It was still white and barely bore any traces of dirt. It was as clean as we would be able to get out here in the forest. For once, I was grateful for the ridiculous feminine fashions required by Ithenmyrian standards.

Grabbing my dagger, I stabbed it into the fabric, running it down in one smooth motion. The petticoat tore easily as a ripping sound filled the air. "Well, let's just say I know some bossy people."

He grinned, but the smile didn't reach his eyes. Xander shifted on the ground, flinching as the movement caused a fresh flow of blood to seep from his wound.

"This isn't exactly how I imagined you taking your clothes off for me again," he said weakly.

Rolling my eyes, I huffed and cut another strip from my petticoats. "Be quiet, you insufferable male."

Once I had three long strips of fabric, I knelt and wound them around Xander's shoulder. Red blood seeped through the white fabric, but color returned to his face as I worked. After I tied a knot in the makeshift bandage, I sat back and studied him.

He had been stabbed before and healed. I knew that. But a dagger was much smaller than a sword, and he looked so pale...

"Are you going to be able to ride?" I asked him quietly.

He narrowed his eyes, grimacing as he pushed himself to his feet. This time, he was able to remain upright.

"Of course," he snapped. "I'm not an invalid. Aileana, I've been riding horses for longer than... for a long time. I'll be fine."

"Good," I said, falling in step with him. If he was going to insist on being stubborn, I wasn't going to push the matter. "Because there's one more thing I want to do before we leave this accursed place."

Eternal Blessings

⌒∽⌒

Daegal, Xander, and I stood around Jo's unmoving body. She was lying on her back, her hands folded over her chest as though she were simply praying.

The Fortune Elf had removed the arrow before wrapping Jo in her cloak. A somber air settled over us. The forest itself seemed to mourn as the animals were silent. Dark clouds covered the stars, and a storm roiled on the horizon.

"Are you sure you can do this, Aileana?" Xander's voice was low as he stood on my right.

I nodded, taking a deep breath. "Yes. I am sure. I *want* to do this for Jo."

It's the least I can do.

I couldn't shake the feeling that Jo wouldn't be dead if it hadn't been for me. More than any of the other ones I'd caused, her death rested heavily on my conscience. It would be a burden I would bear for the rest of my life, of that I was certain.

An owl hooted in the distance as a cool breeze blew past us. The wind blew my hair around me as I stared at Jo's body.

"She can do it, Xan." Daegal's voice was soft as he spoke for the first time since I told him my plan. "Let her."

I smiled faintly at the elf. He had been silent when we had come out of the forest, kneeling over his fallen friend. His vote of confidence meant more to me than I could say. I wasn't used to people having faith in me.

It was new and strange and... entirely welcome.

Xander nodded. "Okay." He brushed the back of his hand against mine lightly, and tingles rushed through me.

Stepping forward, I stood before Jo's body and cleared my throat.

"I haven't been to many of these," I began, altering the truth slightly. The reality was that I hadn't been to a single funeral before in my life, but that seemed beside the point at the moment.

Clearing my throat, I continued, "I wish I weren't here now. It is an honor to say a final farewell to Jo—Josephine. We only knew each other briefly, but during that time, I recognized her as a female of strength, kindness, and loyalty. She was strong, and it was an honor to get to know her. I wish her time on this planet could have been extended."

Kneeling, I grabbed a handful of dirt. It was cold and damp but crumbled as I held it over Jo's chest. The dirt fell on her, the brown specks scattering over her gray cloak. I whispered, "May the goddesses, in all their eternal wisdom, accept your soul with love and affection. May you find everlasting peace and rest in the Next Life."

Once my handful of dirt was gone, Xander stepped forward and repeated my actions.

Xander's voice was low, reverent even as he said, "Jo, you were one of my oldest friends. You helped me when I was lost. You gave me friendship when I needed it, and I am eternally grateful." He took a deep breath, releasing his dirt and resting his hand on Jo's cheek. "May you find peace with Kydona in the afterlife. One day, old friend, we will reunite."

Then Daegal came forward. With his dark skin, he blended into the night. I squinted, his body little more than shadow as he sprinkled dirt on Jo's chest before pushing himself to his feet.

The Fortune Elf cleared his throat. Emotion leaked into his words as he spoke. "Josephine Shaea Prinwillow. You were a female of many words and even more life. You were stolen from us too soon. May you find enduring peace and happiness in the Next Life."

He stepped back, nodding in our direction.

Together, the three of us said, "Until we meet again."

I swallowed. This was it. I wasn't sure I could do this, but I wanted to try for Jo.

Raising my hands, I reached within myself for the pool of power I had sensed earlier. My fingers began to tingle as the same thrum filled my veins.

Ever since the moment in the clearing when I had laid eyes on Xander's kneeling form, I had felt... different. Like some part of me, one that had been locked up for my entire life could finally be used.

Even though I had barely slept over the past two days, I felt more alive than I had in my entire existence.

At first, nothing happened. I was about to give up when suddenly, a green light erupted from my hands. My skin tingled, like feathers were dusting over my body.

Bright emerald ribbons—Earth Elf magic, I was certain of that now—streamed from my fingers. The strips of magic gently wrapped themselves around Jo. They illuminated the night sky, and I watched silently as her body was lifted from the ground. She levitated above the ground, her back bent, as the magic kept her upright.

"Please work," I whispered. Squeezing my hands together, I released another burst of power. Seconds later, the ground below Jo opened up. I kept my hands clasped until the hole was the size of a body and deep enough that animals wouldn't bother her in her endless slumber. "Rest in peace, Josephine."

All I had to do was *think* that her body belonged in the ground, and the ribbons did my bidding. Jo's body slowly descended into the dirt until nothing but her cloak was visible. Then, and only then, did the ribbons gently release her and return to me.

A heartbeat went by before a rumble shook the earth. The dirt moved, rearranging itself until Josephine's body was nowhere to be seen.

Then, on my command, three bright red flowers bloomed over the fresh grave. They glowed despite the late hour, their radiant color a vivid contrast to the greens and browns of the forest.

I exhaled, and the light slowly retreated into my skin as a feeling of pure *life* rushed through me. It was exhilarating. The magic was empowering in a way that I had never known existed. It felt at once like nothing I had ever experienced and something I could get lost in forever.

I stared at the ground. It was *calling to* me, whispering my name.

Aileana.

Come to us, Protectress.

Stay with us.

Come.

Without thinking, I dropped to my knees. Spreading my fingers, I dug into the cool dirt beneath me. It felt like everything I'd ever needed.

Behind me, I could hear voices speaking, but I couldn't understand what they were saying. Their words were nothing more than murmurs that brushed up against my consciousness.

At that moment, I was *more* than just Aileana. I felt my consciousness stretch out of my body until I was at once Aileana and not. My heartbeat pounded in my ears, my skin tightened against my frame as part of me *became* the earth.

At once, I was the trees in the forest, the leaves they bore, the insects crawling over the ground. I was the dirt and the bugs and the plants. I was the roots of the forests and the birds that flew high above the trees. The foxes in their dens, the rabbits in their burrows, the bears resting for the winter.

I *was* the woods themselves.

Knowledge and understanding filled me unlike anything I'd ever experienced. My fingers tingled, and my soul flew over thousands of miles at once. Dozens of emotions flooded me as the flora and fauna acknowledged my presence. They crowded around me, their presence pulsing through my veins. Their song was intoxicating as they drew me deeper into themselves.

Protectress.

Giver of life.

Welcome home.

I was myself, but not. And I could get lost in here forever.

Seconds passed, but they could have been minutes or hours. I knew then that I could spend *years* connecting to the earth. Decades. Centuries.

I could dive so deep into their existence that nothing else would ever matter again. I would never be the king's pet again because I would be *more*.

I would be life itself in Ithenmyr.

But... something was holding me back. And so I struggled against the pull of the earth. Forced it to let me go.

Above me, thunder roared through the sky.

It snapped me out of my reverie. Like a ribbon being pulled taut and then released, I was back in my body. The grip of the earth was gone, and I was myself. Only myself.

I was Aileana and no one else.

Blinking, I wobbled as my legs seemed unable to support my weight.

"What was that?" Xander asked urgently. His voice still sounded far away, as though he was underwater. I felt his warm hand on my arm as he pulled me to my feet. He put his hands on my cheeks, drawing my face up to his. I stared at his golden eyes as he repeated, "Aileana, what was that?"

I blinked at him, my feet still unsteady. "I-I don't know," I whispered.

He stared at me for a long moment before Daegal spoke. "Whatever it was, we have to go. Can you ride with your shoulder like that, Xan?"

Xander pressed a hand to his shoulder, wincing. "I'll manage. Sunshine, you'll ride with me."

I turned and glared at him. "What? No question? Maybe something like, 'If it pleases you, Aileana, would you like to ride with me?'"

He crossed his arms, scowling. The bloody bandage on his shoulder didn't exactly help his air of aloofness as he loomed over me. "Are you being serious right now? Do you want to pick a fight about this? There are only two horses."

"Seriously," I replied. "Stop being so bossy and ask me what I want."

Huffing, he shifted on his feet. "Fine. If it pleases you, Aileana, Protectress of the Woods, Last Earth Elf, and Most Infuriating Female I have ever met, will you do me the *honor* of riding with me?"

My mouth tilted into a smile, and I raised a brow, curtsying in jest. "Thank you. I will."

Despite my attitude, I was thankful Xander was willing to ride with me. At least I didn't have to explain to him I didn't, in fact, know how to ride a horse.

That would lead to far too many uncomfortable questions than I wanted to answer. Even though I felt more comfortable around Xander than before, I still didn't want to explain how I had been raised in a tower, away from everyone and everything.

Daegal cleared his throat. "If you two are just about done with whatever this is, it would be great if we could get going."

They exchanged a look, communicating silently.

"The Pines?" Xander asked.

The Fortune Elf nodded. His eyes took on the silver gleam that I was slowly getting used to. A full minute passed before the glow cleared, and he said, "Yes. Of all the possible courses of action, it's our best bet. Let's hope Teroth has forgiven you."

A grim chuckle escaped Xander's lips. "I hope so, too. How much of a grudge can Teroth hold?"

Daegal blinked at Xander. "You *burned down* a cottage."

"It was an accident!"

My gaze flew back and forth between them. "Was anyone hurt?"

Daegal shook his head. "Thankfully not, but your husband here got himself kicked out of The Pines and had to promise not to return."

"A promise that I will now be breaking," Xander pointed out helpfully.

"I see," I said. "And you think this is our best bet?"

They both nodded.

"It is," Daegal said. A moment passed before he added sadly, "Jo would have known exactly what to say to Teroth."

"Yes, she would have." Xander agreed, sighing. "We'll head over there and regroup. Make a plan." He fingered the cord around his neck. "Now that we have the second piece of the map, it's time to keep going. Look for the third."

I cleared my throat. "I want to come too."

Both of them stared at me, but it was Xander who spoke.

"Aileana," he said my name slowly, "do you honestly believe we will leave you alone in the middle of the woods? After what just happened?"

I shook my head. "No, I mean, after. I want to help. Find the map." I gestured to Xander's chest. "Do whatever it takes to fight back against the king. I couldn't help Jo, but whatever you're doing, maybe... maybe I can help you?"

I was realizing that helplessness was almost as bad as being trapped in a tower. Freedom meant nothing if I kept to myself. Actions, doing things, working with others... those things were important. More important than anything else. More important than just trying to save myself from my fate.

High King Edgar was... horrible. A sadist. A murderer. Over the length of his reign, he'd killed countless people.

And his son... shudders ran through me. Somehow, Remington was even worse. I didn't think all Death Elves were evil, but I knew those two were the worst of the worst.

And maybe, by helping Xander, I could do something about it. That thought filled me with a sense of rightness. I *knew* this was the right course of action.

For a very long moment, I held Xander's gaze. It was as though the two of us were the only ones in the entire world as we stared at each other.

Daegal cleared his throat. "Well," he drew out the word like it was a whole sentence. "This is... awkward. I'm going to get ready to go."

I nodded slowly, never removing my eyes from Xander's. "Okay."

Once the Fortune Elf was out of earshot, Xander spoke slowly. His eyes were glued to mine. "You want to... help me?"

"Yes," I replied, nibbling on my lip. "The last few days, the soldiers... I don't want to run anymore, Xander. I want to help. I think I can be useful."

And wouldn't that be an amazing thing?

A small smile graced his lips as his golden eyes studied me.

"Okay," he said. "Welcome to the team."

He held out his hand, and I shook it. Sparks flew between our hands, and my lungs tightened. Xander's mouth parted as his gaze dropped to where our hands were joined.

Did he feel it, too?

I parted my lips to ask, but before I could do more than inhale, Xander released my hand. He moved swiftly around me, walking to where Daegal stood with the horses. I followed, my thoughts still centered on that spark.

When we were in front of the horse, warm hands landed on my waist. Xander's voice was gruff as he asked, "Are you ready, Sunshine?"

I nodded, my heart beating strangely at Xander's proximity. He was so close. I could feel every inch of where his hands touched me. They seared into my skin, those large hands on my hips.

He was far too close. And yet, not close enough. I wanted to grab him, to press myself against him, to push him away. I wanted so many things.

A moment passed that felt like an eternity as I fought a battle against myself. Every time we grew closer, the lines between us became more muddled. Blurry. Everything was confusing.

Swallowing the lump that had appeared in my throat, I whispered, "I'm ready. Let's go."

"Your wish is my command," Xander said. His grip on my hips tightened as he lifted me onto the back of the nearest horse.

I forced myself to ignore how my insides twisted as he spun me around. The saddle was large but clearly not meant for skirts like mine. I straddled the beast, spreading my skirts so I could hold the reins in front of me.

"This is Stormflier," Daegal said as he rejoined us atop his own horse. He patted the horse's black flank, leaning over and adjusting his position on the horse. "And you two are riding his brother, Thunder."

"Hmm," I murmured. I was incapable of any other words because, at that very moment, Xander decided to join me on Thunder. He swung up into the saddle behind me in the fluid movement of a confident horseman.

The male responsible for all my confusing feelings leaned forward. If I'd thought he had been close before, I had been wrong. *Now* he was close. His chest pressed against my back, and I could feel the hard ridges of his muscles as his breath tickled my ears. "I hope you're ready to travel, Sunshine. It will take us at least a week to reach The Pines."

"I'm ready," I replied. My voice was calm, and I was grateful it didn't betray the way I was feeling inside. I was incredibly aware of every part of his body as it pressed against me. My nerves felt like they were on fire, and it was because of him. His proximity.

Gods, he even *smelled* good. How was that possible after days in the forest?

Sucking in a deep breath, I wiggled in the saddle to find a more comfortable seat. I shifted my bottom, huffing at the burn that was already making itself known in my legs.

Beneath me, Thunder whinnied and stomped his feet.

Xander blew out a long breath. His voice sounded oddly strained as he said, "I quite agree." He leaned in close to me, his arms reaching around to box me in as he grabbed the reins on either side of me. "If you would do me the favor of no longer wiggling your ass, *wife*, this journey can begin."

A dozen questions flew to the tip of my tongue, but before I could voice them, I *felt* the reason for Xander's discomfort. It pressed up against my lower back, and as he shifted, the movement sent a jolt down my spine.

He *wanted* me. That much was clear. He might not have liked me very much, but he wanted me.

Perhaps it was the stress of the past day or the sheer ridiculousness that Xander thought I was attractive, but I giggled. Memories of whispers and tidbits I'd gleaned for too-loud servants flooded me. I might have been sheltered, but I knew what that hardness meant.

My quiet sounds of amusement soon dissolved into raucous laughter as all my emotions seemed to push out of me at once.

Grief for Josephine's untimely death mingled with a deep sense of relief that we were still alive. Thankfulness that I was not in Remington's clutches danced alongside the odd sensations that being so close to Xander brought forth within me.

Beneath it all, I felt a writhing deep within me. Warmth pulsed within my core. It was new and not entirely unpleasant.

And it was because of him. Xander.

Something had changed in me earlier today, and I knew I would never be the same. I wiggled, my laughter giving way to silent gasps of air as Xander shifted behind me. He clicked his tongue, and Thunder began to move beneath us.

Warm breath tickled my neck as Xander leaned in close. "Aileana," he growled, "for the love of all that is good in this world, *please* at least try to keep still."

I sucked my lip through my teeth, trying to ignore how riding with Xander felt so *right*.

"I'll do my best," I finally forced out through tight lips.

"Thank you," he said.

We fell into a companionable silence as Thunder galloped through the forest.

SOON, I couldn't have spoken if I had wanted to. Stormflier and Thunder seemed to make it their goal to move as fast as possible through the dark woods. I held on tight as they raced towards our destination. The storm had cleared, leaving a starry night to guide our way.

Led by the light of the moon, the horses seemed to know exactly where we were going. The thought was comforting because everything looked the same to me.

I vowed to learn what each and every tree and plant in Ithenmyr was named. The newness of being free from my tower was turning into something more. I was learning so much about the country in which I lived—both good and bad things.

Eventually, the movement of the horses lulled me into a restless sleep. I saw the faces of the dead behind my closed lids. The Winged Soldiers. Jo. The human slave. The Earth Elf. And behind them was another face.

My own.

I stared into my lifeless eyes, my red hair flung around me. My face was paler than a piece of paper as I lay prone on the forest floor. Like a discarded doll, my limbs were haphazardly placed all around me.

My gaze dropped, and my breath caught in my throat as my heart pounded in my chest.

Not real.

Not real.

Not real.

Every beat seemed to echo this call, and yet... this looked far too real.

A long, smooth cut ran beneath my jaw, from one ear to the other. Blood was everywhere. My blood. It streamed from the cut of my neck and coated the forest floor. The land itself seemed to mourn my passing as distant thunder roared overhead.

And then, a branch snapped, and the horrible scent of sandalwood filled my nose. My lungs seized, and my hands grew clammy as High King Edgar's voice became the only thing I heard. "The only thing that comes to pets who escape their owners is death."

I couldn't help it. I screamed.

"Aileana, are you okay?" Xander's voice rumbled through me as he pulled me tight against him.

His voice was softer than normal, not as barbed. Something else had shifted that evening between us, something that I didn't want to acknowledge. It felt heavy, frightening, and wholly consuming.

Hating Xander had been simple. Clear-cut. Easy to understand. I was good at hating. Hating was like an old tunic you put on after a long day. It conformed to your body, slipping over every curve and instantly knowing exactly how to hug you. Hatred was comfortable. It was an old friend. It fed me with the fire of a thousand flames.

And this... whatever this was that lay between us now was definitely not hatred. It was not comfortable, nor was it easy.

The events of earlier today had taken that old tunic of hatred and ripped it into shreds, presenting me with something else. Something I didn't want but was forced to wear. Something new and entirely unexpected.

It was as though the entire plane our relationship had rested on had shifted, leaving me standing uneasily on a rocky mountain. I couldn't see what was coming, which scared me more than anything else.

I shook my head. "No," I whispered. "I'm not okay. I don't know if I'll ever be okay again."

Xander rubbed his hand down my arm. "I won't let you go," he murmured. "You're safe with me."

I wanted to believe that. I did. And yet questions still plagued my mind. How could he keep me safe against the most powerful Death Elves in Ithenmyr?

Why did he want to?

The weight of these questions pressed down on me, and soon, every single part of my body felt heavier than before. I yawned, shoving all thoughts of non-hatred away. Those pesky feelings would be tomorrow's problems.

"Sleep, Sunshine," Xander said softly, lifting a hand off the reins to wrap around my middle. His arm was warm and comforting as he whispered, "I've got you."

I was too tired to protest, so I slipped into the welcoming embrace of sleep.

That night, lulled into a deep sleep by the rocking motion of the horse and the warmth at my back, I dreamed of the earth.

A Long Journey

It turned out that if you had never ridden a horse before, traveling for days on end was not an easy task. Especially when the aforementioned travel included going through forests that spanned entire mountains.

Who knew?

Not me.

With every passing day, I was becoming painfully aware of the extent to which I had been sheltered. I had known my education had been limited, but the reality of it shocked me. I knew so little about the world in which I lived.

The king had ensured I knew how to read and write, but what good was a formal education when I didn't have basic skills like riding horses? I knew Ithenmyr boasted of endless mountains and forests, while the Western Kingdom of Ipotha was as flat as the eye could see.

I knew how to properly pour a cup of tea to please my husband, but I did not know how to swim. What good was the fact that I had committed the entire *Ballad of Light Elves* to memory when I couldn't tell which plants were safe to eat?

When we stopped to make camp the first night, I quickly extended my list of things I didn't know how to do. Building a fire and making camp were both foreign concepts to me. At that rate, it would probably have been easier to list things I knew how to do.

I learned early on that "making camp" was a loose term. Because of the constant threat of our pursuers, we didn't dare risk a fire. We slept in shifts underneath whatever greenery we could find, remaining in one place just long enough to get enough sleep to keep going.

Waking up after the first night we made camp was not a pleasant experience. Every single muscle in my body hurt, including ones that, until this point in my life, had remained hidden and unused. Riding horses, I was learning, was not easy on the body.

Or at least on my body.

Both Xander and Daegal seemed unfazed by the entire situation. They moved with ease, not uttering a singular complaint about sore muscles or painful movements.

That was irritating, to say the least.

By noon on the second day, I learned males were terrible travel companions. They didn't understand the need to stop and stretch my legs. Not only did they seem to consider my need to relieve myself every few hours a nuisance of epic proportions, but they thought the way the black flies and other insects swarmed me was amusing.

When I dared to mention my hunger, Xander thrust stale bread and cheese at me out of a pack.

Daegal seemed distracted, but Xander...

Whatever had shifted between us seemed to have been thrown to the wayside because he seemed to be as angry with me as ever. If anything, his temper was shorter than before.

Despite my many attempts to engage Daegal and Xander in conversation, the only responses I ever got were grunts and monosyllabic answers.

"How did you accidentally burn down a cottage?" I asked Xander after we'd stopped so I could relieve myself for the third time since lunch.

"With fire," he replied unhelpfully.

Narrowing my eyes, I turned in the saddle to glare at him more effectively. "I figured that much out on my own," I snapped. "Do you care to elaborate on the particulars of the situation? Was it an accident?"

"No, I don't, and yes, it was."

"Unbelievable," I huffed. Crossing my arms, I tried for an air of what I hoped came across as Highly Aggravated Female. Not realizing my desires, Thunder chose that moment to break into a gallop. I lurched to the wayside, my stomach roiling, as I slipped in the saddle.

The ground drew near, but before I could slip off the saddle completely, a warm hand latched onto my arm.

"Careful," he growled, pressing me tight against his chest. The breath caught in my throat as he murmured, "Falling from a horse is the last thing we need from you right now, Sunshine. I'd hate to see you break that lovely neck of yours."

"That makes two of us," I said as I tried to subtly adjust myself in the saddle. Xander was so close to me that I could feel the ridges of his chest muscles against my back. I glanced down at his arms, gripping the reins. His knuckles were white, and he was as rigid as a board.

A low rumble came up through Xander's chest that I felt ripple through my entire body. "Are you trying to drive me out of my mind, Aileana?"

I blinked. "I.. uh... not intentionally," I replied honestly.

"That makes it even worse," he murmured, tightening his arm around my middle. His voice was husky as he said, "You don't even know how much you drive me crazy."

I drove him crazy?

I had no idea how to reply to that. Should I have told him I was thinking of him far more often than was necessary? That he haunted my dreams? That he made me feel completely—and inexplicably—safe?

In the end, I decided not to say anything.

We spent the rest of the day in tense silence.

ON THE THIRD DAY, it rained.

That was when I learned that riding horses became exponentially worse when you added bad weather into the mix. If I had thought they had been temperamental before, the three of us were downright angry when the sun set on the third day.

We were all soaked to the bone, our cloaks doing little to ward off the chill brought on by the torrential downpour.

The only good thing about the rain was that after a full day of riding over muddy trails, Xander and Daegal decided we would finally stop for the entire night and sleep for more than a few hours at a time.

We had just pulled off the trail when the rain tapered off, leaving a cool, cloudless evening.

I stumbled off Thunder, relieving myself in a nearby bush before returning to the others. They had tied the horses to a tree and were in the process of rubbing them down as I walked back. They were talking quietly, clearly unaware that I had returned.

"... the university in the Western Kingdom," Daegal whispered.

"Last time I was there..." Xander's voice dropped off suddenly as I accidentally stepped on a twig. It snapped, and blood rushed to my cheeks as they turned at once.

"I hope I'm not interrupting," I said hurriedly.

Xander shook his head, his silver-white hair plastered to his face by the rain. He raised a brow, his gaze traveling over my body. "Not at all," he replied. "We were just discussing how much longer it'll take to arrive at The Pines."

He was lying to me. Why?

What did he not want me to know?

I narrowed my eyes, but before I could figure out a discreet way to ask about the university in the Western Kingdom without it looking like I had been eavesdropping, Xander smirked.

"You look like a drowned rat." His golden eyes twinkled in the twilight before he returned his attention to the horse.

I put my hands on my hips, ignoring how the sodden fabric squished under my fingers. "*I* look like a drowned rat?"

He nodded, the corner of his lips twitching. "That's what I said."

"How rude," I exclaimed. Part of me knew he was purposefully trying to get a rise out of me, but I couldn't help but take the bait. He was just so... easy to fight with. "You are one to talk. You look worse than me."

It was a lie.

Despite being soaked to the bone, I couldn't help but notice the way the rain accentuated Xander's muscles. His shoulder had healed far faster than I had thought possible, and he had shed the bandages earlier that day.

Xander's muscles tensed with every stroke of his hand down the horse's backside. He moved with the ease of someone who knew they were big and was confident in their size. It was incredible.

He was incredible.

For a long moment, I just... watched him. I was drawn to him like a moth to a flame. Since Xander had shown up in my life, he had thrown everything I had known out of the window. I knew I shouldn't have been watching him, that he would likely be upset by my attention, but I just couldn't help it.

For years, watching other people had been my only source of interaction with the outside world. I had stood at my window in the tower as everyone else went about their lives.

I had known everyone's schedule by heart. The young boy who brought milk from a nearby farm every morning after the sun rose. The farmer who made the day's journey from Thyr three times a week with enough supplies for me and the two dozen guards and servants who resided in the nearby keep.

I had watched on the first Sunday of every month as the king had made his monthly procession to my tower to check on me. To check on his pet.

I had spent the past twenty-three years watching.

But I had gotten out. I was free. I was living. Learning. *Being.*

My thoughts were so consuming that I didn't notice when Xander stepped away from the horses. I didn't hear his feet walking over the forest floor, and it wasn't until he was standing right in front of me I even realized he was talking to me.

"... sleep for the night," he finished. He stared down at me expectantly as though waiting for a response.

Dammit. Why did I have to choose this moment to dive into my thoughts?

I stared at him, blinking. I had two choices here. The first was to admit that I had been distracted and hadn't been paying attention. The second was to pretend I had heard him and agree to... whatever he had said.

In an effort to save whatever face I had left, I went with the latter.

"I'd be happy to," I said firmly, nodding as though I knew exactly what I was agreeing to do.

Xander tilted his head, studying me for a moment longer, before shrugging. "Okay, I'll get the soap."

Soap.

That meant... I swallowed. Suddenly, I wished I knew exactly what I had agreed to. My breath quickened in my chest as I surreptitiously raised my arm and sniffed.

Instantly, I recoiled.

I would definitely be adding how difficult it was to maintain hygienic practices while traveling to my list of new things I'd learned.

The desire for cleanliness pushed aside everything else I was feeling. I followed Xander through the trees, picking my way over fallen logs and around low-hanging branches.

By now, I was used to the constant brush of branches against my dress. The nearly constant need to pluck small thorns and other pieces of wood from my skirts felt normal.

I'd grown used to the constant whisper of the wind. The way the trees brushed up against me, calling for me. Whenever I heard the quiet call in the back of my mind, I pushed it away.

I had no idea what was happening to me.

Not for the first time since we had realized I was an Earth Elf, I wished someone could tell me if what I was experiencing was normal. Was the call of the wind and the thrum of magic in my veins what every Earth Elf had experienced before High King Edgar had ordered them killed?

Or was I different?

Was that why he hadn't killed me too?

"Aileana," Xander called out, his voice panicked, "Watch your step."

I looked down just in time to see a long black and white snake slithering on the ground mere inches from my toes. My breath caught in my throat as I stifled a scream. I could barely make out the snake's body in the failing sunlight, but what I saw was terrifying.

"Oh my gods," I whispered, staring at the snake. The creature was as thick as my hand and slithered quickly along the forest floor.

When I was younger, maybe eleven or twelve, there had been a red bird that had made a nest in the windowsill of my tower. It had laid three eggs, and I had watched in fascination as the tiny chicks had come to life. The mother had brought them worms and insects to eat before they grew strong enough to leave the nest. When I'd asked my tutor about them, Orvyn told me that worms were tiny snakes.

Well, he had clearly been misinformed. This snake looked *nothing* like a worm. It looked like a thing of nightmares. And considering just days earlier, Winged Soldiers had attacked me, I knew a thing or two about nightmares.

I stood, paralyzed by fear, as the reptile continued on the path before me. It was at least the length of two males, and every second felt like an eternity as it slithered past me.

My chest felt tight, my hands clammy as I stared at the snake moving quickly through the forest. Even when it was no longer right before me, I couldn't pull away my gaze.

When a large hand landed on my shoulder, I jumped.

"It's just a leaf-eater," Xander whispered in my ear. "It won't hurt you. I promise. They only eat things that grow in the forest."

I blinked, forcibly lifting my gaze from the forest floor. Xander's brows were furrowed, his mouth pinched in a straight line as he studied me. "It's okay, Aileana."

"Forgive me if I don't take your word for it," I said as sharply as I could muster. "I'd rather not put the snake to the test."

He nodded, holding out his arm, and his mouth twitched. "In that case, Sunshine, will you allow me to escort you the rest of the way? It's a few minutes out. I promise I will do everything I can to keep you safe."

I laced my arm through him, and the moment our bodies touched, tension began to seep out of me. The two of us walked for a few more minutes in silence, picking our way through the forest. Thankfully, we didn't see any other snakes.

"Here we are." Xander came to a stop, putting his hand on mine. "What do you think?"

I thought I couldn't do this. My heart raced as I stared at our surroundings.

"I-I can't... I don't...." My words failed me as I stared at the water before us. Memories of the currents in the river pulling me under filled my mind. Suddenly, my lungs were tight. It was becoming difficult to breathe again. I turned to him, my tone accusatory as I hissed, "Why would you bring me here?"

"To wash," he said. "That's all." Shaking his head, Xander stepped forward and crouched. He dipped a hand in the water before looking back at me. "I told you, Aileana. I will keep you safe. You have my word."

His word. The promise sent a shiver through me. Although Xander seemed to go out of his way to irritate me, he had fought the Winged Soldiers for me.

He had been willing to die for me.

Surely he wouldn't try to drown me a second time?

Even if he wasn't planning on it, I wasn't keen on the idea of getting back into an unknown body of water. I would be perfectly content to never feel the pull of a current again in my entire life.

Xander must have noticed something on my face because he stepped back, taking my hand. "Sunshine. It's okay. The water here is shallow and doesn't get deeper than my waist."

"Are you sure?" I bit my lip, shifting away from the water's edge. It had been days since I had last been in the water, and I wanted to be clean, but this... I wasn't sure I could do it. Acrid fear coated the back of my tongue as I stared at the calm, unmoving water.

"I wouldn't have brought you here if I wasn't sure," he said. "Do you trust me?"

"Yes," I breathed. I didn't know how I felt about him, but I knew I trusted him.

"Good," he whispered. "Then please, believe me. I've been here before. I always try to stop here when I go to The Pines. This isn't just some regular pond, you know."

I raised a brow, happy for the distraction brought on by curiosity. "Oh? What is it?"

He chuckled, the sound warming me from the inside as he squeezed my hand. "You'll just have to get in to find out."

Clasping my hands in front of me, I stared at the water. It was still and looked so different from the river. Even in the fading light of the day, I could make out the tall reeds that stood sentry on the edge of the pond, like long, thin soldiers. In the middle of the water was a large, smooth rock.

It looked... calm. Peaceful, even. But I couldn't shake the memory of water filling my lungs. My heart twisted at the very thought of getting back into the water.

"Is it really safe?" I asked again.

"It really is," he replied. I looked between him and the water, twisting my hands in front of me. A beat passed before Xander breathed out a heavy sigh. "I'll show you."

The last word was barely out of his mouth before a rustle of fabric came from behind me. My eyes widened, and I turned just in time to see Xander pull off his tunic and throw it on the ground. He met my gaze, his hands going to his trousers as he slowly undid one button, then the next.

My breath caught in my throat as I watched him kick off his shoes before letting go of his grip on his trousers. They fell to his feet in a puddle of fabric, leaving him in a pair of white undershorts. They clung to his body, leaving very little to the imagination.

Even in the falling darkness, I could see the evidence I'd felt behind me in the past few days. He still wanted me.

I sucked in a deep breath, staring at him.

And then he put his hand on the waistband of his shorts.

"Xander," I hissed. My fear of the water had been forgotten, shoved aside for the fresh anger, shock, and... warmth brewing within me. "What in Kydona's name do you think you're doing?"

He chuckled, his voice deeper than before. "I'm going to wash," he said matter-of-factly. He was little more than a shadow as he gestured toward me. "You should, too. Traveling on horseback isn't easy, and we likely won't reach The Pines for another three days. This is our last chance to get clean before then."

And then he pushed down his shorts.

I gasped, blood rushing to my cheeks as I slammed my eyes shut.

"Oh my gods," I whispered. "You're naked."

A throaty chuckle was his only reply as a splashing sound came from in front of me.

"How astute of you to notice, Sunshine," he said. More splashing, and then he asked, "Are you just going to stand there?"

I found myself torn between wanting to flee this space and wanting to open my eyes and look at him. Join him. See if his chest felt as hard under my fingers as it had while we'd been riding...

What is wrong with me?

My mind began ticking off all the reasons I should turn around and leave. First off, Xander was nothing but trouble. He had also tried to kill me. Or, at the very least, he had attempted to commit involuntary manslaughter. Not only that, but he had made his dislike very clear.

I knew these things were true. They were valid reasons. Good ones, in fact. But even as I acknowledged them, I knew I didn't want to turn around.

"Are you trying to make me uncomfortable?" I asked, my eyes still squeezed shut.

"Are you uncomfortable?" he asked innocently.

"Xander," I hissed.

He hummed, making a clicking sound with his tongue. I heard another splash, and I peeked. I caught a glimpse of him as he ducked his head underwater. My cheeks burned as I averted my gaze once more.

"What's wrong?" he retorted. "Haven't you seen a naked male before, Aileana? I thought you weren't a maiden."

Damn.

I had forgotten about that particular lie. It was getting harder and harder to keep them straight.

If I left, Xander would win whatever game we were playing. I wasn't sure I understood the rules, but I knew I didn't want to give up.

He made me uncomfortable, but I remembered how his jaw had clenched in the cavern when I had been standing in nothing but my shift. The way he had felt as we had ridden together these past three days. The dark gleam in his golden eyes as he watched me when he thought I wasn't looking.

I dared a glance back at the water. Xander had walked further into the pond, and I could barely see him. But I *knew* he was there. I felt his presence like a brand on my soul.

"Well," he taunted, "are you coming?"

Yes. Whatever game this is, I am not done playing yet.

Having reached a decision, I unclasped my cloak. It fell to the mossy floor in a pile, my dress and petticoats following quickly behind.

Soon, I was standing in nothing but my shift. I could feel the weight of Xander's gaze on me as I stood at the edge of the water, staring straight ahead.

This was it. I had to get in. I didn't want to lose.

But it was more than that.

I *wanted* to get in the water. I had lived most of my life surrounded by fear. Fear of what the king might do if he tired of me, fear of pushing the king too far, fear of the unknown.

And now, I was free. I would *not* allow a fear of water to control me.

"Turn around, Xander," I ordered in a firm voice. I was grateful my tone didn't betray the nervous butterflies flitting about in my stomach.

"I live to serve, my lady." His voice was deep and raspy as small splashes told me he had complied with my wishes.

I waited until his back was turned before I reached down and grabbed the hem of my shift. Without giving myself time to think, I yanked the rough material over my head.

Instantly, goosebumps erupted all over my breasts and stomach as I bared myself to the world. The only thing remaining on my body was the necklace from Nonna. It was thin, the chain light as it bumped between my breasts.

Other than that, I was as bare as the day I was born.

Lifting a toe, I held it over the water for a single heartbeat before hesitantly lowering it, inch by inch.

You can do this.

A Truce and a Tale

⌒∽⌒

T he water was warm.

Not just warm, but hot. It was almost pleasant as it lapped against my skin. A soft moan slipped out of me as I lowered myself into the pond's welcoming embrace. As promised, the water didn't reach higher than my waist.

Within mere moments, the heat permeated my body. I knelt on the sandy bottom, exhaling as the water lapped at my bare shoulders. Tension I hadn't known existed left my body, and for a moment, I forgot that there was a very naked, very large male standing on the other side of the pond.

Basking in the quiet peacefulness of the night, I blew out a long breath. A small smile crept on my face as I ran my hand through the warm water.

"I told you it was safe."

Xander's voice broke through my meditative state.

I jumped to my feet, wrapping my arms around my chest as I tried to contain my bare breasts. It was a futile effort, so instead, I lowered myself into the water once more before turning to glare at him. I could just barely make out the form of his body a few feet away from me, the water lapping around his waist, but I was fairly certain he could see in the dark.

"You shouldn't sneak up on people," I hissed, rubbing a wet hand down my face. Blood rushed to my cheeks once more, and I shuffled backward, studiously averting my eyes. "It's rude."

"I called your name three times, asking if you were okay," he replied. I could hear the question in his voice.

"Oh." I hadn't heard him. My voice softened as I said, "I'm sorry."

He coughed. "Kydona have mercy upon me. Aileana just apologized for something. The world must be ending."

I laughed at the tone of his voice, splashing him as I backed up. "Don't be so ridiculous, Xander. It's not like I've never uttered an apology."

"You've never apologized to me," he pointed out.

"That's true," I conceded. "You're right. I will endeavor to apologize to you more frequently in the future."

"I'm not going to lie to you, Sunshine. I *really* enjoy hearing you tell me I'm right." His voice was gruff, husky even.

I inhaled sharply as his words settled within me. My insides coiled tightly, and a small splash came from his direction.

He was coming closer.

And we were both completely exposed to each other. Naked. Alone.

"What are you doing?" I whispered. Even in the darkness, the intimacy of this moment didn't escape me.

He took one step closer, then another. A low sound like a growl rumbled through him as the water rippled around us. The air seemed even thicker as we stood in the water with only a few feet between us.

I had never appreciated the barrier that clothing had provided until this moment. Perhaps this was the purpose of those ridiculous Ithenmyrian fashions for females. To stop them from finding themselves alone in a heated pool with a naked male.

A small voice in my head chose this moment to speak up.

You want this. To be alone with him. To take this further.

Further. What, exactly, would that mean?

I'd lied to Xander before. I'd never been with anyone. If someone had so much as touched me, I was certain King Edgar would have had both of us executed at once. But I knew the logistics of two people joining as one. As part of my "education" as the prince's betrothed, I'd been subjected to an explanation of what would be expected of me as the prince's wife.

I knew what sex was. I knew how to act. The directions I'd been given had been clear enough. I'd even been forewarned that the joining would hurt, but it was necessary for the prince to place his seed within me.

Honestly, I wasn't exactly sure what the big deal was. Sex, as it had been described to me, sounded horrible.

But if it was so horrible, why did I feel all tangled up inside when Xander was naked near me? Why was I spending hours on the horse daydreaming about his touch and the way it would feel if he ran his hand down my shoulder, my breasts, my stomach, and lower?

I sucked in a deep breath. Warmth pooled deep in my core, and I shifted as a realization struck me.

I wanted that. I wanted *him*.

"Aileana," he whispered. My name was a prayer and a plea on his lips. That warmth in my core tightened even further as his voice made his closeness known.

"Yes, Xander?" I murmured. My voice was deep, husky, and betrayed the thoughts swirling around in my mind.

He stepped closer to me, and my stomach coiled. The warm water lapped at my breasts as I knelt, and I sucked in a deep breath.

"Give me your hand," he murmured.

I kept my hands at my sides.

He growled my name. It had never sounded so much like a warning as it did then.

I knew he was staring at me. But I wasn't upset. In fact, I was the very opposite of upset. I was... intrigued.

Here we were, naked and alone. Very alone. Based on the deepness of his voice, I was fairly certain he was acutely aware of that fact.

Keeping my eyes where I thought his gaze was, I smiled. "One moment," I said.

He snarled something inaudible, a splash coming from his direction, as I dunked in the water. I waited until my hair was soaked before pushing myself to my feet. Water sluiced off me as I stood tall, my long hair falling to cover my chest as the water lapped just above my hips.

Heat coursed through me as I remained standing, my breath coming heavier as the night insects chirped all around us. An owl hooted, and somewhere in the distance, a wolf howled.

Seconds ticked by as we stood mere feet from each other, with only the forest animals as our witnesses. My heart pounded in my chest as I waited for... something. Our breaths were like shouts in the silence, and my skin felt too tight as we stared at each other.

"Sunshine," he repeated. His voice was deeper than before, his words barely more than a rumble.

"Hmm?" I blinked, trying to clear my head. What was wrong with me?

"Please give me your hand."

This time, I complied instantly, raising my right hand out of the water. He stepped forward, coming close enough that I could make out the distinct shape of his very masculine chest as he stood less than two feet from me. Some would probably describe his chest as sculpted. My breath caught in my throat, my lungs tightening as I felt lightheaded.

Something small and rectangular landed in my outstretched hand, a strong floral scent filling my nose.

Soap. It was soap. My stomach plummeted as disappointment bloomed within me.

That was *not* what I'd been expecting.

Blowing out a long breath, I tightened my fingers around the scented bar. "Thank you," I whispered, trying to keep the disappointment out of my voice.

A moment passed before Xander coughed. "I'll give you some privacy. Don't take too long."

"So bossy," I replied, but there was no bite in my words.

Not anymore.

THE NEXT FEW days went by in much of the same way. We rose with the sun, rode all day with minimal breaks, and rested at night.

The only difference was that something had thawed between Xander and me at the hot springs. Ever since that night, we seemed to have reached a truce of sorts.

It wasn't that we were no longer at each other's throats. If anything, we were bickering more than before.

But our words weren't barbed any longer. Laughter filled the air as we rode, and both Xander and Daegal talked with me. A sadness still permeated the air around them, and it had Jo's name on it.

I was no expert in grief, but I thought it was probably normal.

A small part of me recognized it was special that there were people who mourned Jo's passing.

Who would mourn me if I died?

I wasn't sure that there was anyone at all.

By the afternoon on the third day after the hot springs, the path through the woods had become something that loosely resembled a road. It had widened enough for both horses to ride side-by-side, and the trees were thinning.

The mountains leveled into hills, and the trek became easier. Xander grew more relaxed by the hour, and I knew our destination was near.

"Tell me how the two of you met," I requested after we shared yet another meal of hard bread and cheese. "There must be a story behind it."

Daegal chuckled, his voice in a loud whisper as he leaned in. "You might find this hard to believe, but your husband and I weren't always friends."

"No," I gasped in mock shock, my hand flying to my heart as I gripped the saddle horn with one hand. I was getting better on the horses, and my legs were no longer burning at the end of the day. "Xander is the picture of serenity and kindness."

I snorted, barely able to keep a straight face as Daegal broke into outright laughter.

Behind me, Xander shifted. His thighs tightened around me, pressing my body into the saddle as his breath brushed the back of my neck. I stiffened instinctively as he growled, "I *am* kind to those who deserve it."

I chuckled, patting his thigh gently. He tensed beneath my touch but quickly softened as I said placatingly, "Of course you are, Xander. The absolute image of kindness."

"That's right, I am," he said.

"Perhaps then you'd be so *kind* as to take over the storytelling and tell me how you and Daegal met?" I asked sweetly.

The Fortune Elf coughed. "You walked right into that one, Xan."

Xander blew out a long breath, muttering something inaudible before he acquiesced. "Fine," he huffed. "We met after an especially long winter in Breley some years ago."

"Breley is the capital city in the province of Midena, correct?" I asked. I had never been there, of course.

"Yes. In fact, our destination is not too far from where we first met. The Pines are on the border of Midena and Nin."

Interesting. I stored that information away for later. They had been very secretive about our destination, but I was slowly gathering more information about it. From what I could understand, The Pines was a secluded location they presumed would be safe from our pursuers. How they knew this, I wasn't sure.

Daegal interrupted, amusement lacing his voice as he said, "Enough with the geography lesson. Keep telling the story."

"So impatient." Xander rubbed his hand over his face, chuckling. "As I was saying, it had been a very long winter. I was in Breley for business when, all of a sudden, I heard an outcry coming from the town square. Naturally, I was intrigued."

"Naturally," I muttered under my breath.

A sound of amusement came from the Fortune Elf, but Xander ignored us both. "As soon as my business was concluded, I made my way to the square. You can imagine my surprise when I saw a tall, slender Elf telling fortunes in the middle of the market. A large crowd surrounded him, and people were forcing their way forward to have their fortunes told.

"I watched for quite a while as the Elf told one fortune after another. Eventually, the sun began to set, and the crowd thinned. Only then did I approach the elf. When I got close, he looked up at me. Silver glowed from behind his eyes, and it felt like he was looking right into my soul."

I knew that stare. It felt unsettling. I found it fascinating that Xander had felt the same when he'd first met Daegal.

"Interesting," I murmured.

"Very," Xander agreed. "After a few moments, the silver in the elf's eyes cleared. He blinked, tilting his head toward me before saying, 'You shouldn't be here, son of Aranuil. Your time—'"

Xander's voice trailed off, and the horses stopped in the middle of the path.

I held my breath as a strangled cry rose deep in the woods. The sound sent shivers down my spine as I twisted in the saddle. I gripped Xander's arm. "Did you hear that?"

Xander nodded, his voice low. "I did, but I'm not sure we should—"

"Someone's hurt," I said briskly. "And we need to help them."

"I'm not so sure that's a great idea," Xander said. "There could be more Winged Soldiers in the woods. It might be a trap."

"Or someone could be dying, and we might be the only ones who can save them," I argued.

"Aileana—"

"I'm going," I said. I slid down the horse, my dismount much smoother than it would have been a few days ago.

Still seated on Thunder, Xander snarled, "Kydona, save me from this infuriating female." He glared at me, his golden eyes flashing. "Why can't you do as you're told for once?"

I made a face at him. "Doing what you're told only makes sense if the thing you're being commanded to do isn't ridiculous." Patting my skirts and feeling the reassuring hilt of my daggers, I put my hands on my hips. "Like it or not, Xander, I will investigate the noise. The question is, are you coming?"

After a few more words that I chose not to hear, Xander dismounted. He kept the reins in his hands as he glared at me.

"Of course, I'm coming," he snapped. "What kind of husband would I be if I let my wife wander off into the woods alone?"

A fake one, I wanted to retort, but just then, the strangled cry came again. I swallowed my words as Daegal took the reins from Xander, looking us both over as his eyes went glassy.

A minute went by before the silver cleared.

"We aren't far from The Pines. I'll go get help," Daegal said. His voice was low as he tied Thunder's reins to Stormflier's saddle. "We don't have much time to waste. The Red Shadow draws near. Be careful, both of you."

I swallowed, the warning echoing in my soul, but I pushed it aside. The sound came again from the forest, but this time, it didn't stop.

Someone needed our help.

The Sound of Death

⁓⊱⊰⁓

Xander and I crept through the forest in the cry's direction. With each step, they grew louder. More harried.

My heart pounded as memories I had shoved away forced themselves to the forefront of my mind.

Pain erupted on my back, and I screamed. The sound echoed through the circular chamber as the high king laughed.

"What a stupid bitch," he snarled. The scent of sandalwood swirled all around me as he came closer. The whip cracked in the air, and I shuddered. My back clenched involuntarily. I knew what was coming. "Only good for spreading her legs."

A snap in the air was my only warning before the fire erupted on my bare back.

"Please," I whimpered.

But he just laughed. "My son is going to have a fabulous time bringing you to heel, pet."

I bit back a sob as another scream tried to inch its way out of my throat.

"Aileana."

Xander's voice sounded urgent, and I forced myself out of my night-marish memories. He touched his hand to the back of mine, sending a shock of awareness through me. "We are getting close," he said. "Are you going to be okay?"

Was I going to be okay?

I wasn't sure I'd ever been okay.

But I would survive. I would force myself to keep on living. And maybe one day, the horrible memories of what I'd suffered would be just that. Memories. Distant. No longer able to bother me.

Maybe.

"I'll be fine," I said gruffly. At that exact moment, another cry came from before us. We were close now, and the wailing was distinctly feminine. Shivers ran down my spine. They sounded so similar to my own. "We have to help her."

"We will." Xander nodded, pulling his sword from the scabbard that hung on his hip. "Can you at least try to be careful, Aileana? I'd rather not have to rescue you today."

I withdrew my weapon.

"Bold of you to assume that I would be the one in need of rescuing, *darling*," I retorted.

My fake husband snorted, but before we could say anything else, my eyes caught sight of something ahead of us. A thousand curses rushed through me as we set upon a small clearing.

My nostrils flared, and my grip tightened as the source of the cry came into view.

Behind me, Xander snarled. "Dammit."

I nodded, but words wouldn't come to my mouth. My eyes were glued to a long, thick wooden pole staked in the middle of the clearing in front of us.

Ten, maybe fifteen feet from the stake, was a tiny cottage. It was even smaller than Nonna's, which was saying something. It also had the distinct honor of looking even worse than the murder cottage. The structure boasted a crumbling chimney, two tiny windows, and a door hanging off its hinges.

But that wasn't what stole my breath away.

No, that happened when I saw the emaciated elf who knelt on the ground. Enormous, translucent blue butterfly wings adorned her bare back, but they lay in bloody tatters around her. The elf's arms were outstretched above her head as a braided leather cord bound her to a stake.

A human, nearly twice her size, stalked around her. His back was to us, but I could see the whip he gripped. His clothing was as brown as the dirt beneath his feet. The elf wept as she lay shuddering on the ground. He was ignoring her cries as he stalked around her.

"How dare you disrespect me?" he roared as he pulled back the whip. It made a smooth arc, rushing through the air towards her. I cringed, sucking in a deep breath as I stumbled backward.

"I'm sorry, Raithian." the female cried out. "Please, don't. I'll be goo—"

Her pleas were cut off as the whip slashed through her wings and across her back once more. She screamed, and my heart shattered. The cry that came out of her mouth was the sound of death.

I bit my lip, blood filling my mouth as I stifled the matching scream that threatened to come out of me. Beside me, Xander tightened his grip on his sword as he looked between me and the elf.

"You stupid Light Elf whore," Raithian swore. "I took you in, married you, and this is how you repaid me?"

"No," she wept. "I swear to you, I was never unfaithful. The baby is yours."

She's pregnant?

A shudder ran through me, and beside me, Xander stiffened.

"Liar!" Raithian bellowed. He raised the whip again, and I knew. I just knew. He wasn't going to stop until he killed her and the baby.

And there was no way in the seven circles of hell that I would let that happen. Not while I still breathed. Not to this poor elf.

Tightening my grip on my dagger, I darted out from the trees. Behind me, Xander groaned. "Dammit, Aileana."

The leaves rustled, and I knew he was following close behind me.

"Stop!" I commanded, advancing on Raithian. I stepped into the clearing, stopping between two large, ancient-looking trees as I called out, "Don't you dare touch her again."

"What the hell?" Raithian cursed, turning around. The moment he looked at the two of us, the disgusting human widened his stance. A wolfish grin appeared on his face as he stared at the two of us.

"Step away from the elf," I ordered.

Raithian tilted his head, exposing yellowed teeth as he sneered, "She's my wife. According to the laws of this land, I can do whatever I want with her. Not only that, but you have no right to stop me. This is *my* land, and the two of you are trespassing."

Xander stepped forward, the sun catching on his sword. "Even so, we would ask that you stop harming her."

Raithian laughed. No, laughed was the wrong word. He cackled, the sound mirthless and without joy. It was the embodiment of evil.

He would get along with my fiancé, I thought suddenly. *The two males would probably find sadistic joy in being around each other.*

"You *ask.*" Raithian turned, flicking his hand towards the injured elf trembling on the ground. "Did you hear that, Hironna? These two have *asked* that I stop."

Hironna moaned as rivulets of blood continued their path down her tattered wings. My heart shattered at the sound of her faint voice.

"Please listen to him," Hironna said softly, her words broken up by pants. "You're just going to make it worse."

Raithian nodded, returning his steely eyes to us. Pure violence emanated from him. "Leave now," he ordered.

"No," I shook my head, tamping down the fear rising within me at the sight of the whip. My skin felt too tight for my body as memories of past hurt collided with the present. "We can't."

The human moved his gaze to Xander, sneering. "Are you going to let your wife speak for you?"

"She's not exactly easy to deal with," Xander muttered.

I huffed, shooting my fake husband a look that told him exactly how I felt about his comment.

Hissing under my breath, I tightened my grip on my dagger. "Really? You want to do this right now?" Shaking my head, I took a step toward the evil male. "This is your last warning. Leave her alone."

The horrible male tilted his head, his eyes flashing. "No, I don't think I will. She is my wife, and her life is in my hands. I will do with her as I please."

I sighed, forcing a mask of cool indifference to cover my features. In reality, my stomach was twisting in knots, but there was no way I would show that. Not to this human who so clearly thrived on fear and pain.

It was apparent he was intent on killing someone today.

"Fine," I said.

I peeked over my shoulder, noting the resigned expression on Xander's face as he lifted his sword. He shrugged, seeming to say, *go ahead. Let's get this over with.*

Nodding, I sent silent prayers to all the goddesses that this would work.

Widening my stance, I slide my dagger into its sheath before placing my palms on the rough bark of the trees on either side of me. The trees seemed to come alive under my fingertips, humming their approval.

Protectress of the Woods, the wind whispered in my ear.

Something within my veins thrummed as I called forth the magic within me.

As I dug deep within myself, time itself slowed to a crawl.

The clouds parted as the afternoon sun shone on me. I felt a stretching within myself as the wind picked up around the clearing. My skin tingled as though hundreds of needles were pricking it at once.

Leaves, dirt, and debris swirled as a cyclone of air descended upon the four of us.

Hironna cried out as my skin began to glow green. Her tattered wings fluttered as she struggled against her binds.

Her husband's eyes flashed dangerously as he stepped toward us.

"I am going to kill you," he growled in Xander's direction as he bent, picking up a discarded sword that had been lying near his feet, "and then I'm going to play with your whore of a wife for a *very* long time." Raithian eyed me lecherously, and I shuddered.

"Over my dead body," Xander hissed. His fists clenched at his side as a tremor of fury roiled through him. "My wife is not a whore."

Raising his sword, Xander lunged toward Raithian.

The sound of metal against metal filled the clearing. The two fought, their swords clashing together over and over again. My breath caught in my lungs as they sparred. They danced together, the larger male soon panting as he fought my fake husband. My hands were still on the trees as the awareness of the earth rushed through me.

Myhhena? I cried out in my mind.

The wind carried her answer to my ears mere moments later. *My sisters and I are here, Protectress.*

I need your help.

Of course, Protectress.

A wave of power unlike anything I'd ever felt, flooded through me. The sudden surge of energy rushing through my veins was overwhelming, and I gasped as I felt my control over my body slip through my fingers.

Part of me knew there had to be a way to manage the raging currents of power rushing through my veins, but I had no idea how. All I knew was I wanted Raithian to stop everything. Stop hurting his wife. Stop inflicting pain.

And the magic *knew* what I wanted.

Seconds passed as I stretched my awareness through the forest.

Shall we rid you of this evil human, Protectress? Myhhena asked. I could have sworn her voice sounded almost... giddy in my ear.

Yes, I commanded, *do it.*

Your wish is our command.

No sooner had the last word echoed in my ear than the ground shook. My eyes widened, my hands still on the trees, as dozens of brown roots burst out of the dirt around the evil human. They wrapped around his feet, dragging him backward.

"What in the seven circles of hell?" Raithian cried out as he fell to the ground. His fingers dug into the dirt, scrambling wildly for purchase. "What kind of sor—"

The horrible human's words were soon nothing more than a gurgle for air as countless branches, brown and green, burst *through* his body. Within moments, his corpse was covered in dozens of leafy twigs. Only his boots remained, sticking out of the brambles.

Bile rose in my throat as I stared at the death I had just caused. Another death on my conscience. Another nightmare that would undoubtedly haunt me for the rest of my life.

We are here to serve you, Protectress. Myhhena's voice echoed through me.

I just... nodded. I was incapable of anything else. The currents of unconstrained power continued to run through me. Inexplicably, it was even stronger than before.

The thrum within my veins increased, and suddenly, I realized my entire body was glowing a vivid green.

My head felt light, and my limbs were little more than air as I sank to my knees. The earth softened beneath my feet as I dug my fingers into the dirt.

Somewhere outside of myself, I heard Xander's voice. He was yelling and calling out to me, but I couldn't make out his words.

The magic was too strong as it flooded through me.

My mind *became* the woods once more. The magic poured out of me, encouraging new growth throughout the land. I could *feel* tiny trees sprouting to life. But it wasn't enough.

I became aware of a yearning that existed deep in the earth. The ground itself called out to me as roots erupted from the dirt. I screamed, my voice little more than air, as they tangled around my ankles. My heart pounded as I was dragged back into the woods.

My fingers scrabbled for a handhold as the wind whispered in my ears. *We have lost all the others. We won't lose you too. Stay with us.*

The ground cried out, its deep voice almost primal as it reverberated through me. *Stay with us, Protectress. Let us nourish you. We* need *you.*

And then, all the life within the forests of Ithenmyr cried out to me all at once. Their voices traveled thousands of kilometers, ringing in my soul as they spoke to me.

The land's voice was eternal, ethereal, and ancient. It was deep and earthy and filled with power.

One word echoed through me, over and over again, until it was the only thing I heard.

Stay.

Stay.

Stay.

Roots continued to climb over my body as the rushing currents of magic increased in power. I gasped as they threatened to pull me under. Somehow, I knew that if I gave in to their call, it would be the end.

There would be no coming back if the earth claimed me for its own.

In the back of my mind, another thought rose to the surface.

This isn't what I want.

As I battled my will against that of all the natural life in Ithenmyr, something else flickered in the peripherals of my consciousness.

Bursting through all the green and brown was something hot and fiery. It was burning. The fire was summoning me, calling me towards it.

The scent of ash, smoke, and trees filled my lungs, but it didn't scare me. Instead, it made me feel... safe. Warm. Cared for.

I pushed myself towards that feeling of safety.

My body grew warmer as I neared the heat, but the earth itself was fighting my every move.

No, it screamed, pouring the depths of its rage into every word. *Don't leave us. Not again.*

I'm sorry, I cried out to the land. *Please, I can't stay. I don't want to.*

In response, the roots tightened their grip against me. The wind howled against me, battering my body.

We need *you.*

"I won't leave you," I whispered. "I promise."

The moment the words left my mouth, a tingling sensation ran up my arms. I looked down as matching dark green whorls appeared on both my wrists. They flashed for a moment before disappearing into my skin.

We will hold you to your promise, Protectress of the Woods.

Then, the bright green light faded as the yelling grew louder. I tried to move, but I couldn't. Every one of my limbs felt too heavy for my body.

My eyelids fluttered shut as the magic coursing through my veins disappeared all at once. My chest tightened, and my heart pounded as darkness crept into my vision.

I was stuck within a shell of myself.

"Help me," I whispered before everything went black.

Wedding Bells and Darkness

※

"You must wake up, my lady," a chipper voice said from above me. I slipped back into consciousness, the fuzziness of my dream ebbing away.

I blinked, my eyes adjusting to the sudden onslaught of light as I stretched out my hands.

What?

My brows furrowed as I pressed my fingers down. This wasn't right. Dirt wasn't soft or bouncy or smooth like fabric. And above me...

This wasn't the early morning sky, kissed by the rising sun. No, I was lying under a crimson canopy. And beneath my fingers...

This wasn't dirt. This wasn't right. Nothing was right.

My heart pounded as I croaked, "Where am I?"

The same voice tittered, "Why, you're at home, of course!"

"What?" I exclaimed loudly, jolting upright.

Home.

No.

This wasn't my home. This had never been my home. But these circular walls. The black and gray stones. The four-poster bed.

It couldn't be.

I blinked, rubbing my hands over my eyes. This had to be a dream. A nightmare. A hallucination. Gods, this couldn't be real.

But I pinched myself, and nothing happened other than the burst of pain that rushed through me.

The servant stared at me, her head tilted to the side. She was pleasantly plump, her thick middle covered by an apron as she held a tray bearing food. "My lady?" The question was evident in her voice. "What is the matter?"

"No," I whispered, my heart breaking as my lungs seized. I had no other words. Not right now. This achingly familiar room. This bed. The memories of punishments that stretched into hours and days. My voice cracked as I moaned, "No."

"My lady? Are you feeling alright?"

Alright. I wasn't alright. I would never be alright again. How could this happen?

Ignoring the servant bustling around me, I looked down. My eyes widened as I stared at the white lace nightgown adorning my body. The dress from Nonna and her pendant... They were gone.

"It can't be," I whispered.

"What's wrong, my lady?" The servant tilted her head, watching me closely.

"I... I shouldn't be here. This is wrong."

I had escaped and gone out the window. Found Xander and ventured into Thyr. This wasn't supposed to happen. I wasn't supposed to be in this tower ever again.

I must have said the last part out loud, for the servant said, "Not to worry, ma'am. You won't be here much longer. After all, today's the day you've been waiting for!"

I blinked. "What day?"

A horrid suspicion grew within me—an aching, terrible, horrifying suspicion.

She grinned, her gap-toothed smile proudly displayed as she said the words that brought my entire world crashing down around me.

"Why, your wedding day to the prince, of course!"

No.

No.

No.

It couldn't be. I couldn't be back here. Not after everything that I had gone through.

Seemingly ignorant of the absolute turmoil rushing through me, the servant placed the tray on the nightstand. She patted my hand as I stared blankly at her.

"Eat up, my lady. I will return in a quarter of an hour to help you dress. We mustn't delay. Everyone is waiting for you."

Everyone.

"No," I gasped, drawing the covers around myself as my gaze darted around frantically. My heartbeat was echoing in my ears as panic threatened to overtake me. "I can't." Shaking my head, I raised pleading eyes to hers. "I won't."

She nodded, her eyes soft as she reached over and enveloped my hand in hers. "Of course you can, my dear. Everyone is nervous on their wedding day, but I promise you, it will be okay. Just do what he tells you tonight, and I promise it will get better after the first time."

"The first time," I echoed.

The servant smiled. "Who knows? Perhaps you might find you enjoy married life."

Married life.

To Remington.

Oh, my gods.

My lungs tightened in my chest as tremors overtook me.

"Eat," the servant ordered. She patted my hand, tittering as she walked to the door and knocked. I heard a lock click before the door swung inwards. She curtsied in my direction. "I'll be back soon, my lady."

Then she was gone. And I was alone.

Reaching behind me, I grabbed a pillow and brought it to my face. Pressing my nose against it, I screamed.

I screamed and screamed and screamed until my throat was raw. I screamed until I had nothing left. Then I screamed some more.

This could not be. How could this happen?

The whole thing... had it been a dream? If so, it had been the worst kind of dream. The type that dangled freedom before my very eyes before yanking it away.

My screams gave way to sobs. Deep, heart-wrenching sobs ripped through me as I broke. Defeat and despair filled me, shoving everything else out. I had nothing left.

I wrapped my arms around my legs and pressed my eyes into my knees.

And I wept.

I didn't move until the lock clicked, giving me a moment's warning before multiple footsteps heralded the arrival of many people.

"You didn't eat anything." The same servant as before stood before me, her hands on her hips as she tutted. "Well, it's too late now. It's time to get ready."

"No." I shook my head, pushing myself against the headboard. "I won't go. I don't want to marry him."

The servant shook her head, pity lining her eyes.

And then the scent of my worst nightmares reached my nose. A whimper ripped through me involuntarily, and my back locked up as my heart seized in my chest.

From the doorway came a dark voice that haunted my every nightmare. It was tinged with violence, pain, and death. "You'll get off that bed and get dressed, *pet*. Right this second."

I swallowed, keeping my eyes ahead as I whispered, "Please don't make me."

Tears filled my eyes once more. My hands shook as I refused to look at the doorway. At *him*.

Footsteps rang on the stone floor as my heart pounded in my chest. A moment passed before he stood before me. The scent of sandalwood assaulted my senses.

"Look at me." His voice thundered through the room.

I shut my eyes, trying to breathe normally through the fog of memories I'd long forced away.

"Look at me!" he bellowed.

I took a deep breath and obeyed. My stomach twisted in knots as I stared at High King Edgar.

"Yes, Your Majesty?" I willed my voice to be strong as I stared at the king who held my fate in his hands. His curly brown hair did nothing to hide the gilded caps covering his pointy ears. His eyes were filled with promises of pain if I didn't obey.

History told me he wouldn't hold back from any "training" his pet might require.

The king cleared his throat. "I will only say this once, Aileana, so you had better listen closely. Do you understand?"

I nodded, staring at the sword hanging off his belt.

What are the chances I could grab that sword and run it through him before he stopped me?

Not very high.

"You will marry Remington. Today. If you do not, I will tie you to the stake and light the pyre myself. This union is the only reason you are still alive. Refuse once more, and you are worth nothing to me. Do you understand?"

This threat was new, and new things were bad. They were unpredictable. I had no idea whether the king meant the threat or not.

For my entire life, King Edgar had told me I was being kept until the day I could be a good wife for his son. That when I reached Maturity, I would finally be of use. That was why he kept me all these years.

To *breed* like a goddess-damned animal. That's all I was to him.

A *pet*.

King Edgar had killed those who served me to prove a point. My tutor Orvyn had died for teaching me things outside of the king's "approved curriculum." I wasn't sure that the high king would go through with having me burnt at the stake, but I also wasn't sure he *wouldn't* do that.

Maybe he really was done with me.

Unwilling to completely throw my life away, I shut my eyes briefly before nodding.

The king thundered, "Say it!"

I opened my eyes to see red sparks dancing around his fingertips.

King Edgar's voice echoed through the room as the servants cowered behind him. "Say it now, Aileana, or I swear I will burn you alive today."

The dam broke, releasing the treacherous tears as I opened my mouth. "I understand," I said softly. "I will marry him."

"Today."

All the fight left me as I nodded wearily. "Yes, my king. I will marry Prince Remington today."

THEY DRESSED ME LIKE A DOLL.

Tears continued to streak down my face as I stood limply in the middle of the room. I sucked in heaving breaths as the servants tugged off my nightgown.

I didn't fight as I stood naked before half a dozen servants. I was a statue while they plucked me like a chicken, rubbing scented oils all over my body. My nose wrinkled at the horrible smell, but I didn't stop them.

Pursing my lips together, I didn't move as they forced me into layers of petticoats. Instead of stays, the servants pulled a restrictive corset over my breasts. They directed me to hold on to the poster of my bed as they pulled the strings tight.

So tight.

I couldn't breathe.

But I didn't care. Not anymore.

Once my chest was properly constricted, the servants pulled a long, blood-red gown over my head. It swept over me, covering me in the king's colors. The colors of the House of Irriel. To whom I would soon belong. Because I was nothing more than a possession. A pet.

Someone to be owned. Bred like an animal. A wife.

But it was better to be a wife than dead.

Right?

Right?

If I had been in a better frame of mind, I would have ripped the fabric right off me. I would have torn it to shreds with my bare hands. I would have screamed.

But I was not in a better frame of mind. My escape had been nothing more than a dream, and I would never escape this prison.

I wept silently as they pulled my hair into an elaborate updo.

Remaining still, I didn't even flinch as they yanked my hair this way and that before they painted my face.

I didn't fight them as they clasped thick, black bracelets around my wrists.

They look like manacles, I thought morosely. *How fitting that I will wear them on my wedding day.*

When one of the servants whispered about the prohiberis, I didn't react.

Because I had nothing left.

WEDDING BELLS RANG through the tower as I descended the winding steps. With each step I took towards my doom, my stomach twisted in knots. I trembled as I walked down the stone steps, counting them silently.

There were five hundred and seventeen stairs. Five hundred and seventeen. What an odd number.

Eventually, they, too, came to an end.

I didn't let myself think about the fact that this was the first time I had ever been allowed to walk down these stairs. I didn't let myself think about the freedom I thought I had found.

Staring straight ahead, I barely breathed. I was a shell of myself and nothing more. I knew if I stopped to think about Xander, even for a single moment, fear would paralyze me. And if that happened, I wouldn't be able to move again.

And so, I didn't think about him. I didn't think about his golden eyes, silver-white hair, or infuriating personality. I didn't think about the way he had fought for me.

Instead, I thought about how I would like to get my hands on a weapon—any weapon—and how I would use it. I would ensure King Edgar and his horrible son did not live long enough to terrorize me or anyone else.

As I stepped out of the open tower door, my thoughts swirled around with murderous daydreams. My mind was so focused on my thoughts I didn't realize that something was wrong until it was too late.

I took a step forward. One foot was on stone, and the other was on... nothing. There was nothing there.

It was a void.

Where the ground should have been was complete and utter darkness. I screamed as I tumbled into emptiness.

My heart thundered in my chest, and my hands were sweaty as I reached out and tried to grab onto something, anything, to slow my descent.

But there was nothing there.

I fell and fell and fell into the inky blackness.

I DIDN'T KNOW how long I was lost in the pit or how far down it went. Every second felt like an eternity, and every hour felt like it went by in the blink of an eye.

I tumbled, somersaulting through the void until falling was the only thing I knew. The wind blew past me, roaring as I descended into darkness.

My blood-red gown, the colors of Irriel, billowed around me like a parachute. My hair came undone as the heavy bracelets they had forced on me hung like a weight on my wrists, dragging me down.

I screamed until my voice was raw, and then I continued to gasp for air. My hands clutched for something to grab onto, but nothing was there.

Eventually, a voice broke through the never-ending darkness.

They called me as the scent of ash and smoke and the deep woods filled the air around me. A familiar heat brushed up against me, and I felt a pull towards it.

"Don't give up," the voice ordered. It was so quiet—I had to strain to hear it over the rush of wind blowing past my ears. "Fight. You have to fight this."

Give up. I didn't do that. That was something other people did. Not me. Swallowing, I forced myself to head toward the voice.

Something was dragging me down, pulling me with it. Nothing about this situation was right, but I felt... utterly and completely out of sorts. *Wrongness* was forcing its way through my body.

Don't give up, I commanded myself. *Think. Fight.*

How could I fight when I didn't understand what was happening?

Taking a deep breath, I shut my eyes. With them closed, I could forget for a moment that I was falling through a never-ending pit.

I began to go through a list of all the things around me. What could be causing me to feel so wrong? The dress they had forced me into was just that—a dress. My hair was being held up by a few pins, but that was it.

Other than that...

An audible gasp escaped me as I realized where the sense of wrongness was coming from. The bracelets on my wrists grew heavier with every passing moment, as though they were dragging me down.

That had to be it.

Sucking in a deep breath, I grabbed the one binding my left hand.

Pain ripped through my fingers when I touched the band. Burning tears rushed to my eyes. Forcing myself to keep working despite the agony, I yanked on the bracelet.

Soon, my fingers were a mottled red mess as I continued to seek the clasp in the darkness. Seconds ticked by into minutes as I fought for my freedom. My lungs seized as I struggled to remove the weights dragging me down.

After what felt like an eternity, my ravaged fingers finally found the smallest indent in the otherwise smooth material. Gritting my teeth, I shoved my nails into the clasp and *pulled*.

My fingernails broke under the pressure of trying to undo the clasp as a sharp, shooting pain shot through my hands. I gasped, trying to steady my breathing as I pushed past the complete feeling of *wrongness*. My fingers grew slick with effort, and still, I yanked on the bracelet.

In the back of my mind, I could hear the same voice calling for me.

"Fight," they said. "Please, come back."

And so I did. I fought. With every last drop of strength, I fought.

I had no idea how long I struggled with the bracelet, but eventually, I felt the slightest loosening around my wrist. Moments later, the bracelet fell off my wrists. I blew out a long breath as it tumbled off my hand, disappearing instantly.

The moment the manacle was off my left hand, I felt *life* beginning to flood back into me.

Bolstered by the sense of vitality rushing through me, I turned my attention to my right hand. Once again, the manacle burned my fingers. But this time, I knew it could come off.

And so I used every drop of my energy to find the clasp. My fingers were bloodied and burned as untold amounts of time went by. I sobbed as I struggled, but I never gave up. I wouldn't give up.

I knew the taste of freedom. I wouldn't stop fighting until it was mine again.

Minutes, hours, days, or years went by. But eventually, I was free. The second the other bracelet tumbled off my wrist, the darkness began to recede.

When I opened my eyes once more, I was no longer falling.

The Pines

I groaned, throwing my hands over my eyes as brightness leaked through my shut lids. Every part of my body ached. My limbs were heavy, my head pounding as I lay on something soft.

"Thank Kydona," a husky voice said from somewhere beside me. The scent of smoke and ash and trees was stronger than ever, filling me with a strange sense of safety. A warm hand landed on my arm, sending tiny sparks along my skin. "Can you hear me?"

My throat was hoarse as I rasped, "Yes. I can."

"Can you open your eyes?"

Pursing my lips, I thought about the question. "I can try."

Opening my eyes had never been so difficult as it was at that moment. The task felt monumental as I commanded my eyelids to obey my will. It felt like an entire minute went by before my body complied with my demands.

My eyelids opened slowly, revealing bright light and a pair of concerned golden eyes.

"Xander?" I asked. Stretching my fingers, I pressed them into the lumpy mattress beneath me. There was no richness in this small wooden room. Thank the gods.

Rubbing my eyes, I tried to push myself up. Every movement felt like agony as my muscles screamed.

Weak.

I was so weak.

"Yes," he rasped. "It's me. Don't move. You've been through quite the ordeal."

That seemed like an understatement. But lying in that bed, I realized I wasn't the only one suffering.

Bags lay under Xander's eyes that hadn't been there before, and he was hunched over, his frame folded in on itself as he sat on a low wooden stool. His eyes were dark. His mouth was pinched in a straight line as he reached beside him. I stared at him, unable to look away for even a moment.

Had it really just been a dream? It hadn't felt like a dream. No, it had felt like so much *more*. My fingers still burned from the manacles, and my heart still raced from falling through the pit.

Something had definitely happened. But what? As I was pondering the complexities of the dream that hadn't been just a dream, Xander cleared his throat.

"Aileana, drink this," he ordered gruffly, shoving a wooden cup toward me.

I eyed its contents warily, pursing my lips. "What is it?" I asked as I avoided the cup. It smelled unpleasant, and I could see something floating around in it.

"It'll help you," he said, avoiding my gaze.

I stared at him, furrowing my brows as I shook my head. "I'm not going to drink something without knowing what is in it."

He huffed, his nostrils flaring as his muscles tensed. "Of course." His grip on the cup tightened as a vein in his jaw popped. "Of course, you are going to be testy with me."

"I'm not being testy," I said. "I just asked a question."

"Aileana," he snapped, his eyes widening. "You have been unconscious for two days after you lost control of your magic. Two days. Is picking a fight really the first thing you want to do?"

I widened my eyes, blinking.

Two days?

Glaring at Xander, I pursed my lips. "I wasn't aware that I was the one *fighting*. I was just asking a question. If anything, you're the one who is fighting with me. Just tell me what is in the cup, and I'll drink it."

"Kydona, have mercy on me," Xander hissed through clenched teeth. He slammed the cup down on the nightstand. The contents sloshed as he pushed himself off the stool. He stood, muttering something about incorrigible females as he strode towards one of the two doors. Opening it, he barked, "Morwen, your presence is required."

A response came in another language, one I hadn't heard before. Xander paused, tapping his foot on the ground before responding in the same tongue.

He can speak more than one language?

I tucked this interesting piece of information away just as a tall, slender elf entered the room. She was easily the most stunning being I'd ever seen. Her sepia skin almost glowed in the sunlight, and a pair of small, bright green wings extended from her back that fluttered as she walked into the small space. Snow-white hair fell to the floor, covering all but the high peak of her ears.

"Ah. How wonderful to see you have finally awoken. We were quite worried there for a few moments," Morwen said. Her voice lilted over me, sounding like music to my ears. She had a tight accent that made all of her words sound clipped. White swirling tattoos ran from the tips of her fingers all the way down her dark arms, over her collarbone, and down her face.

She sat elegantly on the stool Xander had occupied only a few minutes earlier. Her dress was slim, the blue complimenting her wings perfectly as she sat primly beside me. "How can I be of assistance?"

Xander crossed his arms, glaring at me as he stood sentry by the door. "My *wife* refuses to drink the medicine until she knows what is in it."

"I'm not trying to cause a problem," I interjected, focusing on Morwen instead of my glowering fake husband in the corner. "As I attempted to explain to Xander, I don't want to drink something without knowing the contents."

"Of course not," Morwen replied, her voice soothing. "I would be happy to explain it to you."

And she did. Once I was satisfied that I wasn't going to be poisoned, I sighed. "Thank you. I'll drink it."

Morwen smiled, patting my hand. "You are more than welcome, my dear. Anything for Xander's wife."

She stood, walking over to the door. With her hand on the doorknob, she turned. "Make sure she rests," the elf commanded. "The magic tore through her, and she can't get up yet. It's too dangerous."

Xander nodded curtly, stepping towards me.

"I'll do my best," he replied. "But trying to tell her what to do is like attempting to herd wild cats."

The medicine worked quickly. Too quickly, perhaps. My limbs felt heavy, my head fuzzy as remaining awake was becoming more difficult by the moment.

"Maybe if you were kinder," I forced out the words as weariness pulled at me, "I'd be nicer... to you."

He replied, but I didn't hear his words as sleep pulled me under.

This time, I didn't dream.

THE NEXT THREE days passed in a blur of medicine and dreamless sleep. Every time I woke up, Xander was beside me. He held my elbow and helped me walk to the privy whenever I needed it, taking care to give me privacy. He brought me broth and bread to eat alongside the daily tonics prepared by Morwen.

I didn't think he slept at all.

Why would he keep a vigil next to someone he hated?

"I NEED to get out of this cabin," I argued, crossing my arms in front of my chest. "It's been four days since I first woke up, and I am bored!"

Xander glared at me as we rehashed the same argument we had been having for the past hour. He was standing near the only window in the small cabin. In the sunlight, he looked... gruff. Stubble dusted his jaw, and his entire face seemed to rest in shadows. "Morwen said you would need at least a week to heal."

I sighed, running my hands through my hair. "I don't just want to sit here doing nothing!"

"You're not doing nothing."

I glared at him. "What would you call this?"

"Recovering."

"I feel fine," I said. It was a partial truth. I felt... better. But fine?

I wasn't sure I'd ever been fine.

Being cooped up in bed the last few days had given me enough time to think, really think, about everything that had happened to me.

And now I knew what I was going to do. I had a new purpose: I would kill High King Edgar and his son if it was the last thing I did. The

High King would never be able to hurt me or anyone else ever again. I would make sure of it.

I could already imagine the shock in those blue eyes when he realized his pet killed him.

Xander growled under his breath. "I don't believe you, Aileana."

"Really," I insisted. "I'm fine."

Xander shook his head. He cleared his throat as he rubbed a hand on his temples. "You didn't see yourself after we rescued Hironna from her husband. For the goddess' sake, Aileana, when Daegal arrived with Teroth, you were lying unconscious on the forest floor. I had to *cut* dozens of roots off of you. They were crawling from the ground, trying to take you away."

"I—"

"Sunshine," he snarled, running a hand through his hair as his golden eyes flashed. "You're not listening to me. It was as though the forest didn't want you to leave. Your magic was pouring out of you, and you were *dying*. Your heartbeat was slowing as the woods seemed to claim you as one of their own. In all my years, I have never seen anything like that. So yes, you need to rest." His voice hardened as he snapped, "Forgive me for caring."

"Why *do* you care?"

The question burst out of me far more harshly than I had intended, and he flinched. Xander's hands balled into fists at his sides. He took a deep breath, staring at the ceiling.

I repeated the question. "Xander. Answer me. Why do you care?"

"You know why, Aileana," he hissed between clenched teeth.

I stared at him. Did I know? I had my suspicions. I thought perhaps Nonna hadn't been lying when she had seen something between us.

But to *know* something was so profound and powerful. To give something life by speaking it out loud was to give it power. And I wasn't sure I was ready to give Xander that kind of power over me.

So I bit my lip and kept my mouth shut. I forced the words back down my throat. I shoved them out of my mind where they couldn't bother me anymore.

And neither of us acknowledged what we both knew to be true. I gave up my fight to leave the room for another day. He didn't push me.

Minutes later, when Daegal came rushing in with a tip about the location of another piece of the map, Xander left without a word.

We didn't see each other for the rest of the day.

"Here."

I blinked, rubbing my eyes as something was dropped on my feet. I pushed myself up, reaching over to grab the dress Xander had unceremoniously dumped on the cot. "What's this for?"

"You need to get dressed if you want to look around The Pines," he replied carefully as he stared out the window, his back to me.

That got my attention. Eagerness filled my voice as I swung my bare feet onto the wooden floors. My toes curled as the morning air ran up my legs. "Do you mean it? I can finally leave this infernal cabin?"

He nodded, turning around. "As long as you are careful, Morwen thinks you should be able to get up." Xander frowned, adding as an afterthought, "Besides, I know how much you hate being cooped up."

"Careful, Xander," I said, trying to keep my voice light. "I might be tricked into thinking you like me."

Xander's eyes flashed, and he opened his mouth as though to reply before seeming to think better of it. He shook his head, gesturing to the clothes.

"Get dressed," he said gruffly. "I'll wait for you outside."

"So bossy," I replied as he left the cabin, but there was no bite to my tone. Not anymore.

As I ran my finger down the fabric of the cream-colored dress he had brought me, the thing left unsaid between us grew even more.

THE MOMENT we walked out of the cabin, I was struck by the beauty of The Pines. It was clear where the settlement had gotten its name. The namesake trees were everywhere.

The ground was hard and firm beneath my feet, but thankfully, there wasn't any snow in sight. We were in the middle of a forest, and I counted eighteen log cabins.

A hum of conversation filled the air as people hurried past us. They barely spared us a glance as they went about their days. Xander led me slowly through the settlement at a pace that could only be described as turtle-esque.

Before we had left the cabin, he had insisted I tell him the moment I felt the slightest bit of exhaustion. That wouldn't happen, but I didn't tell him that. Not after it took me days to convince him to let me take a walk.

The fresh air invigorated me even though the dress Xander had gotten me was far tighter than I used to. I'd had to squeeze into it, forcing it over my curves. The scoop neckline was cut so low—I felt my ample cleavage was only moments away from falling out of the dress and giving the people of The Pines a show they weren't paying for.

There was only one petticoat, and after spending time in the dress from Nonna, I felt practically naked. The dress didn't have pockets, and there was no room for my daggers. I felt bare without them, unprotected.

As we rounded a corner, I tried to adjust the gown on my frame for what felt like the tenth time.

"Stop fidgeting," Xander whispered in my ear. "No one could tell you were moments away from death less than a week ago."

"I wasn't aware that 'moments away from death' was a measurement for judging how one looked," I retorted, trying to mask my discomfort in the new clothes. Despite the cloak covering my shoulders and the muff around my hands, I shivered as a brisk wind blew past me.

Xander loosened his grip on my arm. "Aileana," he whispered. "You're beautiful. Anyone with half a brain can see that."

He thought I was beautiful?

Warmth flooded through me at his words, and I blushed.

"Thank you," I said after a moment. I elbowed him in the side. "You don't look so bad yourself."

His lips twitched, and that warmth within me expanded. After being cooped up, it was so nice to be outside. To breathe in the fresh air. To just *be*.

We walked in silence for a few minutes, past a row of log cabins and carefully tended gardens.

"How many people live here?" I asked Xander after we passed a group of small children kicking a cloth ball between them. They seemed so free. Growing up, I'd never played games. I wasn't even sure I knew how to have fun.

Having fun hadn't exactly been a priority for the king's pet.

"It varies. Anywhere from fifty to a hundred people, although I've seen the population swell to nearly two hundred. Right now, I think there are about sixty people here, including twenty children."

"And it's safe?" I asked.

He tightened his grip on my elbow, leading me around a puddle. "Yes. The people who live here have sought the seclusion of The Pines for a long time. It's a... retreat of sorts. A place where the king's laws don't reach."

I paused, considering. "That's why the people seem freer here than in Thyr."

"Yes," he nodded. "After the Females' Rebellion, a few places like this were created throughout Ithenmyr. A place for people to be themselves."

"I didn't know that places like this existed."

I was going to say more when I spotted Morwen out of the corner of my eye.

The elf—I'd since learned she was a Light Elf and an exceptionally gifted healer—grinned and walked over to us. "Hello, Aileana. Xander." She nodded at both of us. "It's so nice to see you up and about."

Smiling shyly, I twisted my fingers in the muff. I was still getting used to talking to people, and I wasn't sure how to go about conversations without sounding... odd. "Thank you. I was wondering..."

My voice trailed off, and I glanced at Xander, unsure what he would think of my request. It was a thought I'd had when I was lying in bed.

"Go on," Morwen replied.

I sucked in a deep breath, then plowed ahead. "Do you have a library? Or even books? I'm hoping to look into the history of Ithenmyr. I've recently become aware that my education growing up was... lacking."

And hopefully, I can find out more about Earth Elves and my magic, I added silently.

She grinned. "Of course! I'm sure your husband would be delighted to show you the library."

I blew out a long breath as the tension left my shoulders. "Thank you," I said.

We exchanged a few more pleasantries before Morwen was called away. I watched her go, remaining silent until Xander cleared his throat.

"The library?"

I nodded warily. "Yes. Do you have a problem with that, *darling*?"

He shook his head, his mouth twitching. "No, I just didn't know you liked to read, that's all."

I raised a brow. "There are many things you don't know about me."

"Don't I know it," he muttered under his breath.

But there was no bite to his words, and I smiled. Finally, things seemed to be going my way.

Research and Whispers

〜⚬〜

"Ugh, how can there be nothing here?" I shoved the book back in the stack, crossing my arms over my chest.

Every day this week had been the same. I went to the library early in the morning and stayed there well into the evening. Xander and Daegal had spent the earlier part of the week training, but the Fortune Elf had disappeared three days ago.

When I'd asked Xander about Daegal's whereabouts on the way to the library that morning, the silver-haired male had shrugged. "He does this sometimes. He'll be back."

I had narrowed my eyes but hadn't replied. I had been too preoccupied with searching for anything that might tell me about myself. My people. My magic.

Unfortunately, it was beginning to feel like a lost cause. Over the past week, I found books about Death Elves, Light Elves, and Fortune Elves, but none of them even mentioned Earth Elves.

It was as though we had never even existed.

I rested my head against the wooden bookshelf, rubbing my temples. "Please, Kydona," I murmured. "If you care about me at all, will you help me?"

For a long moment, nothing happened.

Of course not.

I was beginning to lose all hope when something caught my eye. Tucked into the back of one of the bottom shelves was a small book bound in worn leather. It was dusty, and the yellowed pages spoke to its age. Something about it called to me.

Crouching, I reached out and ran my finger down the spine.

The Females' Rebellion: What Went Wrong?

Curiosity filled me, and my breath caught in my throat. Grabbing the book, I slid down onto the floor. Crossing my legs, I began to read.

And read.

And read.

I read the book from cover to cover. When I reached the end, I turned back to the beginning and started over.

I'd thought I had known all about High King Edgar. Who he was. I'd thought I'd known why they called him the Crimson King. I had known he was a sadist who found perverse joy in whipping young, helpless elves.

But it turned out he was far worse than I'd ever imagined. As I flipped those dusty pages in the quiet library, my desire to remain in Ithenmyr and fight increased tenfold.

THE FEMALES' Rebellion was exactly what it sounded like. After finding the first book, I discovered two more tucked behind it. What I found between those pages was horrifying.

Nearly three centuries ago, when High King Edgar was still a young king, he had enacted a set of stringent laws declaring that all females, no matter their species, were second-class citizens in Ithenmyr.

According to the priests, the king had received a vision from the gods. They had told him, in no uncertain terms, that females were only good for one thing: breeding.

As such, they had no use for education. The day after the king's vision, laws were passed banning females from all learning centers and public spaces.

Fifty years later, the females had risen up. The details of the actual rebellion were scarce, but the result of the uprising had been two-fold.

First, they were allowed in schools once more. But as punishment for the uprising, High King Edgar had also enacted the Accompaniment Law.

A shudder ran through me as I found a letter tucked between the yellowed pages. Clearing my voice, I read it out loud to myself. My voice sounded too loud in the quiet library.

"If you're getting this letter, it means the worst has happened to me. They are coming for me. For all of us. Because of our... meetings.

"Yesterday, the Winged Soldiers took Mari. She was walking to the market with her brother, but he ran ahead to see his friends. In his youth, he forgot. He left her behind. He didn't do it on purpose, of that I am certain. But that was all it took. One moment of youthful forgetfulness cost Mari her life. She had been alone for a minute before one of the king's guards snatched her off the street.

"Her father, my cousin, pleaded with the guards to release her. They turned a deaf ear to him. She was beheaded at dawn. Her blood painted the streets. Her crime: walking down the road. What can we do? How will we survive? Get out of Ithenmyr while you still can. I hear the border to the Western Kingdom is still unguarded."

I sighed, putting the letter down and rubbing my eyes. This story...

It was horrible. Terrible. The High King did this.

When I got the courage to continue reading, I found dozens of stories like Mari's. The details were different, but they all ended the same. Execution. Deportation. Separation. Death.

So much death. So much suffering. The one thing they all had in common—High King Edgar. I knew that not all Death Elves were terrible. Just like not all Light Elves were good. People were more than just the labels placed on them at their birth.

But High King Edgar and his son... They were the epitome of evil.

They had to be stopped.

But how?

THE NEXT DAY, I hurried through breakfast. I gulped down my tea, and Xander smirked at me from across the table. "Do you have somewhere to be, Sunshine?"

I nodded. "The library."

He raised a brow. "Did you find something?"

"Maybe," I said, shrugging. "Not what I was looking for, but something of interest."

"I'm glad." He reached into his pocket and pulled out an apple. I watched as he bit into it. I couldn't help it. No matter where we were these days, I *always* knew where Xander was. He swallowed, placing his hand on the table close to mine.

I stared at our almost-touching fingers. The air around us was thick as the noise from the other residents of The Pines faded away. Suddenly, it was just the two of us and our almost-touching hands.

I wanted to pull my hand away. I wanted to grab his hand and never let go. To call my emotions complicated at that moment would have been an understatement of epic proportions.

Xander cleared his throat. "I have to leave for a few days, Aileana."

And just like that, I was back in the present.

"Leave?" I echoed.

He nodded. "Yes. Daegal has Seen something. He sent word this morning."

I lowered my gaze to his chest, where I knew the two pieces of the map lay beneath his tunic. "About the map?" I whispered, my words barely audible.

"Yes." Xander sighed, running his hand over his hair. His brows furrowed, and concern laced his tone as he asked, "Are you... will you be okay here for a few days?"

Would I be okay? I considered the question.

A few weeks ago, my answer would have been completely different. But now... something was growing between us.

Not only that, but I felt safe in The Pines in a way that I had never before.

There hadn't been a single sighting of the Red Shadow or the Winged Soldiers, and we were so far in the woods... I thought that maybe, just maybe, I was in the clear. Perhaps the king had given up the search and decided I wasn't worth it.

A girl could hope.

"Yes," I nodded. "I will be fine."

His lips tilted up softly. "I'll be back soon. I wouldn't want you to miss me."

I smirked. "Confident of you to think I'd even know you were gone."

"Oh, Sunshine." He patted my hand as he stood and winked at me. "I know you'll be thinking about me."

I didn't deny it. We both knew he was right. And I wasn't sure how I felt about that.

THE NEXT THREE days went by in relative peace. I read, devouring the books on the Females' Rebellion, and another that I'd found that detailed the history of the Western Kingdom.

I still didn't find anything about Earth Elves.

By the time the sun set on the third day after Xander left, I felt hopeless. After another long, fruitless search, I was trudging towards the dining hall when I heard a familiar pair of voices. I stopped in my tracks, looking around.

They were coming from behind a log cabin.

I knew those voices. My chest seized, and my heart sped up at the sound of Xander's deep grumble.

I hadn't even known he was back.

Why hadn't he come to say hello? How long had he been back? Why did I care?

Xander was whispering, his voice too low to make out the words. I narrowed my eyes, lifting my skirts to creep along the path.

"... We will have to go south..."

Another voice. "What about..." Daegal coughed, and I inched closer. "... Can't just leave her here."

Her. Was that me? Were they talking about me? The audacity of it all made my blood boil. This was what came from treating females so poorly. Males forgot we even had thoughts or opinions. My vision turned red as I clenched my fists at my side. I barely caught Xander's reply.

"... Attachments are dangerous... Important..."

"... Dragons... Can't just..."

They continued their conversation, but my mind had stalled. It was as though I couldn't breathe.

Dragons.

That's what I'd heard. I was certain of it.

Dragons?

A Brief (and Incomplete) History of Dragons

I had been taught that dragons were long dead. Extinct. A thing of the past.

I scoffed. What were Xander and Daegal doing talking about an extinct species?

When I was growing up in the tower, the long history of Ithenmyr's people had been one of the few approved topics of conversation.

High King Edgar was strange like that. He had wanted me to know how to read and write, to learn the geography and history of his kingdom, but only when it had suited his needs. When Orvyn had pushed my lessons too far, he had paid for that mistake with his life.

I learned a lesson the day Orvyn lost his head. Knowledge was the most dangerous thing one person could give another. It was powerful in ways we could not imagine. And if someone was withholding knowledge, they could not be trusted.

That was Orvyn's last lesson, and it had remained with me ever since I had seen his head on a spike.

Never, ever trust the king.

However, that wasn't the only lesson he'd taught me. When it came to the history of dragons, I knew a fair amount.

I had been taught that dragons had been a plague on the people of the Four Kingdoms for centuries. They had flown over villages and cities, burning forests and crops wherever they went. The beasts killed and ate small children, leaving only bones for families to find.

I knew dragon shifters were coarse people who chose to speak their language over the Common Tongue. They isolated those around them who weren't dragons, choosing their own company over others.

Dragons had lived in isolated villages, away from the good people of Ithenmyr. If a wandering elf or human had ever found their way into the dragons' villages, they were dead within minutes.

Not only had dragons been the worst kind of murderers, going after children and the elderly, but they had gone unchecked for years. The fire that had run through their veins had made them practically unstoppable.

I knew dragons hadn't had access to magic like elves. Our magic came from the goddesses. No one knew where the dragons had come from, but it had been understood that they were *not* from the goddesses.

Dragons had been the worst kind of evil.

When High King Edgar had sought to destroy them, no one had fought him. Together, he and his army of Winged Soldiers had fought to wipe dragons from the face of Ithenmyr.

And they had succeeded. There hadn't been a single dragon seen in Ithenmyr for over a century.

No one even spoke of them.

And yet, these two were discussing them in broad daylight.

What was going on?

You are Mine

~~~

I cleared my throat. "Hello?"

Instantly, Xander and Daegal stopped talking. I heard a rustling sound before they both appeared from behind the log cabin. They exchanged a long, meaningful glance before turning back towards me.

"Hello, Sunshine," Xander said. He took a step forward, wrapping his arm around my waist. I stiffened but didn't pull away. "Did you miss me?"

Did I miss him?

Honestly, yes. I had missed him every moment of every day. It was new for me. Missing someone. I found the entire situation rather disconcerting.

The strange feeling had followed me from dawn until dusk, from the moment Xander had left until just a few minutes ago.

But I wasn't going to say that.

"I suppose I missed having someone to talk to," I said. A glimmer appeared in Xander's eye, but I looked around his shoulder and winked at the Fortune Elf. "It's nice to see you, Daegal."

Xander growled, and Daegal laughed.

"I think that's my cue to leave," the Fortune Elf said. Daegal stepped forward and brushed his lips over my palm before whispering, "Nice to see you, too, Aileana."

I just blinked at him, staring until he disappeared from sight. When we were alone, Xander turned to me and crossed his arms. "You didn't miss me?"

"Well," I hedged, "I didn't *not* miss you."

A flicker of a smile flashed across his face. "Aha! I knew it." He stepped towards me. "I'm glad."

"Did you get what you were looking for?"

"We found some interesting information, but no." He shook his head. "We didn't get the next piece of the map."

"I'm sorry."

"Don't be. We have some leads, and something will turn up sooner rather than later. Until then..." Xander stepped towards me, crowding into my space. I sucked in a deep breath, gazing up into his golden eyes. His voice deepened into a low growl as he said, "Why don't we talk about something else?"

My chest tightened at the sight of the desire swimming in his golden eyes. I rasped, "What do you want to talk about?"

He chuckled, the sound low and husky as he said. "You."

"Me?" My voice squeaked, and blood rushed to my cheeks.

"Yes," he breathed. Xander stepped forward, and suddenly, I realized my back was pressed up against the log cabin. "Let's talk about you."

My heart pounded, and the air between us grew thick with anticipation as Xander closed the distance between us. He inhaled deeply, lifting a gloved hand and running it down my cheek.

I pressed my face into his touch, staring at him.

I hope he kisses me again.

As soon as the thought appeared in my mind, I jumped. Where did that come from? Xander wasn't supposed to be kind. I wasn't supposed to want this. He was supposed to be a means to an end.

We had an agreement, the two of us. That was all. There weren't supposed to be any feelings at play in here.

None.

So why was I leaning towards him, opening my mouth? Why was I staring at him, closing the distance between us?

He wasn't moving. Why wasn't he moving? Why was I pushing myself up on my tip-toes as my breathing grew ragged?

I had no answers. I didn't understand this. All I had was a pulsing desire that seemed to grow every time we were together.

"Aileana," he whispered hoarsely.

"Yes?" My voice sounded as ragged as the wind that swirled around us.

He leaned in close until our breaths mingled. He smelled faintly of smoke and trees, and I wondered where that scent came from.

"I missed you," he murmured. His eyes were dark, his voice husky as he drew me against him. His body felt firm beneath me, and I placed a hand on his sculpted chest. He sucked in a deep breath, a growl rumbling through him. "I didn't want to. Goddess knows I tried not to. But I did."

He sounded almost... angry about that.

I tilted my head. "How does that make you feel?"

"Frustrated," he replied instantly. "You make me feel so frustrated. I don't know whether I want to yell at you or kiss you."

"Why don't you?" I asked.

He blinked at me. "What?"

"Kiss me," I whispered. The words were barely audible over the pounding of my heart. I repeated, a little louder this time, "If you want to, kiss me."

He groaned. No sooner was the last word out of my mouth than his lips were on mine. There was nothing gentle about this kiss.

This kiss was everything. It was life-changing. To call it merely a kiss would be a disservice to what it was. It wasn't just a kiss. It was a claiming. A declaration. A saying of things unsaid between us.

It was a proclamation of things to come.

As we came together, I felt something within me shift. The piece of myself that had been unlocked earlier when the Winged Soldiers attacked finally clicked into place. This was *right*.

Xander's lips were warm as they moved against me, pushing me. He grabbed the back of my neck, tilting my head so I was positioned just how he liked it. It was as though he had thought about this moment before.

Maybe he'd missed me as much as I had missed him.

A growl rumbled through his chest as he ran his hand down my front. He touched me over my dress, leaving a trail of sparks in his path. I pressed myself against him, seeking relief for something I couldn't identify. My insides twisted as the now-familiar heat began low in my stomach.

I wanted more. I needed more. Him. I needed him. In whatever way I could get.

"Xander," I whispered. The word was more than a name. It was a plea. A prayer.

The moment my lips parted, a tiny gasp escaped me. He chuckled darkly as his tongue swept into my mouth. My entire world tilted on its axis as he *claimed* me. There was nothing gentle about Xander. He tasted of smoke and spice and the earth.

It wasn't enough.

A whimper escaped me as I ground myself against him, seeking relief from the foreign feelings taking residence within me. I moaned, my nerves feeling like they were on fire when he pulled back.

He stepped back, putting space between us, and I stared at him. I felt cold. So cold. I yearned for the feeling of his body against mine once more.

I stepped towards him and tilted my head, a question in my eyes.

Xander held up his hands, shaking his head as he stumbled back a step, then two. He was panting, his eyes wide as he ran his fingers through his hair.

"Dammit," he said gruffly, "That was... I didn't mean to... I can't do this."

He shook his head, his mouth pinched as he breathed raggedly. My heart squeezed tightly as I realized what was happening.

He regretted it. This. Whatever this was. He regretted *me*.

Just like that, it was as though someone had poured a bucket of cold water on the fire Xander had lit between us.

"Don't worry about it," I snapped. Crossing my arms in front of my chest as though they could protect me from him and the *feelings* he stirred within me, I continued. My voice was as hard as steel as I said, "I know how you feel about me. Nothing has changed."

Lies.

All lies. Everything had changed. Nothing would ever be the same again. How could I hate someone who made me feel this way? I didn't hate Xander. Not even close.

But obviously, he didn't feel the same way. Because he regretted this. I wasn't enough for him.

A long moment went by as we just.... stared at each other. Xander's jaw was clenched, his eyes dark as he stepped toward me. "Aileana," he started, "it's not..."

I shook my head, holding up a hand to stop him from talking. "Forget about it. I don't want to hear it. Will you just walk me to the dining hall?"

Xander blew out a long breath before nodding. "Okay. I will."

He offered me his elbow, the picture of a perfect gentleman, and I took it.

We walked in silence. He didn't talk, and I didn't want him to. I wouldn't let him hurt me any more than he already had.

"HOW MUCH LONGER ARE YOU going to be avoiding Xander?" Daegal asked.

He was standing in front of me, his eyes sharp as he held a sword aloft in the air.

I passed my sword from my left hand to my right, tilting my head as I considered the question.

We circled each other, creating a trail in the damp grass beneath our feet as we eyed one another. The taller elf watched me carefully, but I knew from our previous sessions over the past week that he would wait for me to make the first move.

"I'm not avoiding him," I lied. I shifted my feet, adjusting my stance. Fabric rustled as I moved, the same cream-colored gown hugging my curves. I felt like I was getting used to it.

I had asked Laeanna, one of the humans, for a tunic and leggings, but she had refused. It "wouldn't be appropriate for a female," she had told me reprovingly.

Sword-fighting in a dress was *not* ideal, but I wanted to practice. I needed to practice. To take my mind off everything else. Dress or no dress, I wouldn't be left defenseless.

The Fortune Elf raised a brow. "You two have barely spoken a word to each other since he and I came back a week ago. You've been spending every day with Morwen and her friends in the weaving hut or the library.

He's been moping around, barely talking to anyone. You two do know we're supposed to leave tomorrow, right?"

Right. Tomorrow. We were going south to follow a clue about the third piece of the map. I hoped that we might also find more information about Earth Elves in the southern provinces. I knew so little about myself, what I could do, or who I was.

I narrowed my eyes, tightening my grip on the sword before lunging towards Daegal. "I wasn't aware our... marital problems were so obvious."

It grated against me that Xander and I were still upholding this ruse of our fake marriage. Especially since his reaction after our kiss made it clear he didn't want to be with me.

I did not know why Xander hadn't come clean to Daegal about the reality of our marriage, but I would not be the first one to lose at whatever game we were playing.

Daegal lifted his sword, easily blocking my attack before coming around on the other side. Our swords clashed, filling the clearing with the sound of metal on metal as we fought.

The Fortune Elf chuckled. "No one else has noticed your problems. But I know Xander very well. And I'm beginning to know you, too. This respite at The Pines has been very enlightening, in more ways than one."

"Is that so?" I blocked Daegal's blow, twirling around and extending my sword towards his left side.

The Fortune Elf nodded as he ducked underneath my extended arm. "It is so."

After that, we stopped speaking, giving in to the warrior's dance. Our swords became nothing more than extensions of ourselves as we sparred.

My heart pounded in my chest, and my hands grew sweaty. Even so, we trained. Strands of red hair plastered themselves against my face as I moved, but I didn't try to get rid of them.

A welcome weariness came over me. I didn't fight it. Instead, I fell into it.

If I was tired, I didn't have to think about him. About the way he made me feel. About his rejection. And about the aching hole in my heart that had been growing since he had broken off our kiss a week ago.

Fighting was easy. It was good. It hurt, but not in a bad way. The burn in my muscles reminded me I was alive. And right now, I needed that reminder more than anything.

I lost track of time as we sparred. It could have been minutes or hours before the Fortune Elf stepped back and bowed. "I think that's enough for today, don't you?"

I panted, wiping my hand on my brow. "You're giving up?"

He shook his head. "Not giving up... calling a truce."

A branch cracked behind us, and my neck hairs prickled. The air seemed to grow heavier as an awareness washed over me. I knew without turning around that *he* was there, right behind me.

"What do you want, Xander?" I asked through clenched teeth. I kept my gaze trained on the elf before me, who had sheathed his sword and was wiping his brow.

"I want to talk with my wife," the infuriating male replied. His voice sounded... hesitant as if he didn't know what I would say.

I snapped, "I don't want to talk to you. I'll see you tomorrow."

Daegal shifted awkwardly on his feet. He opened his mouth to speak when a hand landed on my shoulder.

I stiffened, sucking in a deep breath through my clenched teeth.

"Please, Aileana," Xander whispered. Goosebumps appeared on the back of my neck as he came toward me. "Let me explain."

I don't know if it was the tone of his voice or the absolute exhaustion pounding through my body, but I sighed. "Okay," I said without turning around. "I'll talk to you."

Daegal nodded, stepping around us. "That's my cue to leave."

I heard him clap Xander on the back before whispering something that sounded suspiciously like "good luck." I waited until the elf's footsteps retreated into the woods before asking, "What did you want to talk about?"

Xander cleared his throat. "I want to talk about what happened between us."

I tightened my grip on the sword, glad I still had something to hold. "Oh?" I hardened my voice. I refused to let him know he had hurt me.

A large pine tree stood roughly twenty feet in front of me. I glared at the thin green needles, trying to avoid thinking about Xander. "Whatever could you want to talk about? I thought you made your revulsion extraordinarily clear after you kissed me. I don't need you to tell me again that you regret it."

He sighed, the sound long-suffering as it escaped him. "Aileana, I don't regret kissing you. At all."

"No?" I turned to scowl at him. "You sure have an odd way of showing you don't regret something. Why have you been avoiding me?"

"It's a long story..."

I narrowed my eyes, waving a hand in the air. "I've got nowhere to be. Enlighten me."

He crossed his arms defensively, widening his stance. "Will you even listen to me?"

"I'm listening right now," I snapped.

Xander shut his eyes and pinched the bridge of his nose. "I mean, really listen to me. *Please*, Aileana. Listen to me."

There it was. That word again. Xander seemed to know exactly how to wield it to his advantage. Did he know no one had ever asked me to do anything before? That the word please had been foreign to me? Or perhaps he was just being kind?

I sighed, running my free hand through my hair. "Fine. I promise I'll listen."

His gaze dropped to my other hand, which was still clutching my sword. "Could you maybe put that away?"

"I don't know." I glared at him. "Am I going to need it?"

He shook his head, his voice betraying his tiredness. "No. I'm not here to fight with you."

Something about his tone made me look at him. Really look. Bags were under his eyes that hadn't been there before, and his face was long. Drawn. His shoulders were slumped, his fists clenched at his sides. He looked broken. Desolate. Sad.

Did I do that to him? Was it possible he felt as upset about how we had left things as I did?

"Okay." I nodded. Walking over to a nearby tree, I placed my sword on the ground before I slid down and rested my back against the trunk.

As had become the norm, the tree hummed behind me. *Hello, Protectress.*

Absentmindedly, I patted the bark of the tree, making a mental note to talk to Morwen about my... abilities before we left. I needed to find out what exactly was happening to me.

Xander dropped to the ground in front of me, extending his hands behind him as he stretched out his legs. We didn't touch, but the air was thick like mud. The inches that separated my feet from his hips felt like miles as we stared at each other. We sat like that for a long moment, our legs outstretched but neither touching the other.

I knew that if I touched him, the same fire from before would erupt beneath my skin. And if he touched me... I might burst into flames.

It would be hard to stay mad at Xander if that happened.

And I was mad. Furious. His audacity enraged me. How dare he kiss me, tell me he missed me, and then walk away? How dare he make me feel this way and then tell me he couldn't do *this*? What did that even mean?

The more I thought about it, the angrier I got.

Eventually, I broke the silence. Clearing my throat, I raised a brow. "Well, what did you want to say?"

"I want to apologize," he started. "I shouldn't have left things the way I did."

I shook my head. My voice was stern as I replied, "No, you shouldn't have."

He sighed. "Aileana, I—"

"No." I held up my hand. "I need to say this, Xander. You *hurt* me. You can't just go around handing out mind-blowing kisses to people and then tell them you changed your mind!"

He smirked, his eyes gleaming as he leaned in closer to me. "You thought the kiss was mind-blowing?"

I snarled at him, placing my hands on my hips. "That's what you got out of what I said?"

"I can't help it if you think I'm a good kisser." He shrugged.

I leaned in close to him, tucking my legs underneath myself as I hovered within a foot from his mouth. He sucked in a deep breath, and I could smell him. The deep, smokey scent he seemed to carry around with him wafted toward me, and I willed myself not to melt into his arms right then and there. My voice lowered, and I held his gaze as I whispered, "I don't think you're a good kisser."

It was the truth. Mind-blowingly incredible at kissing? Yes. Fantastic? Yes. Experienced? Also yes.

When Xander kissed me, nothing else in the world mattered. I knew I was inexperienced. I was painfully aware of the fact. It pained me to think about Xander pressing his lips, his body against that of someone else. If anything, the past week had given me ample opportunity to bemoan my inexperience.

Xander tensed, his gaze lowering to my mouth. His voice was husky as he asked, "Is that so?"

I leaned in closer, my heart racing as our bodies practically touched. Gulping, I lied through my teeth as I said, "It is so."

A half-strangled noise that was entirely *male* escaped him as he stared at me. I held his gaze, opening my mouth. A rumbling began in his chest as we remained inches from each other.

"Xander," I whispered, hoping he couldn't hear how my heart was pounding.

"Aileana?"

I leaned in until we were all but touching. The air between us felt electrified. Heat was coming off him in waves, and my stomach clenched in anticipation.

"Xander," I whispered, "I need you..."

"Yes?"

I licked my lips, never breaking eye contact. "I need you to tell me why you said we couldn't kiss. Tell me why you've been avoiding me."

His eyes widened for a moment before his expression shuttered. He sucked in a deep breath. "Fine."

I sat back just enough to give him room to think. "Go ahead." I waved a hand in the air, tucking my legs underneath myself. "I'm listening."

Xander groaned, rubbing his hand over his eyes. "Goddess, you are so much. I was avoiding you because... because..."

His voice trailed off as his eyes grew soft.

"Go on," I prodded. "Tell me why you avoided me, Elyx."

I don't know what prompted me to say his name, but when I did, it was like a barrier shattered between us.

Xander sucked in a deep breath, pushing himself to his feet. His face contorted, and his eyes widened as though he was in physical pain as he ran his hands through his hair. He turned around, slamming his fist into a tree, before returning to glare at me.

"You want to know why I've been avoiding you?" he snarled.

"Yes!" I yelled. "I need to know."

Xander's voice rang out through the clearing. "I've been avoiding you because you're my goddess-damned *mate*, Aileana. Do you even understand what that means?" He snarled, baring his canines and widening his eyes as a flash of green crossed his pupils. "You. Are. My. Mate."

I couldn't breathe. My heart felt like it was trapped in my chest. I couldn't move at all. I was a statue, held firm by the wave of disbelief washing over me.

He said it.

How could he? Words had power. Had no one ever taught him that? How dare he voice the words that had hung between us since we'd encountered the Winged Soldiers in the forest?

He had given them life, and now they existed, and he couldn't take them back. We couldn't take them back.

Everything between us felt... different. Transformed. Irrevocably changed.

Xander groaned, the sound full of torment as he continued to speak. It was as though every word caused him physical pain as they forced their way out of his throat. Agony, absolute and utter agony tainted each word as he whisper-yelled, "I am yours, and you are *mine!*"

My voice finally returned to me as I pushed myself to my feet. My legs shook beneath me as I took a shaky step toward Xander. This male who had hurt me and avoided me.

My mate.

"I know," I whispered. And I did. The truth of his words was painfully clear to me. Achingly so. I understood this more than anything.

"Xander, I *know*." My voice broke as I repeated the phrase that had been churning within me all week. "I am yours. You are mine."

The words echoed within me as they left my lips. My vision grew blurry as I moved toward him, but he held up a hand.

"This wasn't something I signed up for," Xander growled. His brows were furrowed, his eyes hard as he stared at me. "A mate. A goddess-damned mate."

"You think I asked for this? I was doing just fine before you came along, Xander."

He ignored me, continuing on his rant. "You don't even like me. From the moment you came into my life, you have been nothing but trouble."

"If it's so much trouble, being my mate, then don't accept the bond," I hissed, my heart pounding. "No one is forcing it on you."

It was common knowledge that mating bonds couldn't be forced on anyone. Even when a bond existed, it had to be accepted by both parties. Then, and only then, could the bonding ceremony take place.

Of course, the logistics of such ceremonies were secret, but I knew they existed. Presumably, it didn't matter because he didn't want to be my mate. Perhaps in time, the bond between us would fray if we didn't solidify it.

Or perhaps we would be left yearning for each other for the rest of our lives, unable to find love or peace without our match.

Considering my luck, it would probably be the latter.

Xander paced before me, his words coming out as a cross between a whisper and a plea, "You are my mate, and you don't even like me."

I sucked in a deep breath, but before I could reply and set him straight, he shook his head. All the emotion disappeared from his face as he pulled the cold, steely mask back over his features. My heart plummeted in my chest as he snarled, "Don't. Just don't. This was a mistake. I can't... I'm not ready to talk to you right now, Aileana."

He turned on his heel, following in Daegal's footsteps as he disappeared from my view.

A mistake.

"Xander, wait," I cried out, but it was too late. He was gone. My heart seemed to break in my chest as a crack of thunder came from above. The sun slipped behind clouds as rain began to fall.

I slumped to the ground and lay my head in my hands. I stopped fighting the tears that had been threatening to come ever since Xander began to speak.

Minutes gave way to hours, and I wept.

I wept for the way my life had turned out. For my inability to express myself. For my mate, who thought I hated him.

The rain soaked me to the bone, and I wept for the situations that had brought us to this point.

He was my mate, and I wept.

The Red Shadow

❦

I didn't move from my spot in the clearing until the thunderstorm had abated. I couldn't. At that moment, moving felt like too much. I was exhausted, drenched, and out of tears. I felt... drained.

Xander was my mate.

The words kept running through my mind.

Mate.

Mate.

Mate.

I stood, hugging my soaked arms around myself as shivers wracked through my body. My teeth chattered as I bent and picked up my long-forgotten sword, sheathing it in the scabbard that hung at my hip before grabbing my wet hair and twisting it into a semblance of a bun on the top of my head. Picking up my cloak, I threw it over my shoulders. It was soaked, but at that point in time, I didn't care.

I had to go back, and yet, nothing was better. Tomorrow, we were going to leave. Head south, with this weight between us. This very heavy, very complicated weight. Nothing about our relationship was uncomplicated.

That would have been too easy. There was no easy solution to the problem that lay between us.

After all, what kind of simple solution was there to having a mate who thought being attached to you was the worst kind of torture? I had thought our arrangement had been painful before. Pretending to be his wife was bad enough.

But now that he had spoken those words out loud, it was impossible to ignore them.

We were *mates,* and he hated me.

At that moment, I wasn't too fond of him myself.

I WAS PICKING my way through the woods, taking my time returning to The Pines, when a soft *meow* came from behind me. My breath caught in my throat as I slowly turned around. Another cat was standing less than ten feet away from me, leaving tiny paw prints in the wet mud.

"Hello there," I whispered as I crouched, extending my hand. "Aren't you darling?"

The black cat approached me, purring softly as it rubbed its head against my hand, begging for a scratch. I complied, enjoying the softness of the animal's fur. A few moments later, the cat lifted its head.

Wait.

What?

I narrowed my eyes. This cat had a half-moon under its chin, just like... I pulled my hand back as though I had been burned.

"How did you get all the way out here?" I asked the cat. This wasn't just any cat. This was *the* cat. I was sure of it. The one that had visited my tower every day growing up.

The animal stared at me, blinking its large green eyes, before a deep masculine voice said from somewhere in the trees, "Why, he came with me, of course."

I jolted upright.

My heart stopped beating in my chest.

Scrambling backward, I watched with wide eyes as the cat jumped to attention and slinked toward the voice. It prowled away, standing on the forest's edge, when its body began to blur. It darted behind a bush. Seconds later, a white flash of light filled my vision.

When the light receded, the cat was gone. In its place was a stout male. He was as bare as the day he was born, the greenery from the leaves barely covering his nakedness. He grinned lecherously at me as he bowed before he turned, scurrying off into the forest.

A shifter.

"Don't tell me you don't recognize my voice," the hidden person said. The timber of their voice sent skitters down my spine, and I forced myself not to throw up right then and there. He continued, "It would be a shame for me to have traveled all this way and find out my fiancée didn't know me."

"No," I whimpered as a cold sweat covered the back of my neck. "It can't be."

Even as the words left my mouth, I knew. He had found me. Goose-bumps covered my flesh, and my blood ran cold.

Everything within me screamed at me to run. I had to run away. To not look back. I had to act.

And yet, I was frozen on the spot.

Of all the times for my body to fail me. Why now?

"Oh, but it is." An eerie chuckle filled the air. "I've been looking for you."

That voice. I knew that voice. It haunted my nightmares. It came to me in the worst moments when I thought about what my married life would have been like, next to *him*.

I began to shake, slowly at first, but then harder and harder as leaves crunched behind me.

Branches snapped, heralding his arrival, and my heart seized.

"Did you miss me, my sweet?" the voice asked.

The trees still hid him, but I knew. I knew who it was. And this time, there was no question.

This was not a dream.

In reply, I screamed. I clenched my fists at my side as I turned around.

"Xander!" I yelled at the top of my lungs as panic threatened to overtake me. "Xander, help me!"

My heart thudded as I reached for the sword sheathed on my hip. I grabbed the hilt, but before I could do anything more than slide it out, thick red cords of magic twisted around me.

The magic yanked me off my feet, forming thick ropes that tightly bound my arms and legs.

"No." I moaned, struggling against the bonds. I tried to pull my hand up, but the magic cut into my skin. Every time I moved, the red ribbons tightened.

Soon, I couldn't move at all.

My own two feet were barely holding me upright. I knew if he released the hold on his magic, I would tumble face-first to the ground.

My eyes widened as I sucked in a deep breath, opening my mouth to scream again when the branches in front of me shook. His voice was louder than ever as he hissed, "None of that, sweeting."

My blood ran cold as the Red Shadow finally emerged from the forest.

Like a living nightmare, he stood tall in his black tunic. His black wings were nowhere to be seen—as one of the most powerful Death Elves in Ithenmyr, the Red Shadow was also a full-blooded shape-shifter—but even without the wings, he was frighteningly imposing.

His blond, curly hair was tied back as he loomed over me. Two pointy ears were visible, covered in matching crimson caps. Long, obsidian horns curled away from his forehead, pointing to the sky.

The cat—the *shifter*—was perched on the elf's shoulders, licking its tiny paws. It seemed completely unperturbed by the red sparks dancing on the Red Shadow's skin.

"Get away from me!" I huffed.

He raised a blond brow. "You're rather feisty for someone tied up, aren't you?"

"I will never go anywhere with you. Run home and tell your father I'm not coming back. The two of you can perish in the seven circles of hell, for all I care."

Chuckling, the Red Shadow produced a handkerchief from his pocket. I snarled at him, but he just laughed as he stepped forward. I tried to bite him, but he evaded my teeth. He wrapped the handkerchief around my head, tying it at the back of my neck. It tasted horrible, like salt and dirt and sweat.

I can't believe this is happening.

He patted my head, tutting. "There now. That's much better. I always liked you better when you couldn't speak."

I glared at him, telling him exactly what I thought he could do with himself. Unfortunately, the gag meant my words came out as incoherent mumbles. But I knew he got the idea when his hand flew through the air. It seemed to move in slow motion as it approached me. Staring at it, I vowed I wouldn't flinch. I kept my back straight and sucked in a deep breath.

It wasn't enough to prepare me for the moment his palm met my face. A clap rang through the forest, and I saw stars. Pain ripped through me, but I didn't give him the satisfaction of hearing me cry out. He thrived on the suffering of others. I knew that from personal experience.

"Don't you *dare* disrespect me again," he spat. His blue eyes darkened with fury. "You need to be able to spread your legs for me and bear my children. That doesn't mean you need to be able to walk or that your pretty face needs to remain unscarred."

I lurched back as far as the bonds would allow. Fear as cold as the rain that had been pouring from the skies earlier ran through my veins. Swallowing the lump in my throat, I nodded.

He smirked. "Ah, I see you understand me. Good. It's time to go."

Staring at him, I tried to figure out if there was a way to stall. Maybe, if we waited long enough, Xander or Daegal would come looking for me.

As if he could read my mind—I was fairly certain he couldn't. At least, I'd never heard of a Death Elf capable of telepathy—the Red Shadow chuckled. "Oh, you think they're going to rescue you? That little boy and his Fortune Elf." He shook his head, a glimmer entering his eyes as he flicked his hand.

The strands of magic holding me tight lifted me off the ground, and I began to *float* alongside him as he strode through the forest. "No, I'm afraid that's not going to happen. You see, they're quite... busy right now. I made sure of it. By the time they realize you're missing, you and I will be long gone."

I struggled against the gag, freeing a corner of my mouth. "If you hurt any of them..."

The Red Shadow laughed. He bent over, slapping his knees like I had told a joke. Behind the gag, I fumed. "I'm serious," I spat. "Don't hurt them."

"Oh, my." He chuckled. "Has the king's pet grown some teeth? What will you do, Aileana? Bite me? I'd like to see you try."

I shook my head, speaking around the fabric as I seethed, "I'm going to kill you."

One moment, he was in front of me, and the next, my head was twisting back. His palm slammed into me twice as hard as it had before, and this time, I couldn't help but cry out as the bark cut into my back. Stars erupted in my vision as pain ripped through my head.

Behind me, the leaves stirred, and I could feel the earth's pulse beneath my bound fingertips. Clenching my teeth, I tried to summon the magic that had saved me before.

It wasn't working. I had no idea how to use my gifts, and I would lose my freedom because of it.

"You will do no such thing," the Red Shadow seethed.

He reached up, red sparks flying over his hands as he readjusted the gag around my mouth. Then he bent and unbuckled the scabbard from my waist. I watched, wide-eyed, as my only weapon fell silently to the forest floor. "I was going to let my magic carry you along, but now I see some physical exercise might help you come to terms with your new situation."

The Red Shadow waved a hand, and the restraints around my legs dissolved into thin air. I fell to the ground in a lump, my knees unable to support the sudden weight of my body. He scoffed, reaching down and pulling me up roughly.

"Walk," he ordered.

I sucked in a deep breath, my vision blurring, but I didn't fight back. I heard the cutting-edge in his voice, the threat of barely contained violence simmering under his calm facade, and I didn't push him further.

Tears slipped down my cheeks, but I didn't fight against the magic binding my arms against my sides. I ignored the tight hold of the gag around my mouth.

I pushed all thoughts of Xander out of my mind.

He wasn't coming, and I had to accept that. He regretted kissing me, and he had made it clear he didn't want me as his mate.

I had tried to be free, and look where that had gotten me. I had caused Jo's death, and now I was at the whim of the Red Shadow. We weren't even at court, where prying eyes would presumably keep me safe. No, here in the forest, he could do whatever he wanted to me. No one would stop him.

I'd seen what red magic could do.

And so I walked.

My muscles ached, my lungs burned, and my heart pounded as I lifted one foot and placed it in front of the other. A seemingly never-ending flow of salty tears ran down my cheeks, dampening my gag.

And I walked.

THE DAY SLIPPED AWAY as we trekked through the woods. I stumbled and fell countless times. Dozens of scratches covered my cheeks, and tiny tears ran through my dress, but we didn't take a break.

Marching through the forest became the only thing I knew.

Shivering in my damp dress, I stared at my captor's back. I found solace in imagining what it would look like with a multitude of daggers sticking out of it.

I tried to remember how far The Pines were from my tower. We'd been on horseback and had journeyed for at least a week. The problem was, I wasn't sure if the Red Shadow was taking me back to the tower or his...

No.

Stop, I commanded myself.

I was not going to think about that. I *could not* think about that. Giving those thoughts life, even in my mind, would let him win. Allowing that poison to fester within me would give him a foothold. And if that happened, if I stopped and thought about it, I knew I would stop. My legs would cease moving, and I would collapse to the ground.

I would not let myself think about what was to come.

Instead, I focused on the way my every muscle seemed to ache. I had never been in so much physical pain in my life. The excruciating burn in my body reminded me that I was still alive. Even though the Red Shadow had me, I was alive.

When he finally turned and grabbed my arm, I jumped.

He looked... fine. It was as though hiking through the woods for hours hadn't affected him. A product of Maturity, I assumed. He could do so much more than me. He was so much more dangerous than me.

"We're going to stop for the night," he said gruffly. "Are you going to try anything?"

I wished I could have. With every heartbeat, my body was yelling at me to fight back. But I wasn't yet Mature, and I was very aware of my limitations.

I shook my head, my eyes heavy.

He lifted a hand, yanking the gag off my mouth. I winced at the sudden relief of pressure. The Red Shadow grabbed my hair, yanking my head back until I stared directly at him. "What was that?"

"No," I whispered hoarsely. "I won't try anything tonight."

"Good girl," he said, patting my cheek before he reached over and lifted me off my feet.

And Thelrena help me, but I didn't pull away. I was so tired and weary that I let him lay me on the cold, hard ground.

I tossed and turned all night as visions of fire filled my mind.

Not So Naïve Anymore

❧

"Wake up." A gruff voice reached into the depths of my nightmares moments before smooth hands roughly shook my shoulders.

I blinked, trying to swat away the person so rudely waking me, when my hands snapped back to my side.

No. It was real. It had been real.

A sob threatened to rip through me as I stared at the blond curls that haunted my nightmares. The Red Shadow smiled, the expression on his face nothing less than terrifying as he crouched before me.

His eyes were hard, and there wasn't a trace of kindness on his face as he said, "We leave in ten, sweeting. Take care of your needs over there."

Tilting his head, he gestured to a cluster of rocks that hadn't been visible at night. I did as he asked, coming out from behind the rocks a few minutes later.

"We?" I asked.

He nodded. "We. You didn't think High King Edgar would be so foolish as to only send a few Winged Soldiers after you, did you?"

I had hoped so, but I didn't say that.

The Red Shadow chortled. "No, those soldiers you killed were just a few of the ones Father sent all over Ithenmyr. Nice trick, though," he said thoughtfully. He tapped his chin before turning on his knees. "Kolvar, bring me the bracelets. We can't have my fiancée playing her little games with us while we travel."

There was a rustling sound before the shifter appeared beside my captor. He was back in his human form, and his cat-like eyes gleamed as he bowed. "Here you go, sir."

Resting in Kolvar's hands were two thick black bracelets. They gleamed in the early morning sunlight, and an aura of complete wrongness emanated from them.

A chill ran through me as I stared at the bracelets. It couldn't be... It had been a dream. They hadn't been real.

"No," I whispered, my shaky voice betraying the fear running through my veins.

The Red Shadow hummed. "I see you may have learned a few things during your little journey, pet. Perhaps you're not so naïve anymore. Do you know what these are?"

I continued to stare at them. The more I looked at the black bracelets, the more my stomach twisted in on itself.

"I... Please don't. Don't put them on me." My eyes widened as I looked at the Red Shadow pleadingly. "Please, if you care even a little for me, you won't put them on me."

"Oh, sweeting," he murmured, running a hand down my face. His fingers were cold. So cold. So unlike Xander's. I cringed at the scarlet sparks that jumped from his fingers, as though even his magic didn't want to be associated with him. He whispered, "I do love it when you beg."

For a moment, just a moment, I thought he would do what I asked.

But then he grabbed my shoulders and twisted me around painfully. My head slammed into the dirt, and I cried out.

"No!" I yelled as I tried to wrench my arms away.

But it was too late.

I heard a clicking sound, and when he finally released me, a black bracelet adorned each of my wrists. The Red Shadow pulled down the sleeves of my dress, hiding the bracelets from sight.

But it didn't matter. I knew they were there. Their wrongness permeated my skin, and I felt lightheaded.

A sob wrenched through me as I lifted my fingers to the bracelet. Instantly, my hands felt like I had thrust them into a raging fire. I cried out, pulling my fingers back as I stared at the manacles on my hands.

The Red Shadow shrugged, his eyes gleaming. "A new improvement to the prohiberis. I had to ensure you couldn't pull anything like your escape again. Not after we kept you away from the earth all these years. Do you like it? I had my witch spell them against you, specifically. If you try to take them off, they will burn you from the inside out. They are keyed to my blood, so only my father and I can remove them."

I shook my head, whimpering.

The Red Shadow leaned in close, whispering in a low voice as though we were sharing an intimate secret, "I did so love seeing you beg, sweeting. Next time, you'll be begging when you're on your knees in front of me."

Red filled my vision at the thought, and I spat at him. My aim was true, and he recoiled. I snarled, "You are a *pig*. I will *never* go to bed with you."

His eyes widened as he lifted a hand to his cheek. "Bitch," he snarled.

Sparks pulsed around him, and the air seemed to crackle with his anger.

"You will learn to show me some goddess-damned respect." He

cracked his neck as he stepped toward me. "I am to be your *husband*. You will *never* do that again."

This time, I saw the blow coming.

I watched as his closed fist came toward me, and I braced my teeth for the impending impact. Even though I knew what was coming, it didn't make it hurt any less. A cry rose in my throat, but I tamped it down. I forced myself to breathe through it.

But then... he didn't stop. He didn't step away. This time, he kept going. He hit me until I tumbled to the ground, my legs unable to hold my weight against his assault.

Even so, he didn't stop.

I curled into a ball as his fists pounded into me. He hit my chest, arms, and face as he called me every degrading name in the book. He hit me until the pain was my only reality.

I was no longer Aileana. I was pain, and pain was every part of me.

When the blackness came for me, I fell into it willingly.

THE MURMUR of voices was the first thing I heard.

Everything ached. Agony was my only reality. I took in a breath, my lungs seizing painfully. Something felt broken in my chest.

Wincing, I opened my eyes. Even that hurt. Everything hurt.

I tried to shift my hands, but they didn't move. I frowned as I saw the red bands of magic still binding my arms to my side.

"No," I whimpered. I was still bound, still captive. That meant that *he* was nearby.

A deep voice said, "Stop the cart. She's awake."

Cart. We must have left the woods.

Instantly, I wished I had kept my mouth shut. The Red Shadow's gleaming blue eyes appeared in my field of vision as the vehicle rattled to a stop. He was riding atop a dappled gelding, studying me with a wolfish smile.

"Hello, sweeting," he purred. "Nice of you to wake up and grace us with your presence."

I sneered at him. "Don't call me that."

He narrowed his gaze, a look of malice crossing his face as he drew closer to me. He opened his mouth to say something when he lurched backward.

"Ugh," he huffed. "You smell horrible." Wrinkling his nose, he called to someone I couldn't see. "Fenris, come here."

A shuffling sound came from outside the cart moments before a reedy voice answered. "Your Highness?"

"Help my fiancée out of the cart." My captor waved a hand, and the red ribbons of magic binding my arms to my sides disappeared. My weary muscles cried out in relief as I flexed one arm and then the next.

Finally.

The Red Shadow continued, "She'll need to get cleaned up before we reach Hiset. She stinks, and I won't marry someone who smells like a pig."

What?

My eyes widened in panic as I sucked in a deep breath. This couldn't be happening. My heart pounded in my chest as I shook my head. "Marry?" My voice squeaked.

He turned his gaze back to me. "Yes, sweeting." He sneered. "After your little disappearing act, we're getting married right away. You will be bound to me forever. When we get home, I'll lock you up in a tower so dark, you'll forget you ever knew what the sunlight felt like on your skin."

The world disappeared from beneath me as his words settled upon me.

No.

NO.

Kydona help me, but Hiset was nearby. Two or three days of travel would likely bring us there.

I could not marry him. I wouldn't. But how could I get out of this? I needed to escape; that much was clear. But these prohiberis bracelets were going to make that difficult.

I'd have to find a witch to get them off later.

My mind swirled when that reedy voice replied, "Yes, sir."

I tensed, balling my hands into fists, when a tall, lanky elf appeared before me. He had olive-colored skin and long brown hair, but there was an air of familiarity about him. I stared at him, my brows furrowed as I tried to remember where I knew him from.

"Don't take all day, Fenris," the Red Shadow snapped. "I want to get back on the road."

"Yes, Your Highness," Fenris said. The elf reached into the cart, grabbing my arm with calloused hands. His grip was rough as he wrenched me upwards. "Come here."

I struggled against his grip, but there was no use. The elf was much taller than me and clearly much stronger. He must have been Mature. The fact that his upper body hadn't been bound by magical ties for hours on end also gave him an advantage.

I frowned as Fenris tightened his hold on my elbow and dragged me towards the bushes.

"Let me go!" I yelled, digging my feet into the ground in an attempt to slow us down.

He ignored me, yanking me over roots and small stones despite my best efforts to stall him. My eyes were wide as I looked around, trying to take in my surroundings.

We had stopped on a dirt road, and we were surrounded by nothing but trees and rocks. Besides the Red Shadow and the cat shifter, I counted the elf dragging me into the woods and a fourth rider.

The fourth one had short black hair and sat silently on his horse. He was watching me with something that looked like pity in his eyes, but I couldn't be sure.

Four. There were four of them, and I didn't have any weapons. What could I do against four assailants?

The road gave way to the forest, and I was soon surrounded by trees and bushes. Despair threatened to overwhelm me as the elf continued to pull me into the forest. Even the wildlife was silent as I struggled. What had become the familiar call of the trees was nowhere to be found. The bracelets on my arms choked off my connection with the woods, and I felt its absence like a growing hole in my chest.

I was completely and utterly alone.

The elf yanked my arm, dragging us through thick groves of trees. I knew that even if I did fight back, no one could hear me. But that didn't stop me from trying. I *would not* go down without a fight.

Yanking my elbow away from the elf, I screamed.

I screamed and screamed until Fenris slammed his hand over my mouth. I tried to bite him, but he wrenched his palm away from my teeth at the last moment.

"Shut up," he hissed in my ear. "You must be even stupider than I had thought. Are you trying to make him kill you?"

Was I? Maybe. Death would be better than marriage to *him*.

I ignored the elf's question, asking one of my own. I could hear water rushing nearby. "Why should I listen to you?"

Fenris halted, his hand tight on my elbow as he looked around wide-eyed. He dropped his voice, whispering, "Because we are alike, the two of us."

"I'm nothing like you," I snarled.

The elf shook his head as he forced me to follow him through the forest. I was still racking my brain, trying to figure out where I knew him from.

"You would be surprised," Fenris said. His voice had a tinge of sadness, but it was hard to focus on that when he dragged me through the woods.

A branch slapped me in the face, and I spat, "You work for him."

A mirthless laugh erupted from Fenris as he tightened his grip on my arm. I tried to shake him off, but he was too strong.

"What's so funny?" I asked through clenched teeth.

Fenris just shook his head. "You. You think you're so brave."

"And?"

"I have news for you. There's a reason they call him the Red Shadow."

Fenris yanked me over a fallen log as I said, "I know who he is and what he can do. He can't hurt me anymore than he already has. He and his father have already taken everything from me once before."

The elf sighed. "You sound brave. But around him, no one retains their bravery for long."

"You can say his name," I said, trying to rile Fenris up. Anger was easier than fear. It felt safe. Familiar. And if I could make this elf mad, maybe he would slip up, and I could get away. So I buried my fear under bravado and hissed, "Remington."

"You shouldn't say his name," Fenris warned as he dragged me through the woods. "You shouldn't be pushing his buttons. It'll only make things worse for you."

I swallowed. There was a tinge of something that sounded oddly like concern in the elf's voice. "Why are you telling me this?"

He blew out a long breath. "I don't know." A long moment passed as the creek I had heard finally came into view. "I suppose it's because I'd rather not be witness to the murder of the last female of my kind."

The last female of his kind.

That meant...

"You're an Earth Elf," I gasped as he shoved me to the ground. I repeated, my voice gaining strength. "You. Are. An. Earth Elf. And you work for *him*?"

"Don't speak those words aloud," he said. "Are you stupid? The High King will have us whipped within an inch of our lives if people know what we are."

I knelt in the damp mud, staring up at him. Anger flooded through me as I clenched my fists at my sides. My nostrils flared as I hissed, "How dare you? You call me stupid? I'm not the one working for the House that wiped our entire people off the face of the planet!"

Fenris narrowed his gaze. "You think I have a choice? That I wanted to forsake Thelrena and all that she stands for?"

The traitorous elf rolled up the sleeve of his tunic, unveiling the swirling green tattoos that ran from his wrist up his left arm. They twirled, forming intricate markings.

As I watched, they shifted on his skin as though they were alive and trying to rearrange themselves.

I snarled, drawing my gaze away from his arm. "We always have a choice."

He shook his head, running his hand over his face. "Not me. By the time High King Edgar got to me, I had already watched my entire clan be murdered. I wasn't even Mature when his guards swept through the land and took everything from us."

"That doesn't explain how you are here, and the rest of our people are not."

For a long moment, Fenris didn't respond. He stalked away from me, his cloak billowing in the wind. I watched the elf—the Earth Elf—and I wondered about Remington's audacity. Did the prince feel so secure that he didn't care if the last two Earth Elves in Ithenmyr spoke without supervision?

The answer came to me instantaneously. Of course, he did. He was confident in his power.

Prince Remington, also known throughout Ithenmyr as the Red Shadow, son of the Crimson King, was renowned for his cruelty and power.

His father, the High King, was the only Death Elf with more power. Rumor had it that their power was unmatched even in the entirety of the Four Kingdoms.

I called out to Fenris' retreating form, "How can you work for him?"

"He made me!" the Earth Elf yelled. He huffed, his nostrils flaring as he pivoted on his heel, marching towards me. His face contorted as he stared down at me. "You understand *nothing*."

"Try me," I spat.

Fenris thrust a cloth at me that he pulled from his cloak. "Not. Now. You need to wash. There's dried blood on your face. I can't take you back looking like this."

Dried blood. From the beating. Anger, fresh and new and powerful, swept through me.

I splashed the cloth in the water, wincing as the material came in contact with my face. It did feel good, though, so I dipped the cloth three more times, wiping it on my tender cheeks and then my hands.

I peered into the water, staring at my reflection. Purple and blue bruises covered most of my flesh from my shoulders down. My face held a mark from Remington's hand and was swollen, but I thought it would probably go down in a day or two.

But my eyes.

My green eyes reflected the utter despair I felt in my soul.

Shuddering at the look in my eyes, I dragged the cloth through the water, disturbing the reflection. As I washed, something came to me. I stilled for a moment as memories of my time in the tower flooded through me.

When I was done and felt more like myself, I turned to the other elf. He was pacing nearby, his back to me.

My voice was calm and steady as I pushed myself to my feet. "I remember you, you know."

Fenris stilled. "What?"

"It came to me while I was washing. I remember watching you from my tower. Every time the king came to visit me, you came with him. I always wondered who the elf was, dressed in fine velvet and sitting atop the king's horses. You used to wander off into the King's Forest for hours at a time. You didn't look like you'd been coerced then."

Fenris returned, a mirthless laugh escaping him as he gestured to the woods around us. "The High King keeps me fed and clothed while he drags me around his kingdom to do his bidding."

"Why?"

He huffed. "Don't you get it yet, Aileana? The reason you and I are still alive?"

"He wants to breed me," I whispered as a shudder of disgust roiled through me. I'd been told my purpose from the moment I could talk. "I've always known that."

Fenris shook his head, a wild look in his eyes. "He *needs* us."

"What?"

"The bastard didn't realize it until it was almost too late. The land needs to be fed by Earth Elves, or it dies. Surely you've felt the call of the earth?"

"I hadn't until..."

Until I'd escaped.

The unspoken words swirled around the clearing.

He nodded, his eyes glimmering. "The king kept you surrounded by prohiberis for your entire life. It blocks the call of the wild."

I lifted my arms, studying the bracelets. Fenris had just confirmed everything I'd thought, but to hear it spoken out loud... the weight of the manacles felt heavier than ever before.

Returning my gaze to the elf, I narrowed my eyes. "You don't have any on you."

"Not anymore." Fenris rubbed his wrists as though invisible shackles bound them together. He shook his head, shaking the cloud of memories that seemed to have settled upon him. "Come on, we have to go."

"What? No. I'm not going back." I stood, shaking my head as I took a step back. I hit a stump, and my fingers flicked behind my back as I grabbed a piece of wood I'd seen earlier. "You shouldn't either. You basically just told me you're as much a prisoner as I am. What if there are more Earth Elves out there? We could find them."

A flash of longing passed over Fenris' face before he shook his head, scoffing. "Don't be ridiculous. There is no one else. You and I are the only ones left."

"No, we're not." I shook my head, my eyes widening. "I was in Thyr, and the priests executed an Earth Elf just a few weeks ago! He couldn't have been the only one left. We can work together, the two of us, and find freedom. What do you say?"

I stared at Fenris, watching as my words settled upon him. He didn't immediately reply, and a sliver of hope grew within me. Was he considering it? Could this be the answer I was looking for?

Then, a branch snapped in the distance, shattering the silence into a million pieces. He shook his head, his voice hard. "You are coming back with me. If you don't, High King Edgar will..." Fenris' voice trailed off, and he paled. "It doesn't matter what he will do." His voice hardened. "I'm not going to let that happen."

I widened my stance, leaning forward slightly. "I'm sorry to hear that, Fenris. We could have been friends, you and I."

His gaze narrowed, and he cocked his head. "What are you—"

Before he could finish his thought, I flung the piece of wood toward the elf. It smacked him in the head, and he cursed.

Turning on my heel, I ignored the stinging of branches as I fled. I ran through the trees and over fallen logs, past thickets and brambles as my heart raced.

I ran as my lungs burned in my chest and my heart pounded. I was so focused on getting away that I didn't hear him until it was too late. Suddenly, the forest floor softened beneath my feet.

Brown roots erupted all around me, grabbing onto my feet and dragging me backward. I sank *into* the ground, the earth solidifying around my ankles.

I was trapped.

"No!" I cried out as I tumbled to the ground.

A panting Fenris appeared a moment later. He held a hand to his still-bleeding head as he stared down at me.

"You shouldn't have done that," he said almost mournfully.

He twisted his free hand, and a green glow erupted from his palm. Instantly, the ground softened again, and the roots released their hold on me. I squealed as he reached down, grabbing my elbow. I squirmed against his grip, but it was no use. Even injured, he was much stronger than I was.

Even so, I wouldn't go with him without a fight. So I kicked and screamed as he dragged me back to the camp. This elf, who could have been an ally, returned me to my captors.

"The bitch tried to run," Fenris spat as he shoved me towards the prince.

I stumbled but remained upright. Clenching my fists at my sides, I dared a look at the Red Shadow. When I saw the look on his face, I knew I'd pay for my insolence in pain.

But I didn't care.

Because there was an ache in my chest with Xander's name on it, I knew it would only get worse.

I Would Rather Die

❦

The Red Shadow stalked around me. His jaw was clenched, and his black horns reached into the sky. Red sparks surrounded him, and I watched in horror as a ripping sound filled the air. Moments later, wings as black as the night unfurled from his back. They blocked the sun from view as he loomed over me.

He looked like violence and death personified.

"You thought you could get away from me?" he thundered. Red sparks flicked as magic swirled around him like a red storm.

I bit my tongue against the curses that threatened to escape me. Clenching my teeth, I seethed, "I will not be your bride, Remington. I will keep fighting. Keep pushing back. You'd be better off leaving me alone than trying to make me yours."

"Is it really going to be this way?" He shook his head, sighing dramatically. "You're going to make me drag you back, kicking and screaming the entire way?"

"Yes," I hissed. I could see the anger coming off him in waves, but I couldn't help it. I wouldn't marry him without a fight. Not after I'd tasted freedom. Not after I knew just how horrible his father was.

No, I would do everything I could to kill Remington and the evil king, even if it was the last thing I would ever do. "I will fight you every inch down the aisle."

For a moment, we just stared at each other.

Remington looked at me, really looked at me for the first time in his life. His brows furrowed as he studied me intently. "Why?"

I snorted, taking a good look at the red magic surrounding him. With one blow, he could kill me. "Are you joking right now?"

The prince shook his entitled head. "No. Why are you fighting this? When you marry me, you will be a princess. The wife of the High King's Heir. You will have a comfortable life. I will provide for you and our children. Keep you safe."

"Is that all you think about? Providing me *comfort*? No one ever asked me if I wanted to marry you!"

"That's why you're angry?" He sounded legitimately puzzled, as though he couldn't fathom anyone being upset simply because their consent wasn't sought.

"Of course, that's why I'm upset!" I huffed.

He stepped closer, his wings snapping behind him. "If that's all—"

I recoiled. "No! That's not all. You stupid, selfish, pigheaded oaf. I don't *want* to marry you. It doesn't matter if you asked me nicely or not. Your father kept me prisoner for my entire life, and you knew about it! I was known as the king's pet. You're both murderers! Of course, I won't ever give you my consent to marry you!"

I was aware of the three others gathering around Prince Remington, but I ignored them. My entire field of vision was filled with red.

Remington stared at me as though no one had ever spoken back to him in his entire life. I seethed, "I would rather *die* than see myself wed to you."

Truth. It was an absolute truth. I felt it in the core of my being.

My words rang through the air as the weight of my declaration settled upon us. The wind stopped blowing. The birds stopped chirping.

For a very long moment, no one spoke.

Then, red lightning flickered around me as bands of red flew out of Remington's hands. They wrapped around me like deadly snakes, tightening around my entire body until I could not move at all. Only my face was left unbound.

The Red Shadow prowled towards me, clenching and unclenching his fists at his sides until he stood right in front of me.

"So," he said in a low, careful voice devoid of all emotion, "you would rather die?"

Gulping, I nodded. "Yes," I whispered. "I won't marry you. Not now, not ever."

He chuckled darkly before waving his hand behind him. "Leave us," his voice thundered. He never removed his eyes from mine, and I tried not to flinch under the weight of his gaze.

One of the others—Fenris, I thought—cleared his throat. "Your Highness, are you certain?"

A strand of red magic flew from Remington's fingers as he stared at me. I heard a strangled sound from behind me before the prince repeated. "I won't tell you again. Leave."

He twisted his fingers, and the choking sound stopped. Rapid footsteps, followed by silence, spoke to the fact that we were alone. The prince stared at me, and I pointedly looked anywhere but at him. I noted the blue, cloudless sky, the shining sun, and the number of trees that surrounded us.

I stared at all of them instead of at the dangerous prince standing before me. I ignored the way his wings cast large shadows over me.

A minute passed before I felt his fingers on my chin. I recoiled at the touch, but he dragged my face up to his.

"You want to die?" he asked slowly.

How was I supposed to answer this question? With the truth? That was likely to get me killed. Lie? A life attached to Remington was likely to be a death sentence in and of itself. Marriage to him...

Every time I thought about it, golden eyes flashed in my vision. Xander's words echoed in my ears.

I am yours, and you are mine.

No matter what I chose, I knew I would be the only one losing here.

Because neither answer would get me any closer to my mate. The ache in my chest would only grow. I didn't know what happened to people who found their mates and then lost them, but based on the physical pain in my chest, I was sure it wouldn't be good. We hadn't even solidified the bond, and I was already missing Xander with every part of me.

How much worse could it get?

"Aileana," Remington growled. By his tone, I was sure that wasn't the first time he had said my name. I must have gotten lost in my thoughts. "Tell me."

He grabbed my shoulders, shaking me. His eyes flashed as his nostrils flared. His wings retreated into his back as red sparks of magic flew all around him. Even through the material of my gown, I could feel the ice that seemed to reside under Remington's skin.

He was *nothing* like Xander. Nothing like my mate, who burned with the heat of a thousand suns.

"You know the answer," I replied.

He slapped me. The sound of flesh against flesh echoed through the woods. I bit my tongue to keep from crying out as the coppery tang of blood filled my mouth. Remington snarled, "Do you want me to kill you?"

I swallowed. "I want you to let me go."

"That is never going to happen!" he roared.

"Then if death or marriage are my only options, then I suppo—"

Just then, a large winged shadow blocked the sun.

I looked up, tilting my head as I stared at the bird-like form flying off in the distance. It was too far away to make it out clearly, but the creature must have been enormous. I had never seen anything like it—but that wasn't especially unusual.

What was unusual was the tremor of fear that went through my horrid fiancé as he gripped my shoulders.

"Oh my gods." He inhaled sharply, following my gaze and staring at the sky where the shadow had been.

"What was that?" I asked.

Remington paled—impressive for a Death Elf—and stepped back from me. The moment he released his grip on my shoulders, I began to inch backward. Considering the bindings wrapped around my entire body, it was exceedingly difficult, but I managed to shuffle along inch by inch.

I wanted to put as much room between myself and this dangerous prince.

He didn't seem to notice me as he stared at the sky, shaking his head back and forth. He muttered as he paced like a caged animal, running his hand through his hair. "No. That isn't... How..."

The Red Shadow's voice trailed off as his face hardened. He turned to me, his eyes steely. "Do *you* have something to do with this?"

I wrinkled my brows. "No. I don't even know what that *is*."

Just as quickly as it had appeared, the fear on Remington's face disappeared. He prowled closer to me, tilting his head like a hunter watching its prey.

"Aileana," he snarled. "Do. You. Have. Anything. To. Do. With. That?"

"No!" I said again. Then, because my heart was racing in my chest and my lungs had trouble drawing in air, I repeated, "I don't know what that is. Please, I didn't do this."

Remington's eyes were hard. The promise of violence was etched into his every feature as he studied me. His jaw was clenched, and his eyes narrowed as his nostrils flared. Red sparks covered his skin like tiny bolts of lightning.

I only had a moment's warning before Remington lunged toward me. His eyes flashed as red filled his pupils. "If I find out you had anything to do with this…"

He left the threat unsaid, but it swirled around us, ringing through the air.

I will make you wish you were dead.

I shook like a leaf as fear gripped me, unable to open my mouth.

A beat passed before Remington twisted his hand. I watched, my heart racing, as he spooled his magic like a thread. The bindings around my feet loosened just enough for me to walk, and I took a hesitant step forward.

"Come with me," he snarled, yanking on the bonds like a leash. Hard. Everything hurt as he tugged me along.

Gasping, I went stumbling after Remington as he pulled me behind him. I struggled against him, but it was no use. I could not fight the strength of his Death Elf magic. Not with the manacles on my wrist.

Instead, I focused on the only weapon I had remaining in my arsenal. My mouth.

"Where are we going?"

He refused to respond, giving my bonds a firm tug as he strode to his horse. He looked at the sky, but the shadow was nowhere to be seen.

I tried again. "Are you going to explain what's going on?"

Still no response.

"What kind of bird makes a shadow like that?"

That did it. He turned towards me, his eyes flashing angrily as the binds around me tightened. I struggled to breathe as they compressed my chest, pushing against ribs, still bruised from his earlier assault.

"Shut up!" Remington bellowed. His breath was ragged as he waved a hand at me. His cool composure was completely and utterly destroyed.

Whatever had made that shadow seemed to have shaken the prince to his core. He snarled, "It's time you learned your place, you little bit—"

"Your Highness!" the black-haired male shouted as he ran towards us. I still didn't know his name. He was panting, his hands on his knees as he pointed to the sky. "Did you see it?"

The Red Shadow nodded once. "I did."

Fenris stepped forward, his eyes flashing as green ribbons of magic laced around his fingers. "What does it mean?"

Remington shook his head. Anger seeped into his every word as he said, "Nothing good."

"What is the plan, sir?" Kolvar asked.

Remington growled. "She's going to have to ride with me."

"No!" I shouted.

The prince ignored me, speaking to others as though I hadn't said anything. "Cut the cart loose," he commanded. "We will need to ride as fast as we can."

"Yes, Your Highness." Kolvar went off to do what he was told.

Remington waved a hand at the traitorous Earth Elf. "Fenris, come here."

Fenris stepped forward without missing a beat. I sent him a look that told him exactly what I thought about his horrifying behavior. The Earth Elf avoided my gaze as he stood with his hands clasped behind his back. "Yes, Your Highness?"

"My father needs to hear of this immediately. We are changing course and heading to Vlarone at once. Nothing is more important than this. Everything will be lost if that thing finds the missing pieces before we do."

"Yes, sir," Fenris nodded.

The Red Shadow put out a hand, placing it on the elf's shoulder. "You need to go ahead of us. Ride as *fast* as you can to the capital. Do whatever it takes to reach my father as quickly as possible. Tell him he may need to prepare his contingency."

"Sir." The elf dipped his head. "It shall be done."

Without waiting for a reply, he strode to his horse and hopped onto the saddle. I glared at the elf who could have helped me. Fenris left us without a glance, galloping down the road.

The other two jumped to action, doing what the prince commanded. They threw me onto the horse in front of the Red Shadow. With a flick of Remington's hands, the bonds around my upper torso twisted, becoming red ropes that tied my hands together at the wrists.

"Hold on to the saddle," he commanded gruffly. "We'll talk about your death wish later. Perhaps I can *persuade* you to see things differently."

I snorted, ignoring the way his chest pressed against my back. He felt nothing like Xander had when we had ridden together.

The thought of the silver-haired male made me sick. How I wished I was still with him. I would take fighting with Xander over being with Remington any day.

With that thought empowering me, I hissed, "I will never marry you."

"We'll see about that," Remington snarled.

Then, before I could say anything else, he withdrew the gag from his pocket. The moment I saw it, my stomach twisted. I tried to get away from it, but the ropes around my hands held firm.

"Please, no," I said, tears welling in my eyes. "I'll be quiet."

"It's too late for that," my horrid fiancé replied. I nipped at him as he came too close to my mouth, but it didn't stop him. He cursed, replacing the gag around my mouth before tying it to the back of my head.

"Let's go," Remington snapped. "Kolvar, you ride ahead. Phrin, you will follow us. Make sure no one is in our path."

The three horses quickly moved to a gallop, taking us down the road with alarming speed. I held the saddle horn with both hands, trying desperately not to fall.

As we rode, I thanked the nameless shadow for providing me with a temporary reprieve. Whatever it was, it had bought me some time. Time I desperately needed if I was going to think of a new plan.

Vlarone was on the other side of the kingdom, and even if we rode as hard as we could, I knew it would take at least two weeks to get there.

My wedding day would have to wait a little bit longer.

Thank Thelrena for small mercies.

THE SHADOW APPEARED TWICE MORE that first day.

Like before, it flew above us as we rode down the roads. Every time I saw it, it seemed to be getting a bit larger. I watched the shadow carefully. I had never seen anything like it in my life.

Whatever it was, it seemed to scare Remington. He tensed behind me, his words becoming more clipped as the day wore on.

He was afraid.

And that, more than anything else, caused a spark of hope to grow within me.

WHEN WE STOPPED that first night, I practically fell off the horse. My entire body ached.

Remington loosened the bonds so I could rest, but he tethered my ankle to a tree instead. He took the gag off long enough for me to eat and drink, quickly replacing it when I was done.

"You can relieve yourself behind the tree," he growled. "Don't try anything, Aileana. We don't have time to go chasing you through the woods."

I glared at him, my eyes filled with fury, but he just turned his back on me. Whispers rose as Remington spoke with his companions long into the night. I couldn't make out what they were saying.

As I lay in the cold, hard dirt, I thought I saw a strange blue glow coming from underneath my dress. My brows furrowed, I turned from the others and peered beneath the neckline of the now very dirty gown.

Nonna's necklace looked the same as it always had. I sighed, rubbing my hands over my face. It must have been in my head.

As I slept, nightmares of burning villages and a tall, silver-haired male haunted me.

ON THE SECOND DAY, I saw the shadow three times. The bonds around me became looser the further south we traveled, as though Remington was losing the ability to concentrate.

I spent every waking second of that day trying to remove the prohiberis from my wrists. I tucked my hands into the fabric of my gown, hiding them from sight as I fiddled with the heavy bracelets. Every time I touched them, it felt like I was jabbing painful needles into my fingers, but I didn't stop.

I couldn't stop.

Soon, small blood spots joined the mud, dirtying my dress, but I didn't care. I would not go down without a fight.

By the time we stopped to make camp that second night, my kidnappers were casting each other worried glances as they discussed the shadow.

That spark of hope grew into a little flame.

Stand Your Ground

W hen the third day came around, my abductors were well and truly spooked. It had rained the night before, and everyone was in a foul mood. We were soaked, having not found any shelter before the skies opened up, and the shadow had swept over us four times already. Even the horses seemed jittery.

I sat quietly astride the horse, watching the seemingly never-ending procession of trees as we rode towards Vlarone. By the time the heat of the spring day had burned off the chill of the morning, Remington was shifting nervously in the saddle behind me.

"We need to get off the road," he ordered, shattering the tense silence. "Leave the horses. We will have to travel on foot. Let's see if the beast can follow us, then."

Beast. What exactly is *following us?*

I looked around. It wasn't as though we were in the middle of civilization. The road itself was barely more than a dirt path. Trees surrounded us on both sides, their looming presence casting deep shadows across the road. We hadn't met a single person since yesterday.

They hadn't put on my gag that morning, and I wouldn't remind them by speaking.

"Yes, sir," Kolvar said. He dismounted, leading his horse to us before taking the prince's reins.

Remington followed suit, stretching his legs before yanking me off the saddle. I stumbled as my feet touched the ground. The prince made a sound of derision as he grabbed my shoulders roughly, forcing me to stare into his eyes.

"I'm going to undo the bindings around your wrists now," Remington growled. "I need you to be able to move as fast as possible once we get into the forest. But before you get any ideas, let me show you who will come after you if you run. Kolvar?"

The cat shifter handed the reins to the prince before winking at me. A white light flashed, and Kolvar disappeared. I swallowed my shriek as I stared at the place where he had been standing.

Before me was a giant tiger. It was unnaturally large, the size of a pony. It had razor-sharp teeth and paws the size of my face.

"Oh my gods," I whispered. My hands trembled as I stared at the creature, suddenly wishing he was the tiny black cat again.

At least then, he'd appeared harmless.

Remington chuckled darkly, his grip on my shoulders tightening. "Thank you for the show, Kolvar. I do believe my fiancée understands."

The tiger roared, the sound sending shivers down my spine before the flash of light returned. When Kolvar shifted back, he bowed.

I stared at him, fear and revulsion battling within me. This was the first time Kolvar had shown his true colors, and to say that I was scared would have been an understatement.

Now more than ever, I knew I needed to get the prohiberis off me. And soon.

Kolvar had remained in his human form the entire time I had been with them, but now that I knew *what* he was... I itched just thinking about all the times I had played with that cat growing up.

Bile rose in my throat when I thought about the times he had been present as I had engaged in the most private matters. He'd watched me while I had gotten dressed... and undressed. He'd watched while I had washed and Slept.

He had intruded on my life for years.

I wouldn't be sad if I got the chance to drive a dagger through Kolvar's heart.

The other one, Phrin, had barely spoken since we first saw the shadow. I was fairly sure he was human, but there was no real way to tell. He was quiet and seemed withdrawn. A sword hung from his saddle, and I wondered what his position was in the Red Shadow's retinue. Whenever I looked at him, he was eyeing the sky. He emanated nervousness as he rode, passing his reins back and forth between his hands.

Now, he dismounted warily. Phrin glanced at the sky as he grabbed his sword before he handed his reins to Kolvar. The shifter took all three horses and tied reins to their saddles before slapping the steeds on their backside. They whinnied before taking off in a run down the road.

"They'll make it to the city," Phrin said as he watched them go. "But I'm not sure about us."

Red ribbons of magic snaked from Remington's palms, wrapping around Phrin and lifting him off the ground. "Shut up, you fool. I'm the Red Shadow, for Kydona's sake. We are in no danger."

I raised a brow. The prince was awfully jittery for someone who wasn't in any danger.

Phrin nodded, his face pale. "Of course, Your Highness. My deepest apologies."

Remington sighed, releasing the male. The red ribbons rushed back into the prince's skin as Phrin went tumbling to the ground. He stood quickly, dusting off his cloak and tunic.

Keeping my thoughts to myself, I pursed my lips as I tried to figure out how to use this fear to my advantage when Remington grabbed my arm and yanked me after him. My cloak billowed after me as I hurried to keep up with him. He was taller, and it took two of my strides to keep up with each of his.

"Enough chit-chat," the prince said gruffly, marching towards the forest. "We need to leave."

We were just about to enter the forest when suddenly, a screech came from overhead. My neck hairs bristled at the sound. It was so loud that the trees all around us shook.

Then, even though it was the middle of the morning, the sun suddenly disappeared from the sky. I looked up, my brows furrowed as I sought the source of the sudden darkness.

The shadow was back.

But this time, it wasn't far away.

No, this time, I could see exactly what it was. I blinked once, then twice, wondering if I had gone mad.

A dark green, enormous dragon was circling above us, descending rapidly. Wide-eyed, I stared at the enormous wings extending from the beast's body. Twin horns extended from the middle of each of its wings, adding to the creature's deadly aura.

Kolvar swore. "Dammit. The dragon found us."

The creature was magnificent in a way I hadn't known was possible. It continued to descend towards us until even its scales were visible. They were massive, the size of my hands.

Another roar and my heart pounded in my chest. Our rush into the forest was forgotten as Remington released my elbow.

He fumbled as he summoned ribbons of red magic. "Ready your-selves," he snapped to the others. "It won't go down without a fight."

Phrin and Kolvar stared at the dragon. Their gazes were transfixed as their weapons lay forgotten at their sides.

Remington roared, "Pick up your weapons!"

They jolted and withdrew their blades, the weapons zinging in the air.

I took a quivering step away from the three of them, my eyes darting between the dragon and my unwanted fiancé.

Death by dragon certainly seemed like a better way to go at this point. That, at least, would be quick, unlike the painful, drawn-out torture of being repeatedly taken to Remington's bed. I had heard stories about what this sadistic prince did in the bedroom, and I wanted no part of that. I would not return to my gilded cage.

It wasn't that I thought death by dragon would be painless. On the contrary, I imagined that being burned alive would be somewhat unpleas-ant, but hopefully, it would be over quickly.

Unlike my marriage. Once I Matured, I could live for a millennium. A thousand years of long, drawn-out torture.

No, thank you.

Right then and there, I made a promise to myself: I would never marry Remington. Even if it meant slitting my own throat, I couldn't do it.

Crimson sparks flitted through the air as Remington raised his hand. He threw his cloak to the ground, his black wings unfurling from his back as a whip made entirely of red magic appeared in the Death Elf's hands.

"Come here and fight me properly, beast," he roared.

The animal huffed, shaking its head as it continued its descent. With every beat of its wings, the dragon commanded our attention. It was incredible. Two horns curled from its head, winding towards the sky as a row of spikes ran from the top of its head, disappearing from view.

It looked like death itself.

And Remington was a fool for challenging it. A complete and utter fool.

The dragon roared, and I gasped. The air, which had been warm before, turned scorching. Bright red flames erupted from the dragon's mouth. They immolated the leaves around us, showering us in black and gray ash.

The dragon continued towards us, growing larger by the moment. It was the most immense beast I had ever seen—easily the size of four horses. It made Kolvar's tiger look like a mouse.

"Is that all you can do?" Remington cried out. He flicked the whip, which unfurled in the air. The barbed red rope had to be at least fifty feet long.

I watched, a silent scream in my throat, as the whip cut into the dragon's flesh.

The beast *roared*. The sound was full of pain and agony, and I flinched.

Something inside of me broke at the sound of the dragon's suffering. It was drawing so close now that I could make out its enormous claws.

"Your Highness," Phrin's wobbly voice reached my ears. "It's going to land. What would you have us do?"

"Stand your ground," Remington ordered. He flicked his wrists, his whip disappearing into thin air as his magic rushed back into him with a *whoosh*. "We will fight."

With that declaration, Remington grabbed my arm, pulling me back as the dragon descended.

I struggled against his grip, but he was too strong. I could only watch as the dragon came plummeting towards the earth. With every beat of its wings, it drew nearer. The shadow had appeared massive, but this...

This beast was awe-inspiring.

Fifty feet separated us from it.

Forty.

Thirty.

Twenty.

Ten.

The ground itself quaked when the dragon finally made contact. It landed in the middle of the road, cutting Remington and me off from the other two. A roar escaped the beast as its long tail extended behind it, knocking trees down in its path. From here, I could see the spikes extending from its head all the way to its very long, very large tail.

For a long moment, it seemed like time itself stilled.

The magnificent beast loomed over us, and I stared at it. Waves of heat came off of it as the sun glistened on its scales.

The animal was panting as small puffs of smoke came from its mouth with every exhale. Glistening red blood dripped from its side where Remington's whip had slashed into it. Each drop of blood that fell on the ground sizzled as though it, too, was made of fire.

The dragon was beautiful.

To say that it was simply green would be a disservice to the color itself. It was like the forest had been picked up and bottled before being formed into scales. Some were light, and others were dark, but together, the beast was incredible.

I continued to stare at it, unable to comprehend the size of this enormous animal. It was massive, but it seemed so... aware. Sentient. Even the way it moved its tail seemed planned. My gaze lifted from the animal's scales to its head, and I jolted.

A large, golden eye with a slitted pupil stared back at me. The beast looked into my soul as I took a wobbly step forward.

Then, a deep, rumbling sound came from within the dragon.

It shifted, each step shaking the ground beneath us. I stumbled as it opened its mouth, showing off rows of razor-sharp teeth. It seemed to... smirk at me before turning and facing the others.

The dragon's tail flicked back and forth, not unlike a cat's, as the scent of smoke filled the air a second before red-hot flames erupted from within the beast. There were screams, and then there was... silence.

Complete and utter silence.

When the fire disappeared, all that was left of Phrin and Kolvar was ash. I searched inside of myself for a modicum of pity for the cat shifter, but I couldn't find any. For Phrin, I felt... sad.

I thought that he might have been kind at one time in his life. But obviously, something had happened to him. Both he and Kolvar had been more than willing to stand by while the Red Shadow dragged me back to his home and forced me into a marriage I didn't want.

For that reason, my lips tilted up as I watched the wind carry away their ashes. But then the dragon turned back towards us.

And I looked my death in the eyes.

Death Smells Like Smoke

❦

The dragon tilted its head as it lifted one giant, taloned claw, then the next. It prowled towards me, but I stood my ground.

I would not quake in the face of death.

Not after everything I had been through. I would face my fate head-on.

Bravery, I was learning, was not about being fearless. Rather, it was standing in the face of danger and not running away.

Beside me, Remington bellowed, "I will not go so easily, beast!"

The dragon roared, shaking its head as it glared at the two of us.

The air crackled as the prince pulled spools of magic from himself. "You need to run," he snarled, turning to me.

I involuntarily took a step back. The blue of Remington's pupils was completely gone as red sparks flitted *through* his eyes. He was violence incarnate.

Right then and there, I knew *this* was the origin of his name. This was the reason everyone was afraid of him.

The Red Shadow looked like he had danced with death and won.

"Run," he ordered, his voice reverberating with deadly power.

"No," I refused, widening my stance. "I'm not going to run." Extending my bound hands towards him, I asked, "Why don't you remove my bindings and let me help?"

He scoffed, his voice gruff as he shot red bolts of lightning toward the dragon. The beast roared as Remington turned and glared at me. "You are an absolute idiot."

"With words as sweet as yours, how could I ever refuse your proposal of marriage?" I quipped.

A flash of red magic shot towards me, shoving me back against my will. Remington snarled, "I am Mature. I can fight him. You will break within moments if this beast gets close to you."

I had already made up my mind. One way or another, I was not leaving this road alive. There was no way I would marry Remington. If the dragon saw fit to take care of my problematic fiancé, well, then... good.

I certainly wouldn't protest the sudden change in my situation.

Shaking my head, I widened my stance. "No. I'm not going anywhere."

"Stupid bit—"

The Death Elf's response was cut off by a roar as the dragon turned. For such a large animal, it moved so quickly.

I watched with wide eyes as the dragon lifted its tail in the air. The appendage's shadow fell between Remington and me, marking its path.

My lungs tightened in my chest, and I scrambled to the side just as the massive tail came towards the ground. It hit the ground with a bang as the dragon roared. The sound echoed through me as though it was calling to my very soul.

Something about this dragon felt... safe. Which was odd, considering it was trying to kill me.

I filed that thought away as something to deal with later. If there would be a later. At that very moment, I was fairly certain I was looking at my executioner.

Stumbling back, I clenched my fists at my sides. I wished I had a weapon—any weapon. At this point, I'd even settle for a single dagger to help me defend myself. Although, what good would a dagger do against a dragon?

I made it three steps back when suddenly, long red ribbons snaked between my legs.

"No!" I yelled, but it was too late.

Remington's ribbons dragged me back. There was nothing gentle about the magic he sent to bind me, and within moments, I found myself with my back against a tree. My heart raced as I struggled against the binds, but they continued to tighten.

Soon, I couldn't do anything but watch as the dragon and Death Elf faced each other. The dragon was so much bigger than Remington that it barely looked like a fair fight. The sight would have been almost comical if it wasn't for the small matter of my fate on the line.

The Red Shadow's wings beat in the air as he hovered a foot over the ground. He twisted, snarling in my direction. "I'll deal with you later. But first, enjoy this show of your future husband's strength. Who knows? Maybe this will make you change your mind about me."

"I doubt it," I replied. "Unless you plan on completely changing your entire personality, there is no way in the seven circles of hell the two of us will ever marry."

"We'll see about that," he said before summoning a ball of red magic in his hand.

I watched as he shaped it into a spear, launching the weapon at the dragon. It sailed through the air, and the beast roared when the spear made impact. Billows of thick, gray smoke came from the animal's mouth as its body writhed in pain.

Death smells like smoke and ash.

The thought popped into my mind as I tried to free my hands from Remington's magic. The dragon didn't even seem to notice me. Its golden gaze was firmly on the prince.

On the other side of the beast, the prince in question was spooling his magic into another whip. He took a step away from the beast just as the dragon raised a taloned claw in the air. Then, a crimson light erupted from the Death Elf as his whip cracked in the air.

A pain-filled roar echoed in my ears as the dragon lurched backward. Fire erupted from its mouth as the Red Shadow erected a shield around himself. Even though I knew red magic could be shaped and pulled, I'd never seen it work like this.

I had no idea Remington was so powerful.

The next few minutes seemed to pass in the blink of an eye as Death Elf and dragon fought. I watched, wide-eyed, as they engaged in the timeless dance of bloodshed. It was evident only one of them would be leaving this deadly arena alive.

A mix of smoke and fire, blood and ash, filled the air as beast and Elf attacked each other. They moved so fast that I could barely see them. Every time they slowed, more blood poured from their bodies.

I had no idea who would survive.

Fire and magic clashed over and over again until the air was filled with the scent of ash and copper.

And then, something happened.

Remington turned.

He turned, and he flew away from the dragon, who was lying bleeding on the road. For one blessed moment, I thought Remington was retreating.

"Coward," I whispered. "Are you running from your death?"

Then, as if he heard me, he landed on the ground. A wolfish grin appeared on Remington's face that was visible even from here. His shield dissolved as he twisted his hand in the air. Blood dripped from his shoulder, a long claw having run through his chest, but he was still standing.

His death magic pulsed once before it gathered in his fist like a bright ball. Sparks like tiny bolts of lightning filled the air around the sphere as the Red Shadow pulled back his arm.

"My father did the right thing wiping you and your kind out a century ago," he roared. "I will finish what he started now."

"No!" I cried out as my stomach twisted and bile rose in my throat.

He would kill the dragon, and then...

And then...

And then...

He would force me to marry him, and I would never be free again.

"Fight!" I yelled at the dragon. I begged the beast, inserting every ounce of feeling that was roiling through me into my words. "Please, don't give up."

I didn't even know if the creature could understand me, but for a moment, it seemed like maybe it could. Its golden eye met mine before it let out a cry of distress, flapping its wings as it gained enough power to take off once more.

The wind stirred my hair, blowing red locks into my face as the dragon lifted off the ground. Red blood pooled beneath the beast as it rose, and I stifled a sob. The magnificent beast looked like it was in so much pain.

But perhaps this was for the best.

For one brief moment, I thought the dragon might be able to escape. Maybe Remington wouldn't win. Perhaps evil would not triumph on this day. I would die, but maybe the beast could survive.

My breath caught in my throat as the dragon lifted five, then ten, then fifteen feet in the air.

"Go," I whispered. "Live for both of us."

It looked like it was getting away, but then Remington roared. The sound sent shivers down my spine as he released his grip on the sphere of magic. He lobbed it through the air towards the retreating dragon.

I watched in absolute horror as it arched perfectly through the air. "No," I whimpered.

Too late.

Everything moved slowly. So slowly. Too slowly.

The sphere inched towards the dragon, its path clearly marked against the bright blue sky.

The injured dragon let out a cry of distress, flapping its wings as it tried to fly faster. It moved higher in the sky, stirring the wind around us, but it wasn't fast enough.

I screamed, the sound of my voice blood-curdling, as the sphere continued on its deadly path. I had seen magic like this before. It left holes —giant, deadly holes that went straight through bodies.

My legs shook as the ball hit the dragon right under its left wing. The magic exploded, coating the creature's entire body in bolts of red lightning.

A thunderous roar erupted from the beast. The rocks shook, and the trees trembled as the magnificent beast cried out in agony.

My heart clenched in my chest as the dragon went tumbling to the ground. Its injured wing dragged as it tried to right itself. My lungs seized as I struggled against my bonds, wanting desperately to help the poor animal.

Remington laughed.

He *laughed* as this magnificent animal plummeted back to the ground far faster than it had before. The dragon landed in a movement that could only be described as ungraceful. Crimson blood poured from its wing, staining the ashy ground beneath it.

The Red Shadow was already spooling more magic in his hands.

"After this, they shall call me the Dragon Slayer," he thundered. "Just think about it, sweeting. You shall be the wife of the Dragon Slayer. Imagine the glory that will be bestowed upon us both at court."

"There is no glory in slaying innocent creatures," I spat. "I will never marry you. You are a horrible, conniving bastard and I despise you. The blood that stains your hands will never come off. How could you find joy in killing such a splendid creature?"

A sob wrenched through me as I stared at the dragon. It was lying on the road, its golden eyes shut as it heaved heavy breaths. Blood poured out of its wounds, staining the ground beneath it. It appeared to be moments away from dying.

Remington stopped short. His mouth opened and closed as a look of incredulity crossed his face. "Do you... Do you care for this animal, this *beast*?"

"Yes," I replied. My voice wobbled, but I continued. "No living creature deserves this kind of treatment. Certainly not something as impressive as this dragon."

The Red Shadow stalked towards me, his eyes flashing in anger. He gestured to me, the injured beast momentarily forgotten, as he drew near. Now that he was closer, I could see that not only was there a cut down his chest, but Remington was limping. A long cut ran down one of his wings, and soot covered him from head to toe.

Remington stopped five feet away from me, and his wings disappeared from view. His fists were clenched as red sparks still danced over his skin. The magic pulsed around him as though it were alive.

He lifted his hands, and the ropes binding me to the tree disintegrated. I fell forward, throwing out my arms to slow my landing. A rough, icy hand landed on my elbow, yanking me up.

"Look at me," Remington ordered. His voice was firm, steady, as though he hadn't just wielded an untold amount of power. I knew elves got their power from the goddess, but I wondered why he wasn't exhausted. Why wasn't he passed out, like I'd been after saving Hironna?

When I'd been with Xander.

A pang went through my heart.

Pulling my gaze to his face, I stared at the male who had just fought a dragon. He glared at me, his eyes wide with violence and bloodlust.

"I'm looking," I stated. In my peripheral vision, I saw something twitch. I held my breath as the dragon moved. It was still alive. At that moment, I knew I would do anything to keep Remington's attention on me. "Are you going to throw your magic at me, too? Was killing a dragon not enough for you today? You need to take out your anger on a defenseless female?"

Remington slapped me. I was coming to understand that this was his automatic reaction to everything. Pain. Suffering. Torture. I winced at the throbbing in my jaw, and he *smiled*.

"Don't test me," he hissed between clenched teeth. "There is nothing I would like more than to teach you a lesson, but unfortunately for me, I *need* you alive."

I swallowed, nodding. Alive. To breed.

Behind Remington, the dragon was pushing itself to its feet. Its golden eyes were open, and I could have sworn it looked right at me.

"Okay," I said quickly. Anything to keep Remington's attention on me. A plan began to form in my mind. A completely crazy, absolutely insane plan. But he had released me from my bonds, and there was no way I would go with him willingly.

Over the prince's shoulder, I caught a glimpse of the dragon's open mouth and razor-sharp teeth. It was standing on two unsteady legs now and seemed to be... waiting.

"Okay?" Remington repeated, disbelief lacing his tone.

I nodded. "Okay." Smirking, I tilted my head, raising a brow. "You'll just have to catch me first."

Before the last word was even fully out of my mouth, I took off running. I refused to look behind me even once. My cloak billowed in the wind, but still, I ran.

When heat—hot, infernal, horrible heat—erupted at my back, I continued to run. When cries of absolute agony came from Remington's direction, I didn't stop. I kept running until the cool breeze embraced me.

Only then did I whirl around.

And I screamed once more.

My voice shattered the silence as a throbbing pain fissured through my chest. I gasped for air, my heart breaking as I stared at the scene behind me.

Remington—what was left of him—lay prone on the ground as horrific burns covered his body. He was very clearly dead.

But that wasn't what made me scream.

The dragon was nowhere to be seen. And in its place...

I sobbed, my chest tightening painfully as I stared in disbelief. I blinked once, then twice, but nothing changed. The horrifying scene in front of me remained the same.

A very familiar head of silver-white hair was lying on the ground, a few feet away from the very dead prince. Crimson blood stained everything in sight.

How is this possible?

My heart seemed incapable of beating properly as it stuttered in my chest. I couldn't breathe. I couldn't think.

My feet carried me to Xander's body of their own accord. My soul felt as though it had shattered into pieces.

He was lying before me. Bloody and bruised and broken.

And now...

A sob ripped through me as the weight of the cuffs around my wrists felt heavier than ever before.

My mate was dead, and I was alone once more.

I'm So Sorry

❧

I fell to my knees in front of Xander's battered body. Blood covered nearly every inch of his very naked form. The only thing on him was the necklace containing the two pieces of the map he had shown me.

A sob wrenched through me as I averted my eyes, reaching to my neck to unclasp my cloak before settling it over his legs and hips.

At least in death, he would have dignity.

A moan, low and deep and heart-wrenching, ripped through me as I stared at him. He had come for me. He had cared. After everything, he had still come.

And now he was gone.

Everyone always died.

I reached over, gently taking his blood-soaked hand in mine and squeezing tightly. Even in death, Xander was burning hot. Now that I knew what he was, I supposed the heat didn't surprise me. I rubbed my thumb down his hand, pressing it to my cheek.

"I'm so sorry," I whispered against the back of his hand. Tears ran down my cheeks, dampening his skin as my shoulders shook. His torso was a mess of blood and dirt, and I couldn't bear to look at it. "Kydona only knows how sorry I am."

I had no idea what I was going to do. Remington was dead. Xander was dead. There was a huge gash in Xander's side, presumably where the magic had struck his wing.

His wing.

Xander was a dragon, and he had wings. That was *not* what I had expected.

And now...

Now I was alone in the forest. Somewhere in the middle of the province of Nin. The only other person who even knew I was here was Fenris, and he was long gone. Not to mention the fact that the Earth Elf was a traitor, and I knew I couldn't trust him.

Despair leaked into my voice as I whispered, "What am I going to do?"

"Why don't we start by getting off the road?"

I dropped Xander's hand, stumbling back as his golden eyes blinked open.

"What?" I whispered, my voice wobbling. My eyes darted back and forth across his face as his eyes met mine. The faintest smile appeared on Xander's face as I asked, "How?"

"Hello, Aileana." He coughed, his voice rough. "Did you miss me?"

I blinked, staring at him. "I thought you were dead."

Xander tried to push himself up to his elbows, but he dropped onto his back. He winced, a grimace overtaking his features as he said, "Honestly, I did too. But apparently, it's harder to kill me than I thought."

"I'm glad," I replied instantly. "I didn't think..." I shook my head as my voice broke. Clearing my throat, I continued. "I didn't think you were going to come for me."

A deep groan came from Xander as he stared at me. He planted his hands on the ground, shoving himself up.

I gasped, putting a hand on his arm. "Stop! You'll hurt yourself." Even as the words left my lips, I noticed the quantity of blood pouring from his chest was slowing down. Furrowing my brows, I insisted, "You shouldn't push yourself."

He shook his head, continuing to try to sit up. "I need to look into your face as I tell you this."

"But you're—"

"Aileana," he growled, pushing himself into a seated position. He reached over and placed a finger on my lips. "Be quiet."

"So bossy," I whispered around his finger.

He smirked, some life returning to his eyes. "I am. And here's what is going to happen. You are going to listen to me when I tell you this."

I nodded, staring at Xander. "Okay," I whispered. "I'm listening."

"Aileana, I will *always* come for you. There will never be a moment where I don't follow you."

"But our figh—"

"Shh." He shook his head. "Not yet. I'm not done. People fight. We will fight. Goddess knows, fighting with you is the most amusing pastime I have ever had in my life. But that doesn't mean that I won't come for you. Aileana, I—"

He coughed, his words getting lost as a trickle of blood came out of his mouth. I gasped, shoving his hand away from my mouth.

"You're bleeding," I said accusingly.

His lips tilted up into a wry smile as he blinked. "Very astute of you to notice, Sunshine. Did you see the dead elf, too?"

Yes. I had, in fact, seen the burnt body that was no more than ten feet away from us. I glanced over my shoulder, but it was still there.

"This isn't a moment for joking," I snapped. "You need help."

As I said the words, I realized just how difficult that would be. We were stranded in the middle of a deserted road.

Despite the fact that Xander appeared to be able to heal at an incredibly rapid rate—something I would definitely be requiring a lot more information about in the future—he was bleeding.

Even I, with my limited medical knowledge, knew that continued blood loss was *not* conducive to survival.

"Okay." He nodded. "Give me your necklace."

It was my turn to blink at him. "Excuse me?"

"Your necklace, Sunshine. The golden one from Nonna. If you'd take it off for a moment?"

Wondering what exactly my necklace had to do with anything, I paused. Xander caught my gaze, his tone softening. "Please, Aileana. Trust me."

I wasn't sure which of his words caught me more off guard.

Please.

Trust me.

Either way, something within me seemed to knit itself back together again as he spoke.

I whispered, "I do trust you, Elyxander."

He sucked in a deep breath but didn't move. Under his watchful gaze, I tilted my head and reached underneath my hair. It was a tangled mess after the past few days on the road, but I moved it aside quickly.

My hands were steady as I undid the clasp. The necklace slipped off my neck, the tiny chain light as I pulled it off my chest. Placing the necklace in Xander's outstretched palm, I sat back. "What are you going to do with that?"

"Call for help," he replied.

A hundred questions flitted through my mind, but before I could ask them, Xander pressed the locket against his bloody palm.

Instantly, a radiant pulse of blue light came from the piece of jewelry.

I blinked, covering my eyes for a moment against the onslaught of light. When I uncovered my eyes, I saw not two people before me.

"Hello, young ones," Nonna said. She held a bundle in her hands as she smiled in our direction. "You called?"

I stared at the elderly witch standing before me. "Nonna?"

In reply, she leaned forward and grabbed my arm and Xander's. Whispering something under her breath, everything around us blurred.

When I could see again, I gasped.

One second, we had been sitting in the middle of the road, and the next, we were in a small cavern.

Xander was lying on the ground, his eyes shut. His chest was still moving, and his ragged breathing proved he was still alive. Nonna's bundle was on the ground next to Xander. I reached over and placed my hand on his skin. He was pale and still bleeding, but there was a touch more color in his cheeks than before.

"How did you do that?" I asked the witch as I looked around at our rocky surroundings.

Nonna smiled softly, bending to crouch before Xander. She placed her hands on his chest, humming to herself.

A blue light came from her hands, wrapping around him as she replied, "It's a simple translocation spell, my dear."

I blinked at her. "Trans-lo-what?"

"Translocation. I can't move multiple people very far. We are just on the other side of the woods, but at least now we are off the road. Xander will need to rest for a few hours before he's better."

"A few hours?" I repeated. Incredulity tainted my words as I stared at her. "He has a hole in his chest!"

She tilted her head, her eyes glimmering with amusement as she chuckled. "Does he?"

"Yes, I saw it with my own eyes." I pointed at Xander's torso, where the wound had been only minutes ago. "It was right... here." I stared, my jaw falling open in disbelief. Xander's skin had knitted itself back together under Nonna's hands, as though the injury had never occurred.

Not only that, but all the traces of blood were gone. I gaped. "What? How?"

Xander coughed, his eyes fluttering open as he winced. "Nonna's a witch."

I raised a brow, crossing my arms. "I'm aware of that. But you were... dead."

"It would take more than some stray red magic to kill me." He winked at me, a wry grin on his face.

I wanted to scream at him. Remington had thrown everything at Xander while I'd been forced to stand by, watching. How dare Xander smile when he was bleeding out mere moments ago?

Xander seemed ignorant of my inner turmoil as he lifted the bundle of clothes beside him. "Do you ladies mind turning around so I can get dressed?"

Blood rushed to my cheeks as I nodded. Crossing my arms, I pivoted and stared at the vines crawling up the rocky wall as the rustle of fabric filled the air. While Xander changed, Nonna's magic swept over me. When I looked down, I gasped. My dress and hair were clean, and my skin looked better than it had in days.

Xander cleared his throat. "Your modesty is safe, Aileana. You can turn around." Once I did, he continued, "Almost dead is not the same as dead. I was just... resting while my body's natural healing kicked in."

"Natural healing? Does this have something to do with the fact that

YOU ARE A DRAGON?" I yelled the last part, unable to contain the anger slipping into my voice.

On the other side of Xander, Nonna's gaze darted back and forth between the two of us.

"Aileana, I was goin—" Xander began, but Nonna cut him off.

The elderly witch clucked her tongue. "I think I will take this as my cue to leave." She bent over, kissing Xander on the cheek. "Come see me when the two of you have worked things out. I think we will have lots to discuss in the future."

Then she leaned in close, putting the necklace back in my hands. "Put this back on, dearest. Your blood will work the spell just as much as Xander's. Don't hesitate to call me. I have a feeling I'll be seeing you again soon."

Nonna pecked me on the cheek before standing and clasping her hands together in front of her.

"Oh, and young ones?" We both looked at her. "I see your auras are more intertwined than ever." She winked at us, a wide grin on her face. "I know you don't need my approval, but you have it."

Before we could reply, she muttered another incantation. A puff of blue magic erupted, and when it dissipated, Nonna was gone.

A long moment passed as Xander and I just looked at each other. We were alone, and we had so much to talk about.

"We keep ending up in caverns," Xander chuckled awkwardly. He pushed himself up, adjusting his position until he was leaning against the rocky wall.

I shifted, coming to rest on the wall beside him. Neither of us touched the other, but I was acutely aware of exactly how much room there was between our bodies.

Nodding, I looked around. "It does seem to be a theme, doesn't it?"

Gesturing to the pine needles dusting the floor, I shrugged. "Once you've seen one cavern, it feels like you've seen them all."

A silence fell over us as our gazes met. My stomach twisted as I stared at those golden eyes. With every breath, the tension in the cavern grew exponentially.

A multitude of desires warred within me.

There wasn't enough space between us. There was too much space between us. All I wanted to do was climb onto Xander's lap and hold him. I wanted to scream at him. I wanted to kiss him. To feel his lips on mine. His hands on my skin. I wanted him to hold me until the memory of Remington's icy touch was nothing more than a distant thought.

I wanted too many things, so I settled on what seemed like the most pressing issue.

"You are a dragon," I said after a moment.

He nodded, his face grim. "I am."

"A dragon," I repeated.

"Yes, we have ascertained that to be the truth."

I couldn't seem to think of anything else to say. "You. Are. A. Dragon."

Xander chuckled, reaching over and wrapping my hand in his. I sucked in a deep breath as sparks erupted from his touch. I felt like fire was running through my veins.

"Aileana," he whispered, his voice hoarse. "I think we've established that I am a dragon shifter. Is there anything else you'd like to ask me?"

I blinked. It was so hard to think when he was holding my hand. When he was so close. "I... I don't know," I said truthfully. Biting my lip, I turned my head and studied him. "I have so many questions; it's hard to keep them straight."

"We have time to answer them all."

I nodded as a wave of sadness welled up within me. My chest ached at the thought that we might not have had any time. That Remington might have killed Xander. I tried to keep the tears away, but one escaped down my cheek. I shuddered.

"Xander," I whispered, "I was so scared."

The dragon shifter raised a hand to my face, gently running it down my cheek. My mouth opened slightly from the tenderness in his touch. His hands cupped my face as his eyes swept over me.

Then, his jaw clenched as he traced a sore spot on my cheek. His nostrils flared as he stared at me, and anger filled those golden eyes. He snarled, "Aileana, did he *hit* you?"

I inhaled sharply.

In all the chaos, I had forgotten about the bruises on my face. Apparently, they must still have been visible because Xander's eyes flashed, promising violence.

"Tell me," he growled, his voice tinged with echoes of the dragon that lived within him.

"Yes," I whispered after a moment. "He hit me. But it's not the worst I've ever dealt with, so—"

A growl, deep and animalistic, began in Xander's chest. It rumbled through the cavern, a reminder of the fire-breathing beast living beneath his skin.

Xander's voice was gruff as he snarled, "If that bastard weren't already dead, I would kill him again."

"But he is dead," I said. I reached up and placed my hand over Xander's. At my touch, his anger seemed to soften. "You killed him. He's dead. We both saw his body. He can't hurt me anymore."

Those last words were little more than a whisper, but as I gave them life, a weight lifted off me. Remington was dead. He could never marry me now.

I was free. Free to live. Free to remain with Xander. I would never be held captive again. Remington was dead, and I would kill his father if it were the last thing I did.

"He's dead," I repeated, more to myself than anything else. My voice grew in conviction as I looked over at Xander. He watched me, his eyes filled with deep emotion that flooded me with warmth.

"Xander," I murmured, rubbing my hand over the back of his. "I need to tell you a story."

Stay With Me

A story?" he repeated.

I rested my head on his shoulder. "Yes. It's important, and I need you not to be angry."

Xander snarled, "Am I going to want to be angry?"

Pursing my lips together, I nodded slowly. "Probably. But it will be hard enough for me to tell you without you going all... dragon on me."

A long sigh escaped him. "I'll do my best," he said. He jokingly added, "Besides, I'm a captive audience right now. You heard Nonna. I need to rest for a bit."

My lips twitched as I patted his cheek. "Why do you think I chose to tell you a story now?"

"Fair point." He waved a hand in the air. "Please, Sunshine. Tell me a story."

I snuggled up beside him, letting the heat of his body warm me from the inside out. "How did you start?" Humming, I pulled his arm over my shoulder. "Oh yes. Once upon a time...."

Over the next hour, I told Xander about everything that had

happened to me. Growing up in the tower, being raised as the king's pet, being marked for breeding. I skipped over the various punishments I had received, deciding that now probably wasn't the right time to share those with him.

I told myself it was because I didn't want Xander to get angry. But really, I just wasn't ready to confront the truth of what had been done to me.

One day, when we were both ready, I would tell him.

When I got to the part about Matthias taking me to the attic to train, Xander chuckled. "I was going to ask who trained you to wield those daggers so well. I suppose I have him to thank for the way you stabbed me when we first met."

I winced. "You could, but he's dead."

"Oh," he said.

"Everyone always dies." The words were soft and tinged with sorrow as they left my mouth.

Xander shifted, pulling me onto his lap. His arms wrapped around me, drawing me against him. I didn't fight him. His warmth washed through me as he brushed back a stray lock of hair from my head. Xander pressed his lips to my hair, murmuring, "I'm so sorry, Aileana."

I sighed. "It's... not okay. But it is the way my life seems to go. I never even met my parents. Did you know that?"

He shook his head.

"It's true. My earliest memories take place in the tower. When I was younger, I had a nursemaid. She taught me about Thelrena." I shook as I said the goddess' name, my back clenching in terror even though I knew I was safe with Xander.

He ran a soothing hand down my back as he asked, "What happened to her?"

"One day she just... disappeared. She was there one day and gone the next. Fool that I was, I asked the king what had happened to my nurse-maid on his monthly visit."

After a long pause, Xander growled, "What did he say?"

"The bastard laughed. He said I didn't need her anymore, so he killed her. A liability, he had said. Because she knew too much. She knew *me*."

I blinked, rubbing my hands over my eyes as I remembered how I had sobbed that day. The king had left my tower, and I had collapsed into a ball on the ground. I hadn't even moved until the next day.

I ran my hands over my face. The sleeves of my dress slipped as I whispered, "I don't even remember her name, but I know she used to sing to me at night."

Xander tensed beneath me, his hand darting out and grabbing my wrist. He yanked up the sleeve of my dress, exposing the black bracelet. "Aileana, what is this?"

I stared at the black manacle that seemed to suck the light out of the cavern. I lifted my wrist, staring at it as I said, "Remington—"

A snarl escaped Xander, and I hurried to finish my sentence. "Remington put them on me. He said a witch made them and can only come off with his blood." My voice cracked. "They stop me from using my magic."

"I swear to you on all that I am, Aileana, we will find a way to get these off you."

"We?" My voice cracked as hope, treacherous hope, leaked into my words.

Just as soon as the sentiment appeared, I shoved it away. I still didn't know where things stood between us.

He was a dragon, and I was an Earth Elf. I had promised the woods that I didn't know how to keep.

And then there was the mate bond...

Xander nodded, interrupting my thoughts. "If you'll have me."

I stared at him, drawing in deep gulps of air as though it could help me get through what I wanted to say. "For most of my life, I didn't have anyone. But now..."

My voice trailed off, and I wasn't sure how to finish the sentence. I knew what I wanted to say. I wanted to say that I had Xander. He and I, together, could deal with everything.

That's what I wanted.

But questions flitted through my mind, sowing seeds of doubt as they popped up, one after the other.

Could we even be together? There was no doubt in my mind that we would be hunted now that Remington was dead. Where did that leave us? Was there even an *us*?

The last time we had spoken about this *thing* between us, Xander had left me in tears. Surely, that meant he didn't want me.

I was prepared to shove all my feelings and lock them in a tiny box when I felt his hands on my arms.

He turned me around so I was facing him on his lap. Xander's face was surprisingly firm as he finished my sentence. "Now you have me. I promise you, Aileana, *we* will get these off you."

My breath caught in my throat. This infuriating, frustrating, horribly irritating male tilted his head, running his hand down my cheek tenderly. His lips parted as his golden eyes darkened.

I asked softly, "Xander, I... I need to know. Do you want me?"

"Yes," he answered immediately. "Yes." He pressed his lips against mine, the kiss soft, gentle, and fleeting. "A thousand times, yes. I want you so badly that I have no idea what to do with myself."

"Thank the gods," I whispered.

He pulled back, his eyes filled with vulnerability as he asked, "Does that mean you want me?"

My heart pounded in my chest as I spoke the words that I knew to be true. "We haven't known each other for a long time. And I know this is crazy."

He raised a brow. "Is there a 'but' in there?"

I smiled. "But I want you too, Elyxander. I need you. You make me *feel* more deeply. You have shown me what it means to live." I narrowed my eyes. "Even though you didn't tell me you were a dragon."

He chuckled. "I promise I'll never keep anything from you ever again." Xander pressed his lips against my forehead, and I felt his growing desire for me as I sat on his lap. We were close. So close. My gaze dropped, and I stared at his lips. The scent of ash and smoke and pine trees filled my lungs as time itself seemed to slow.

"Xander," I whispered, raising a hand and laying it on his chest. "What does this mean?"

My dragon blew out a deep breath. He tilted my head with tender hands so I looked into his eyes. "It means that I am begging you. Please, Aileana, stay with me. Be with me. For all that entails. Be *mine*. Say that you'll accept the mate bond. Claim your position by my side. As my part-ner. As my *everything*."

When he said that last word, a flash of green went through his eyes. A reminder of the beast who lived under his skin.

"I am yours," I whispered. "And you are mine?"

"Yes," he growled, the word rumbling through me. "*Yours*."

I nodded, holding his gaze. "Okay."

My mate's eyes darkened as he studied me. His voice was gruff, and his body was firm beneath me as he said huskily, "I want to kiss you."

I didn't speak. I didn't think. There was only one thing on my mind. One being. He was here. And he wanted *me*. I wanted him. I already felt so close to him—I couldn't imagine what it would feel like once our bond was solidified.

After the ceremony, I knew. There would be no going back.

Oh, I wanted him so badly; I didn't even know what to do with myself. A fire burned within me as I shifted in his arms.

Heat coiled low in my belly as I studied him—my mate. My dragon.

He was waiting. For me. That he respected me, even in this, was incredible. And it made me want him even more.

"You are mine," I murmured, lowering my lips until they hovered above his. I could taste the smoke on his breath as I reached out and ran a finger down his chin. "And I am yours."

A low groan rumbled through him as his grip tightened around me. He held still, waiting until I closed the distance between us. Once our mouths touched, it was like he lost all control. He pressed me against him as we kissed. We were nothing but lips, tongues, and teeth as our mouths said everything that was still unsaid.

My hands trailed down his face, touching every part of him as we kissed. I ground myself against him, trying to ease my growing ache.

"Xander," I moaned as his tongue darted out and touched my lip.

In response, he deepened the kiss. This felt so *right*.

My fingers began their perusal of his body again. I ran my fingers through his hair, down his neck, and over his shoulders before he gasped.

I pulled away from him, my eyes wide.

"I'm sorry," I whispered, trying to put distance between us. The moment I pulled away, a chill ran down my front. "I didn't mean to—"

"Don't stop," he growled, grabbing my hands and putting them back on his torso. "For Kydona's sake, Aileana, don't stop."

And so I didn't. I ran my hands over his arms and shoulders and chest as he showered me with kisses. He touched my breasts over my dress, tenderly at first but then with more urgency. The fire within me grew hotter with every passing second, and I squirmed on his lap, seeking relief that wasn't coming.

As we kissed, the space between our bodies was non-existent. He murmured in my ear. "You are mine. My mate.."

"The ceremony," I whispered. "Coming together..."

He shook his head. "There is no pressure here. I will wait as long as you need, Aileana."

Be ready. As much as I wanted that moment to be now, I knew this wasn't the right time. He was injured, and there was still so much to do.

But I wasn't scared. I knew Xander would keep me safe.

And one day, when the timing was right, we would solidify our mating bond. Be bound together for eternity. One day, we would bring our bodies together and become one in a union that no person could rip apart.

A sound of contentment rumbled up from deep within me. I pressed my lips to his exposed throat, and a thrill ran through me as he moaned.

"Xander," I whispered against his skin, "I'm your mate."

My heart pounded in my chest as this thing between us took on a life of its own. Right then and there, I knew nothing would break us apart. We were bound together in a way that was *more* than us.

Fated.

"I'm yours."

"And you're mine."

We kissed until everything else lost all meaning.

WHEN OUR LIPS WERE SORE, and our kisses were nothing more than tender brushes against each other, we pulled apart, panting.

I rested my head on Xander's shoulder as he brushed a lock of hair back from my face. "Aileana, there's still so much to talk about."

I nodded. "I know."

He shuddered, his voice low, "Before... When he took you..."

I put my finger on his lips. "I'm here now. We're together."

Xander nodded, the movement shaking me. "I know, but I need to say this."

He cleared his throat, and I waited.

For him, I would wait forever. We were mates, and I wasn't sure exactly what that entailed, but if it meant feeling the way I felt now, I would gladly wait forever. For *him*, I would do anything.

A full minute passed before he said, "When I realized you were gone... something fractured within me."

"Me too," I whispered, pressing my forehead against Xander's. "I need you to know I didn't want to go with Remington. I fought back. Every single step of the way, I fought."

My voice cracked on the last word, and Xander pressed his lips against my cheek. He kissed away my tears, one by one.

His lips brushed over my cheeks, nose, and eyelashes as he whispered, "I know, Sunshine. There was never a doubt in my mind. I'm sorry for fighting with you. Soon after I got back to camp, there was an ambush."

I gasped, pulling back. I had forgotten about the others in the chaos of everything that had happened. "Daegal? The children?"

Xander nodded. "All fine. Daegal was able to See the attack before it took place. There were a few injuries, but nothing major. Everyone survived."

"Thank Kydona," I murmured. "I couldn't forgive myself if something had happened to them because of me."

"They're all safe." He brushed a lock of my hair behind my ear, his gaze tender. "No lives were lost. Daegal sustained a laceration on his side, but Morwen assured me he would be fine."

"Good. That's good," I said. Pursing my lips, another question came to me. I wasn't sure how to ask it without insulting Xander.

"Go on," he said gently. "You can ask me anything."

"I just..." I took a deep breath. "How old are you?"

My mate laughed. His mirth bounced off the cavern walls, and he shook beneath me. I blushed, trying to get off him, when his grip tightened around me.

"Don't go," Xander whispered. Vulnerability leaked into his words as he said, "Please don't. I... I want to hold you."

I nodded, stopping my movements. "Okay. But will you answer my question?"

He cleared his throat, avoiding my gaze. "I am... not young," he said.

Narrowing my eyes, I placed a hand on his chest. "How 'not-young' are you?"

He leaned over and whispered in my ear.

What are We Going to Do?

"One hundred and thirteen?" I blinked at Xander, trying to wrap my mind around this new information. A small breeze blew through the cavern, and I shivered as I stared at him.

This male... I shook my head. No, he wasn't just anyone. He was my mate. Who was nearly a century older than me?

It could have been worse, I supposed. What was a hundred-year difference when we would both live to see many centuries go by?

If the king didn't kill us first. In that case, I supposed the age difference wouldn't matter, anyway.

With that morbid thought, I shuddered.

"Aileana?" Xander said my name, his tone betraying that this wasn't the first time he had called for me.

Blood rushed to my cheeks. "I'm sorry, I got distracted."

He huffed a laugh. "I noticed." Xander looked away from me, his voice surprisingly serious as he asked, "Does my age bother you?"

Blinking, I thought it over. "I mean... Not really. I just... I haven't

Matured yet, and I don't really know much about dragons. Will you... Are you..." I huffed, dropping my face into my hands. My words were caught in my throat, and I couldn't seem to get them out.

Xander chuckled. "Aileana, are you trying to ask me if I will grow old?"

"Yes," I said into my hands. My cheeks were warm, and I peeked out my fingers to see Xander smiling.

"Not very quickly. Dragons Fade at a slower rate than elves. Besides, it's *very* hard to kill an adult dragon. As you've seen, we heal much faster than elves or humans. I expect to have many years left in my future... as long as a certain feisty redhead stops trying to kill me."

"But..." My mind raced to the story he had told me earlier. That other cavern seemed like it had been a lifetime ago. "Your village. The fire you told me about. The burned buildings..."

He nodded, his gaze distant. "Yes. A contingent of Death Elves murdered my entire village. They had several strong sorcerers with them. Burning their bodies was just a sadistic touch. We are made of flesh, Aileana. Not immortal. But much harder to kill than most."

Pondering his words, I pulled my hands away from my face. I stared at the bump under his tunic where the pieces of the map rested. "Does that mean you've spent the last century trying to get *one* piece of the map?"

My mate coughed. "Yes, well. I didn't *just* look for the map, you know. After Saena and I escaped the village, we wandered for many years."

"Where did you go?" I tilted my head. "Surely it couldn't have been safe for the two of you to remain in Ithenmyr. Not after what High King Edgar did to you and your family."

He shrugged. "We spent some time in the other Three Kingdoms."

"You've left Ithenmyr?" I gasped. "What was it like?"

"It was... Everything that I thought it would be and nothing like I thought. The other kingdoms... They are dangerous, Aileana. In many ways, more dangerous than Ithenmyr. Saena and I went into the Southern Kingdom together, but only one of us returned."

"I can't imagine the pain, Xander." My vision blurred as I pressed my lips against his hand. "I am so sorry."

His eyes were hooded as he nodded. "Thank you. After I lost Saena, I was broken. Nonna found me wandering in the woods a few months later. She took me in and raised me. Dragons don't Mature as fast as elves. It takes upwards of fifty years for dragons to grow into adulthood."

My brows raised. "Nonna must be...."

"Ancient," he finished for me. I made a sound of agreement, and Xander continued, running his hands up and down my arms. "Even I don't know exactly how old she is, but I know she's a very powerful witch."

"Clearly," I said.

Before I could say anything else, a brilliant red light came from outside the cavern. It was followed almost instantly by a rumbling of thunder as the ground itself shook beneath us.

I shot to my feet, my eyes wide as I stared in the direction the light had come from. "What was that?"

"I don't know." Xander swallowed, pushing himself to his feet and widening his stance. He clenched his fists as he tilted his head. "Whatever it was, it can't be good."

"Nonna said we weren't far from the road..."

"And that looked suspiciously like Death Elf magic," he finished for me.

The implications of what that meant flitted through me. Fear began to take hold of me, squeezing my heart as Remington's face flashed before my eyes.

We stared at each other for a very long moment.

"Xander," I whispered. "If that was... What are we going to do?"

He stepped forward and laced his fingers through mine. His touch was hot as our skin met.

That *thing* between us grew even further as he said, "Whatever it was, Aileana, we will tackle it together."

"Because we are mates," I whispered.

This bond between us, the intertwining auras that Nonna had seen, felt like a living entity that pulsed as we stared at each other.

I could have sworn there was something tangible binding us together. Every point where our bodies touched felt like it was on fire. He made me feel safe. Warm. Like I could do anything as long as we were together.

Xander drew me towards him, his lips meeting mine as we melted together. He kissed a trail down my cheeks and jaw as he murmured, "I am yours, and you are mine."

His words settled within me, and I knew. Whatever that flash was, whatever it meant, we would tackle the problem together. We would take things one step at a time.

As he lifted his lips to mine once more, I smiled. This vexing, sarcastic, irritating dragon shifter was also fiercely kind, loyal, and protective.

And he was *mine*.

That knowledge produced a sense of rightness within me, unlike anything I had felt before.

My heart pounded in my chest as I pulled back from the kiss.

"Xander." I pressed my hand against his chest and forced him to look at me. "That light... it can't mean anything good. Whatever is happening out there is not going to be easy to deal with."

He blinked at me, a wry smile coming over his face. "I know," he said. "But right now, it's okay. Right now, it's just the two of us." He pressed his forehead against mine. I inhaled his familiar scent and reveled in his closeness. "Can we just *be* for one minute?"

"Okay," I whispered. "Let's just *be*."

And we were. For that moment, there was nothing else. There was no flash of red magic and likely impending doom. There was no fight with forces we didn't yet understand. At that moment, we weren't trying to figure out what lay between us or how to unlock the cuffs binding my magic.

At that moment, we were just *us.*

That minute was everything to me. It felt like it lasted for an eternity, and yet, it was gone in the blink of an eye.

Too soon, it was over. I tugged on his hand, and we walked out of the cavern together. With him at my side, I wasn't afraid of what we might find.

Because I was free, and I wouldn't let anyone put a leash on me again. I wasn't the king's pet, and I would *not* do what he wanted of me.

And my mate? He would be with me every step of the way. With the power of those words settling within me, I took a deep breath.

I knew who I was and what I had to do. We weren't done, of that I was certain.

My mate and I had a lot to do. I had a high king to kill. Prohiberis to remove. Pieces of a map to locate.

I was Aileana of the House of Corellon. Earth Elf. Daughter of Uhna. Granddaughter of Niona. Mate of Elyxander, the Last Dragon. Protectress of the Woods.

And with Xander by my side, I knew I was ready for whatever was coming our way.

The End... for now

THANK YOU SO MUCH FOR TAKING THE TIME TO READ OF

EARTH AND FLAME. I CANNOT EXPRESS TO YOU HOW MUCH IT MEANS TO ME.

REVIEWS ARE SO IMPORTANT FOR INDIE AUTHORS, AND I APPRECIATE EVERY SINGLE ONE.
THANK YOU FOR TAKING THE TIME TO LEAVE A REVIEW!

ARE YOU WONDERING WHAT XANDER'S THOUGHTS WERE IN CHAPTER 15: THE FEELING WAS MUTUAL? YOU CAN READ A BONUS CHAPTER FROM HIM HERE!

ALTERNATIVELY, COME HANG OUT WITH ME AND MY READERS ON FACEBOOK! JOIN ELAYNA R. GALLEA'S READER GROUP

The next part of Aileana and Xander's story is out now!

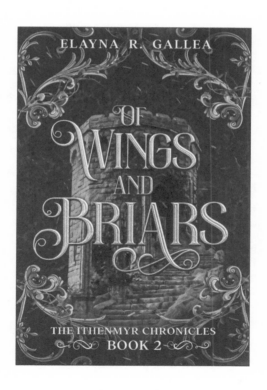

ELAYNA R. GALLEA

OF WINGS AND BRIARS

THE ITHENMYR CHRONICLES
BOOK 2

Find out what happens next!

Before you go, did you know there is another series set in the same universe? Tethered is an arranged marriage, forced proximity, vampire fantasy romance.

Read Tethered here!

Acknowledgments

Writing a book is not unlike having a baby. I should know, I've done both. Unlike having a baby, there are a *lot* more people involved in the book making process.

It would be foolish of me to think that I could list every single person that ever played a role in my books.

But I'm going to try.

To my writer's group. Thank you. A million times, thank you. For proofreading, for being there to bounce ideas off of. For laughing and crying with me. Thank you. Without your encouragement, this book wouldn't be where it is today. You are so important to me. Thank you for including me in your lives. We talk every day, and I know that these stories wouldn't exist without you.

To the FaRo community. I am so blessed to be part of such an amazing global community of authors.

To my alpha, beta and ARC readers. You know who you are. Thank you so much for putting up with my many questions as you read my books. I appreciate your comments and your patience when reading my stories.

Thank you to my husband, Aaron. Because he puts up with me every day.

To Britanny and Jack. For letting me be your mom. I love you so much. One day, you'll be allowed to read this book.

And to you, my reader. Because you are the one entering my world.

When I tell you that it means everything to me that you are reading my words, please know that I speak the truth. I so appreciate the fact that you are here, spending time in Ithenmyr.

Thank you so much.

About the Author

Elayna R. Gallea lives in beautiful New Brunswick, Canada with her husband and two children. They live in the land of snow and forests, in the Saint John River Valley.

When Elayna isn't reading or writing, she can be found doing indoor things. Because she hates bugs. And she loves to eat. Chocolate, cheese and wine.

Not in that order.

You can find her making a fool of herself on Tiktok and Instagram.

Also by Elayna R. Gallea

The Binding Chronicles (*A complete series that place in the Four Kingdoms at the same time as Of Earth and Flame*)

Tethered

Tormented

Treasured

The Choosing Chronicles

A Game of Love and Betrayal (2024)

Legends of Love (New Adult Standalones)

A Court of Fire and Frost (a Romeo and Juliet Retelling)

A Court of Seas and Storms (a Little Mermaid Retelling)

A Court of Wind and Wings (a Hades and Persephone Retelling)

The Sequencing Chronicles (Young Adult) - a complete series

Sequenced

Rise of the Subversives

The Wielder of Prophecy

The Runaway Healer (a prequel novella)